THE WAXING MOON

THE AREEKYAN CHRONICLES
VOLUME 1

BARRY S MARKWICK

For all those who have been told you can't. You can.

CONTENTS

MAP OF AREEKYA

theareekyanchronicles.com

THE WAXING MOON

BOOK 1

PROLOGUE

I watched as he sat hunched over his books for the final time. Most of his days were spent poring over the old, thick tomes. Reading, re-reading. Looking for what exactly, I was at first unsure, but he kept searching; hour after hour, day after day. Studying the secrets held within them, as he had done nearly every day that I had spent with him. He didn't know it, but today was to be his last.

I had conflicting feelings for the man I was as close to as any. I was amazed at the knowledge he held. In awe at his outlook on life, always finding the tiniest glimmer of Sunlight in the gloomiest sky. But there was also something else; darker, insidious, becoming stronger the more I stayed here, watching, learning, waiting. A contrast at first difficult to reconcile, but no longer. It would have to be done today. I'd taken all that he would give willingly, and even a little more unwillingly. This afternoon is when it would be. Before he leaves for the ceremony and has any chance to discover my plans.

He closed his books and returned them carefully to the shelves from where they came: everything meticulously placed. He walked towards the stairs, his graceful gait not revealing his many years. I once tried to guess his age, but he was impenetrable.

"Numbers and sums won't bring you any closer to the truth," he'd said, as I fumbled for answers.

As he ascended the stairs almost effortlessly to the Watching Room, I thought back to the first time he took me up there, one morning, many Moons ago:

"You see my lad, there are two Magicks in this world: Sun Magick and Moon Magick. To fully know one is to know the other; but to misunderstand one is to misunderstand both. One is dependent on the other. They are intertwined, in balance with nature. If you are patient, you can learn. With your patience will come reward. If you want to know the true secrets of the Magicks, this is to understand fully the nature of, well, everything," he'd lied. I didn't know that he wasn't being truthful at the time. I don't think I knew it for a long time, but he wasn't.

"And how long until I know it?" I replied. "How long till I get everything?" I was hungry. I wanted everything I could get.

"Patience comes first. Time has no hold over those who know, the initiated few. Time is but one dimension of life that can be manipulated by Magick. But come, enough for now."

As he finished, his words lingered in my thoughts; drifting into images in my mind's eye, exploding into vibrancy and clarity I had never experienced. Words transposing into colours infused with an effervescent energy that touched me deeply. I was standing on the balcony of the Watching Room, looking out for miles over his part of Areekya that he had carefully cultivated over the years. The panoramic view from the top was mesmerising. An awe-inspiring vista: the rolling hills, the green and yellow meadows and fields, the icy blue water of the lakes and fjords. This part of the world was beautiful, the colours vivid, all crafted by the Magicks. And the feeling was tranquil, powerful and addictive. The Watching Room balcony gave vantage points for the Sun and Moon rises, Sunsets, and wonderful nocturnal views of the magnificent, pulsating stars in their glorious constellations; all essential to gain the illuminated insight of the Magicks. The images that were dancing around my mind like nymphs prancing around a midsummer's morning's first ray of light were immediately erased with the sharp, shrill voice that ended my ecstasy.

"Come on, lad. Plenty of time for all that," he cried out from halfway down the stairs. It snapped me out of my thoughts. I stood wondering what had just happened. The one pervading thought remaining was: I want more.

Many Moons and Suns had passed since that first time up on the balcony. Each Moon brought more knowledge, but moved me further from him. It didn't take too long to discover what he had been hiding, what he had never told me at the beginning. It seemed that as I stumbled upon these secrets, he made them more opaque. The closer I got, the harder it seemed to find more. This was just my imagination, though. He had no idea of the long nights I spent reading as he slept. Once I found the Lunar Runes, the hidden became uncloaked and unveiled itself; slowly at first, carefully, selectively, as if it were being controlled by something, someone, guiding me to the truth. Then, when the mysteries of the Sacred Shapes revealed themselves, the secrets cascaded down upon me, quenching my long-held thirst; raining on me like the first torrential storm after a long, dry summer drought.

Now, I waited down below until I could hear him

moving about in the Watching Room above before I took out my knife. I had covered it with the Lunar Runes, as I had learned to do. I had practised this many times. At night, lying awake, I had perfected it in my mind, and in the meadows, rehearsing my grip with imagined figures. As well as hands-on practice with the pigs in the forest. Soon, the final obstacle would be removed and the secrets would be mine alone. His meticulous nature and obsession with ritual would be his undoing. The day of every Full Moon was always the same, down to the minute. And what irony; his favourite day of the month would be his last. Moon Magick would be overcome on Moon Day, making way for what should always have been. The secret hidden away in old books like a skeleton lying in a grave, whispering to be found again. Only those that could hear chose not to. They wouldn't dare to out of fear, and those who had the courage were unaware of its existence.

I could hear him coming back down the stairs. As his long, willowy frame descended and came into view, the affection that I once carried for him pulsated within me. For a brief moment, it stirred before I crushed it with the knowledge of the secrets he had hidden purposefully for all these years. It was pushed down and replaced by something else: excitement. The time was here. It was my time now, the time for a new Magick. No more hidden secrets, no more deceit and camouflage. The gatekeeper will be gone, and soon the dam will be breached. The secrets will flow like water flooding into an empty lake that had been selfishly kept parched.

"Let's go then. All ready?" He sounded particularly

cheerful, as he always did on Moon Day. He looked at me with the kindness that I remember in the beginning. The feeling rose again within me. As I looked into his eyes, I remembered the love, the patience, the wisdom he had shown me. All wasted. I pushed it back down, ignoring the guilt, preferring to focus on the knife I had prepared. Waiting. Ready.

"Yes. All packed. I have everything we need in the bags in the hall. All set," I replied. I had to go through with the pretence of preparing for the day. He was too smart and would've noticed if I didn't.

"Well then, time to go. Cannot be late, not today, not on Moon Day. People will be waiting." As he said this, he looked at me and there was excitement in his eyes, too.

Moon day, the day of the Full Moon. The most important day of the month, and today was the most important Moon Day of the year. Every month he went to the Midnight Forest, to the standing stones that had been there for generations, long before the forest, it is said. The stones were arranged in a five-pointed star: the Pentagon. This was one of the Sacred Shapes, the one all around us if you had been taught to see it. The pattern of the Sun Star in the sky. Every five years, the Sun Star, usually at its brightest at Sunrise and Sunset, traced out the Sacred Pentagon in the sky. And once a year, the Sun Star rose and set in synchronous harmony with the movements of the Full Moon: today. Finding out the power of the Sacred Shapes was the start of the end. The key that unlocked the secrets that were hidden. The secrets he kept hidden.

As he walked past me, towards the door to the stairs leading down to the hall, I grasped the hilt of my knife with my left hand. I followed him, gradually getting closer. He opened the door and started to walk down the twenty-two steps to the hall. I followed patiently. Waiting, fighting the guilt, while carefully raising my knife and preparing my other arm to grab him round the neck as I had practised many times before. As I reached out my right arm, the knife plunged in and out of the rib cage; I felt the warm liquid ooze from the gaping hole it had left. He turned his head to face mine. My eyes centred on his piercing gaze; the kindness gone, replaced by something else. For a moment it looked like pain, but quickly turning into something else altogether; the excitement I had seen before was back in his eyes. The corners of his lips upturned, breaking into a smile, even, the kindness usurped by a look of malice. Yes, malice, and something else. Something less obvious.

The cry sounded so unfamiliar, so unexpected, that it took a few moments to register that it was mine. The sharp pain proliferated to all parts of my body, making me scream in agony. I fell, still grasping the knife that wasn't given a chance to find its mark. I felt my knife drop as my head hit the stairs, my body tumbling down. He was standing over me; one or two steps above, looking down, his eyes burning into mine. He still held the knife that he had thrust into my rib cage.

"To misunderstand one is to misunderstand both. You had enough hunger to misunderstand this, and not enough patience to fulfil your desires." He walked down and grabbed my knife, holding it up to examine the Lunar Runes closely.

"Yes, good. This will do. It will suffice. To work with the Secret Magick is dangerous. You become exposed to its powers, and it is best done from afar. There's too much risk for me to reveal myself to its power directly and this, at least, you could do. Many Moons I have waited and now we are here, Moon Day, the day these runes will be at their most potent."

I kept my eyes fixed on him; the pain growing duller. A feeling of numbness replacing it. I was drifting. Drifting away.

"Yes, this will do nicely." He stepped over my ever increasingly lifeless body and moved down the stairs towards the hall. He opened the door, picked up the bags and stepped outside. The light from the door seared into my eyes as he loaded the bags onto his cart. He turned, looked one last time, expressionless, and closed the door. The pain had now subsided altogether. I could feel my eyes closing, slowly closing, reaching out for sleep. Reaching out for death.

JUK THRI

The darkness was all-consuming. It engulfed every instinct he had except the one for survival. He felt his body contort, his sinewy fingers grasping for the void at the same time, grabbing for life. The water flowed into his lungs and now he knew he was close to death. His mouth opened once more, gasping for one more lungful of drowned air, his body stretching out in pain, reaching out for relief, for salvation, for the void. Juk could hear a voice; it was crying out in pain, then another, and another. Three voices, crying from the void. The dimly lit crescent Moon hovered in the distance, too far and dark to see clearly, but he sensed its presence. One final time, he reached out in desperation, for relief, for the void.

Juk Thri awoke from his fitful sleep. He threw off his old, dark brown bearskin covering and sat up. He glanced around the camp and saw the guards looking out across the field. Juk liked his men to see him sleeping outside, roughing it with them; no relative comfort of the tent for him. There had been many early mornings started like this in the last weeks and Moons. The dreams, the nightmares, were becoming more vivid, more terrifying, but he cared less each day. Juk stood up and walked towards the early morning watch, taking over from the guards he had posted hours earlier. He could see the banners being stretched, as they flapped wildly in the wind; dark brown banners with the proud insignia of a bear with two crossed swords in the foreground and one bright star above it — the 1st Regiment's banner, reflecting the Chinsap region he and his men called home.

Captain Juk Thri had worked hard for his position in the 1st Regiment; the front line cavalry regiment sent out to bring peace to Areekya. Juk was a tall, thin man with angular features: sharp, high cheekbones, a nose that was slightly too big for his face, and blue piercing eyes that gave his friends reassurance, but filled his foes with intimidation and uncertainty. This morning was the two hundred and sixtieth since he was last home in Chinsap; miles away to the north east. In those two hundred and sixty days, Juk had become tired. He pulled three flowers out of his chest pocket. Moons ago, when he last saw his family, they had given them to him. Every time he looked at the dried, blue cornflowers, he thought of his family: his wife Maca, her long, chestnut brown hair falling almost to her waist, and twin daughters, Dek and Mek, who had the same long hair as their mother. As he stared at the flowers, he could feel his tear ducts fill and he quickly placed them carefully back into his pocket. It had been too long since he had seen his family. He missed his wife's loving touch and longed to hold his twin daughters in his arms again. He needed to do so.

The wind must have been biting the skin of the shadowy figures just visible on the western horizon from where Juk was now standing, as it gnawed away at his own. It was the third Moon of the year, and the weather was still inclement. Spring was slowly crawling her way back into existence again, taking her inevitable place in the cycle of the yearly dance of the seasons.

Juk was shivering slightly. He was straining his eyes; trying to focus, trying to make out the movements the shadows were making. He had been waiting for this moment to arrive, waiting for it and dreading it. He looked over his shoulder and saw the faint red glow of the early spring Sun now visible in the east. It was another morning which would be met with blood and battle; the colour of the Sunrise mirroring the savagery of the battle to come, thought Juk.

In the early years of the War, joining was a simple decision. Fighting to protect what you had is an instinct that came naturally to people from Chinsap, the poor mountainous region in the north east of Areekya, where Juk was born and raised. Pride was a favoured trait and encouraged in Chinsap when he was a young boy; pride of your home, of your people, and pride in yourself. Juk had left to join up nearly five years ago, and the two hundred and sixty days since he had last seen his family felt almost as long again. The Juk Thri that left Chinsap to protect what was his nearly sixty Moons ago, was not the same man that saw the blood-red Sunrise today. Doubt had replaced certainty, and shame had eclipsed his pride. He was not the same smiling, rough, aggressive soldier of those days; he was still killing, but he was no longer smiling.

As the Sun climbed slowly higher in the east and its dim, early morning rays fell over the landscape, the shadows on the western horizon were less opaque. They revealed themselves to be man-sized figures, some on horseback, strung out along the edges of the marshy bog that separated them from Juk and the 1st Regiment. Juk and his men were at the top of a large hill, staring across the marshland from less than six hundred yards away. It provided a natural advantage and afforded Juk views of the surrounding area. From his lofted position, he could see in all directions for some distance. Under other circumstances, he would have admired the rolling green hills to the north and the flat grasslands that lie beyond them in the east. From here, westwards lay a large area of marshy land, called the Wetlands, and from this observation point, it looked serene and solemnly beautiful. To the south east he could just about make out the trees of The Midnight Forest in the distance.

"What next, Juk?" asked a large set, tall man who appeared beside him.

Juk turned his head to reply. "We wait, Chik. We'll give the poor bastards until full Sun to decide. Then, well, then we'll move in." Juk turned back to the west.

"Full light? Moon's sake, you're softening in your old age. We could finish this by then. Why wait? Why do you think they've stopped here? So close to their homeland? Don't trust Wetlanders," Chik replied.

"We'll wait, Chik," Juk said softly to his friend and lieutenant, Chik Srin.

"Why didn't they stop here, on the hill? Best place to make a stand, if they were true. Something's wrong, Juk. Don't trust Wetlanders, never have!" Chik's voice became louder as he finished his point.

As he asked all these questions, Juk saw Chik's eyes were burning bright with the anticipation of battle that once shone in his own. "Wait until full Sun and then we'll move," the Captain replied. *Why wait indeed?* thought Juk. There was no need for it, other than his own desire to delay; doubt was devouring his self-belief. As Juk continued to stare across the marsh, a small number of the figures rode towards them. One was holding a pole with what looked to be a white cloth attached to it.

"Chik," Juk said quietly. "Bring ten men here at once. There's movement."

Chik nodded. "Cap!" Chik hurried off, leaving his senior countryman alone. As Juk's eyes traced the band of men heading his way, his apprehension receded for a fleeting moment. It was replaced by something else; not by hope, but by something less negative than doubt.

Chik returned with the men on horseback. He brought Juk's horse, too. A beautiful, tall grey stallion. Juk jumped up and quickly scanned the men Chik had brought. Some of the best fighting men the army had; any army in Areekya had. Trained on the battlefield, they killed without remorse, carried out orders without thinking, unwavering followers; just as Juk once was. The 1st Regiment always fought on horseback. They were skilled horsemen. The ancestors of the Chinsap men had moved to the mountainous region from the spacious, meadow-filled lands of the Greenscape a few generations ago for the protection the mountains offered. The affection for horses was brought with them; the Chinsap men still retained their love of horses and the skill to ride them.

"Sir!" The men announced their arrival.

"Looks like we've action. I want you all to stay

close to me. Chik, you do the talking." Juk nodded to his friend.

The men fanned out either side of Juk and Chik, sitting proudly atop their mounts, wrapped in the black bear fur for which the regiment was known. Juk and his men rode out to meet the oncoming figures.

"Hail! Who rides before the 1st Regiment?" Chik shouted out.

"Ashran, head of the Clan Grash. These are my clansmen with me. We come to talk."

"You come to die. Tell us, Wetlander, why should we not kill you and your raggedy-arse band now? We can finish up the cripples and the rest later," Chik spat back. "We are many, you are few. How many do you have? Two, three hundred? We have three times your number, and you have led us on this hunt for three nights. This is the last Sunrise you'll see. You know why we've hunted you down for days. Talking time is over."

"We are beaten, we are tired, some are sick, and we had to leave the wounded to die two nights ago," Ashran replied, locking his eyes on Chik. "What we're asking for is mercy. Do you have that?" Juk watched closely from beside Chik. He saw the clan leader's long, broad frame covered by his long sheep-skin coat, with dirty white hair down to his back. He brought four of his men with him. They were all staring at the floor, their blood-covered faces unable to hide the tiredness the last three nights had inflicted. Ashran's grey eyes were full of emotion as he gave his speech, a speech no clan leader would ever want to give.

"Mercy?" Chik laughed and looked over his shoulder at his men.

"We stand before you asking for mercy," continued Ashran. "We surrender, you have the victory, but we won't come crawling on all fours like some whipped dog. Yes, you have the numbers, but that doesn't mean we won't reduce yours if it comes to that. If we wanted a slaughter, we would've camped there and put up a last fight." As he finished, he pointed over Chik's shoulder to the hill where the 1st Regiment was waiting.

"Victory? What victory is this? For three nights and days you've been running, three blood-red Sunrises need appeasing. Surrender don't appease nothing. Fucking Wetlanders." Juk could see the hatred in Chik's eyes and heard it in his voice.

"Tis any victory that you care to name it, friend. I have lost kin, friends, loved ones. I wish to lose no more. But I'll do so if needed and with it my own life for what it is," Ashran said, the emotion in his voice now not so clear. "But it doesn't have to come to that, I hope. You'll have our allegiance in the coming wars. Let us leave and return to our homes. Name your price, if that's not enough."

"Enough life has been lost, too much blood spilt," Juk interjected. "You speak well, Ashran of Clan Grash. Well enough for a man lost. You have your mercy and we have our victory, as I name it such. Return to your people and surrender yourselves back here before full Sun. Surrender to me in the name of Lord Runkarn."

Juk felt his younger lieutenant'[CP1]s eyes on him. "Captain?"

Juk ignored Chik and continued. "We'll escort you back to the Wetlands, and you'll agree to fight when it is asked, and you'll send grain every harvest to the capital; to Magdil."

Ashran nodded, smiled, and his men turned and rode back the way they had come. Juk looked towards Chik. "Back!" he ordered, and he rode back to his regiment's position. The men followed, with Chik pulling up alongside the leader, his face flush and his eyes wide.

"What the Sun was that?" Chik asked.

"It was time to end it. And watch what you say. You're a good friend, Chik, a close one, but there's a line. Don't cross it, least not in front of the men."

Juk saw Chik staring at him as the younger man replied. "I've never seen you that way before. We're the 1st Regiment, remember?" The junior man continued, "We're known for killing, not showing mercy. That's what we do. The men will like this less than me. Five years we've been together fighting this War, and for I don't know how many Moons before that, we've been friends. We loved the same things: fighting, wine, and fighting." Chik's eyes never left Juk's face.

"Tell the men to stand down. I need to think." Juk rode back towards the hill, but veered to the right of where the 1st Regiment were waiting in formation, proud banners still wrestling with the blustery wind. One thousand of the best fighting men the People's Army had to offer. Men that Juk had helped train to fight. They wore light armour and attacked at high-speed. Their swift, aggressive style of combat meant they regularly caught their opponents off guard. They were the most effective regiment in the army and as such, were often sent to trouble spots all around Areekya. They were well trained and well disciplined; men that followed without question. They were men that lived to fight. Men that he knew wouldn't like the news Chik was telling them as he rode towards the small copse a hundred yards or so away.

Juk dismounted and tied his large grey stallion to a tree. He patted his horse a few times and reached into his pocket and gave him an apple. He watched as the horse greedily devoured it. The people from Chinsap took good care of their horses; they loved and protected them as they would their own family. Stallions were rare to be used for warhorses due to their difficulty in riding them into battle. Juk's horse, Noble, had a gentle enough personality for a stallion. It was mild most of the time, but when battle came around, Noble was the first horse to sense the upcoming trouble and relished it.

The wooded area was fifty or sixty yards wide and about as long. The trees were not tall, but gave Juk some shelter and the solace he needed. The first morning's light was seeping through and made the leaves sparkle with the early morning dew. Juk could smell the sweet aroma of the local flowers, starting to wake for the onset of spring. He sat down on the uneven carpet of leaves and small sticks that had gathered there, and a momentary feeling of peace washed over him. Juk wasn't sure how long he stayed there, deep in his own thoughts, but he was suddenly aware of a noise; leaves crumpling under foot. He turned and saw Chik walking towards him.

"Juk, I thought you could do with some company," Chik said as he continued walking towards him.

"How'd the men take the news?" Juk thought he already knew the answer, but asked anyway.

"As you'd expect they would, the same as I did. No, worse. I'm not sure what happened back there. Is there a plan? Is it a double-cross? Like we did with the Hillmen that time?" Juk thought he could see a flash of excitement in Chik's eyes at this question.

"It's no trick. I thought it was time to end it, that's all," Juk replied, watching his younger friend closely.

Chik was three years younger than Juk. A few inches taller and more muscular. His long, dark curly hair fell past his shoulders and framed his square face with grey eyes and red cheeks. They left the north east together five years ago to join the fight to protect their home; to fight the enemies of Areekya before trouble came to Chinsap. *Fight abroad now, or fight at home later* they were told. It would only take one year. A year to push back the traitors. To bring back peace and calm to all. Well, one year turned into two, then three, four, five. During that time, they had grown closer, reminiscing about home, about their wives and families. Juk had risen quickly, and he brought Chik with him. A good fighting man, a strong, hard man in an army of hard men. Chik was a very capable lieutenant; good enough to have his own command. Juk was sure he'd get it after this.

"The men are confused. I told them it's all under

control. Is it? Is it under control, Juk?" The younger man's eyes didn't have that excitement now. They were full of emotion, but not excitement.

"Tell them we'll break open the last of the ale tonight, Chik. That'll keep them happy. They'll be riding back today, once the terms are agreed. The fighting is done here." With this last comment, Juk walked back to his horse, untied it and mounted the beautiful grey beast.

"That'll only keep them happy until tomorrow, Juk. Once the ale wears off, they'll still be angry. They're owed a fight, and they feel cheated. They want to finish the job."

"It is finished, Chik. Tell them it's done. I'll say no more. Tell them to enjoy the victory. It's over." Juk trotted back towards the camp. He could hear Chik's footsteps following him; no words, but he knew his friend wasn't happy.

ASHRAN

Ashran of the Clan Grash, his clansmen on either side of him, slowly crossed the distance back to the two hundred or so men keenly waiting for his return. As his still proud battle horse trotted through the boggy marshland, his thoughts were of his men. He was glad he had brought about an end to their torment, but with this came the shame of surrender. He dismounted his large grey horse and as he did so, it let out a cry; an exhale of emotion that Ashran wished he could echo.

"It's done, boys," Ashran said to his waiting men. "Make ready for movement. We need to be on the move before full Sun. It's as agreed. They will accept our surrender and they'll allow us to return home. Let's do it with heads high." Ashran looked at his men. He thought he saw relief, but sadness was there, too. "As soon as can be we'll move," he added as he turned and lay his hand on his exhausted horse's head. "Well done girl, take a rest now and we'll be off again soon."

Most of his clan rode geldings: male horses that had been castrated. They were known for their ease of handling, particularly in battle. But Ashran had always felt that the horse chose the rider. And even though mares were thought to be more difficult to handle, Ashran's magnificent girl, Grace, had a personality that had attracted him to her many years ago; and she accepted him immediately.

As he turned around and looked back across the marshland, he thought of the last few days and how tired he felt. He was sure his men were feeling the same. Five days previously, they were camped in the Midnight Forest, hiding, waiting for the enemy to ride across the plains. Their scouts reported the army was five hundred strong, no more. Ashran's army was nearly double that number and his best men were with him. The mage had told him the extra protection the forest would provide all but ensured victory.

They had left their home in the far north western corner of Areekya a week earlier. Ashran knew Magdil's army was coming. His plan was to draw them away from his clan; the women and children would at least be safe. It would give them time to find whatever stores they could and hide in the wetlands of Lendir, their home for generations. Many lives of men had passed since they first lived in those Wetlands. Most would tell you those years were not good years. War, famine and disease tore the land apart. The Clan Grash survived those years by farming the wetlands, fighting when they had to, but mostly living of what they could tease from the land, sometimes not much, but enough to survive.

The enemy surprised them that night in the Midnight Forest. They had cut off their way home to the west. They'd approached from both the south and the west under the cover of a Moonless night. Ashran felt shame for allowing that. He had let down his clan, his people, his honour. The battle was over in less than two hours. Three hundred of his best men cut down dead or left to die as they retreated north. Hunted down for three days and nights, losing more men; leaving them to die in the surrounding hills and grasslands. Now he was leading them into the enemy's hands, into surrender. As he looked into his horse's eyes, he saw the tiredness there that mirrored his own. Ashran felt almost overcome with fear and anxiety, and was close to becoming paralysed with dread. His upbringing in the Wetlands was the only thing that would pull him through this moment. Wetlanders knew how to deal with hard times. They had to learn that as younglings, eking out an existence from the land living in fear of the uncertain future. This moment wouldn't break Ashran of Clan Grash. Today wasn't the day he would succumb to fear. He may have surrendered to the enemy, but he hadn't surrendered himself, not today.

"So, it's accomplished, then?"

The voice came from behind, but it was unmistakable: soft, melodic and with a deep baritone, it was that of Rivan.

"Yes. As you said, it didn't take long." Ashran turned to face the mage. "We have a short while to get ready. They'll escort us home."

"You had no choice, Ashran. It had been written."

Ashran studied the tall mage's face. Dark brown, almost black almond-shaped eyes revealing no emotion. He had a kind face, but there was a sense of something else below the surface that he did not allow to be shown. Ashran looked down at the floor and said, "Well, for good or no, it's done. At least the woman and children are safe. We ride back today."

"Yes, yes, good, very good," Rivan replied, smiling as he walked past the clan leader. "I need to leave before then. I'll away soon."

Ashran turned, his eyes following the mage. "Leave?" Ashran's lip curled up on one side. "Where? Why? What do you mean?"

"I have to leave before they come. That is of great import. I mustn't be seen. I'll ride away as soon as I am able," the mage said without turning his head.

Ashran's eyes were fixed on the back of Rivan's head as he walked away. A flush of anger rose within the clan leader, which he managed to contain. Long ago, Ashran had learned not to second guess or try to control the inscrutable mage. He had known him for many Moons, turning up on Midwinter's Eve a long time ago. Ashran was barely old enough to hold a sword when he first saw the tall stranger enter the Sacred Circle. Rivan spoke to Mushran, the Clan Leader of the time, and then sat, watching silently for the rest of the night. The mysterious stranger was gone the next day, but intermittently showed up from Moon to Moon. Ashran had seen more of him since becoming Clan Leader himself, years ago. Ashran never felt he knew him or his motives well, but over the years, Rivan had steered the clan well with advice, mostly spiritual, but sometimes on all manners of things from conflict to health. He had never steered them wrong, except for the Midnight Forest, five nights ago. That night, Rivan wasn't seen. Last night he reappeared with his plan for surrender:

"The past is gone, the future is never here, now is now. Now is when you choose," Rivan had offered as reason

last night. *"Choose now. Choose to protect the families. The battle is lost. Do not lose now, do not lose the present,"* the Mage had urged. In truth, Ashran had been half-glad to hear this counsel. He was tired, and the fear had begun to rise in him. It had engulfed his thoughts. He was ready to hear the advice the mage gave.

Ashran walked towards his men. His eyes scoured the remnants of his clan, less than three hundred, nearly half wounded. He fixed his eyes on a small, wiry young man of only twenty years. "Ashron, are the men ready?" the clan leader asked his son.

"Yes, Father, almost. The last of the wounded are being patched up. We'll be ready for the off soon."

Ashran looked at his son and smiled. He had fought well. Ashron was small, but he had skill with his sword. Ashran had tried to keep his son out of trouble, keeping the strongest on either side of him in the battle. But in the milieu, Ashran had become disoriented and was happy to see his son survive the main onslaught. He had kept him close by his side during the retreat, and Ashron had done well looking after the wounded. "We're moving as soon as we can. Be quick, eh?" Ashran walked towards his large mare, climbed up, and trotted towards the front of where the men were waiting.

In a short while, Ashron moved up next to his father. "All set."

With that, Ashran slowly trotted towards the rising Sun, not yet fully risen in the sky. It was a deep burning red colour this morning, as it had been these last few mornings. A bad omen. Red mornings were a bad sign in the Wetlands; trouble usually followed:

'Red morning, clan's warning', was the saying in Lendir. Ashran was hoping there would be no trouble this morning. The remains of the clan rode slowly across the marshy bogland to the waiting army at the foot of the hills. As he rode, Ashran thought about what this surrender would mean. He knew it wouldn't be good, but at least he had kept the clan back home safe from harm. He would have to ride out to fight for Magdil, for Lord Runkarn, every once and in a while. Grain and harvest would also have to be sent to Magdil every season, as payment, food they couldn't spare, but it was done now. At least the women and children were safe.

"Whoa," Ashran said and brought his horse to a stop. "I, Ashran of Clan Grash, present myself to the People's Army in surrender." Ashran just about allowed the words to escape his mouth. "I agree to present myself to you under the terms already agreed. We'll fight in your wars, and we'll send grain every year to Magdil." Ashran held eye contact with the blue-eyed man atop a horse about ten feet away. "We lay down our weapons to be returned upon our arrival home." A clan member rode forward and dropped three large sacks on the floor.

"It's done then. Now we'll escort you back to your home." The blue-eyed man yanked his reins, turned, and said something to the younger man to his right. Ashran couldn't make out what was said, but the younger man looked shocked at what he was told; his eyes were wide and his brow furrowed. With that, the blue-eyed man rode forward, followed by about a hundred of his men. He raised his hand in a gesture that Ashran was to follow.

THE LADY OF MIDSCAPE

She observed him closely as he pulled back the cream silk sheets, got out of the bed and gracefully walked over to the far side of the room where his clothes were. She watched on with a smile at his slender, smooth body as he got dressed, replaying the previous night's experience in her mind. Once he had finished dressing, she turned her gaze to the window and saw the Sun had just crept over the Mountains of Dawn to the east, its orange glow faintly lighting the eastern sky. She always loved this time of the day; so much promise, so many opportunities lay ahead. The early morning Sunrise was her favourite part of the day.

She continued to stare out of the window at the wonderful Sunrise while she spoke. "Be sure you're quiet on the way out. I wouldn't want to wake my husband if I were you," she barked at the young, handsome boy as he pulled the door open and quietly made his way out of the bedroom.

Lady Livian Masterton-Greenaway was the matriarch of the city of Midscape, the capital of Areekya before the War. Before Runkarn beguiled her father with his whispers and lies and before Runkarn brought 'peace' to the land. After the death of her father, brothers, and her first husband in the War, Runkarn had also made her wed her current husband, Dennis Greenaway; a minor lord of Areekya. Dennis Greenaway had done well out of the War, winning plaudits for his bravery from Runkarn, but getting nothing but contempt from Livian Masterton. A constant reminder to Lord Greenaway and a point of pride to Livian was that she kept her family's name after the marriage. It was accepted to give credence and reassurance to the people, and Livian saw it as a minor victory. They hadn't spent more than a dozen nights together in the two years they had been wed, and those were nights she would rather forget.

She got dressed and made her way to the dining hall, and sat down at one end of the long oak table for breakfast. Livian was a tall, slim woman. She looked and acted as someone of noble birth should: proud, confident and beautiful. Livian had long, black hair which flowed down past her shoulders to the middle of her back. She was in her mid-thirties, but retained the youthful, dark-skinned looks she had developed and flaunted since her teenage years. She had realised her beauty at a young age, using it to get what she needed and much that she wanted. She found that it all came easily to her.

She was served dark bread and fish by the young, handsome, blond-haired serving boy who had left her bedroom minutes before. As she pulled off a piece of bread and put it into her mouth, she heard familiar footsteps coming into the main hall.

"Couldn't you be a bit more discreet with your fucking?" Dennis Greenaway aimed this jibe at his wife, while keeping his eyes fully focused on the serving boy. "His clunking and clanging woke me this morning. Lucky for him I have to be up early today, else he'd be on the end of a pike instead of serving you breakfast. Boy! Bring me one half loaf and two fish. Oh, and I want some dark beer with that."

"I see you had a pleasant night's sleep," Livian said, continuing to eat. "Do we have to start this early? We usually wait until your late afternoon drinking before the arguments start." Livian kept her eyes on her food, not looking at her husband at all. "Anyway, what business is it of yours with whom I sleep? Do I enquire of whom you are sharing your bed with this week? It's best if you keep to your bedmates and leave me to do as I please."

"My dear, I couldn't give a fig who you are fucking, but I do care what the servants think," Dennis said, staring at the serving boy again. "And if they think I don't care, well, well, that won't do. Your problem is you think your family is still at the top table. You need to remember that you are all that's left of your precious family, and that you are — all you fucking are — is some brood mare married off to me to keep your fucking bloodline alive. A lot of good that's done! Sun's mercy it was me and not some other cunt of a lord who you got stuck with." Lord Dennis shifted his gaze from the serving boy to his wife.

Livian lifted her eyes. She felt that well-directed barb from her husband, but defiantly decided not to show it. She looked up at him. "Mercy, was it? Well, that's more than you and Runkarn with his cronies showed my father, brothers, and my husband at the Moon Bridge, my dear."

"I trust I can count on you today. With the Magdil

lot turning up. On your best behaviour. We can get back to the bitter resentments tomorrow." Dennis half smiled.

Livian watched her husband as he devoured his fish and bread. His short, stout frame with red, receding hair barely squeezed into his chair. He wasn't much more than a peasant, elevated to the position of the Lord of Midscape for his conduct in the War. She had detested him from the first moment she set eyes on him; his low-born position, his looks, his manner, just about everything about him had repulsed her. Added to that, the humiliation of marrying one five full Suns younger than her. She continued to watch as he finished his goblet of beer and his cheeks changed colour to match his hair. "Have I ever let you down with my service? I'm not planning on starting today. Even if they are they sending that toad Ruperk and his cronies. Why they would send that cretin all the way here, I don't know. Something must have happened over there in Magdil." Livian continued to eat.

"The message said little," Dennis replied, taking another large gulp of beer from his almost instantaneously refilled goblet. "Just keep quiet, and let me do the talking. It might be good news." He burped loudly as he finished the sentence.

"When have you ever known that snake to bring good news? You should prepare yourself. He's not bringing good news, of that I'm sure." Livian left the remains of her breakfast, placing her knife and fork on the plate.

"He's a fucking snake, for sure. Runkarn's never

been the same since that fucker wormed his way into his inner circle. I know that, but we're still on good terms. Maybe not like the old days, but I would've heard if it was something really bad. Just an administrative adjustment, grain or tax raise, I'd wager," Dennis said through a mouthful of bread, fish and beer.

Livian, appalled at her husband's manners and language, left the table, walked over to the exit and just about heard the end of the sentence as she made her way out of the hall and back to her room. She sat at her drawing table and gazed out the window. From her bedroom, she could see the Mountain of Serenity in the distance and beyond that, the foothills of the Mountains of Dawn. The morning Sun was rising over the mountains and the yellow rays of light caught the Mountain of Serenity at this time of the day. The summer Sunlight glistened. And there, in its incandescent elegance, the tip of the mountain shimmered in its beauty. Her ancestors were buried on that mountain, not her father, husband or brothers, though. They were not given the honour of a burial, their bodies burned with the other poor souls who fell at the Moon Bridge over three years ago. But her mother was buried there. On the mountain in her rightful place, albeit too soon. She died as the War started, years ago. Livian's mother was an outwardly strong person, but that belied her nervous disposition. The War had proved too much for her and she succumbed to illness just after it started.

Livian thought back to the day of her mother's funeral. Her husband had not yet gone off to fight in the War. He was acting as counsel, together with her two brothers, for her beloved father and Lord of Areekya, Lord Sydric Masterton. She had only been married two months at that point, and soon after, she was alone, as all were sent to fight. But on the day her mother was buried, the entire city came out in respect and condolence for Lady Elena Masterton. The city mourned the loss heavily. It signalled a turning point in the history of Midscape. A generational shift. The familiar, the traditional, the known were all lost that day, replaced by war, change and the unknown. It seemed to Livian, now reflecting upon the past, that the whole city cried for her mother that day. Maybe they were crying for the city, too. Life had never been the same since that day. War came, men were lost, and women cried.

The mountain was her mother's place of reflection and tranquillity, just as it had become Livian's. She rode out there sometimes to be alone, to be away from her life in Midscape. As she sat by the window, gazing at the tranquil vista in contemplation, her mind all too quickly drifted back to Magdil, and its impending visitor, Ruperk. The snake with two heads, her father used to say of him. He was one of his vassals until things turned ill against Runkarn. His double-cross at the Moon Bridge was the last wave of the unrelenting tide that had been coming for a few years. It led to the death of all that she cared for, and the end of her family's hold on Areekya. For that, he held a special place on her list of people she intended to pay back for all the ills that had befallen her; he was one of many.

For all the resentment she had for Dennis, she had noticed a shift in his feelings towards the capital of late.

In the two years since he was ordered to marry her and move to Midscape, his relationship with Runkarn had cooled. It had become more distant, and this she could use to her advantage. She would bide her time, though. Planning, preparing, observing, waiting for the time to push, but her patience was beginning to bear fruit, she thought. Just be patient a little longer, she told herself. Just a little more.

JUK THRI

He felt intense pressure on his chest. His heart felt as if it was being hammered; wrought and twisted. His blood felt as if it were pumping around his veins and arteries at double speed. He felt his breathing slow as he gasped for air in the darkness that engulfed him. Slowly, he felt himself sinking into the earth, not by some force pushing him down, but by the weight of his body, like large anvils tied to each arm and leg drawing him down. Down into the cold dirt. There was something else, too. A smell of burning; he could sense the smoke flood his senses, getting more intense with each passing moment. The odour became stronger and stronger until it overwhelmed him.

"Captain, Captain, it is getting on, and you said to wake you before first Sun." Juk felt himself shaken awake by one of his men.

He sat upright and stared into the glowing embers of the fire, that was petering out as the smoke swirled and snaked past him upwards into the dimly lit sky, the fading night stars preparing to hand over duty to the first hint of daybreak. "Yes, is everything prepared? Are we ready to go?" Juk looked away from the fire as the last word left his lips.

"Yes, Captain, the Wetlanders are being roused now. We'll leave before first light."

Juk Thri stood up and climbed on his horse. He

rode towards the front of the makeshift camp they made at Sundown yesterday. At the head were about half of his men, the other half waking the prisoners. Before too long, they were set, and they started off.

Ashran rode up front with Juk. There had been little discussion between the two men. Juk had been lost in his own thoughts for most of the journey. It was nearly at an end now, just a morning's ride to Lendir. The weather had become wetter the nearer they got to the borders of Ashran's home; the Wetlands justifying their name. By Mid-Sun they should reach the borders of the Wetlanders' home. The journey had taken almost a whole Moon's ride, stopping only when they had to. Juk had no desire to dally.

"I am a proud man. Defeat is a difficult pain to bear. I have lost men, good men. Such is the way with War, whether it comes unlooked for or not. But I want to say thank you," the older clan leader said. Juk felt Ashran's gaze upon him.

"For what?" Juk replied, continuing to stare straight ahead into the distance.

"For allowing me, for allowing us, to return to our families. Showing mercy to your enemies is a virtue. Not one your men share, I feel." Juk could still feel Ashran's eyes fixed on him.

Juk turned his head and met the clan leader's stare. He thought of his own family, his wife and daughters waiting for him in Chinsap. "War is a terrible thing. You refused the service of Lord Runkarn, you paid the price, your men paid the price. It was time to stop. You are now in the service of Magdil. No thank you is needed."

"Well, needed or no, it's yours. Family is important to the Clan Grash. For years, we've struggled and suffered. The one thing we've always had is family. The only thing that made the suffering bearable. I let down my clan. The only comfort I take is my family is safe, my men's families are safe." Ashran broke eye contact and looked down at his horse, Juk noticed.

Juk Thri said nothing in reply. He looked ahead and allowed himself to think of his own impending family reunion. Before too long, he would be home. He would be in the arms of his wife. Family was important to him, too.

"When we arrive, will you allow us to give you the hospitality of our clan?" Ashran asked, looking over at Juk. "We can provide you with some food and drink; it's not much, but you'll get the best we have."

Juk shook his head. "We have no time for hospitality. We must be away as soon as we reach your borders. Your weapons will be returned to you, and you can ride the rest of the way with your men. Keep your food and drink for your families. It's been a tough winter, and the spring will hardly be any better for you." Juk made eye contact with Ashran once more.

"Sun be good, we'll have a good harvest this year," Ashran replied.

Juk smiled. "You have a tough road ahead, Ashran of the Clan Grash. I suggest you prepare well for it. Magdil will call on you before too long. Once it has you in its jaws, it doesn't let go." Juk's eyes remained fixed on Ashran; he saw the soft grey eyes of the heavy- set man riding next to him, and the tiniest and briefest of warm smiles flashed across the clan leader's face.

Ashran replied, "We may have been enemies on the field of battle, but that part is done now. I wish happiness and the blessings of the Sun and Moon on you. I hope that if we meet again, it'll be under warmer circumstances. We have been dealing with lords and rulers for generations. We'll survive; at least the clan will. That's as it must be, that's as it always will be." They rode in silence for the rest of the journey. Before too long, the ground became damp and to the north west a large forest came into view. They had reached the borders of Lendir, with the Wet Forest towering over the marshy Wetlands.

"Your weapons are returned," Juk announced as three men came up from the rear and dropped the assorted swords, bows, axes and clubs to the ground. "Leave them on the floor until we ride out of sight. You will then be free to ride home. A messenger will be sent soon, by Runkarn, Lord of Magdil. And then you'll know what needs to be done. Farewell, Ashran of the Clan Grash, may your tidings be better in the coming Moons." Juk Thri pulled on the reins of his horse as he turned its head and rode back the way from which they had come.

There came no reply from Ashran or his clan members. The 1st Regiment rode off and was heading back out of the marshy boglands as Mid-Sun approached. The rays of the Sun were now becoming warmer. Spring had fully announced herself and the bright flowers were easy to spot as they rode the rest of the day in silence. Juk rode at the head of the group, as his men rode in double formation behind him. They continued to ride in an eastward direction for the next few weeks, stopping only at night to camp and feeding on the locally caught game they found along the way. Small game mostly; rabbit and pheasant, although on one occasion two of the men managed to fell a medium-sized deer. By the next full Moon, they could see the hilly area where the Wetlanders surrendered looming up ahead.

Juk raised his arm and rolled his fingers into a fist. "Halt! Gather round, men. Here we must part. I must ride to the east. You must return to Magdil, and to the regiment." There were puzzled looks on the men's faces, but none spoke for a few moments.

"Captain?" muttered a rider. "Leave you alone? That doesn't sound right. Will you not take an escort? Take a score or more with you. 'Tis better safe than not, eh?"

"I'll ride alone. That's an order. You are to return to Magdil. Lieutenant Chik will have need of you. I'll be fine, I'm in no danger. I must ride off to the east today. You'll head south to Magdil from here. You have fought hard, so stop at a tavern or two and enjoy your victory. That's an order." Juk smiled at his men. "You'll be in the capital soon enough. There you can get some rest and be ready for the next battle to come."

"Captain!" the men shouted as one in deference to the order given.

Juk Thri flicked his heels into his horse and rode away from his men. His mind was full of conflict. He thought of his family waiting for him in Chinsap. His father and mother long dead, his wife and children were what mattered most to him now. Juk thought of the army, and the implications of his decision came flooding over him in a wave of anxiety that he had kept down before this moment. The uncertainty and angst he had been feeling washed over him with the dread of a condemned man, finally realising his plight and allowing the guilt to consume his whole being. He thought back to when the change in his mind had occurred. He was sure he'd fought willingly at first, but those early days were difficult for his mind to reconcile with today. How had it spiralled out of control? What decisions had he made that were wrong? Were they wrong?

All these questions and more flew through his mind as fast as his horse was now galloping. He kept riding; the tears formed in his eyes, dropping onto his cheeks, and splashing away as his horse galloped across the firm earth underfoot and headed towards the grasslands of the Greenscape.

CHIK SRIN

The distance back to Magdil was a little more than a Moon's brisk ride, but Chik and his men took their time. Chik wanted to give Juk time. He wanted to give his friend time to think, time to reconsider, time to return. Chik was still in shock at what his old friend and Captain had told him as he left to escort the Wetlanders home. Chik and his men stopped at every small town, tavern and brothel. They rode at a leisurely pace. Apart from his main reason, it gave the men some well-earned down time. They could drink, relax, and try to forget about things for a while. They even indulged in the Midsummer celebrations in a small village near the end of their journey. It was over three Moons before they were within a day's ride of Magdil. The weather had improved during their journey, and now with the seventh Moon approaching, Chik decided to camp out in the open for the night and enjoy the summer weather. They'd make an early start at Sunrise and the men would be fresh when they entered the city.

"Let's camp here for the night, boys." Chik looked around. There was tree cover to sleep under, and the Spindle Sea, which was to the east, provided them with protection. Not that Chik thought they'd need it here, less than a day's ride from the capital, but old habits died hard in the young lieutenant. "Break open the ale, lads. Let's enjoy our last night on the road, eh?" Chik smiled as he dismounted his horse and tied it to a tree.

Some men had caught a few wild animals during the day and they were busily preparing them for supper.

This night would allow him to get his story straight, too. To choose his words carefully for the account he would have to give tomorrow. Chik had thought hard about it since that morning when Juk, his Captain, his friend, his fellow countryman, had told him he was quitting the army. No reason was given and Chik could still feel the shock he felt that morning. Chik wanted to convince him to change his mind, but Juk didn't give him any time. His friend and Captain had quickly grabbed a hundred men and rode off to escort the prisoners home to the Wetlands. For over three Moons, Chik had wrestled with how to report Juk's decision to do that to Lord Runkarn. It was not a Captain's job. It could have — it should have — been carried out by a junior man. Chik had decided that he would say it was his suggestion to do so. This would buy Juk some time. Chik was sure that given time, Juk would see reason. He would come to his senses and return. Chik planned to report that Juk had escorted the Wetlanders back after talking to him; they'd both agreed it was the right thing to do. That would buy his friend some time.

The next morning, Chik and the 1st Regiment readied and left at first Sun. It was about half a day's ride to the capital. Chik wanted to arrive before mid-afternoon. The ride to the capital was a pleasant one from their overnight camp. There a vast area of lush green fields with magnificent coloured flowers growing in them. The colours were glittering in the early morning summer Sunshine; it gave Chik some relief from the apprehension he was feeling. Just after midday, Magdil came into view. They were at the beginning of the wide, tree-lined approach to the capital, which led to the gigantic stone walls of Magdil. On either side of the approach, massive pine trees stood as proud sentinels, guiding the way into the capital. From the outside, the city looked an impressive stronghold. The tall, red walls were nearly fifty feet high, with arrow slits every twenty feet.

Mountains surrounded the city and enclosed within, the city stretched out in multiple directions. The capital housed five thousand people. Up high, atop a hill to the north of the city, stood the main castle. Towering above, it was protected by another set of red stone walls, nearly as tall as the ones that protected the city, with battlements every ten feet. The castle stood proud, looking down on the organised, neat roads and avenues of the city. It was no wonder Magdil had never been breached; it was difficult to imagine an army that could do such a thing. Chik and his men waited at the main gate, as was customary for any returning army. Each successful returning regiment had to be announced by the guardsmen at the gate by the blowing of trumpets, followed by the pronouncement of the regiment's name and Captain.

The trumpets rang out, and the head guardsman bellowed, "The 1st Regiment returning home victorious once more, and at its head, Captain Juk Thri."

The gates opened and Chik led the regiment in. There were the expected cheers and shouts from the crowd that had gathered. Nobody seemed to notice that the regiment wasn't being led by Juk Thri, as Chik led the men to the east of the city towards the barracks.

As the men continued to their barracks, Chik veered to the left and headed north to the castle. The drawbridge was slowly lowered to cover the large expanse of water that surrounded the huge, intimidating castle up high. Chik rode across it, rehearsing in his mind what he was going to report. As Chik rode his large white horse up towards the main castle gates, a single bead of sweat rolled down his forehead and dropped into his eye. Chick wiped it away and regained his composure. *Just keep it simple*, he told himself.

Chik was led into the counsel room by two large guards suited in silver armour with purple breastplates. Sitting at the head of the table at the far end of the room was Runkarn, Lord of Magdil and Areekya. Chik stood with his hands behind his back.

"Well met, Lieutenant Chik Srin," said the tall, older man with short, greying hair dressed in a tunic the same colour as the guards' breastplates. He remained in his chair.

"Hail, my Lord Runkarn. I bring you another victory from the 1st Regiment. The Wetlanders were defeated. They gave us a little runaround, but nothing we couldn't handle," Chik replied, keeping his eyes firmly on Runkarn's. "They finally surrendered and agreed to favourable terms."

"I see. Tell me, where is your Captain? Where is Captain Juk Thri? I heard the guards announce him, yet it is you bringing me this news." Runkarn stood up and sauntered towards the young lieutenant. "I would have thought the death of one of my Captains would have reached me sooner."

"Juk Thri is not dead, my lord. He escorted the remaining Wetlanders home. We thought it needed a strong command. He took a hundred men to ensure there would be no problems. You know Wetlanders, stubborn bastards!" Chik answered, maintaining eye contact.

Runkarn was standing right behind Chik now. "Yes, I know them well. When shall he return? I wish to see my Captain to congratulate him on another victory."

"The Wetlands are more than a Moon's ride from where we caught them, and there is some heavy ground from there to here, so it could be a while yet, my lord. But I am here at your service. If there's anything you need of the 1st Regiment, we are here to serve. A couple of days' rest and repair, we'll be ready to go again," Chik said, trying to say as much as he could while protecting his friend.

Runkarn placed his hand on Chik's left shoulder. Chik felt it stroke across his shoulder and saw the thin fingers with long, clean nails drape down the top of his arm. "Get some rest, Lieutenant Chik. You have done well, enjoy it, and we shall speak again soon." Runkarn withdrew his hand, then walked back to his seat at the head of the table and sat down. "Rest well, young man. Bring news when you hear it."

"Yes, my lord. It was all done for the honour of Areekya, in the name of Runkarn the Great." With this, Chik turned and moved towards the door.

"Tonight, the city is yours. Tell your men the taverns are at my pleasure tonight. I shall see it so," Runkarn declared from his seat.

"Thank you, my lord. From all the regiment, thank you."

And with that, Chik left and made his way back to the barracks in the east of the city. *Something's off*, he thought. That went too smoothly, too trouble-free. He hadn't had many dealings with Runkarn — that was mainly done by Juk — but what he knew of the man, he was insightful and suspicious. That conversation seemed to be unhindered by awkward questions, and that didn't seem right. Still, he was tired and relieved it was finished, and he had a night of drinking ahead of him, a night all the regiment deserved and would fully take advantage of.

That evening, Chik accompanied the men to the Witch's Broom; the closest tavern to the barracks, and the most soldier-friendly in town. Usually, Chik indulged with the men in the almost ritual homecoming onslaught of raucous drinking that took place, but this time was different. He sat in the corner of the tavern, watching the men drink while he quietly drank on his own. The smell of stale beer and jasmine filled the air; the sweet aroma of the flower used mainly to overpower the odour of the beer, but failed to do so. Before too long, Chik was deep in his cups and found he had the company of a young serving girl.

"One more, mister?" asked the young girl, barely in her twenties.

Chik looked up at his companion and nodded. "Yes,

one more — two more, you join me." He looked back down at his empty mug.

The girl returned with two mugs of ale. "Two more, mister." She plunked herself down tightly next to Chik.

"Now, let's drink. Let's drink to me, to you, to Juk." Chik picked up his mug and took a huge gulp.

The girl did the same, before asking," Juk? Who's Juk? Is he here?"

"No, not here. Gone. Gone home. Given up, he has. My friend, my Captain, given up." Juk kept his eyes on his half-empty mug, not lifting them once. "I didn't stop him or try to." Then he gulped the remaining beer down and waved his mug at his newly found friend. "One, two more!" he said, his raised voice leading to a few heads turning in his direction.

"Two more, mister." The girl walked over to the bar.

Chik looked up and looked around. He saw his men enjoying their night, as they should. It had been a long ride, and they'd had a hard battle. They deserved to enjoy themselves. He thought differently of himself, though.

"Two more, mister." The girl returned and sat down again. "Gone home? That's good innit? Why the sad face?" She took a sip of her ale.

"My Captain, my friend, went home. I let him. I didn't stop him. I lied." Chik took another big gulp.

"Lying don't matter none. Keeps us safe from harm

sometime, it does. Best thing ever, I reckon," the girl said with a smile on her face.

"Lying don't matter? It does matter! When it breaks a man's honour, it matters." Juk emptied his mug and banged it on the table. "Two more," he slurred, the words just about forming and leaving his lips.

"Two more, mister? I ain't done with my one," the young girl replied, eyes wide.

"Two more," Chik repeated, lifting his eyes and looking directly at the serving girl. He noticed her long black hair and almond-shaped face. She had an earthy beauty, reminding Chik of the girls from Chinsap. Hard-working beauties they were in Chinsap, strong, hard of heart, and beautiful. Chik watched the serving girl as she walked over to the bar, her large arse showing through her baggy dress. He smiled and kept his eyes on her as she returned with two mugs of ale.

"Two more, mister." She put them on the table and smiled back at Chik.

"Now, let's drink. Drink to you, me, and Juk!" Chik picked up his mug and finished the ale in one. As he banged the mug on the table once more, his head followed, knocking his empty mug and the girl's full one to the floor. For a brief moment, the chatter of the tavern stopped and focused on Chik's table. The girl was quickly on her knees, picking up the mugs and clearing away the ale. As she stood up and walked back to the bar, the chatter started up again and everyone carried on as before. Chik stayed still, head on the table. He'd passed out.

When Chik awoke the next morning, he was back in the barracks, in his own bed. He had no idea how that had happened, but was glad it had. Slowly, last night came back to him. He remembered drinking. Drinking too much until someone started talking to him. A woman; he remembered her beauty, and that was it, nothing, until this morning. It was late. He could see the Sun climbing outside. It was nearly Mid-Sun.

"He's awake," came a shout from the opposite side of the barracks. "How do you feel, Chik? That was some night, eh?" the voice continued.

Chik looked over and saw one of his men, Klaw, smiling, looking over at him. "Yes. How'd I get home?"

"We carried you back. It was tough to keep you quiet, though, Chik. Not sure what you were going on about, but you wouldn't shut up. About Captain Juk, mainly. That's right isn't it lads?" Klaw looked around at the men all nodding in agreement.

"Well, I was drunk." Chik stood up, and immediately regretted it. His head was pounding. He made his way to the bathing area and thrust his head into the tub full of water there. He felt the ice-cold sensation race through him at once.

"Oh, Chik. You have a request to report to the castle when you awoke. An early messenger this morning. New orders, I reckon!" Klaw shouted from his bunk. "Looks like we're on the move again." Klaw didn't sound too happy.

Chik's mind began to race. His gut told him this wasn't a usual summons. What did Klaw mean about

Juk? Chik knew he talked too much when in his cups. Had he been talking about Juk? Who had heard? He could think about nothing else while he got dressed. It didn't matter how much he searched his memory, he couldn't recall anything more of last night. Chik was now worried. By the time he was being led in to the counsel room to see Runkarn, he had convinced himself he'd been caught in his deception and was thinking of the best way out of it.

"My lord," Chik greeted Runkarn. Even though there was a chill to the room, a bead of sweat formed, and Chik felt it run down his forehead.

"So, Lieutenant Chik. How is the spirit of the regiment? I take it last night went some way to helping." Runkarn got up out of his chair and walked towards Chik as he finished his sentence. "And news of your Captain?" Runkarn had his back to Chik, looking out over the courtyard below. "Before you answer, think very carefully. Late last night, Captain Juk Thri's men returned without their Captain." At that moment, Chik knew. He knew he couldn't lie any more. He couldn't protect his friend, and himself. He had to choose. "Juk Thri has gone home, my lord. He headed there after taking the Wetlanders back." Chik looked down at the floor, staring anxiously, thinking about what to say next.

JUK THRI

The voices in the distance were difficult to make out. They sounded like children shouting. Whether it was children at play or some other activity, they were too far away to tell. It made Juk Thri feel uneasy, though. He made his way towards the voices, walking at first, and then he tried to run, but his feet wouldn't move. They felt heavy, as if they were rooted to the ground like some tall sentinel oak. He tried to move again, but he felt his body held back by some unseen force. He could sense its malevolent presence, grabbing at him, pulling him; invisible hands clutching at his tired, anchored body. The voices moved further away, further and further, until he could hardly hear them anymore. Juk now felt himself pulled backwards. He reached out; he grabbed onto a branch of a tree as he felt himself being dragged away further from the children, further from the voices. The branch snapped. His head hit the ground and his body lie stationary on the floor. The voices, gone. The uneasy feeling remained; a presence lingered behind him, towering over him, seeping through him.

Juk Thri woke with a start. He felt the cold sweat dripping from his forehead. He stared straight ahead and saw his horse, Noble, tied to a tall oak tree eating the grass. It was still early, the first rays of the early morning Sun shimmering through the branches of the tall oak. Juk heard the morning songs of the local birds. Here in the Greenscape, the birds were plentiful, using the vast green flatlands and tall trees to make their home. Juk untied his horse and set off again. They had been riding hard together for nearly three Moons, Noble showing none of the fatigue and anxiety Juk felt. By Mid-Sun he would reach the northern city of Stoneguard. It was now the seventh Moon of the year, and the scorching midday Sun was burning his skin as he rode. He could feel its powerful, fiery rays on his face as he rode north, which traditionally had a more temperate climate, but this year the Sun was fierce and its glistening rays beat down on Juk.

Stoneguard had been used as protection from the northern hill tribes many Moons ago. Now it was mainly used by Magdil as a northern recruiting and military training centre. It was where Juk and Chik had started out. It was home to Lord Janson Brok, a northern noble and long-time friend to Juk. They had campaigned in the north together many Moons ago. Juk was tired, cold and hungry. He thought a night's rest in more comfortable surroundings would do him good. Juk wasn't certain what kind of reception he would receive from his old friend. It was four Moons since he left Chik to ride back to the capital, so he couldn't be sure if Magdil had sent any word. But his friendship with Janson Brok was long and close, and Juk felt the level of trust between them made it a small enough risk worth taking.

As he approached the city, he could see its tall, protective stone walls. There, hanging down proudly either side of the entrance, were the banners of House Brok: a castle and a tall tower on a green background; on both sides of the tower was a tall mountain peak. It was a banner that brought back a sense of familiarity to Juk; an intimate feeling he had been missing. Dead ahead, at the main gates of the city of Stoneguard, he saw two guards standing on either side of the main entrance. They noticed his army uniform and 1st Regiment insignia, and allowed him to enter without any words needed to be exchanged. A silent nodding of heads was suffice. Juk rode through the main gates and continued straight, past all the hustle and bustle of the afternoon market, and headed straight for the tower in the centre of the city. The tower was surrounded by a moat which was crossed by a drawbridge. This was controlled from within the tower itself. Juk stopped at the city side of the moat and gave the guards instructions to signal the lowering of the drawbridge.

"On whose orders, Captain? Who are you here to see?" the senior guard asked.

"I'm here to see Lord Brok. I'm an old friend. Tell him Juk Thri, Captain of the 1st Regiment, is here to see him." It felt strange for Juk to hear these words leave his mouth now. They almost caught in his throat, and he let out a cough.

"Aye, Sir. Wait here," the guard replied and signalled to the guards on the other side to lower the drawbridge. When it had descended, the guard walked across and Juk could see him talking to the other guards. After a while, he gestured for Juk to follow him.

"I'll escort you there now," the guard said, and led the way. When they had reached Lord Brok's hall, the guard halted. "My lord is expecting you inside." With that he turned and walked back the way he'd come, leaving Juk standing by the doors.

The door guard opened the door and motioned for Juk to enter. Juk walked through the wide entrance and saw Janson Brok sitting at the head of the table in the middle of the room.

"My Lord Brok," Juk greeted his friend.

"Well, bless the Sun thrice. Juk Thri, what an unexpected pleasure this is, my friend. Come, sit. Tell me your news. Why have you come? How are you? What's the news from the capital?"

"I have taken leave for now, my lord. I'm on my way home," answered Juk to the first of the three questions as he made his way over to the table and sat down next to his friend. "All is well, with me and the capital," he quickly answered the second two. "But, my lord, tell me, how are you? How long has it been?" Juk quickly diverted any focus on his unexpected presence.

"Ha! Older, fatter, slower. Too long, Juk. Wine?" Lord Brok raised his large hand and pointed to his old friend as a young boy scurried over with a jug of wine and began pouring it into the silver goblet on the table. "Leave the jug there, boy. Let's drink to old friends and old memories. Sun, how long has it been? The days and Moons go so fast. Nearly twenty Moons ago we were at Windwatch fighting the remnants of the Hillmen, and if I remember aright, they didn't put up much sport, did they?" Brok let out a loud, booming laugh. "And that's enough of the my lord nonsense. I get enough of that here. Come Juk, let's drink and remember the old times, soldier to soldier, friend to friend."

Juk took the wine goblet from the serving boy and took a long gulp. "To old friends. It's good to see you Janson, it has been too long. Bloody Hillmen didn't know what'd hit them. I remember the first time we headed north together, too. Nearly five years ago. Those were good times, better times," Juk replied.

"Better times? What's better than now? We have peace finally. We have full bellies, full cellars. Good times, but surely better now, yes?"

"Yes, better now, of course," Juk replied, keeping his eyes on his wine goblet. He felt blood rush to his face and took another long gulp of wine. "I mean, we were younger then. Not better, different." Juk raised his eyes and looked at his friend. Janson was staring at him, a large man with his shock of black hair receding slightly. He was starting to show his age. Lord Brok was pushing fifty years old, although he still looked like a man under forty. He was blessed with boyish looks, fading now, but still looking a lot better than Juk felt.

"Come Juk, let's drink like we're five years younger then," the older man said, smiling, revealing the crow's feet around his eyes Juk hadn't noticed before. "Drink to the old times, drink to the new times, let's drink!" Janson refilled both men's cups. "So, what brings you to Stoneguard, then? You came from Magdil? Is he keeping you busy there, huh?"

"No, from the Wetlands. We had to put down some trouble in the west. I've been rewarded with a few Moons away from the capital." Juk took another long gulp. "I'm on my way home, and thought I could do with a warm bed and some good company." Juk held up his cup and his friend filled it once more.

"Ah. Wetlanders, I always thought they got the worst of things. Had a few friends back in the day from out that way. In fact, the wife's family is from near there. Lady Brok hasn't been there for a while, though. I'm surprised they gave you any trouble; normally a peaceful bunch, as I remember." Juk felt Janson Brok kept his eyes on him as he spoke.

"A little trouble. Nothing we couldn't handle," Juk replied. His mind was racing. He didn't know what to say and what to reveal. He wasn't used to not telling the truth, especially to a friend. "I think the men were a little disappointed in the end. Chik was, I know for sure; he wanted more blood. I let them surrender, and we escorted them back to Lendir. They agreed to pay tribute, food and men, when called upon." Juk looked up and tried to gauge his friend's response.

"Surrender, eh? Well, you got the job done, that's the most important thing. Sun and Moon, there's been enough blood over the years. Let's celebrate the peace. Let's drink to that." Janson raised his cup and together both men sank their wine in one, and refilled the cups again. "Peace!" he shouted.

"Peace," Juk said in unison. Juk was now feeling light-headed. The effect of the hard riding and little food made the wine go straight to his head. "Janson, food. I need some food."

"Of course, I'm sorry." Janson looked over to the serving boy. "Bring bread, meats and fruits," he said and pointed to Juk.

Juk took another gulp of wine and presently, the food was put in front of him. He ate some of the bread and meat, feeling the energy return to his tired limbs.

"You eat like a man who hasn't seen bread for Moons," Lord Brok said as he took a long gulp of wine, his plump face now reddening with each gulp. "Now, tell me why you're really here? I've known Runkarn as long as you have, maybe longer. When has he ever rewarded a skirmish with a Moon away, let alone a few? Never, is when I can tell you. Never have I seen it." Janson was staring at Juk, not taking his eyes off him at all.

The next morning, Juk opened his eyes to look around at the unfamiliar surroundings. His head hurt, he felt it throbbing, and the memory of the wine came back to him. He tried to sit up, but his head wouldn't allow it. As he lay in his bed, half-dressed, he thought back to his conversation last night. Juk remembered he had confessed all to his friend. Had he said too much? Juk thought Janson reacted to him sympathetically. He had never been a big supporter of Magdil; he enjoyed the peace that it had brought, but he had no strong appetite for their methods in winning that peace. A knock on his bedroom door brought this self-reflection to an abrupt halt.

"Captain? Lord Brok wishes to see you as soon as you can. I'll wait here to take you to him," came a voice from the other side of the large wooden door.

"Now? Before breakfast and a wash?" Juk shouted back.

"Breakfast will be served with my lord. He's

waiting for you."

Juk picked up his clothes, strewn on the floor last night, and quickly got dressed. As he opened the door, he saw two guards waiting to take him to breakfast. "Well, let's go then," Juk said gruffly.

They went down the hall and entered a large, spacious room with views overlooking the moat and drawbridge. "My lo... Jansen," Juk greeted his friend.

"Juk. How's the head?" Lord Brok gestured to his guards. "You may go. Leave us alone." The guards walked out and closed the door behind them. "So, do you still intend to go home? You were pretty sure of it last night, with a belly full of wine." Juk could feel his friend eyeing him closely.

"I am, yes. That decision was made long ago. There's no turning back now."

"Well then. Is there nothing I can do to change your mind? I have to ask, Juk. You're my friend, and I have to ask one last time." Jansen's eyes were still firmly locked on Juk.

"No. It's done. There's nothing to do or say. For good or ill, it's done." Juk looked up and saw his friend still staring at him, and continued. "There's one thing you can do. Speak to no one of this, unless you have to. I don't want any trouble to come your way, but the sooner Magdil hears, the sooner things may go worse for me."

"Of course, my friend. I am here for counsel, if you should need such a thing. But have no fear, this news is ours only. Moon and Sun, nobody wants my opinion on anything anymore, anyway. News travels slowly into, as well as out of, Stoneguard these days. No one will hear this from me." Jansen Brook smiled and Juk thought there was a look of kindness on his face.

"Thank you, old friend," Juk replied, matching his friend's expression.

"I'll have your horse ready after breakfast, but come now, let's eat and remember one more time." They sat down and ate black bread and cold meats together, washed down with a glass or three of hair of the dog.

"Now, that was a breakfast, Jansen. But I must be off. Chinsap is still half a Moon's ride and I want to get home before my news does. I'll bid you farewell." Juk stood up and walked towards his old friend.

"Farewell, Juk. Safe travels, and even safer tidings when you get home," Jansen stood up and embraced his friend. They held each other a few moments longer than Juk expected. And when they parted, they locked eyes and grasped each other's arm and said farewell once more.

Juk Thri rode out of Stoneguard, his head clearing in the morning's air. He rode for many days and slept rough for many nights. In the summer there in the north, the evenings were not usually pleasant; especially when the wind blew. But Juk found them temperate enough to sleep comfortably under normal circumstances. Juk Thri did not sleep well. The angst he felt deprived him of that. It was a long time since he had slept well.

After about a half a Moon's ride from Stoneguard,

the Red and Yellow Mountains came into view. These mountain ranges had kept Chinsap protected from outsiders. The natural barrier they provided proved to be better protection than any castle or man-made fortification could ever provide. The only way to approach from the west was through the Valley of Widows, the scene of many bloody battles over the years; many wives had lost husbands here, giving the place its name. As the morning Sun rose over the mountain ranges ahead, the rays bounced off the snow-capped peaks and glistened red and yellow, producing an awe-inspiring sight. Juk found this sight mesmerising every time he witnessed it; on too few occasions over the last few years. At nightfall, he camped at the foot of the mountains, at the entrance to the Valley of Widows. He was finally allowing himself to think of the future; the worry was giving way to hope.

CHIK SRIN

Chik tossed and turned all night. His physical discomfort mirrored the turmoil in his mind. Chik couldn't get any sleep at all. He got out of bed with the sound of the dawn birdsong. He washed, dressed and made his way to the stables. Chik had arranged to meet his men after breakfast, but he couldn't stomach any food, and he wanted to get started early. Chik had been at the stables for over an hour when the men arrived; twenty hand-picked men to ride out for Chinsap. Lord Runkarn had ordered him to ride out with his best men. Upon hearing the news that Juk Thri had ridden home, Runkarn demanded more information, and Chik provided him with it; all of it. He had told him everything he needed to know; he didn't leave any question unanswered, and volunteered a bit more besides.

"Where we off to, Chik?" one of the men asked as he looked around.

"Captain Chik," Chik replied, "It's Captain Chik now."

"Yes... Captain. Where we going, Sir?"

"Chinsap. As soon as we can. It's no holiday, though. We'll ride every day. And in the summer heat, it will not be a pleasant ride. We have an errand for Lord Runkarn we must complete as soon as we can."

"Can we know what it is? Can we know what it is, Captain?" the man said, correcting himself.

"We're to escort a delegation to Midscape. Half a Moon's ride," Chik replied. "Then we're to bring back Juk Thri to Magdil." Chik looked at the men carefully, as he said this, watching closely for reactions. The men looked at each other, but said nothing. "Juk's men arrived back from the Wetlands two nights ago, as you probably know."

Klaw broke the silence from the men. "Juk's men, yes, we saw them yesterday. Didn't see Juk, though; was the Captain not with them?"

"No, Juk has ridden home to Chinsap."

"Well, why do we have to bring him back? Don't make a lot of sense to me," Klaw said as he looked around at the men gathered there.

Chik ignored the question. "We've got to escort Lord Ruperk Stonefish to Midscape. After that, we'll ride on to Chinsap, to Juk. We leave this morning. Get ready. I want to be on the road soon."

Within the hour, Lord Ruperk's party arrived at the main gate; nine riders in total. Ruperk, wearing a purple tunic in the style and colour of Magdil, was accompanied by two dark-haired men with tattooed faces. They were also garbed in the purple colour of Magdil, loud and garish. There were six men from the 2nd Regiment. The regiment was mostly made up with soldiers from the Spine region; a mountainous area in the south, known, like Chinsap, for its rough, hard, resilient men. Three men rode on either side of

Lord Ruperk and his two companions. With no word, Chik led his men out the main gate, followed by Lord Ruperk's retinue.

By the end of the day's Sun, Chik, his men and the delegation had reached the edge of the Spindle Sea. Within a few days, they would cross Runkarn's Bridge. The bridge was built after Runkarn moved the capital to Magdil from Midscape. It provided a more convenient way to travel on horseback to Midscape; which, for a while after the move, was still vital for the administration of the land. On this occasion, it also provided a more direct route to the north east; to Chinsap.

After a couple of weeks, they had reached the Mountain Tower, a hundred miles from Midscape. The tower was many hundreds of feet high and had stood as protection from the south for the city for generations. It was ideally situated between the Mountain of Serenity and the surrounding hills to be utilised as a watchtower, as well as act as the first line of defence against any incoming army. It was less than a day's swift ride from Midscape, and following convention, as soon as anybody approached the tower from the south, a speedy rider was sent to the city to announce their impending arrival. Soon, Chik thought, if they upped their pace, they could reach the city the next day and then continue straight on to the north. They could reach Chinsap before Juk or even better, reach Juk before he got to Chinsap.

By Mid-Sun the next day, they'd reached the city of Midscape. The city was the largest in Areekya. For years it had been the capital and the home to its ruling family, the Mastertons. The city had two huge concentric stone walls, separated by a large water-filled moat, only crossable by one iron drawbridge in the centre. Sitting atop the city was a tall stone castle, surrounded by another forty-foot-high stone wall. Within the castle resided the Lord and Lady of the city's accommodation and the offices of the city's administration.

Chik and his men escorted Lord Ruperk and his delegation through the main gates and they crossed the lowered drawbridge into the main city. From there, they were met by a company of Midscape guardsmen, and escorted into the castle. They were greeted by Lord Dennis Greenaway, Lady Livian, and a reception committee.

"My Lord Ruperk, a pleasure as always." Lord Dennis bowed and instructed his wife to lead the delegation through to the guests' quarters. "I shall allow you to wash and clean up. A meal will be prepared in an hour. I will join you then. Your men can take their rest in the city barracks. My guards will show them the way." Lord Dennis smiled widely as he spoke.

Lord Ruperk nodded without a word, and with his two companions, followed Lady Livian. His six riders from the 2nd Regiment were led towards the barracks by Lord Dennis's men.

"Bless the Sun! Chik Srin, how the fucking Moon are you?" Lord Dennis shouted out once his men had taken the delegation out of earshot.

"Lord Dennis! It's good to see you. I'm well, and all the better for seeing you again," Chik replied, dismounting, and genuinely pleased to see his friend again.

"And tell me, where's that Captain of yours? Where's Juk? I've missed that old bastard. I didn't know you were bringing Fat Ruperk up here." Lord Dennis looked over his shoulder as he hugged his friend.

"Ah, Juk's not with us. He has business elsewhere. I think you'll be discussing the details of that at dinner with Fa... Lord Ruperk," Chik replied, remembering his men were right behind him.

"Good business, I hope. It's been too long since I've seen Juk. And you! What times we had, eh? Would that I could have those days back again. Fighting in the west and south, fucking, and fighting some more. What days they were. And look at me now, getting fat and lazy, living out my days as an administrative clerk." Lord Dennis's smile slowly turned to a frown.

"You look like you're doing pretty well from where I'm standing, my Lord. Domestic life suits you; you'll live longer anyway," Chik said, noticing that although Lord Dennis still had his shock of red hair, he was a lot fatter than since he last saw him.

"Ah! Don't get old, that's all I can tell you. You young lads, living the soldiers' life! Best years of my life they were. If only I could go back, back to those days..." Chik saw Lord Dennis's eyes widen and his smile return as his words drifted off. "So, how long are you staying? Once I get old Fatty out of the way, we can catch up, yes?" Lord Dennis continued.

"We have orders. I'm sorry, Lord Dennis. Once the horses are fed and watered, we'll be off. Orders from the very top," Chik replied, also frowning now. "We wouldn't mind a bite ourselves if that isn't putting you at out all,"

"Ah, shit. Really? That's pissed on my fish, I can tell you. Stuck between a sour old ice maiden and fat Lord Ru-prick, it looks like tonight then. I'll have my men send you some salted meats, fresh dark bread, and some ale. How does that sound, eh?"

"That will hit the spot, my lord," Chik said, smiling again.

"Well, I have to get back to fat Ruperk now, but promise me you'll come back when you can, and bring that bastard Juk with you next time." Lord Dennis's frown had returned.

"Yes, as soon as I'm able, my lord." With that, Lord Dennis and Chik said their farewells, and Chik headed to the stables. Within an hour, Chik and the 1st Regiment were off again.

"Time to up our pace, boys." Chik looked back and directed the men. "Time to go home."

By the next New Moon, they had reached the Valley of Widows. Chick decided to camp here for the night. Even this far north, the summer nights were comfortable for Chinsap men; pleasant enough to sleep outside. He sent some of his soldiers out to hunt something decent for supper; the game and fowl had always been good in the valley. The men went about quietly setting up camp for the night, happy to be in sight of the Yellow and Red Mountains; so close to home. They had an excellent supper of wild hare and pheasant, and washed it down with a keg of black beer. It was the happiest Chik had seen the men for a long time; a very long time. He didn't share the happiness. Chik knew that there was business that had to be taken care of. Business that he wasn't looking forward to. Chik had hardly eaten any of the food, but had drunk the beer and felt his stomach churning over. The beer had also gone straight to his head; he felt light-headed. He was thinking about tomorrow, about meeting Juk again, about what he would say and what he would do. Chik knew he wouldn't get much sleep this night.

After supper, the men were content, with full bellies, and singing songs of battles past and songs from their homeland. They were happy to put the War behind them for one night. For one night, they were free from the worry and stress; for one night they could enjoy their youth. *For one night,* thought Chik.

Before long, the men were passing out around the camp. One by one, they dropped, smiling. Chik could see they were all in a good mood, glad to be home, and he wished he could feel the same.

LORD DENNIS GREENAWAY

Lord Dennis Greenaway looked across the courtyard and saw four men making their way towards him. The first was one of his personal guards, and of the other three, he only recognized one: Lord Ruperk Stonefish; a portly, middle-aged man with grey hair and a flushed face. He was the Lord of the Gate Citadel and the closest, most trusted advisor to Lord Runkarn. Ruperk Stonefish was a man of great sway and power in the capital, indeed the land. Truth be told, Dennis couldn't stand the man. The two men that flanked him looked alike: shoulder-length dark hair, blue eyes, and both adorned with a tattoo of a mountain tip across their right cheeks; a sign of the Spine region of Areekya. Dennis wasn't sure whether he had seen the two men before, or at least he didn't recognise them. He'd noticed their tattoos earlier at the main gate, and felt a glimmer of recognition, but Dennis was a man known for his drinking, and it's entirely possible they had met at some or other engagement at Magdil where Dennis had been too deep in his cups to remember.

"My Lord Ruperk, I trust you and your companions have freshened up, and all is as it should be." Dennis walked towards his guests, beaming and using the most deferential voice he could muster.

"My Lord Dennis. Sober, I see. Well, that's a good start. I was just telling my friends here about your prestigious bouts of drinking. It is indeed a surprise we find you sober this fine afternoon, though you do seem to be expanding sideways to a large degree," Ruperk replied. The men either side of him snorted out a laugh. "Shall we continue to your main hall? Urgent business calls, and I don't want to stay any longer than I have to." Ruperk looked at his companions and smirked as he finished his sentence.

Dennis continued to smile. "Ah yes, very good. We have much to be thankful for in these peaceful days, and much to celebrate. It has never been said of Lord Dennis Greenaway that he doesn't indulge in a celebration when one is warranted. And of course we shall attend to this business immediately. Please follow me, my lord." Dennis showed Ruperk and his two companions through to the main hall. The guard blushed and headed back the way from which he had come.

The four men entered the main hall and sat down at the large, round mahogany table that was in one corner; Dennis sat on one side, the three guests choosing to sit on the other. Midscape's main hall was a long rectangular shape, with the banners of House Greenaway adorning each wall, hanging down from the ceiling and almost touching the floor. The Greenaway sigil was comprised of a green background with a white-tipped mountain in the middle. There was a large, brown, bearskin rug in the centre of the room.

"So, Lord Ruperk, what's this urgent business? What is worth taking the time of a man as important and valuable to Lord Runkarn as yourself to travel all the way out here to tell me?" asked Dennis. "And who are your companions? I don't believe we've met before."

"Lord Dennis, your flattery is as obvious and as odious as the extensive amount of wine you consumed last night. Let's not pretend, eh?" Ruperk ignored Dennis's last question and continued, "I am here... I am only here because my Lord Runkarn demanded I come. I am here to ask you about your good *friend* Juk Thri. I noticed your very warm reception to his former Lieutenant, Chik Srin, earlier. Somewhat more convivial than that you showed to me and my companions." Ruperk looked at the men sitting on either side of him, still failing to introduce them, both nodding in unison.

"My lord, Chik Srin is a man I hadn't seen for a long time. We stood side by side in many a battle in defence of the peace. A soldier doesn't easily forget a bond made in blood. A bond like that isn't easily broken. Please forgive me if I offended you and your companions. I can assure it was not meant." Dennis's brow became furrowed, and continued, "Former Lieutenant, you say? Chik still wears the 1st Regiment's colours. I saw them myself this very day."

"Indeed," answered Ruperk.

"Then what is this game you play? What do you mean, former Lieutenant?" Dennis shifted his eyes between the three men opposite him.

"When did you last see Juk Thri?" Ruperk asked, his tone demanding and blunt.

"Juk? I've not seen Juk for nearly two whole years. Why? Is he well? Is he in trouble?" Ruperk said nothing in reply. Dennis's face flushed red and an alarmed look came over him. "What is this?" he continued.

"No contact for two years? None at all? No messages in all that time?" Ruperk continued his minacious line of questioning.

"None." Dennis was now becoming irritated, his soldier spirit coming to the fore. "Ruperk, tell me. What's going on here? What are you asking? More to the point, Why?"

The three men sitting across from Dennis Greenaway looked at each other for a few seconds, exchanging some unheard words before Ruperk looked up and said, "We are concerned that Juk Thri has become hostile to Magdil. That he is now an enemy to Lord Runkarn. News has reached us of his treachery, and we have to be sure you play no part in it. Forgive me if you find this line of dialogue somewhat combative. I know for a soldier like you, it can seem so."

"Juk Thri? An enemy to Runkarn? You've lost your mind, man! What in the name of Sun and Moon...?" Dennis stood up and pushed his chair back against the wall. "Juk Thri is one of the finest, decent, most honourable men I know."

"Indeed, so it is said. Yet, he has quit his post, left his men, and has not been seen or heard for many Moons."

"Nonsense. There must be some explanation," Dennis interrupted.

"Furthermore," Ruperk continued, "Captain Chik Srin told Lord Runkarn himself that Juk had relinquished his position in the 1st Regiment. He abandoned his men and fled back to Chinsap. How honourable does that sound, hmm?" Ruperk did not take his eyes off his host.

"I don't believe it. The Juk Thri I know, well, he wouldn't do these things. I don't believe they're true. They can't be." With this, Dennis clicked his fingers to get the attention of his serving boy. "Are you sure of these things?" The serving boy brought wine and four goblets. Dennis grabbed one, and the boy started pouring.

"We're sure," Ruperk replied. "And must you drink?"

"You're telling me Juk Thri is a traitor, and expect me not to take a drink. Sun and Moon!" Dennis finished his cup in one long, large gulp and held it out to be refilled. "Again boy." He looked at the three men, who all refused a cup, and continued, "If this is true, it's the first I've heard of it. If, mind you. I'll still not have it. Won't have it." He took another long swallow of wine and drained his second cup.

"I think our business is done for now," Ruperk said. "I trust you'll be serving dinner after Sundown. And I trust you'll be sober, Lord Dennis. We can continue our discussion then." With that, the three men got up from the table and moved towards the door.

"Dinner just after Sundown, my lords." Dennis drained his third cup, and continued, "I shall look forward to it, my lords." As he finished the sentence, the door closed as the three men left the room. "Cunts," he muttered under his breath. "Cretinous cunts." He drained his fourth goblet of wine and sat staring at the wall.

LADY LIVIAN GREENAWAY-MASTERTON

Livian Greenaway-Masterton sat by her window in her bedroom. Her long black hair was being combed carefully by her maid. After showing Ruperk and his company to their quarters, she returned here to escape the formality of official visits. She remembered when her father, Lord Sydric Masterton, would entertain all the minor lords and ladies from all around Areekya. How they would bow and curtsy in front of her mother and father; not unlike snakes slithering on the ground, she always thought.

She had pride in those days; she was the object of their attention, currying favour with the lord's favourite daughter, trying to get into the grace of the Lord of Areekya himself. Various suitors were always being offered to her father; always rejected. "She's too young and too precious to me," her father replied. Out of his love for her, he had allowed her to choose her own husband. No arranged marriage for the favourite offspring of the Lord of Areekya. She looked out of the window and reflected. *My father would never have married me to one as low as Dennis Greenaway, even if his life had depended on it. He would have killed him rather than marrying me to him.* Lady Livian was certain of that.

But that was a different time. A different Lord of

Areekya now ruled; one that cared little for Livian's well-being. The two men that accompanied Ruperk Stonefish were two other such men who did not meet her father's approval. Brothers, offered by their father, Berak Veerak, as prospective suitable matches to Lord Sydric Masterton, Lord of Areekya's favourite daughter before the War. Livian thought back to the time her father had told her of it. The laughter in his voice, mixed with incredulity: "Sons of Berak Veerak, marrying my own kin! Rock smashers and collectors."

Miners from the Spine region had become rich in the mountain range the name comes from, but they weren't good enough for his daughter. The Veerak family had grown in influence since then. Never forgiving her father for the slight. Rising up against him, when the tide turned in favour of Runkarn and his cohorts. It was no surprise to Livian that the two brothers, Madnan and Walnak, accompanied Ruperk to Midscape. A nest of vipers, slithering and sliding, acting as if they were from the same high stock as her.

She waved her maid away and left her bedroom, and made her way down the long, winding stone staircase to the parlour. Even though she had been married to Dennis Greenaway for two years now, he didn't know and would never know all the secrets of Livian's family home. Secreted in a cove in the corner of the room, on the wall about halfway up, was a brick. The brick was slightly paler than the rest of the wall, barely perceptible, even when you're looking for it. She looked around the room to ensure nobody was with her and gave it a hard push. This revealed a secret door that opened opposite. She quickly made her way through it and closed it behind her. She lit the torch on the wall, then gracefully and quietly made her way down the passage. Turning first to the left and then to the right, and climbing ever so slightly, until she stopped at the spot she had done so many times before. First, as a child, brought here by her older brother, whilst promising not to tell their father or mother. It was directly behind the main guest quarters. The wall here had purposefully been built with weaker, less dense stone, as to make it easier to hear through the wall to the conversations on the other side. Her father had used this to gather all sorts of information from his guests; friends, as well as enemies.

Quietly she put her ear to the part of the wall that been used for years to gain secrets and whoever knew what. At first there was nothing, then a door was opened and closed. She could hear the footsteps of two men. One sat down, while the other paced up and down the room.

"So, does Greenaway know anything?" said one voice from the far end of the room.

"If he does, he's hiding it well," came the reply. The nasal tone of the voice meant it could only have been Ruperk, a whiny voice that matched his demeanour. Livian had never trusted him, even when he had the favour of her father.

"Fat pig would lie though, wouldn't he? You can't trust him any further than you could throw five sacks of rocks." The owner of the other voice seemed to move across the room. One of the Veerak brothers, the older one probably, Madnan. "Put some real pressure on him tonight. In front of his whore of a wife. See how he likes that? He's had some time to stew," the voice continued.

"Stew or think," replied Ruperk. "He's not as stupid as he sounds. And he's as strong as a mountain bear. We'll push him, but maybe we'll get more from his wife, Livian Masterton-Greenaway." Ruperk laughed as he finished his sentence, full of disdain.

"She'll remember me," said the voice, now moving from one end of the room to the other. "Her father tried to marry me to her near the end of the War. Begging my father, he was. He knew he had lost and was looking for some small mercy. To think I'd marry that!"

"Well, Madnan, we will need you to turn on your charm tonight. I'll get Fat Dennis drunk, and you take care of the lady." Ruperk's tone towards the end of the sentence was once more riddled with disdain. He continued, "Also, I've dispatched your brother with three of the 2nd to pay Lord Brok of Stoneguard a visit. He left not an hour ago."

"Brok? Stoneguard is some way off from here. You think he may know the whereabouts of our good absent Captain?"

"Lord Brok is a good man. And he's at least as close to Juk Thri as Greenaway is. Or was at any rate. Walnak will find out if he's heard anything. He'll have the 2nd with him," Lord Ruperk replied.

With that, Lady Livian heard a door open and close. She stood quietly for another few minutes. There was nothing coming from the other side of the wall, so she elegantly and silently made her way back up the passage, considering all that she had heard. The words percolated into a half-formed plan. Livian continued to ruminate as she looked through the slight gap in the false wall to check no one was in the parlour. She tacitly opened and slipped through the door, then pushed it shut behind her. She walked back to her bedroom and once more gazed out at the Mountain of Serenity. Thinking of her family, she cried. Tears of lamentation; small drops slowly falling down her face, like fragile snowflakes that evaporated as soon as they touched the ground. She sat there crying for her mother, her lost husband, father and brothers; her proud family, all the while plotting her evening, planning her performance, and choosing her words.

Tonight will be the start of it, she thought. Tonight, she would begin to put into place all of her dark desires that had been developing over the long, lonely years she had spent mourning her family. She had felt her city mourn with her, too. The loss of the Mastertons to the city of Midscape had never been forgotten. When she put her plans into place, she would see the city rise up. The people would rejoice in her resurgence; her family's revival. The restoration of how things should be. Tonight, it would start.

JUK THRI

As he moved through the dense woodlands, he sensed the presence of someone or something behind him. Watching, stalking him, waiting for him to stop. He made sure he didn't. He picked up his pace, running, but he found his surroundings became even more compact. The forest seemed to close in on him; the trees squeezing the air from the atmosphere and Juk could feel himself choking, gasping for air. He tried to run faster, looking, searching for an exit. His eyes were drawn to a tiny light to the left of his field of vision. He felt an irrepressible *urge to run towards it. As he turned and headed in that direction, he saw a circular structure in the distance. It was small, but far away on the horizon. Then he felt his legs sinking into the ground. His pace slowed, almost to a stop, as he tried to push on towards the faint light, towards the circle that was drawing him in. The presence behind him was getting closer. So close now, he could feel its breath on his neck. He turned violently, and as he did, a scream escaped him.*

Juk Thri woke and sat upright. His sleep was restless and short. If it wasn't for his nightmare, he couldn't be sure he had slept at all. It was before dawn. The dark sky above reflected his mood. He rode off through the Valley of Widows before First Sun. Even though it was dark, Juk had ridden this path so many times that he could almost do it with his eyes closed. The final night stars were giving way to the pre-dawn darkness, before the first few shafts of Sunlight brought life and warmth back to the world. In past times, there would have been guards posted at the Valley's mouth and throughout. But with most fighting men in Magdil or off fighting in some corner of Areekya, there were too few to do so, and in these times, no trouble had come to Chinsap for many Suns. Juk and the army had allowed Runkarn to see to that. Some means used to achieve this were questionable. Juk never fooled himself into believing they weren't, but even an immoral peace was better than any kind of war. This is what Juk thought in the beginning, and well into his time fighting for 'peace'. That had changed, though, and now whenever he thought about it, he couldn't articulate at all what he thought, not even to himself.

Juk was eager to get home. The journey was straightforward enough, but it had been long. And after an all too brief respite from his fears, he found his anxiety growing again. In fact, there had been a pernicious presence germinating inside of him. A growing danger; an insidious, gnawing, grabbing feeling just out of reach in his mind. It lingered, and haunted both his waking and sleeping awareness. A sense of helplessness and doom, existing just close enough to consume him, but far enough away so it could not be focused on or dealt with.

Just before the end of the day's Sun, Juk Thri was relieved that his home, the town of Chinsap, came into view.

Juk's large grey horse stopped short of the town, at the side of the river that ran through Chinsap. It provided the principal water supply to the town and was essential to its foundation and continued existence. As his horse, Noble, drank, Juk looked towards the town's gates. There were two guards, chatting and paying little attention to the comings and goings of the townsfolk entering the gates and gossiping with one another. There was no real need for the guards anymore. It was more symbolic than anything else, dealing with the odd drunkard staggering in or out, or an angry wife in from the surrounding villages on the hunt for her absent husband; more often than not lost in the taverns or brothels of the town. The gates, in fact, were not needed; the palisades didn't even surround the whole town. The wooden stakes, about six feet high, stretched about a third of the way around. Security wasn't high in Chinsap; there was no need for it to be.

Juk Thri nodded to the guards as he entered and received the customary salute in return. They might not have known who he was, but they saw the uniform and it was an automatic response. As he rode down the main thoroughfare, people were going about their business. In and out of the shops and stalls that were on either side of the street, with fresh vegetables on display outside some of the shops. The healer's hut was busy with customers, but the largest throng of people was around the tavern; men too old to fight, or too young.

After about two hundred yards, he turned towards the right and headed down a narrow, muddy lane with small, one-storey cottages on one side, and tall, thick trees on the other. The Sun was now barely visible as it crept down in the west and the early evening shadows from the trees were flickering across the lane, like long sinewy fingers grabbing out in the dusky, pre-evening hue. The last house at the end of the lane was Juk's. His wife would be bathing the twins, getting them ready for supper and bed. The anticipation that had been building, competing with the unease and growing tension within him, was close to the surface now, and Juk allowed himself a smile. The muscles tightened in his face as his lips turned upwards, and he felt a lifting of his spirits. For the first time in a long time, he felt a sense of happiness and excitement that was a welcome, long-forgotten, but soon-remembered stranger.

As he approached the cottage, Juk noticed the front of the house looked dark. The sentry candles on either side of the door were unlit, as was the one at the side of the house, leading to the back entrance. He dismounted and tied his horse to the gatepost and, not wanting to alarm his wife, he knocked on the door with a smooth double tap — no answer. Juk knocked again, this time louder. Nothing. He pushed the door lightly, and it was locked from the inside. Juk smiled.

"They must be asleep. Maybe they have the fever," he whispered to himself.

It wasn't unknown at this time of the year for whole towns to go down with it. He saw no sign of it elsewhere on his ride in, but the locked door allayed his fears that something was wrong. Juk walked around to the back entrance and tried the door; it was also locked. He called out to his wife. No response. He felt the muscles in his stomach tighten. Juk pulled out his knife and hurriedly sliced the cloth parchment that was used as a covering to the right of the back door. It allowed light in, but provided a level of protection against the elements. He reached his hand through the tear and unbolted the door from the inside.

He stood in the kitchen area, and apart from the darkness, nothing was seemingly out of place. There was no supper preparation to be seen, but if his family was sick, then there wouldn't be, thought Juk. He walked at a quickened pace through to the living area; the hearth was unlit, and the beds were empty. There wasn't any sign of his wife or daughters. A wave of panic now washed over Juk, starting in his stomach and rushing up till it reached his head; he thought it was going to explode into a thousand shards. Juk quickly unbolted the front door and went out to the front of the house, where his eyes darted in all directions, looking for some sign of life. He focused on a light in the neighbour's house. He rushed over to the front door and banged loudly four times in a panic. Two or three voices could be heard. Juk thought they sounded flustered.

"What you want?" came one muffled voice from behind the door.

"It's your neighbour, Juk Thri, back from Magdil. Can you open the door?"

"Juk? Haven't seen you for Moons," the voice replied as Juk could hear the unbolting of the door. "Juk Thri, Well met! How in the name of the Sun and the Moon have you been?" An elderly man of about sixty with a wispy grey beard spotted about his chin opened the door.

"Yes, greetings Makkab. My family, I'm looking for my wife and children. Have you seen them?"

"Your wife?" Makkab asked.

"Yes, and family," replied Juk.

"And family?" The old man squinted as he spoke.

"Yes, my wife and family. Have you seen them?" Juk shouted, his heightened sense of anxiety overflowing into anger.

"Your wife and family? Yes, yes. Saw them yesterday, no, two days past. Just there, behind you." The old man pointed over Juk's shoulder, back to from where he had come. "They was cleaning the front of your house. Had a chat, we did. You know the street's changed, only the other day you never guess what I saw the Siks from the top of the road putting out in the —"

"Yes, my family. Have you seen them since?" Juk interrupted, his voice quick and shrill. "Since two days ago?"

"Why, umm... No, not since then. Are they not home now? Sleeping? It's getting late, you know, and the Sun is getting shorter and —"

"How did they seem?" Juk cut the old man off again. "Happy? Upset? How?"

"Fine," Makkab replied, staring at Juk. "Yes, they was fine, I've been keeping an eye on them you know."

"And not since then? You're sure? Not at all?" Juk's eyes darted about, looking over the shoulder of the old man. "And your wife? Has she seen them? Please, it's important. Can you ask her?"

"Shrin! Shrin! Can you come here?" Makkab looked over his shoulder as his wife came hobbling to the door. "Now, Juk here, he's back from the War, you know.

Hasn't been home for, ooh, how long is it now? Got to be going on a full Sun I reckon. Juk, how long is it…?"

Juk stared at the woman now standing just behind Makkab. "Shrin, have you seen my wife, Maca? My daughters, Dek and Mek? Please, have you?" Juk was speaking quickly now. His words were getting stuck and tripping out of his mouth.

"Yes, I seen them three days past, they was there, cleaning the front of the house there, see?" She pointed over Juk's shoulder.

"Three days? Not two?"

"No, it was definitely three days pas… Now, hang on, it could've been two. Now, yesterday we was cleaning our own front and…"

Juk turned and hurried back to his house, leaving his neighbours debating among themselves. His mind was now racing. He couldn't focus. In a panic, he ran through his house, out the back door, his eyes frantically searching for something. Anything. Then he saw it. In the far corner of the garden, next to where the potatoes grew. He saw a white rag. It didn't look much, but it didn't look right. Something was wrong. He knew it. He rushed over, trampling across the neat rows of crops, and bent down and touched the cloth. It was a piece of a garment, a skirt maybe, or a shirt, he couldn't tell. It had uneven edges on one side, as if it had been torn, and he turned it over in his hand and saw the red spots: blood. Juk felt like he was falling into a deep hole, as if the ground had opened up and he was falling helplessly between the sides, falling, and his mind was racing as everything rushed past him and he let out a scream, a shout, a wail: "Maca! Maca!"

He searched the bushes at the back of the garden. There were no signs of his family. He jumped the low stone wall at the back of his garden and looked around him. He could see the Stone Mountains in the distance, looming large on the horizon. Between them and Chinsap was a rocky valley surrounded by mountains on all sides. The valley lacked vegetation. It was mostly flat, with some larger rocks and boulders providing shelter for the local vermin and insects. To the north he saw a large number of birds; crows, he thought, swooping down and fighting among themselves. He ran as fast as he could over towards the commotion.

What he saw when he got there made him retch. He fell to his knees. There, lying in twisted, unnatural positions, were his wife and twins; lifeless, with faces contorted in torment and pain. His eyes fixed on the scene laid out in front of him. He was unable to look away. His eyes were caught in the horror of what he saw. He stood there, and he found he couldn't turn his eyes away until finally he did, to scream at the top of his voice up into the night sky.

LORD DENNIS GREENAWAY

The long oak dining table looked sparse, with just four people seated at it. At one end was Dennis Greenaway, and his wife, Livian, sat at the other. Ruperk sat on the right side of Dennis, and a dark-haired smiling man with blue eyes sat on the left, both in the centre of the table nearly twenty feet in length. Dennis was already deep in his cups. His almost completely round face was glowing pink, and he was slouching in his chair.

"Forgive my lack of courtesy earlier, Lord Dennis," Ruperk said, breaking the awkward silence. "It was remiss of me not to introduce my travelling companions. This is Madnan Veerak, son of Lord Veerak from the Spine. A good friend of your wife, Lady Livian, I believe."

"Is that so?" Dennis took a drink from his silver goblet. "Friend of my wife, you say?"

"Yes, but before your time. Prior to your rise to such lofted heights," Ruperk replied.

"That would be when I was winning the War for Lord Runkarn, then. Fighting my way to the top," Dennis took another gulp.

"Of course. And Lord Runkarn gifted you a most generous reward for it," Ruperk remarked as he took another sip of his water and a small bite of his meal.

"So, my Lord Ruperk, how is the business of Magdil these days? We so rarely get to visit there now." Dennis took a long, slow swig of his wine and held his goblet up to be refilled.

"Yes, we do so rarely see you there these days. Somewhat surprising given the close proximity, less than a Moon's ride, half a Moon if one desired." Ruperk took a sip of his water.

"Ah, yes, not so far. However, business keeps me occupied here. Running a city large enough to be a capital is no mean feat. I made the trip back and forth to Magdil during the War often enough, as I recall. I think you were mainly based here then. That's right, isn't it, Lord Ruperk? Advisor to my wife's father, as I recall." Dennis was getting combative with his guest. The drink and his earlier conversation had played its part in that.

"Careful, Lord Dennis. Lord Runkarn values your service, but I am the one by his side now." With that, Ruperk put down his knife and fork and sat back in his chair.

"Come now, my lords. The past is the past. Let's talk about the present," Livian interjected. "Captain Juk Thri is absent, my husband tells me. He holds great favour with Lord Runkarn, doesn't he? That seems an odd thing to have done, no?"

"A black bear will always turn to its own nature. That's what we say in the Spine," Madnan Veerak replied. "Bears are savage, wild, solitary animals. It doesn't surprise me he abandoned his men and ran home when it suited him. I've never held the men from Chinsap in high regard, my lady."

"Is that so?" Livian replied.

Dennis took another long drink from his goblet and stared at the man to his left. The serving boy quickly rushed to his lord and refilled his cup.

"Yes, overrated as fighting men and not at all honourable, as has been proven time and time again. And may I say, my lady, the men from Midscape are some of the most virtuous and disciplined I've ever encountered. It's always saddened me, what happened to your family. Most unnecessary, I've always said," Madnan replied, and Dennis could see that he kept his focus solely on his wife.

"So, Lord Dennis. Let's get back to your friend, Juk Thri." Ruperk took another small bite from his plate. Is there anything you can tell us? Anything at all that might help us locate him?"

"Juk Thri is the finest fighting man I have ever encountered. He would never run from a fight, nor abandon his men. In fact, regardless of what this rock breaker may think, the Chinsap men are the bravest, most honourable men in Areekya. Anyone who disagrees is a fucking idiot, by the Moon." Dennis looked directly at Madnan, emptied his cup of wine, and held it up. "Boy!" The serving boy quickly refilled his lord's cup and quietly and meekly backed into the corner, keeping his eyes on Lord Dennis all the while.

Ruperk pushed his plate to the side. "That's as it may be. But here we are. He's missing, and Lord Runkarn presumes him hostile. Yet his close friends have no idea where he is or why he's *run away*." Ruperk stressed the last part of his sentence.

"Run away? Fuck the Sun, Moon and Stars. I'm telling you now, Juk Thri would never run away. Maybe he went home. He got homesick and wanted to visit his wife. Is that so bad?"

"You have heard from him, then." Ruperk and Madnan were now all staring at Dennis.

"No. I said I hadn't heard from him for two years. But has anybody ridden to Chinsap? To check?" Dennis took another gulp of wine.

"Lord Runkarn despatched some men. We have yet to hear from them." Ruperk's eyes still trained on Dennis.

"How long has it been since you've heard from him? Three Moons? Four? Five? I've been in the field longer than that. No one was running around the land looking for me. Fucking nonsense, the lot of it."

"Indeed," Ruperk replied. "And yet, Lord Runkarn thinks it necessary we investigate."

"And what's with all this, anyway? He's a Captain in the 1st Regiment, not some fucking stone breaker from some shithole in the Spine. So what if he's away for a while? He's done as much as anyone to bring about the peace we all enjoy. Leave him be. Let it all be. He'll fucking turn up." Dennis finished his goblet of wine, and the serving boy rushed to refill it.

"My dear Madnan. Tell me, where is your brother? I saw him arriving today, yet he's not joining us?" Livian interjected.

"Ah, my lady. Regrettably, my younger brother

Walnak had to leave on urgent business. He sends his regards, and he too fondly remembers our times together in the past."

Dennis was getting his cup filled again as he shouted down the table. "north to Stoneguard, he went."

"Yes, to Stoneguard." Madnan continued talking to Livian. "He is on Lord Runkarn's business there. He is to meet Lord Brok."

"Perhaps he'll find Juk feasting with his old friend," Dennis added. "Lord Jansen is a fine man, Juk is a fine man, I used to think I was a fine man, all in the favour of Lord Runkarn. But this nonsense has me thinking our good Lord Runkarn has spent too much time cooped up in Magdil. Maybe too much Moon gazing in his tower." The serving boy filled Dennis's cup once more.

"My Lord Greenaway. Be very careful. If Lord Runkarn were to hear such comments, well, let's just say it would do your standing no good. No good at all. Maybe one would think you are withholding information about your friend, no?" Ruperk's tone became more serious. It didn't bother Dennis.

"My Lord Ru-berk, let's do away with the pleasantries, shall we?" Dennis was now deep in his cups; slurring and speaking boldly. "Whatever I say here tonight, good or ill, will be reported back to Runkarn."

"Lord Runkarn," Madnan interjected.

"Let the fucking Moon take you!" Dennis spat across the table. "And," Dennis continued his rant, "I don't care." He took another long gulp of wine. "You come here, *you* come here and, and, tell me, tell *me*, my friend, Juk Thri, one of the fightest fining men I have known..." He trailed off as his goblet was once more refilled by the serving boy.

"Now, my dear," Livian said, "I think it's been a long day and night. What say we all retire to continue this in the morning?" Dennis saw her smile at the guests. "I'm sure we could all do with an early night."

Dennis took another long gulp. "Bed is it? You take the guests, my dear. I'm staying to drink my fill."

"My Lord Ruperk, Lord Madnan, please forgive my husband. He's not himself this evening, and this news you bring has somewhat affected him so." Livian stood up and gestured to the serving staff to open the doors for her guests.

Ruperk and Madnan stood up, bowed, and nodded.

"My Lady Livian," Ruperk said, "the problem is that your husband is exactly himself." And with that, he stormed off.

Dennis looked from the other end of the table at his guest. "Goodnight snake," he muttered under his breath.

Madnan looked down the room at Dennis slumped on the table. "My dear Lady Livian, it has been a pleasure seeing you once again, and I was hoping we shall breakfast together tomorrow. Or even a small nightcap in the drawing room, perhaps?"

A silver goblet came flying across the room and

struck the open door. "Let the fucking Moon take your eyes, rock man," Dennis shouted from his slumped position, "and let it take your slithering friend, too." The serving boy rushed to collect the silver goblet from the floor.

The last thing that Dennis thought he saw was his wife raising a half-smile towards the serving boy, before he passed out on the table.

JUK THRI

Juk Thri sat in front of his hearth, fire blazing, with his wife's head on his lap. He could hear his two daughters playing in their bedroom. He smiled to himself as he stroked his wife's hair. Juk stared at the hearth, the flames flickering and dancing in a wild, energetic fire-dance. The flames grew taller and danced faster and more aggressively. A spark flew out, then another, and another, until one caught on the cloth covering the window. He sat there paralysed, unable to move or scream, but he heard the screams of his wife as the fire engulfed the entire room. And then the cries of his daughters. The smoke reached out, twisted and morphed into a human figure and grabbed at Juk. As the cries became louder, he sat there terrified, paralysed still. Juk was just able to turn to his wife, but he didn't see the fire burning her. He saw her flesh being gnawed at by worms and other insects. He let out a scream, but no sound made it out of his mouth. It only allowed the smoke to rush in, down his throat, and begin choking him. He was gasping for air as he saw his wife's face being devoured greedily, and the screams of his children becoming louder and more terrified.

Juk opened his eyes. He looked around, and the full weight of his situation came bearing down on him. He was still fully clothed in his 1st Regiment uniform, and got out of bed and went into the garden. Juk walked over to one large and two small mounds of earth in the corner of his garden. He replaced the blue cornflowers lying on top of the graves with freshly picked ones. He placed the old flowers carefully in the breast pocket of his uniform. As he looked down at the final resting place of his family, the feeling of numbness he had felt had now given way to anger. *Who? Why?* Many more questions with few answers raced through his mind. The *why* eluded him. Had Magdil got here before him? Who would do such a thing? Chinsap soldiers could not do such a thing, or so Juk thought. Soldiers from the Spine region, perhaps. They had always been close to Magdil, ready to do its bidding. The *how* was the most frustrating unanswered question. He had asked neighbours and guards. None had seen any strangers or heard anything. And, more surprisingly, neither had he. In the two days since he found his family murdered, he hadn't seen or heard anything of Magdil, no word at all. This he found strange. If they wanted him dead, or worse, and they were in Chinsap, why hadn't he seen or heard them?

"Morning, neighbour." Makkab peered over the fence.

"Yes, Makkab. Can I help you?" Juk replied, not looking up.

"No, no help. Only checking you okay?"

"I'll be off soon, Makkab. You can help by keeping your eyes on the place for me." Juk looked up and noticed Makkab was doing that already.

"Ah, off are you? Back to the War, eh?" Makkab said, returning his eyes to Juk.

"Yes, I'm off tonight, so keep your eyes and ears

peeled. Inform the guards if anything comes up." Juk laid the last of the flowers and walked over to Makkab. "And look after the graves for me."

"Aye, I'll do that, Juk. Keep my eyes peeled under Sun and Moon. Shrin will tend to the graves as often as she can." Makkab shouted over his shoulder, "Shrin! Shrin! I was saying you'll look after them, won't you?"

A muffled voice came from over his shoulder. Juk couldn't make out what it said, but Makkab continued, "Yes, she'll look after them alright. And I'll do what I can. When will we expect you back then?"

"Not for a while. In fact, don't expect me back." Juk turned and walked into the house. He changed from his uniform and put on a pair of dark brown trousers and a loose-fitting, brown tunic; the traditional clothes of men from the north east. He placed the blue cornflowers from the grave into his tunic pocket. He kept on his 1st Regiment boots, and kept his sword in its scabbard, securely tightened round his waist. Juk sat down and stared at the hearth in the middle of the room. It was half-full of ash; lifeless, cold, grey. His eyes were fixed on the sedentary fireplace and he could not turn away from it. He felt the numbness return. He pulled out the flowers from his pocket and held them tightly in his hand. He remained there for the whole day, consumed and tormented by the ashes in front of him.

He left Chinsap just after Sundown. There was just enough light that Juk could see if anyone was watching him, but dark enough to slip away without too much attention. He mounted his horse and left through the south gate, but quickly doubled back and headed north towards the Red Mountains. As he rode, he felt a wave of despair wash over him. The days and sleepless nights he'd spent at home had been a mix of despair and anger. Now that he was leaving Chinsap, the anger gave way entirely to despair. He was lost mentally and spiritually, and he felt exhausted physically. Even his need for answers had given way to his need for sleep. It was a long time since he had slept peacefully and to continue seemed like the most difficult thing for him to do.

Each trot of his horse seemed to move him closer to the darkness, to the void. Juk wandered for what seemed like days. It could have been Moons, though it just as easily could have been hours. Time left him; he half-remembered spending sleepless nights under the trees and gloomy, empty days rambling through the fields and foothills of the Red Mountains. He was losing his fight for life; his soldier's spirit waning, and leaving his physical body. It was escaping through his every movement and dark thought in his mind.

Juk had passed through the mountains and was deep in the Northern Hills. Briefly, his conscious awareness returned, and he saw that daylight had drifted away. The first of the evening stars became visible on the horizon, and this was as far as his physical body could go. He dismounted his horse and set up camp in a valley protected from the wind. This much he could do on instinct. His tired body collapsed to the ground and his restless, despondent mind finally gave way, stubbornly, to sleep. He closed his bloodshot eyes and drifted away.

When Juk awoke, the Crescent Moon was rising in

the eastern sky. He slowly sat up and looked around him. The insects of the forest were chirping and singing their night songs, although it hardly registered with Juk. The wave of despair erupted over him once more, paralysing him. He felt as if he hadn't slept at all. This far into the Northern Hills, the landscape became more barren, and the weather could be chilly. The cool night air briefly brought him out of his trance and the need for fire and warmth induced him to get up and look for wood to burn.

Sitting next to the fire he had made, catching the warmth from the glow of the embers, his thoughts drifted back to his wife Maca, and how she loved sitting with Juk in the glow of the hearth at their home. He stood up and retrieved from his horse that which he had prepared in Chinsap; a noose he had fashioned from rope in his garden. He walked into the lightly wooded area next to his camp, looking for a tree tall, strong enough to carry his weight. He was now fully committed to this thing. It had been on the periphery of his plans since Chinsap, but now it was time. He searched for an hour or so in the area around his fire. Every tree he found was too short or too brittle; the constant wind and harsh climate in the north had whittled away at the timber. Juk tested a few promising branches, but each one snapped after a sharp pull, and fell to the floor.

Not finding what he was looking for, he returned and slumped back down next to the fire, now petering out. He threw another few pieces of the brittle wood on the fire and his thoughts once again turned to his family and their love of the burning, life-giving flames. He was pulled from this bittersweet memory when he heard a crunch of broken twigs and leaves from behind where he was sitting.

"Well met, stranger," came a voice from behind Juk. He quickly grabbed his sword and turned to see a figure walking towards him. Juk stood up and saw a tall man smiling as he spoke. "It's unusual to see fires here in this valley; even more unusual to see a man alone sitting next to one."

"Who are you? What do you want?" Juk kept his eyes on the stranger. He drew his sword from its sheath and held it up towards the tall man, now standing still.

"A friend, *friend.* A wanderer, wandering. I often wander these hills. Empty, they are, mostly. But in truth, it is a happy coincidence that I find you here, Juk Thri, Captain of the 1st Regiment."

"How do you know that name? Did you follow me here?" Juk's eyes and sword-hand remained steadfast.

"No, not followed. But I have seen you before. I am known to Ashran of Clan Grash. I spend many Moons in Lendir. I saw you in the west, nearly five Moons gone. You looked better then. What has happened to you, friend? You appear as if you have not slept in a bed for Moons." The tall stranger continued to smile as he spoke.

"You are far from Lendir. What brings you here? My sleep is my own concern, *friend.* Give me your name. Tell me why you are here."

"My name is Rivan, and I am sorry if I startled you. This was not my intention. I often wander these hills, although I have not seen many men of Chinsap or anywhere here for a long time." He pointed at Juk's drawn sword. "There will be no need for that."

Juk's eyes remained fixed on the stranger's, thinking there was something familiar about his voice.

Rivan continued. "I wander and meditate on things, past and present. The solitude of these hills gives me plenty of time and space to think; an action too often overlooked in these peaceful days, wouldn't you say?" Rivan's expression remained friendly, his eyes exhibiting a kindness that matched the melodious quality of his voice.

"A coincidence indeed, you meeting me here, miles from Lendir. Wandering and meditation, you say?" Juk kept his sword drawn.

"Wandering and meditation, Juk Thri, that is all." Rivan continued smiling.

"Well, it's quiet enough for sure. Maybe you are who you say and your purpose is true. But I've no mind for company, friendly or otherwise. Best you go on your way," Juk snapped, as he slowly lowered his sword and sat back down next to the fire.

"A fire to warm the body of an old man for a while is enough, if I may ask this of you." The benevolent melody and rhythm in Rivan's voice lingered. "I'd spend awhile warming my tired bones if you'd permit. Then I'll be off to wander and meditate once more."

Juk looked up at the tall stranger. His short, black hair was partly concealed by a strange-looking silver headband. Juk nodded and gestured for Rivan to sit.

"Not so long, mind. As I said, I'm in no mood for fire-side stories and such. Warm yourself and be on your way." Juk's sword remained by his side.

Rivan accepted his offer and gracefully placed himself opposite Juk, the fire separating the two men. Juk felt himself plunged back into his despair after the brief respite. All he could see and feel was darkness engulfing him, hopelessness all around him.

After a short while, Rivan looked up from the flames and asked, "Won't you share your troubles, friend? I see the pain etched on your face, and it resonated in every word you said, Juk. What is it that troubles you?"

Juk looked up at the stranger across from him and even though he felt the words wash over him, as if they were being sung by a sweet, melodious voice from a children's tale, he was all-consumed by his despair, paralysed by his fear.

"My troubles I'll keep to myself, stranger. They are mine and not to be shared."

"So be it, friend," replied Rivan. "But maybe unburdening yourself of this despair that is clear on your face will be of some comfort."

Juk said nothing at first, his eyes returning to the glowing embers of the fire. Then he spoke. "The despair is mine, too, and I will keep it whole. But it is not despair that troubles me, old man. It is hope. Or lack of it. Lack of hope is a terrible thing. One I wish on no man by sharing or otherwise."

"I have some skill in healing, both physical and

spiritual. The power of the Sun flows through me and can ease your pain, maybe."

"Sun Magick, eh?" Juk spat back. "So you're a mage or wizard or whatever? Didn't know they existed anymore, or ever."

Rivan held out his hands, palms facing Juk, closing his eyes, whispering words that couldn't be heard. Before Juk had had a chance to react, he felt a warm sensation wash over him. It started inside his head and slowly cascaded down his neck and back, revitalising and re-invigorating every part on its way down. Juk was transfixed, the fearful paralysis of his despair replaced by a peaceful, dull numbness permeating through his whole body. He could feel his body shutting down, not falling into the void he had foreseen, but being lifted to a place of passive ecstasy. He felt himself drifting off, his eyes drooping shut, and his tired, broken body and mind finding salvation. Slowly, he drifted into unconsciousness; a deep sleep he hadn't known for many a Moon, if ever.

THE CAPTIVE

He sat chained to the wall in almost complete darkness. The Sun's warmth had not touched his face in many a Moon. How long, he could not say with any confidence, but it had been a long time. He had accepted his circumstances; the submission to the present and nothing else. He lived his life moment by moment, day by day, Moon by Moon, without the hope for anything other than this. He did not allow himself to be seduced by the twisted sisters of fear and hope. His days would be lived breath by breath, within this physical cell just ten feet by ten feet in size. Despair or depression would not enter *his* prison; *his* refuge, the inner-jail he had constructed in his mind. He had prepared himself for the inevitable outcome of his incarceration. This inescapable conclusion of his fate. His ultimate triumph over his condition and the defeat of his difficulties, regardless of his circumstances. The inner-man had been in control for a long time. He had consumed the outer man, and *he* would allow nothing else.

A loud banging on the door was followed by the rattling of keys and the creaking of the door opening.

"Grub's up," came an irritated voice from only two feet away. He could smell the beer on the breath of the guard who dropped the wooden bowl and cup on the floor.

"Treat today," announced the guard. "Bread. Ha!" The guard seemed to enjoy his comment. It had been bread every day, and one-half cup of water, every day, for the whole time he had been chained to the wall.

"And fine bread, I'm sure it is," he replied as he groped for the bowl and cup on the floor.

"Ha! Fine bread," the guard said, as he kicked the cup over, water spilling onto the floor and over the groping hands. "It's as fine as it was yesterday, and the day before that!"

He heard the door slam shut and the key turn in the lock. He was alone again, as he broke off a piece of stale bread and soaked it in the water on the floor before he placed it delicately into his mouth.

"Fine bread it is," he said to the darkness, and received no reply. "Fine bread indeed."

The inner-man had played this role, moment by moment, day by day, Moon by Moon; he was in control.

CHIK SRIN

After just two days in Chinsap, a message arrived from Lord Ruperk. Chik and his men were to ride to Stoneguard. No other information was included. They were to leave as soon as the message was received. Chik had allowed his men to stay in their homes; it had been a long time since they had seen their families, and once they had found out about Juk's wife and children from the local guards, Chik felt it was even more important to spend time at home. This made the news that they had to leave immediately even more difficult to break to his men. And more surprising. How had Ruperk known of the murders so quickly? Would the guards have sent birds to Magdil? Maybe the rumours of Magdil men seen in the days after the murders were true. Or maybe it was a coincidence? The 1st Regiment men seemed to respect their new Captain, and to a man followed this directive, but not happily so.

Chik had enjoyed his time with his family, his wife, June, and young son, Choch. He had been away from them for too long, more than a year. He hadn't allowed his family to enter his thoughts in all that time. He was a soldier in the 1st Regiment. Now a Captain. His soldier's duty had always come first. It was good to see his family, though. And now he was leaving, he knew he would miss them. After receiving the message, he allowed the men an hour to say their goodbyes, and arranged to meet them at the main gate before Mid-Sun.

"Captain Chik, why the rush?" one of his men asked, looking at the dispirited faces all around.

"Orders. We're to head to Stoneguard."

"What did you manage to find out about Cap... Juk? The rumours are he done 'em himself. That's why he left the army, he —"

"Enough!" Chik interrupted. "You know Juk Thri is not a man who could've done that."

The men looked around and muttered to each other.

"They say the Moon took him," another of the men continued. "They say he..."

"Enough!" Chik stared at the men, and his nostrils flared. "I'll have no more of these old maid's tales. I spoke to the neighbours and the guards. There's no evidence that such a thing happened. None! Whatever you've heard is gossip and the whisperings of old fools who know no better. You all know Juk. We've all fought beside him. He could not have done it. I won't believe it and I won't have any more of it." Chik kept to himself the rumours of Magdil men seen asking questions in the aftermath of the murders. That would only add to the men's confusion and concerns. He didn't need that right now. He wished he had time to get to the bottom of these rumours now, though. The immediate summons to Stoneguard had curtailed that.

Chik pulled on his horse's reins and it turned to move through the main gate. "We leave for Stoneguard and we ride as swiftly as we can." For the rest of the day's ride, Chik heard no more from any man. He couldn't abide the thought of his men thinking Juk could be capable of that vile act on his own family. But the thought lingered in his mind just the same. After around half a Moon's ride, the large city of Stoneguard came into view. This place held happy memories for Chik. It's where his journey with the 1st Regiment started. He and Juk were stationed here for their initial training. They had both fought together with the Lord of Stoneguard, Lord Janson Brok, and Chik regarded him as a friend.

He was surprised and happy to see Lord Brok waiting for him at the main gate of the city. He was sitting atop a marvellous looking grey and white horse, with a guard either side of him. There was a third man, who Chik thought looked totally out of place sitting astride his own dark brown horse just behind Lord Brok, smiling widely. He had shoulder-length, dark hair and blue eyes, and a tattoo of a mountain tip across his right cheek; a sign he was from the Spine region. He was dressed out of place for the north, wearing the purple colours of Magdil. Chik recognised him as one of Lord Ruperk's travelling companions from Magdil, although he had never met the man. Chik thought the man's smile looked false, more akin to a hound master beckoning a wild forest dog, before hooking it with a big net.

"My Lord Brok. It's a humble pleasure to visit your fine city once more," Chik said, pulling the reins of his horse softly to bring it to a halt.

"Captain Chik, they tell me now," Lord Brok said and then looked over his shoulder at the man behind him.

"Yes, my lord. Sun and Moon be good," Chik replied, nodding.

"Well, Captain, let's go into the main tower. We have some rather important matters to discuss." Lord Brok pulled at his horse's reins to turn and enter the city.

"My lord," replied Chik. He followed Lord Brok and the two guards into the city. The other Magdil man rode beside Chik.

"Captain Chik Srin, Well met. I didn't get a chance to introduce myself on the trip from Magdil. My name is Walnak Veerak. I'm here at Lord Runkarn's pleasure."

"My lord," replied Chik. He always greeted strangers who were dressed as he was as my lord; it didn't matter to Chik whether they were high born or not; he felt it was the safest way to address someone who could have an influence over you.

"We have many questions to ask you," Walnak continued, smiling as he spoke.

"I'm here to bring honour and grace to Magdil and Areekya, my lord, Chik replied, smiling back at Walnak as they rode towards the drawbridge of the main city's tower.

Chik found himself sitting at a large table in the middle of a large, impressive looking hall. Sitting on one side were Lord Brok and the man from the Spine, Walnak Veerak.

"Well, Chik, how was the ride from the mountains?" Lord Brok asked from across the table.

"The ride was fine, my lord."

"We heard about the terrible business with Juk's family. What did you find out? Do you have any idea who could do such a thing?"

Chik took a moment to steady his emotions. "Horrible business, my lord. I cannot imagine who would do... Do that. No Chinsap man for sure." Chik looked across at the two men as he spoke. He thought Lord Janson Brok had the concerned look of a friend. He wasn't so sure about Walnak.

"And you saw no sign of Juk Thri?" Walnak asked.

"None," Chick answered to Walnak's question, but directed it at Lord Brok.

"Did you gather any information regarding this atrocity, Chik?" Lord Brok asked.

"Well, it seems that no one saw or heard anything. The neighbours saw the family a day or so before. They said nothing was untoward," Chik answered, still looking at Lord Brok. "However, there were reports of men from the capital asking questions. This was days before we arrived." Chik turned his attention to Walnak to gauge any reaction from the Magdil man.

"And Juk Thri? What news of him, Captain?" Walnak wrestled the topic back, showing no reaction to the news of the men from Magdil.

"He was there for two days or so. He discovered the bodies," Chik replied, returning his gaze to Lord Brok.

"Oh my!" Lord Brok blurted out. "Nobody should have to see that, Juk. I wonder how he is. And what's this of Magdil men?" Lord Brok turned to Walnak.

"Lord Runkarn thought it prudent to send the 2nd Regiment to investigate as soon as Captain Chik informed him of Juk's treachery," Walnak stated with no hint of emotion. Chik didn't like the words he used.

"Then why send Chik and his men?" blurted back Lord Brok.

"Why, this you should address to Lord Runkarn himself."

"Sun and Moon." Lord Brok stared at Chik and continued. "Do you know where he went after? Juk, I mean. Is it known where he went after leaving Chinsap?"

"He was seen heading south from Chinsap. That's all we know."

"Yes, that is as my men report it. Although they were more suspicious of your ex-Captain than either of you seem to be," Walnak added.

"What? I mean, excuse me, what are you saying?" Chik shook his head, trying to understand the meaning behind Walnak's statement.

"Do you not think it strange that the family wasn't missed by anyone? Or that they were discovered by a man who hadn't seen them in nearly a year. A man who was acting, shall we say, strangely?" Chik didn't like the tone the man from the Spine was now using.

"I don't understand the question." Chik looked directly at Walnak, although he had a sudden realisation of the meaning behind the questions, and mentally prepared himself.

"Well, it seems to me that if a man deserts his friends, his country, his lord in such an abrupt manner, but then scurries back to Chinsap to find his family slaughtered in such a way, it is incredibly strange and unlikely." Walnak's tone and manner became even more direct.

"That's enough, Walnak!" Lord Brok stood up and interjected. "We had this last night. Juk Thri had nothing to do with this. I told you then and I tell you again, now. Absolutely impossible. Although you failed to tell me about the 2nd Regiment riding out there."

Chik felt a rage grow within him. It took everything he had, all his soldier's discipline, not to stand up and reach across the table at the implied accusation.

"Would you not have said it was impossible that Juk Thri, and in your own words, the best soldier and finest man you ever knew, would desert his men, his position, his country?" Walnak fired back, continuing his blunt line of enquiry.

"That's nowhere near the same thing, Walnak," said Lord Brok. "He had his reasons for that. He needed a break. The reason he did those things is that he wanted to see his family again, he told me himself. This other thing you accuse him of, nonsense. I cannot believe this!"

Chik Srin sat there and watched the two men argue back and forth. It was obvious that Lord Brok had seniority, but he also was deferential to a degree that surprised Chik. It had been a long time since he fought with him in battle and drank with him in the taverns, but Lord Janson Brok was as close to Juk as anyone, except perhaps himself. The fact he hadn't thrown Walnak Veerak out of the window behind them came as a shock to him.

"I see tempers are a little raised. This is a terrible business. You are correct," said Walnak. "I'm sure the young Captain would like to rest and bathe after his journey."

"Chik, follow my men. They'll show you to the barracks, although I'm sure you remember the way." Lord Brok smiled as he gestured Chik to the door.

"My lord."

"I'll send for you later. Once you've cleaned yourself up and taken some rest." Lord Brok smiled and stood up.

Chik turned and followed the guards, his rage still simmering just under the surface. He was glad to have left that room. He was glad to have left without allowing his lack of soldier's discipline to embarrass him.

LORD JANSEN BROK

Janson Brok sat at the breakfast table with his family. His wife, Jenna, sat opposite him and his twin boys, Barok and Bilbuk, were sitting on either side. He sat quietly, eating the bread and eggs before him, thinking. His thoughts were of Juk Thri, Walnak Veerak and Magdil. It didn't sit right with him that Walnak seemed to be withholding something, and he didn't like the way he talked about his friend, Juk.

"Husband, you've hardly touched your food this morning," Jenna softly stated from the other end of the table. "And you were tossing and turning all night last night, too. This Juk Thri matter is putting years on you, my love."

Janson looked up from his meal and smiled at his wife, seeing the concern in her small, brown eyes. Then turning to each son in turn, he took a bite of the loaf. "Well that won't do, will it," he said while the bread tumbled around and out of his mouth. The twins laughed, and it brought a smile to Jenna's face, too.

Janson looked back at his wife. "It's a damned business, this, you know."

"Language!" Jenna looked at Janson and then at both boys, who found it most amusing.

"Sorry, my dear. This is a puzzle I can't get out of my head. I think I shall have to take my men and try to find Juk. I know him as well as I know any man. I'm sure I could find him and get to the bottom of this whole bloody mess!"

"Janson! Please," Jenna said, her face scrunched up into a frown. The boys started giggling again.

With this, Janson stuffed his eggs and the remainder of his bread into his mouth. "Sorry, my dear. I've done it again!" The eggs and bread tumbled out all over the table. This sent the boys into raptures and Jenna laughed, too. Janson didn't want his family to share the burden he felt; this conflict inside of him. He knew he would be away for a while and didn't want his family to feel any concern for him. Janson spent the rest of the morning with his wife and boys. It was time he enjoyed, but he also felt a darkening shadow drawing near. He needed time with his family before he had to confront the coming storm.

Just after Mid-Sun, Janson made his way to the barracks, a guard on either side. It wasn't often in recent times the Lord of the City ventured into the soldiers' confines. Each soldier he passed saluted with a look of surprise. It was Chik Srin he came to see. The guards entered the 1st Regiment's dorm and announced Lord Brok's presence.

"My Lord Brok. It's a surprise and a pleasure to see you here." Chik got up to greet him.

"Yes, it was about time I paid a visit to the barracks. There was a time, long ago mind, when this was where I preferred to be. That was before, though. Walk with me a while, will you, Captain?" Janson walked outside and headed towards the main courtyard. "So, Chik. What do you make of all this?"

"Well, my Lord Brok..."

Janson smiled at Chik. "Janson, please. I've never enjoyed formality, only when it must be followed. Call me Janson, please."

"Well, Janson, to be honest, I haven't thought about anything else since Chinsap, and even before that, Juk's behaviour and actions were constantly on my mind. But I don't know what to think."

"Aye, it's a damned unpleasant business. Could you believe Juk had anything to do with, with... that?" Janson looked down at the dried dirt as he spoke.

"I can't believe he would do it. I don't think he *could* do it. He was acting strangely before, I mean when we were dealing with the Wetlanders nearly six moons ago, but this? No, not unless some madness took him. Even then, I can't imagine he could do it."

"Well, I don't believe it either. I don't like this business of the 2nd Regiment being sent there before you, but we must be careful. Magdil and Lord Runkarn have brought peace to Areekya, and it's difficult to believe he could have sanctioned such a thing. It's a bloody bad business." Janson was shaking his head, still looking down. "The only thing to do, to help Juk and sort this out, I think we have to find him." Janson looked up at Chik.

"Where would we start?" the younger man asked.

"Well, you said he headed south. If you were him, you had just buried your family, and didn't want to be found, would you continue south?"

"I cannot think what *I* would do. He could continue south to Dawngate, nobody would know him there. But why wouldn't he want to be found? What would he have to hide?"

"Grief is a terrible thing, Chik. The Juk Thri I know, would seek solace in solitude, not in a big city such as Dawngate. I've been thinking about this all night."

"The Northern Hills?" Chik stopped walking and looked up at Janson as the question left his mouth.

"That's where I'd go to find some peace. The seclusion those hills offer might attract him there. He knows that area well, we fought there many Moons ago. A man could hide away there without seeing another soul for Moons. Windwatch is less than a week's ride. We could start there and search the area." Janson's voice sounded more confident.

"What about Magdil? What do we tell Walnak?" Janson detected the conflict in Chik's voice.

"Leave him to me," Janson replied. "He'll be told what he needs to be told and nothing more. Tell your men to be ready. We'll leave tonight before last Sun. And tell them to talk to no one regarding this. Let's keep this between us, eh?" With that, Janson nodded and winked at Chik, and gestured to his guards to lead him back to the tower. Chik made his way back to the barracks.

Janson spent the rest of the afternoon with his family. His wife and two boys met him in the courtyard. Looking around, he saw the boys wrestling together with his attentive wife looking on. Her long, chestnut hair, the same colour as her eyes, was blowing in the wind. It was now the ninth Moon of the year, and the north wind blew cold this time of the year. It wasn't as cold as usual today, though. He enjoyed this time with his loved ones. Relaxing with his children brought out the softer side of his personality. He knew what terrible things he had been capable of, and the memories of those experiences still haunted him in his darker moments. This also brought to his mind the things he knew Juk Thri capable of; one of the best fighting men he had ever fought with or against, but he tried to block those fragments of long past horrors.

He wanted to spend time with his family and relax before he had to leave. The smell of the courtyard had always brought him relief when he was younger, as it still did now. The fresh wind that constantly blew through the courtyard carried a sweet aroma from the north; a combination of the pine trees and local flowers. It was a place that reminded him of his family. He almost forgot the terrible things he had done in the past fighting for his country, his home, his family.

By the end of the afternoon, as the Sun dropped in the west and the wind blew colder, he took his family inside, and they had an early dinner together. He watched as his sons and wife ate the food prepared for them by the kitchen staff; the wild rabbit stew, with herbs from the gardens of Stoneguard. He watched, and he smiled. After dinner, he put the boys to bed and kissed his wife Jenna softly on the cheek. He then made his way to his study, finding Walnak Veerak waiting with two guards of the city.

"Walnak, I'm glad you could make it. I'm afraid I

have to leave. I leave you in the capable hands of my good wife, Lady Jenna. She will see you are catered for and any requests you may have will be dealt with as if I were here myself." Janson smiled as he spoke.

"Leave? Where to, my lord? Perchance with Captain Chik Srin?"

"Aye, Captain Chik and his men will accompany me for my protection, and I'll take some of my own men, too. There's trouble up at Windwatch. Reports are some Hillmen have been seen. We'll go and investigate."

"Hillmen, eh? Such is the trouble that the Lord of the City must deal with it?"

"Aye, it should take a Moon or so to deal with. The city is yours till I return."

"A Moon? Or so? That's too long for me to remain in Stoneguard, my lord. Lord Runkarn's called me back to the capital to report on my findings here. And in Chinsap, of course," Walnak replied. Janson didn't detect any surprise in the man from the Spine's voice.

"Well then. Well met and good travels. Pass on my most humble greetings to Lord Runkarn. Sun be good, I'll be in Magdil soon myself to personally bestow my greetings." Janson stood up and accompanied Walnak to the door of his study.

"Until then, my lord. I'm sure Lord Runkarn will be interested to learn of your troubles with, with Hillmen, was it?"

With that, Walnak made his way back to his quarters and Janson closed the door behind him. He knew Walnak didn't believe the Hillmen story, but he was happy enough that he didn't ask too many questions. He knew he'd have to deal with that sooner or later. His priority right now was to find Juk Thri. Magdil's suspicions could wait.

Just before Last Sun, he met Chik and his men at the main gate. Lord Brok also brought twenty-five of his best with him.

"Well met, Captain," Janson greeted Chik.

"My Lord Brok," replied Chik.

Slowly, they all left through the main gate until they were outside of the city walls. Then, with Janson and Chik at the head of the party, headed north at a swift gallop.

CHIK SRIN

Windwatch tower, at the foot of the Northern Hills, was built to protect Stoneguard from attacks coming out of the north. One hundred feet tall, it was built mainly as a watchtower. The tower could hold up to two-dozen men comfortably, but now it was manned with the bare minimum of Stoneguard men. In all the years, it had only been attacked once; by a brigand of Hillmen, two-dozen in total. Birds were sent out to warn the local villagers and Stoneguard. The tower was sturdy enough that the six men stationed there held the attackers off until reinforcements turned up in a day or two from the surrounding villages. That was nearly two years ago. Runkarn's army was very efficient in eradicating the threat from the Northern Hillmen.

"Well, Lord Brok, do we keep heading north, or do you reckon we should split up?" Chik still used the formal title. Although he counted him as a friend, he didn't really feel comfortable enough to use any other with the older nobleman.

Lord Brok surveyed the surrounding area from atop his horse. "You know Juk as well as any man does. You take your men and head north east, as I think it more likely that's the direction he would've travelled. I'll head north, north west. We'll both take a small cage of pigeons from the tower. Send back word if you find anything."

"If he's here, we'll find him. I'm sure of that. At any rate, let's hope we'll find some sign at least." Chik sounded more confident than he felt.

Lord Brok smiled and ordered his men into the watchtower to get the birds. "Let's meet back here in six days. That's the Full Moon. We'll decide what's next then."

"Let's hope for some good news to report." With that, Chik got his men together and headed off at a swift trot.

By Last Sun, Chik and his men were deep into the hills. In the far distance off to the east, the tallest peaks of the Red Mountains could just be made out.

"Okay, boys. We'll camp here for the night. We'll start off again at first light. Set up watches as required." Chik kept his tone upbeat and smiled as he gave his orders. Although that belied his own feelings. He stood staring at the mountains. Clouds were gathering around the tallest peaks. He anticipated a wild storm and envisaged the lightning and the loud rumbles of thunder heading their way.

Morning came without incident. They set off at a slow pace, investigating anything that appeared worthy of a second look; carefully looking for human activity or presence of any kind. The area around the Northern Hills in the north east of Areekya was a desolate place. There was almost a total absence of wildlife; rarely a bird or other creature was seen. It felt empty, dead almost, with the occasional presence of a copse or small valley to protect from the harsh winds that blew all year round.

It was now the ninth Moon, and the wind was cold. The place looked, and felt, forsaken. The Hillmen had inhabited this area for years before Magdil had pushed them even further north. It looked an empty, lifeless place now. Chik could not imagine it ever looking any different. For almost three days they searched, looking for any sign, but found none. Late in the afternoon on the third day, one of Chik's men shouted out:

"Captain, look here." Chik rode over to see the remnants of a fire.

"Well, there's something!" Chik exclaimed. "How long ago would you say that fire was alight?"

"Not recent. A whole Moon. Maybe more. Whoever warmed themselves by this fire have long since gone," one of the men replied.

"Let's search the entire area near here. We've a couple of hours of light left. Report back anything you find. We'll set up camp here for the night." Chick gestured to his men to fan out, and he stared at the ash and charred wood. "Well, that's something," he said again. Not loud enough for anyone to hear, but that imagined sound of thunder seemed to be getting closer. After a while, Chik was called again. Not far from the camp, he was shown the faint existence of footprints.

Two of Chik's men were looking down at the ground. "Two people by the looks of it, and one horse, maybe two. These prints were made a Moon or so ago. It's difficult to be sure," one of the men said. "They headed west in any case, for a few hundred yards, and we lost them. My guess is deep in the hills they went, or even on to the Greenscape."

Chik looked at the prints and then turned his head to the sky. "Well, we'll head back west ourselves in the morning. It's getting too dark to continue today. Maybe we'll find more prints then."

The next morning they set out early, just after First Sun. They travelled slowly, looking for any more prints or signs; they found none. By Mid-Sun, They stopped for a rest. The Sun was directly above them, shining down. Even this late in the year, with the wind blowing, the midday Sun's rays were strong enough to feel its warmth. After the rest, they started off again, but found no more prints, no indications of any sort that anyone had passed this way. In fact, they found no signs of any sort at all during the whole journey back to Windwatch.

As they approached the tower on the evening of the sixth day, Chik could see Lord Brok and his men gathered around a campfire.

"Well met, Chik." Lord Brok stood up and gestured Chik and his men to join them.

"Well met indeed, Lord Brok," Chik replied. "What news? Any signs of Juk?"

"Signs, yes. Of Juk? That's more difficult to be sure of." Lord Brok replied. "We found some prints in the foothills just north of here. Two horses we think, heading south west. We can't be sure as they were more than a Moon old. And you? What did you find?" Lord Brok asked.

"It sounds like the same as you, evidence of a horse, maybe two. Footprints of two men, heading west, so they could've been made by the same people." Lord Brok's eyes shone with this news, thought Chik.

"Well then. What's to be made of this?" Lord Brok posited. "Juk headed to the Northern Hills for solace, and either went with someone or met someone there, and then headed west together? Who can piece this puzzle together?"

"I know not, my lord," answered Chik. "But the more I hear about this, the more I dislike it."

Lord Brok shook his head. "Well, well, if they were Juk's prints, and if he was with someone heading south west, the questions are, who, and where?"

"And *why*?" added Chik. "None of this makes any sense to me, Lord Brok."

Lord Brok looked at Chik and smiled. "Well lad, you look tired. Let's rest here tonight under the Full Moon. We'll all feel refreshed in the morning. But, I must say, as bad as this business is, I have enjoyed being back out on the road. It's brought back some of my old vigour."

"Aye, my lord, we are tired and a good night's rest is what's needed," replied Chik, ignoring Lord Brok's final comments. "We'll head over there to camp for the night." Chik gestured to the east, where he saw a sheltered area on his way in.

"Warm yourselves first, Captain. Then you'll get that good night's sleep you're talking about." Lord Brok continued to smile and gestured to his men to make way for Chik's to get close to the fire.

"Thank you, my Lord," replied Chik, knowing that

no amount of warming by the fire would give him the good night's sleep he required, not with the storm in his mind getting ever nearer.

"Janson, Chik, please, call me Janson. Leave the formal nonsense for the city lads, eh?"

"Thank you Janson," Chik replied as he stared into the flames, knowing the storm was close now.

ASHRAN

Ashran woke early, as he usually did, and got dressed and went outside to the front yard of his house. The chickens and ducks were clucking and quacking as normal as the Sun rose above the hills in the east; It was going to be a dry day. Ashran was glad of that, at least. There was a lot of activity this morning. Everyone was preparing the extra grain demanded from Magdil. A messenger had visited yesterday and wanted five grain wagons to be sent by the end of the week. It had been almost five Moons since Juk Thri had said there would be demands, and he had been proven correct.

"Ashron, my lad. Is everything as it should?" he called out to his son, working tirelessly preparing the extra grain as instructed last night.

"Yes, Father. It'll be tight, but it looks like we'll cope... this time. Let's hope the next message from Magdil is many Moons away, eh?"

"Aye lad, we can hope that. My bones are telling me it might be sooner than we can manage, but let's hope that." Ashran walked over to his neighbours' dwellings, nodding and smiling as he did so; few returned his friendly gestures. He reached the home of Bishran. He had been there with him in the Midnight Forest and the subsequent bloodshed over six Moons ago.

"Bishran, how goes it? Everything as it should?

Would that it didn't have to be done so much in a rush? Will we manage it in time?" Ashran looked kindly at his friend. He had relied on Bishran's counsel many times in the past, and considered him his closest friend.

"Aye, it'll be done. It'll be tight, but it'll be done." Bishran looked up and smiled as he saw his friend. "Damn Magdil to the Moon and Stars for this. And this is just the first of many calls, I'm sure of that." Bishran's smile turned into a frown.

"Let's get these carts off. We can talk about the next call when we have to. Today's not the day for that, old friend." Ashran maintained his smile.

"You're right Ashran. But I'm not alone in thinking this. The others might not be saying it to you, but you can see it in their eyes. I think it's best if you call a Council when this is done. Try to keep everyone together."

"Aye, you could be right there." Ashran tried to keep his friend happy.

Bishran continued to frown and looked at Ashran. "It was tough enough when we got back from the last battle. Well, massacre, whatever you call it. I think they'll need sound counsel after this is done." Bishran turned away and got back to work.

"I'll see what I can do, old friend," Ashran said in parting and continued around the village, offering words of encouragement and comfort as necessary.

Lendir was a village built amongst the marshlands in the west. Most of the dwellings were raised from the ground on wooden stilts, four or five feet high. The boggy swampland that surrounded Lendir had acted as a protective barrier from unwanted guests over the years, as well as being a hindrance for the Clan Grash to find suitable land to settle. The village itself was built on solid enough ground, but the extra height afforded that greater level of protection from flooding from the winter rainfall, which occasionally befell the aptly named Wetlands. There was enough dry land to grow grain, and they also had a decent trade with the villages on the coast of the Endless Ocean to the south.

As Ashran continued to walk around the village handing out words of support and reassurance, he noticed that most villagers were too busy in their work to either notice or care, and this made Ashran feel even worse. He could feel the confidence drain out of him and feelings of guilt and regret rise within him. He got back home after around an hour. Ashran walked up the stairs to his front door, stood for a brief moment to steady himself emotionally, then opened the door to see his wife was getting breakfast ready.

"Morning, my lovely," Ashran said, smiling widely. "And how is my beautiful wife this morning?"

"Well enough, my dear. How's everyone else? Can't be too cheerful after yesterday's news, I'll wager." Tinkar, Ashran's wife, was busy frying fish and boiling water. She was a short, squat woman with long, black hair and matching eyes.

"Ah, they'll be fine. We'll be fine. What can we do? We're in the grasps of Magdil now. A place I didn't want us to be." Ashran sat down at the table.

"Well, fine, eh? I think they ain't happy. You'll find

that out soon enough if you don't know already. What to do about it is the thing." Tinkar put the fish and bread on the table. "Ashron, get in quick now. Breakfast is ready," she called out to her son.

"I'll call a Council for tomorrow. We'll discuss it then." Ashran broke off a chunk of bread and took a bite.

"A Council? Well, be ready for a lot of talk and nonsense, my dear. A lot of hot air about at the minute. It might be best to let them blow it out first." Tinkar looked at Ashran with some concern. "I think it's best to wait a while. People say things when they're full of bluster that otherwise wouldn't get said. Best give it a day or three, eh?" Tinkar looked out the window to check if Ashron was coming.

"You're probably right, as ever. Let me think on it. Anyway, let's enjoy our breakfast. Give Ashron another shout."

"Ashro—" Tinkar stopped as her son walked in and sat next to his father. "Eat up lad, you can finish loading the carts after breakfast," Tinkar directed her son.

"Father, with respect, the village is not happy at all. Everyone's saying you shouldn't have given in so easily, you shouldn't have listened to that mage, you shouldn't be sending five carts of grain to Magdil." Ashron kept his eyes on the fish and bread as he spoke, finally grabbing a piece of bread.

Tinkar coughed, and Ashran noticed a slight nod of her head. He replied to his son, "Aye, life's hard at the minute. I'll have to do something about that, I know. Today's not the time to talk about it. Let's enjoy breakfast, get the grain carts out, and then we can talk about Magdil and me." Ashran then continued eating his fish and bread in silence.

Just before Last Sun, Ashran was leaning on the wall outside his home as he watched the last of the five grain wagons leave the village. Standing next to him were Ashron, his son, and Bishran.

"Well, that's done. I know it wasn't easy for any of us, but now that's that," Ashran said, looking over at the two men next to him.

"Aye, it's done," said Bishran. "But it's not the end. This is just the start, and it will not get easier; a lot harder, if you want to know my thoughts on the bloody mess."

"I do respect your thoughts, Bishran." Ashran smiled.

"Well, what happens when they come back and we don't have the grain? What about when they want fighting men? Who's going to give up sons, brothers?" Bishran was getting agitated. The physical and mental toughness of the day was showing.

"I do want your counsel on these matters, and more besides, Bishran. But let's leave it for today. Tomorrow's Sun will bring a new day and with it a fresh mind and body. Tomorrow we'll have to talk about getting out of this bloody mess, if we can." Ashran smiled and turned towards his home, with Ashron following him.

"Aye, tomorrow then," Bishran replied. "Tomorrow." And with that, he started off home himself.

—

Tap, tap, tap. Ashran was awoken by the noise of someone knocking on the front door. He jumped out of bed and looked out of the window. He saw two shadows there. Men wearing cloaks, it looked like. It wasn't dawn yet, and it was unusual to be woken at this time.

"Who is it?" Ashran called out from behind the door. "Who's calling at this hour?"

"It is I. Open up, open up. We've much to discuss. I wanted to slip in unnoticed. I don't suppose I'm that welcome after the Midnight Forest," the visitor replied, barely above a whisper, from the other side of the door.

"By the Sun and Moon," Ashran answered as he unlocked the bolt and opened the door. "And who's this you have with you, Rivan? It's unlike you not to come alone."

"Let us in, let us in. You'll see who I bring once we get inside." The two men walked in and uncloaked.

Ashran stared in amazement at the man standing next to the mage. The blue eyes and the tall, slim frame made him unmistakable. "Juk Thri of the 1st Regiment. What the Sun are you doing here? What are you doing here with him?" Ashran directed that last question at Rivan.

"You once invited me into your village. I hope that invitation still stands," Juk Thri replied. "And it's just Juk now, no 1st Regiment. I'm here to offer you my apologies and to seek your help."

"My help? By Sun and Moon. Sit down then, both of you. Let me get you something to drink. Wine? It looks like you've travelled far and not in any comfort by the condition of your cloaks." Ashran grabbed some cups and wine from the side. He poured three glasses and placed some bread and fish on the table.

Rivan broke off some bread and handed it to Juk. "You guess correctly Ashran, we've come far and in some rush, and what's more? Our friend here has suffered a great loss, and he needs refuge for a while, counsel too, probably. And he needs some solace. Would you provide these for him, Ashran?"

Ashran studied Juk closely. He remembered the cold blue eyes of the man he'd met on the battlefield, but something was changed. In front of him sat a gaunt man with a haunted look on his face. The blueness of his eyes had not dimmed, but they seemed empty of the fire he remembered from before. "I can provide a place to stay, friend. My offer stands still. As for the other things you say, well I'm not sure what counsel I could give an officer of the 1st Regiment, but this village is quiet enough. I'm pretty sure the rest of the village won't like his presence here, though. Where are your horses? They would've been seen. There'll be trouble come morning."

"We hid our horses out of town, and we'll be gone before first light. You can talk to the village before we return." Rivan took a bite of the bread.

"I'm not sure I could convince them that having a Magdil man here would be a good thing. That's asking too much, Rivan." Ashran's eyes remained firmly fixed on Juk's emaciated, grim face. "We have a counsel soon. Maybe I could bring it up there, I don't know. We'll need to keep it quiet till then, though."

"Ex-Magdil man," Juk said, looking down at the floor. "I quit my post. I've left that life behind and I'm looking for somewhere to rest for a while. If it is any inconvenience, I'll understand. I shouldn't have come, but—" Juk was interrupted by Rivan before he could finish his sentence.

"Yes, very good Ashran. We'll sleep on this floor tonight. It'll be a lot better and warmer than we've become accustomed to this past Moon or so." And with that, Rivan finished his cup of wine, took another bite of bread, and promptly curled up in the corner of the room.

"Thank you, Ashran," said Juk. "Thank you for the help. I know it's beyond that which I've any right to expect, but it's been a long journey and I need sleep, too." Then he walked over to another corner of the room and dropped to the floor, and instantly fell asleep.

Ashran stood there for a moment or two, looking at the two men in his home, trying to take in what had just happened. He shook his head and made his way back to bed, muttering, "Tomorrow then," he said to himself. "Tomorrow."

JUK THRI

Juk was shaken awake by Rivan. It was still dark, and for a few seconds, he was confused. Then the realisation of his location and situation came to him.

"It's still early, but I want to move before we're seen," the mage said.

"Move? Where to?" Juk was still grappling with his bearings.

"Somewhere else, somewhere safer. Your presence here will not be appreciated. Not at all. Let's wait until Ashran talks to the villagers first. Maybe then we can come back." Rivan grabbed the remaining bread and fish from the table and put them in his bag.

Juk stood up, put on his cloak, and pulled his hood over his head.

"Follow me." Rivan opened the door and made his way outside.

Juk followed. "Where are we heading?"

"We'll grab our horses and head for the Wet Forest. Despite its name, it'll be dry enough this time of the year, and should be safe for a while."

"Is it far?"

"Not even a morning's ride. I left instructions with Ashran. He'll know where to find us if he needs to,"

Rivan whispered. "Come now, quietly. This way."

Juk quietly followed the mage out of the village. The first shafts of orange Sunlight were rising in the east, and Juk felt his spirits rise, too. The village was still quiet, and he was unsure if they'd been noticed, but Rivan seemed pretty confident they hadn't. Before Mid Sun, they reached the outskirts of the forest. Rivan found a dry, comfortable clearing, and they tied up their horses.

"Stay here. I'll get some firewood. We're far enough in, so the smoke will go unseen. I'll make sure of that."

Juk sat down and looked around. In all the rush this morning, he hadn't had too much time to allow his fear and situation to get the better of him. In fact, he hadn't felt it completely overwhelm him for some time. He didn't feel better, just different; numb. Within the hour, Rivan had returned and got the fire going. He had brought back a fair-sized hare, too, and it was already roasting over the flames.

"So, Juk Thri. What do you do next?" Rivan was turning the animal using the improvised spit he'd made.

"I don't know. I need to think. I haven't been able to think clearly since Chinsap." Juk was staring at the fire.

"Well, you are no longer a soldier. What's it to be then? A farmer? Raise some sheep and tend some land," the mage asked as he continued to turn the spit.

"There's honour in farming land," Juk replied. "But I fear I have no inclination for it. For anything."

"Maybe with time. With time you will feel, well, different." Rivan pulled at the hare and tweaked something on the spit.

Juk looked at the mage. "It's *time* itself that I fear. The hope has been taken from me. The despair and misery I can live with. Having my hope taken from me. My wishes for my family, for me. This will not change."

"There's honour in avenging your family, Juk. Do you not want to get back at them? These people who did this. Make them pay for what they did to your wife, your daughters?" Rivan continued to turn the roasting hare.

"If I knew who *they* were." Juk kept his eyes on the burning wood.

"Well, who else could they be?" The mage stopped turning and pulled the hare off the spit and split it into two pieces in one swift movement.

"You mean Magdil? Runkarn?" Juk went to pick up his half of the hare and quickly dropped it again. "Sun and Stars! That's hot."

"Yes, sorry. I barely feel heat and cold after all these years," Rivan apologised. "And yes, I mean Runkarn. Isn't it obvious? Your soldiers got to Magdil long before you reached Chinsap. You told me there was time for that, to get there before you."

Juk stared again into the flames. "1st Regiment killing Chinsap folk? Impossible."

"Is it?"

"Yes, completely unthinkable. My men, or I should say the 1st Regiment, are Chinsap born and bred, to a man."

"And no Chinsap man has ever killed another?" Rivan took a sizeable chunk out of his half of the hare.

"A woman and two children? For no reason? No, I can't believe it." Juk put his meat down on the ground next to the glowing fire.

"Well, who else is there? And maybe they thought they had a reason?" The mage took a bite of the freshly cooked meat.

Juk continued to look deeply into the flames, as they jumped and danced their wild dance. He sat and said nothing. He thought back to his wife and daughters. Who would do that to his family? Juk thought. *How* someone could do it was easier to understand. His soldier's life had seen worse than that. He pushed those thoughts from his mind, took a small bite of the meat, and stood up. "I'm off for a walk,"

"Don't go far. We're safe here, but if you wander too close to the edge, you may be seen," Runkarn said while finishing his hare and picking up Juk's half.

Juk was walking for no longer than a few minutes when he saw a narrow stream, only three feet across. He sat down next to it and listened to the gurgling, bubbling, frothing water whispering its song. He sat, and he thought. Juk felt his mind wander back to Chinsap, back to his family, back to his grief. He lay down and let the grief overwhelm him, filling every sinew, muscle and bone. It filled his body completely. He could feel it slowly invading his body, and he gave in to its slow, pulsating advance. He allowed the sensation of dread to fill him, and then he felt something else; an undefinable energy pumping out from his chest. It was surging from his heart through his veins to every part of his being. He closed his eyes and saw a vivid array of colours in his mind's eye; brilliant, illuminating colours swirling. With the colours, the energy grew stronger, an overpowering, ecstatic feeling flowing through him and around him. Juk had never felt such an intense emotion. Then the colours in his mind's eye became interwoven with stars and he could see the entire night sky, a crescent Moon glowing in the centre of this vista. He became elated; the dread retreated from his feelings and emotions utterly. He lay there and allowed this intense experience to infuse him unconditionally. Time seemed to expand and compress all at once. He observed this state of ecstasy within him, filling his heart with joy and pleasure never before known.

For how long Juk lay next to the stream, he was unsure. But when he finally opened his eyes and sat up, he saw Rivan standing over him, smiling.

"You looked so peaceful. Your face so carefree. I didn't want to wake you."

Juk blinked twice and stood up. He felt lighter, as if the huge steel anvil he felt he had been carrying around with him had been cast off into the stream beside him. He looked directly at the mage. "I felt peaceful. Something just happened that I don't know how to explain; colours, feelings..."

"Then do not try," Rivan said calmly. "Some things do not have to be voiced to be real, to be felt, to be experienced."

"It was wonderful, no that doesn't fit, it was..."

"Maybe it just was," the mage interjected. "Let's head back. It's nearly Sundown."

Juk followed the mage back to their temporary camp. The fire was still burning, and the air was starting to chill as he sat down and warmed his hands. "You know, I think I have an idea about what to do," Juk said as he looked across the flames at Rivan.

"Ah, that's good," Rivan replied. His eyes flashed as they reflected the light from the fire. "That is very good."

ASHRAN

"So, how often are they going to come calling? Taking our grain. It'll be men they'll be wanting next. You watch!" one of the villagers assembled near the back of the town hall shouted at Ashran.

"Now, now. We don't know that, Finran," answered Ashran. "How long have you known me? All your life. And me and your father were tight as old trees. I'm asking you... I'm asking you all to trust me. I've not steered you far wrong all these years. Trust me, and I won't let you down." Beads of sweat were running down Ashran's neck. The weather had become cool in the west during the ninth Moon of the year, but the atmosphere in the hall was fiery. Ashran was sitting behind a long wooden table at the front of the hall. Next to him was Bishran, his closest friend and advisor. The town meeting had been going on for nearly an hour, and Ashran's back was aching and his head was hurting.

"How about the Midnight Forest? Didn't steer us too well that night, nor that mage of yours," came another shouted complaint, this time from the front of the hall. "And he was seen this morning, skulking around the village, early hours an' all. What's he doin' 'ere? The likes of 'im got us in this mess to start with, if you ask me. And he weren't alone, neither."

Ashran looked at the old man near the front of the crowd. "Avran, yes, Rivan was here last night. He came to see me. He has gone now, and his friend. They left this morning after seeking a place to stay for the night. The question remains, do you trust me to get us through this? We've been through tough times before. Dare say we'll have them again." Ashran looked up at the crowd, four hundred strong at least.

"I say we need to agree, all of us here today, to try to untangle ourselves from this Magdil arrangement," Bishran announced. "This will end up no good, mark my words," he added.

Ashran looked at his oldest friend next to him, smiled, and nodded. He moved his eyes away from Bishran and addressed the crowd. "Listen, we've just sent five wagons of grain. They'll be no more harvest until next year. That buys us some time before they'll come again. Time to plan and time to think."

"And how about if they come for our men or women?" an older woman cried out from the front.

"We'll cross that swamp bridge when we have to. Until then, do I have your trust? Your trust to come up with a plan to improve this situation for all of us?" Ashran asked again.

There was a lot of discontented murmuring. Ashran could see the townsfolk talking to each other, some in a whisper, but most almost shouting. He could see and hear a lot of displeasure in the room. He could feel it, too. As he was scanning the room, his eyes fell on his wife, Tinkar, in the corner, beaming at him, and this gave him strength.

After a while, Bishran spoke again. "Well, I think I

can speak for most here, and I say, this Magdil situation needs fixing. I say we form a clan council to work out how to get through it the best we can."

"That sounds like a sensible way forward, Bishran," Ashran said, smiling, relieved that it sounded as if things were coming to an agreement.

"And we'll give you until the next Magdil visit to get it sorted. Whenever that may be, in a Moon or ten Moons' time," Bishran continued. Ashran could hear approval coming from the hall. "So, what do you say to that, Ashran?"

"I say, aye, that'll do. That will do." Ashran smiled as he spoke.

"There it is then," Bishran said, looking at the crowd. "Does anyone have anything further to say?"

Ashran looked and listened, and apart from a couple of whispered complaints from somewhere near the back, the crowd was silent and seemed satisfied with what was proposed.

"Friends." Ashran stood up and came out from behind the table as he spoke. "We'll start the Clan Council tomorrow. Let's leave all disagreements and ill thoughts behind us for the time being and let's get back to our everyday lives, eh?" There was a muttering of agreement from the assembled townsfolk. And with that, the crowd made its way out of the hall slowly. Ashran could still hear some complaints, but they were few, and he was happy that it had ended.

Bishran stayed behind and smiled at Ashran. "Well, that could have been worse, old friend," Bishran said.

Ashran smiled back and put his arm on Bishran's shoulder. "Aye, let's meet tomorrow morning, early, and we'll get some names together to discuss all this."

"Tomorrow," Bishran said as he made his way to the exit.

Ashran walked over to where his wife was standing. She had now been joined by Ashron, his son.

"Well, family. That wasn't so bad."

"Not so bad," Tinkar replied, smiling.

"So, what say we all go home for a nice cup of tea?" Ashran said as he gestured towards the door.

After drinking his tea at home, Ashran stood up from the table. "I think I'd like to go for a nice walk before dinner. Ashron, would you like to join me?"

"No thanks, Father. I'll help ma with the supper. Some vegetables need peeling."

"That sounds nice," Tinkar said. "When you come back, we'll have supper all ready. I'm doing a nice stew tonight. I've even got a bit of rabbit!" she continued, unable to contain her excitement.

"Well, that all sounds lovely," Ashran said as he put on his coat and walked outside. He walked past his neighbours' houses. It was early evening and he could see them all busily preparing suppers of their own. He had been walking for about ten minutes when he reached the local tavern, The White Horse. From inside the building, Shiker, the landlord's wife, knocked on the window, trying to get Ashran's attention.

Ashran smiled as she gestured for him to come inside. He walked towards the entrance. When the door opened from the inside, Shiker was standing there. "You just saved me a walk, Ashran."

"Oh yes?" replied Ashran. "Why's that?"

"We had a messenger arrive. Not over five minutes ago, he left. After supping a quick jug of ale."

"A messenger?"

"Yes, a messenger. With a message. A message for you," Shiker said, holding the door open as she spoke.

"For me?" Ashran asked. "Who's sending me a message?"

"Yes, for you. Here it is." Shiker handed him the letter.

"Why, thank you, Shiker."

"Won't you come in for an ale? Warm yourself by the fire while you read your letter." Shiker's eyes were full of anticipation.

"I'd better not. Tinkar has a special supper on the go. If she smells the ale, well, that wouldn't go down too well. Thanks all the same." And with that, Ashran waved goodbye and continued his walk out of town. He felt Shiker's disappointed stare boring into his back as he went. He looked at the writing on the letter and got a nervous feeling in the pit of his stomach. The handwriting on the envelope was unmistakable; it was Rivan's. He walked towards a wooden bench just along the path, next to the fishmonger's, and sat down. Ashran slowly opened the letter, hoping it held some good news for a change. As he read the note, he felt dizzy and light-headed, as if the blood had drained from his head down into his stomach. He put the note down beside him on the bench and stared off into the distance.

After a while, his head cleared slightly, and he picked the note up again and read it all one more time, focusing on the last two lines:

Meet us in the east, bring 100 of your best men, and meet us by the end of the eleventh Moon. We'll be waiting in Deadtown, near the Dead Forest. Come by way of the Bloody Pass.

He put the letter in his pocket, got up from the bench and walked home. During the walk home, his mind became distracted by questions, many questions he had few answers for. As he approached his house, he pulled the letter out one more time, read it quickly, and placed it back into the pocket inside his coat. He entered his house and took off his coat and boots. He could smell the rabbit and vegetables his wife had been preparing.

"My dear," Tinkar said, "how was your walk? It looks like it's taken all the life from you. Your face is as white as the summer clouds. Get yourself near the fire and warm up. Ashron's got a nice blaze burning in the hearth."

"I will, my love." Ashran walked over to the hearth, rubbing his hands together. He stared into the flames, and as the roar of the fire warmed his body, he felt the warmth spread from his fingers and toes. He watched as the flames jumped and spat. Under his breath, he heard himself mutter, "The east? The eleventh Moon?" He shook his head and continued to stare into the hypnotising flames, questions running through his mind.

"My dear? Ashran? Supper's ready. Are you alright, my love?" He heard Tinkar's concerned voice coming from the table.

Ashran turned and walked towards Tinkar. "I'm fine, my love. And this smells lovely!"

JUK THRI

After five days, Juk and Rivan had reached the border of the Midnight Forest. The ground had been boggy and a little troublesome, but once they were out of the Wetlands, their steeds could travel at a good pace. The last time Juk was here was the night of the battle with Ashran's men. That felt like a lifetime ago; so much had happened since that Moonless night nearly seven Moons ago.

Juk knew little of the Midnight Forest, only what Rivan had volunteered over the last few days; it held sacred properties for the Wetlanders and the ancestors of Areekya going back hundreds of years. Beyond the forest, Juk could see the vast, vivid flatlands of the Greenscape. Rivan showed no desire to enter the forest and Juk surely didn't, so they rode around it. It held memories of a darker time for Juk, saturated with sadness, remorse and anger. The good times that he shared with his men had all but disappeared in his memory now; replaced by guilt and regret. By the end of the day, they had reached the Greenscape. They found a nice, flat sheltered area and Rivan had caught a small boar for their supper. The temperature had dropped, and the rain that had been following them for two days showed no sign of dissipating. They prepared a fire to dry themselves and keep warm. Rivan was busy preparing to roast the boar.

"In just over a week's ride, we'll reach Stoneguard," Rivan said as he turned the meat over the fire. "Are you confident of a positive reception from Lord Brok?"

Juk drew his eyes away from the fire and looked at the mage. "Positive reception? No. But Janson Brok is a good, principled man. He has a connection with Magdil and he is the man I trust the most for news out of the capital. If Janson has any word of my family's murder, he'll tell me. I'm confident of that." Juk looked away and stared at the fire once more, rubbing his hands together.

"Well, let's hope you're right," Rivan replied.

Juk kept his eyes fixed on the fire, trying to warm himself. "If I may ask, Rivan, what is all your interest in this? In me? You have relieved some of my burden. I cannot deny that, but why? This has me puzzled. And why you are riding with me to Stoneguard is also unknown to me." These questions had been on the fringes of Juk's mind for some time, but until now hadn't formed into words.

"Why?" replied Rivan. "Why indeed? Areekya existed as a peaceful land long before Runkarn brought his War to it. You, Juk Thri, from Chinsap, far from Magdil in the north east, did you see this War before the army came to recruit you into its arms? Was Chinsap not a peaceful place then, more so than after?"

"It's true, the War didn't come to Chinsap. We were far from the battles. The troubles were with the Hillmen and the Wetlanders, and the men in the south," replied Juk, who noticed that Rivan was staring at him.

"And what do you think would have happened to

Chinsap had its men not agreed to join these battles, these troubles, this *War*?" Rivan's eyes opened wide and it seemed to Juk that there was powerful emotion in his words; something Juk hadn't noticed before. The mage continued, "The same as the Wetlanders, the Hillmen and the fishermen who lived peacefully on the Endless Ocean, before the *War* came. Trouble would have come to Chinsap, battles would have come, and the *War* would have come! But who would have brought it?"

Juk studied the tall man now standing by the fire, his long grey tunic ever so slightly blowing with the breeze. The emotion seemed to disappear from his eyes, but his face revealed a crack, a conflict that Juk hadn't yet noticed. "These men you talk of. These men were the problem, we were told," Juk said.

Rivan walked towards Juk. "These men did not want trouble, did not want this War. They did not go looking for this War. Who does? They were given a story: trouble is coming, War is coming, join and fight it, before it comes to you."

Juk kept his eyes on Rivan, transfixed.

The mage walked back and started turning the meat over the fire again. "Why would they want to fight? Why would they want to leave their peaceful fishing villages, their friendly towns and farms? Why? When the best they could possibly hope for would be to come back to live the same lives they had lived for years? Leave their families behind to fight some unknown malice. Fight now or fight later, the army told them. Well, they decided not to fight, not until that same army came fighting its way back to them." The mage pulled the meat from the spit, ripped it in half, and handed Juk his share. Rivan then sat down and started eating.

Juk received the meat from Rivan; it was hot, but he took a small bite. As he chewed, he looked back up at the tall mage. Rivan was chewing as he stared into the fire.

"That is why, Juk Thri. I saw something in you. Or I should say, I *felt* something in you. Something that could make a difference. That is why, when I found you lost in the hills, I had to do something. That is why I'm riding with you to Stoneguard."

Juk carried on chewing his meat. He had more questions, but felt now was not the time to ask. He smiled at the mage, sat, and ate his meal in silence. Rivan did the same.

The next morning, they set off across the Greenscape. It had stopped raining, which Juk was thankful for, and this lifted his spirits. They mostly travelled the rest of the way in silence. Juk was deep in thought. He had many conflicting ideas and emotions running through his mind. Rivan's face had returned to its normal, emotionless state. In just under a week, the Green Mountain range came into view; they would reach Stoneguard by the end of the day's ride.

"Well Rivan. We are almost there."

"Almost. I think it is best if you take the rest of the journey alone, Juk. I'm not sure my presence would assist you with news regarding your family."

Juk stared at the mage for a moment, trying to gauge any emotion; there was none. "As you wish," Juk uttered. He was surprised by this, but he paid it no mind. His mind was full of questions about his family. Juk rode off alone, only turning back once to see the mage ride off to the north.

Juk reached the city walls in the late afternoon, the Sun's orange glow growing dim over his shoulder in the western sky. There was a large concentration of people at the main gates. The guards were keeping the entrance clear. As Juk rode closer at a slow pace, he reached the back of the line of people that had gathered there waiting to enter the city.

"Hail, friend," Juk said, greeting a man standing with his family at the back of the queue. "What's the hold-up?"

"Some big fancy lord's coming, I heard someone say. Too important to be let close to the likes of us." The man spat on the floor.

"Aye," replied Juk, as he quickly pulled the reins of his horse and moved to the side, away from the crowd, to get a better look at the main gates. Juk saw a stream of men, forty or fifty strong, coming down from the north. At its head he saw the banners of House Brok, and behind that, the personal guards of Janson Brok.

Juk sat atop his horse, paralysed by indecision. He had planned to get word to Janson somehow once he got into the city. Seeing him come down from the north had thrown him off. Seeing the company of men, he felt a wave of fear wash over him and he was frozen to the spot. He thought of his dead wife and family. The anguish that had subsided came rushing back from his head down to the depths of his stomach. Suddenly, from behind, he heard a voice, harsh, but barely above a whisper.

"Juk Thri, the Lord of the City wishes to see you."

Before Juk had a chance to turn, he felt a sharp dagger just below his ribcage, and the voice continued, "Best not to make a scene. Ride forward to the gate. The men will let you in."

Juk gently kicked his heels into his steed and trotted forward, slowly towards the main gate, guided by two men on horseback from the rear. Juk glanced behind him and was surprised by who he saw cloaked and smiling.

"Janson!" exclaimed Juk.

"Well, what sort of lord would I be if I didn't know who was coming and going in my own city, eh?" Janson Brok said as he winked directly at Juk.

CHIK SRIN

"Leave us. All of you. Leave us until I call you," Lord Janson Brok ordered his personal guards. He was standing in the courtyard within the city of Stoneguard. The courtyard was outside the main tower, but surrounded by the moat which separated the main city from the inner sanctum where the Lord of the City spent most of his time. Within the moat's border was the accommodation for Lord Brok's family and personal guards, as well as the main offices of power.

Chik looked at his oldest friend, Juk Thri. He looked tired and seemed different from the man he last saw over seven Moons ago. He watched him closely as Lord Brok now addressed him.

"I think we are safe from any of Magdil's birds, here outside in the courtyard. With Walnak Veerak not gone more than five days, I am sure he would have bought off some of my staff to chirp back to Magdil any juicy secrets. In fact, we should assume that the news of your arrival is already flying back to him as we speak."

"Juk, where have you been?" Chik asked.

"On a journey," Juk replied, looking into Chik's eyes. Chik saw a sadness there and immediately remembered Juk's loss.

"I'm so sorry to hear about your family. Maca was a good woman, a good friend to my own wife. Have you any ideas about who did this?"

Juk looked at both men before looking down at the ground. "Ideas, yes, some. I was hoping you and Janson had some news for me. Do you? Do you have any news from Magdil?"

"Well, yes. But you won't like it." Lord Brok looked to the floor as he spoke. "The news from Magdil is bad. They think you did it."

"What? Me? How could they? How could anyone think that?" exclaimed Juk. Chik observed his face recoiling in pain at such a suggestion.

"I know, I know," Lord Brok said. "It's crazy, and that's what we, what Chik and I said. What do you think happened, Juk?"

Juk looked down at the floor and remained silent for a few minutes. Chik could see the hurt he carried. His friend looked years older than the last time he'd seen him.

After a long silence, Juk spoke. "I can't say for sure. But whoever did that to Maca and my children had hate in their hearts. The image of my family lying motionless, pain forever etched on their faces. As I buried their broken bodies—" Juk stopped mid-sentence.

"Bastards!" spat Janson Brok. "May the Moon take their eyes."

Juk looked at both men, pain in his face. "My only guess is Magdil, but I can't conceive of any Chinsap man doing this thing. Have you heard anything of this?

Anything at all?"

Lord Brok looked at Chik briefly, and both men's eyes met for a moment.

"What is it?" Juk asked.

"We were there, Captain. The 1st were in Chinsap. We were sent by Runkarn. After the Wetlands, we rode back to Magdil, as slowly as I could and..."

"Slowly, why?" Juk interjected.

Chik smiled at his old friend. "I wanted to give you time. Time to reconsider, Cap... Juk. I thought you would change your mind and I would see you at Magdil, waiting for us with a smile on your face."

"So no Magdil men were in Chinsap before me? Is that what you're saying?" Juk's face became flushed.

"The 1st were not there before you," Chik responded. "We spent one night in Magdil and then sent to Chinsap. We first rode to Midscape to escort Lord Ruperk and the Veerak brothers there. After that, we rode on to Chinsap. We arrived a week or so after. After the murder."

"Runkarn also sent the 2nd Regiment," Lord Brok said. "To investigate your disappearance."

"Sun and Moon!" exclaimed Juk.

"They were seen days before we arrived, but still after this thing happened, Juk," Chik explained. He looked at his ex-Captain and saw the difference that had come over him: his eyes narrowed, as if his mind were racing away with this idea. His body seemed to shrink a couple of inches, his shoulders sagging, no longer pushed back.

"Chik's right, Juk," added Lord Brok. "I do not think this was done by Magdil. I don't think it *could* have been done by Magdil. Runkarn would not do this to you, to your family. I think he was, and even is, still hoping you will return."

Juk looked around and sat down on a wooden bench. He held his head in his hands and sat quietly for a long while. Chik looked at Lord Brok and left him there for a time. Left him in his grief, to allow him to absorb what he was told. There were many questions Chik wanted to ask his friend, but asking them now would be of no use; they would not be answered.

After some time had passed with all three men keeping their silence, Juk lifted his head, despair in his eyes and face. "I'm sorry, my friends. This talk has brought everything back to me. I let my desperation get the better of me. I'm sorry." Juk stood up again and walked towards Chik and Lord Brok.

Chik watched his friend as he approached him. "Juk, why did you leave? That day, why did you leave us?"

Juk looked up and into Chik's eyes. "There had been something growing in my mind for some time. That day with Ashran, the Wetlanders. I decided I didn't want to fight anymore."

"After all that we had done together? You are the best fighting man the 1st had. Any regiment had. How can a fighting man like you want to stop? How can men like us change?" Chik asked, feeling the same disappointment he felt that day seven Moons ago.

"Chik, I'm sorry. I know I let you down. I'd had enough of the killing. It made little sense to me anymore. I missed my family. I missed my home. I couldn't see the sense in this War. Has their not been enough killing?"

"Enough killing?" Chik replied. "We're protecting our homes, Juk. We are fighting, so our families and homes can remain safe."

"Safe? Where was this protection for my family?" Chik detected the same anger in Juk's voice that he felt himself.

"Chik, Juk, let's take some time to think about this, eh?" Lord Brok interjected. "Juk came to me after the Wetlands and he told me just as he is telling you now, Chik. Men can change, men do change. I'm not sure I understand it any better than you do, why this man, our friend, changed? But what's done is done." Chik felt Lord Brok's gaze fall on him and deferred to the senior man. It didn't change the way he felt, though.

"But Juk, I have to ask one question," continued Lord Brok. "Is there a way back for you? Go to Magdil, speak to Runkarn. He will understand, of this I am sure."

Chik looked at Juk Thri as Lord Brok spoke. He saw Juk remained passive. No emotion, not a flicker of any reaction.

"A way back to fighting? Yes, I think it is time for me to get back to fighting." Juk's face remained emotionless as he spoke.

Lord Brok half-smiled. "Ah, that's good. So together we'll ride to Magdil. We'll talk to Runkarn and then we'll find who did this to your family."

"I will find out who did this to my family," Juk said, "but we'll not go to Magdil, not yet."

Chik continued to stare at Juk. He had heard this voice before, had seen this look in his eyes a long time ago, but he remembered it.

"I'll not go to Magdil until I have the backing of five thousand men behind me. The truth is that I've been fighting for the wrong side all these years. We have all been fighting for the wrong side." Juk's eyes flared with anger. The anger that Chik had seen many times, in many places. But this time the anger was directed not against their enemies, but Juk's enemies alone; Magdil, Runkarn, him.

"Juk! What's this madness?" Lord Brok said, raising his voice. "What nonsense is this? You are not yourself. Has the Moon madness taken you? What are you saying? Do you even know what you're saying?"

"All too clearly," replied Juk. "But I am tired. I have travelled far and with little rest."

"Guards!" shouted Lord Brok.

Two uniformed men hurriedly entered the courtyard. "Take Juk to the guest's quarters. See that he gets food, drink and rest. And make sure he is not disturbed until morning."

"Thank you, old friend," said Juk.

Lord Brok and Chik watched as the guards led Juk out of the courtyard. The two men looked at each other in silence until Chik broke it.

"Sun and Moon. What do you make of that, Lord Brok?"

Lord Brok looked down at the ground and shook his head. "I don't know what I think, Chik. But it cannot be good, can it?"

Chik looked at the older man. "I've had a thought trying to assault my mind, which I have tried to push back for days now, Lord Brok. It's a thought I was ashamed to admit to, but I can now hear it battering down the doors."

"A thought, Chik? What thought?"

"Could Juk have done it? Could he have murdered his family?" Chik looked down as he spoke these words. "A thought that while I am still ashamed to utter it out loud, feels less crazy than it did yesterday, my lord."

Lord Brok did not answer. The two men remained in the courtyard, staring at the ground, silently. Not a word was spoken between them for a long while, until Lord Brok said, "You'd best post two men outside Juk's room tonight, Chik. Moon and Stars!"

JUK THRI

The wind was blowing hard; the trees were swaying back and forth, some almost bending in two. Juk found himself in a dark forest. He caught the fragrant scent of pine trees; it scared him. How he got here, he didn't know. There was only the faintest of light coming from above. He looked up and saw the pale, gibbous Moon, partly obscured by clouds. Opaque, its luminosity was deadened by the surroundings. He felt utterly despondent. The darkness, feeding off the dark, desolate forest, was somehow controlling his mind, his body, his emotions. Then the Moon shone brighter, the clouds cleared, and the Moon glistened, and the dark, desolate trees found themselves covered in light, the leaves sparkling in the newly discovered illumination. Each single branch stretched, reaching out to the light as the Moon grew in size, and with it the beaming rays increased in intensity; pouring down into the forest. The Moon now covered the whole of the night sky. Nothing else could be seen, and it kept increasing in size and brightness. Juk stretched his arms out to the Moon, reaching out, trying to catch the light in his hands; trying to grab the Moon.

Juk woke early with a start. He sat up in his soft, warm and comfortable bed to survey his surroundings. The spacious room he was in had thick rugs covering the wooden floor. At one side of the room were dark curtains, drawn, with the faintest glimpse of the early morning Sun visible through the gap where they didn't quite meet in the middle. To the other side of him was a thick-looking wooden door, bolted shut. Juk got out of the bed and pulled the curtains open to allow the post-dawn light to the room. He stared out of the window for a few moments, taking in the majesty of the view. Seeing the orange Sun, knowing it had risen above the Red and Yellow mountains far in the east, brought him back to the present and then, to the past.

He remembered yesterday's discussions with Janson and Chik, and he remembered his dead family. A wash of despair rushed over him once more. He felt helpless, paralysed; he knew what he had to do, but his body was making it almost impossible. All he wanted to do was to get back into the bed, curl up, and forget his troubles. Juk looked around at the guest bedroom Janson had offered him last night, and he thought about his day ahead. He felt cold, the northern winter seeping into his bones. He urged his body forward, first one leg and then the other. He made it to the washbasin and, fighting his mind's resistance, splashed the ice cold water onto his face. It gave him an upsurge in spirit. He resolved to override his fear and push it down, keep it hidden, and he thought about what he must accomplish today, and how he would do so.

He got dressed and made his way towards the solid wooden door, unbolted it, and made his way out. Immediately to his left and right, he saw two guards from the 1st Regiment, men he knew and who knew him.

"Sir!" They both saluted as he passed. Juk nodded and smiled back. Juk continued down the hall, finally making his way to the main hall for breakfast. As he sat down at the long table in the middle of the room, a serving girl appeared with bread, meat and a goblet of wine.

"No wine for me. Water will be fine," Juk said, and smiled at the young girl.

Juk sat quietly as he ate the food before him, planning the morning ahead, thinking of what and how to say what he felt in his heart. He thought back to the previous evening with Janson and Chik, and was predicting a tough day ahead. After some time, the door creaked open and Janson Brok appeared. The large man smiled as he entered the hall.

"Good morning Juk. Sleep well?"

"I slept well, Janson," Juk lied. "I could always find peace in this city. Many good memories are held here for me, friends made and, well, good times." Juk managed a smile back at his friend as Janson pulled up a chair to sit beside him. The serving girl reappeared with a plate of food and a goblet of wine. Juk noticed Janson look at his water and gestured to the girl to bring him the same.

"How are you feeling today, Juk? Rested? Better?"

"Yes, rested. It has been a long time since I slept in such surroundings. Thank you again for your hospitality, Janson."

"Speak nothing of it. You're one of my oldest friends. No need for thanks," Janson replied as he tucked into his breakfast.

The two men sat in silence, eating their food. Juk could sense the tension in the air, and asked his friend,

"Janson, tell me truthfully, what did you make of what I said last night?"

"Last night? Hmm. Juk, is that what you really want? What you said last night? Against Magdil? Runkarn?"

"It is." Juk stopped eating and pushed his plate to one side, and looked at Janson as he continued, "Can you remember when Runkarn's War started? Do you remember how, or why?"

"Look, Juk, that was a long time ago. You can't be talking like this. How about the peace we have now? Doesn't that count for something?" Janson pushed his own plate aside.

"Peace for who? For the Wetlanders? For the Hillmen? How about for those who haven't this peace you speak of?" Juk kept his eyes fixed on his friend, feeling the tension still circling the room and the conversation.

"Peace for those who want it, Juk. If they choose not to, well, then let the Moon take their eyes."

"Peace for those who want it. They already had it. Before Runkarn came. It was disturbed by him, by his War. Those that yielded got to keep it, keep their peace. But it was on his terms. No longer their own." Juk turned away from his friend as he stood up and walked towards the long bay windows on the other side of the hall.

"Well, I remember the years before Runkarn," Janson replied. "The Mastertons ruled in Midscape. In fact, Runkarn was advisor to Lord Sydric before the

War."

"And what started this War?" Juk asked, looking out of the windows.

"What started it? Well, I know Runkarn took over to bring peace to Areekya. Don't we have peace now, Juk?"

"Well, you have peace, Janson. There seem to be those that have it also, at a price. A price that we have extracted from all over the land, north, south, east and west. And there are those that do not have it. They will not have it; not until they bow down to Magdil, to Runkarn's demands."

"Well, what I know is that now there is peace. This came from Runkarn. This peace is good for Areekya. What about the past? Who cares how it came about, or when, or why? Can we not have our peace? Enjoy it?" Juk sensed Janson was getting irritated. He heard it in his voice.

Juk turned to look at his friend Janson, still sitting down. "What if we've been on the wrong side all these years? What if we've been fighting to disturb this peace you treasure so much? When did you first get trouble from the Hillmen? Was it before or after Runkarn took power? Was it before Magdil became the capital, or after?"

"Juk, this must stop. Do you really think you could fight against Magdil? Against Runkarn? Where are these five thousand men you talked of last night? "

"We could get them together, Janson, from the north, the west, even in the east. I'm sure we could recruit to stop this War. Stop the fighting, bring harmony and real peace to Areekya."

"Stop the fighting, by more fighting? What madness is this? If you continue, it will be your end. It will lead to the ruin of all that go with you, Juk. Please, you are not yourself. You have suffered a great loss. My heart, our hearts, go out to you, but please, I ask you as a friend, let's stop this talk. You are grief-stricken, but this is foolishness." Janson stood up and walked towards Juk by the windows.

"I see then that you will not be with me in this."

"In this what? What is this, Juk? This madness against Magdil? No, I'm not with you."

"And Chik? How does he feel?"

"Chik thinks you should rest. As do I. Rest until you feel better. We're concerned, Juk. Do not do this. Magdil will crush you, and all that go with you, into dust before you even start." Juk could hear the concern in his friend's voice.

"And are you sure Runkarn had nothing to do with my family?" Juk's eyes were focused on Janson's as he stood next to him.

"I cannot be sure what another man does or did, Juk, unless I see it with my own eyes, and then only maybe. But do I think he did this? No. Why would he? I'm sure he would take you back today if you forget this madness."

Juk placed his arm on his friend's shoulder. "Janson, you are a good friend. I'm still tired. I think I'll go back to lie down and perhaps take a walk later to think."

"Juk, the city is yours. Anything you need, just ask, please know that. But rest is good. Take the weight from your shoulders. Your friends are here to help. Take a walk, clear your head."

With that, Juk smiled and made for the door. He proceeded down the hall back to the guest bedroom. He smiled at the two guards who remained outside the door, and they saluted in unison. Once inside, Juk stood and looked out of the window facing east, towards the Red and Yellow Mountains, towards Chinsap, and he felt the Sun's soft winter rays through the window. He turned and lay down on the bed, and sleep took him.

Juk woke up with the late-afternoon gloom visible through his window. He got out of bed and washed his face. Then, he made his way out of the room, the guards saluting as he passed them once more. He continued to walk and made his way out of the tower to the stables. He grabbed his proud, tall grey horse from the stable boy and rode out of the city gates.

CHIK SRIN

"What do you mean, he didn't come back?" Chik barked at the two men standing in front of him.

"He left the room, and he didn't come back," one man repeated.

"You let him leave?" Chik raised his voice.

"Lord Brok said the city was his. What could we do? It's Cap... It's Juk Thri. We were not his jailers, Captain. To be honest, I don't know why we were there."

Chik dismissed the two 1st Regiment men who were tasked with guarding Juk's room and made his way out of the barracks to the main tower. He was shown into Janson Brok's personal office. It was late at night and Lord Brok was sitting at his desk in his nightdress underneath a long woollen gown.

"Chik, it's late. What is it? What can't wait until morning?"

"It's Juk. He's gone," replied Chik.

"What do you mean, gone? Is he not in his room?"

"He's not in his room. He went for a walk late afternoon, and he didn't come back. I've just been told this from the guards."

"Have you checked the stable? Is his horse still there?" Lord Brok stood up and paced the room.

"My men are looking now, Sir," Chik replied.

"Well, it's too late to search if he's left the city. Let's hope he turns up in the morning. For his own sake, Sun and Moon," Lord Brok said, the concern clearly audible in his voice.

"If he's left? What then?" Chik asked.

"Let's climb that hill when we get to it, Chik. Let's hope for the best, eh? Make your way back to the barracks. If your men report his horse gone, then prepare to leave at dawn. Send word here and I'll meet you at the gate."

"My lord." With that, Chik turned and left. When Chik arrived back at the barracks, he was met by three of his men.

"Horse is gone, Captain. Stable boy said some time in the afternoon."

"The Moon has taken him," Chik muttered to himself.

"All men are to be ready to leave before dawn. I want every single man prepared to ride an hour before Sun up," Chik ordered his men and made his way to his bunk. As he lay on his bed, Chik continued to mutter to himself. "What have you done, Juk? What have you done?"

At dawn, Chik and thirty of the 1st regiment were waiting at the main gate when Lord Brok arrived with six of his own men.

"We'll search the surrounding villages and

woodlands," Lord Brok barked. Chik could tell he didn't appreciate being up this early. "Don't go too far. Keep within a five-mile radius. If we find no news, return here at Mid Sun. If you do find out anything, send word as soon as you can."

Chik nodded and said nothing. He took six of his men and rode off to the south. The rest of his men, in groups, dispersed in various directions. Lord Brok rode off to the east with his men, shouting back, "Meet here at midday."

All morning, Chik searched for news or signs of Juk. Chik and his men searched the local villages just to the south of the city, the small farmsteads in the surrounding area; they found no news, not any hint of Juk Thri. On their way back to the city, they came across a tavern. There were a few horses and a couple of horse-drawn carts outside. Chik decided to take a look inside.

"Good day, barman," Chik said as he walked in past the tables where a few patrons were seated. The smell of stale beer was in the air. "Seven ales, if you would be so kind." Chik looked around while the barman poured the drinks.

Chik's men sat down at one of the tables as their ale was brought over by an elderly grey-haired woman, limping as she carried the tray of jugs. Chik stayed at the bar and took a gulp from his jug and placed it back down on the wooden bar. "How's business, friend?" Chik asked the barman.

"Aye, can't complain. People coming and going. Can't complain at all. And what're army men doing in these here parts? Not seen your like for some time."

"On Lord Brok's business." Chik studied the bald, red-faced portly man washing the dirty jugs closely. "We're looking for a friend, in fact. A friend of Lord Janson Brok, a friend of mine."

"Oh aye?" the barman said, rinsing his jugs and placing them under the bar.

"Tall man, thin, with blue eyes and dark hair," Chik continued. "He would've had a big, strong grey horse outside if that helps. Probably wearing a cloak. Have you seen anyone like that today? Or last night?"

"Can't say I have. Then, I don't take much notice anymore. People come, people go, all the same to me."

"Maybe your serving lady, then. Maybe she remembers better than you."

"Wilka? Come here a mo," the barman called out.

"What do you want?" the elderly serving woman shouted from across the tavern. "Busy here, and I've only one pair of hands. Can't you see we've a rush on?"

Chik watched her limp over to the bar, her face grimacing as she did so.

"This man here says he's looking for someone," the barman explained.

"Is he?"

"A tall man with blue eyes and dark hair. Would've been last night or this morning. Do you remember such a man?" Chik asked in as friendly a way as he could.

"Tall man, you say? Blue eyes? I don't know about the eyes, but we've a tall man with dark hair here now, over there." The elderly woman pointed over Chik's shoulder to a corner of the room.

Chik nodded and signalled to his men to join him as he walked to the back of the dimly lit tavern. As they approached, they could see the back of a dark-haired man sitting alone. He looked thin, but it was difficult to guess his height.

"Hail, friend," Chik greeted the man from behind and continued to walk towards the table he was sitting at. He motioned his men to ready themselves for trouble, if it came to it.

"Well met, friend," came the reply in a rich, melodic voice.

In an instance Chik realised it wasn't Juk. And as he reached the table, he could see the dark-haired man drinking from his jug was definitely not Juk Thri. "Well met," Chik responded. "Enjoying your ale?"

"Very much so indeed. It's good ale the landlord serves here. I don't get to sup often enough," the dark-haired man answered with his smooth, deep voice.

"And what business brings you here, if I may ask?" Chik continued.

"Indeed, you may, friend. I am a wanderer, wandering. I come to the north from time to time, wandering."

"Well then, maybe you have seen my friend on your wanderings. Tall, thin, blue eyes, striking appearance. Today or maybe yesterday."

"I have seen no one today except those in this

tavern. Yesterday, I cannot say that I saw such a man. I am sorry."

Chik watched and listened to the man closely. He was accustomed to asking questions of people who didn't want to give answers. Something he thought he had become very skilled at. He saw no lies in the dark-haired man's face or heard any falsehood in his smooth voice. He was smiling as he spoke and his hair was kept in place by a strange-looking silver headband.

"I thank you and please, get back to your drinking. Enjoy your ale." With that, Chik turned and signalled for his men to follow. He scanned the tavern on their way back to the table the men had been sitting at. Quickly, they all finished their drinks. They said their goodbyes to the barman and serving woman, then left.

As they mounted their horses, Chik said, "Let's head back. It's nearly Mid Sun. Hopefully, the others will have better news."

Upon returning, it became clear that none of the men had seen or heard of Juk during their search.

Lord Brok came riding back. "Well? Any news?"

"None. None at all," Chik replied. "And you my lord?"

"Nothing. No sign at all. This area is so busy that tracks are everywhere. There's no knowing where he went."

"He's made his choice then, Lord Brok."

"His choice? What choice has he made?" Lord Brok had a puzzled look.

"I fear he's chosen madness," Chik replied, looking around at his men and then fixing his eyes on Lord Brok.

"Sun and Moon! Meet me in my chambers in one hour, Chik, and come alone." With that, Lord Brok galloped off. Chik sat atop his horse, thoughts running through his mind, thoughts he didn't like.

"Okay men, back to barracks. All men confined there for today," Chik shouted at his men. And with that, they all trotted back through the gates. Chik could hear the men whispering to each other. It wasn't clear what was being said, but he was sure it wasn't good.

Just before the hour, Chik made his way from the barracks to Lord Brok's chambers. He was let in by the guards, and he saw Janson Brok sitting behind his desk.

Looking up, Lord Brok asked, "Well, Chik. What now? What has Juk done? And what can we do?"

"I think he has chosen, my lord. I don't think there is much that can be done now."

"Where do you suppose he has gone?" Lord Brok asked.

"I hope he has gone back to Chinsap. Gone home to grieve for his family. But my hope is not my belief. I fear he has gone looking for allies. To continue this madness," Chik replied, his voice flat and sombre.

"What do we do, Chik?"

"I will send men to Chinsap to check there, if it pleases, my lord."

"Yes, of course. My concern is Magdil, Lord

Runkarn and Ruperk. What will we tell them? It won't be long before they hear. It is better they hear it from me. I'll send word today. And prepare to ride out tomorrow." Lord Brok got up from behind his desk and paced the room.

"Shall I come with you, my lord?" Chik asked as he saw the concern on Lord Brok's face.

"No, you wait here for the return of your men from Chinsap. And in case Juk shows up. You can continue to search the surrounding area and let's hope for the best."

"And if not? What if it's the worst that we're faced with? What then?" Chik's eyes followed Lord Brok as he continued to pace up and down the room.

"Let's hope it doesn't come to the worst," Lord Brok answered as he strode back and forth. "Let's hope that Juk is now riding back to Chinsap to grieve and to reflect. Let's hope that. But if it comes to the worst, then you'll do your soldier's duty, I'm sure."

"And you, my lord? What'll you do?" Chik looked at Lord Brok as he sat back behind his desk, his face ashen and wrinkled, black shadows under his eyes and lines on his forehead. He looked years older than yesterday, as if the Sun and Moon had paid a visit in the night and laid the troubles of the world on him.

"I'll ride to Magdil tomorrow, Chik. And I'll do my soldier's duty."

LORD DENNIS GREENAWAY

Dennis Greenaway was sitting on his favourite bench, staring off to the east. From the gardens inside the city of Midscape, he could see the far-off Mountain of Serenity. This time of the year, in the late afternoon, the sky turned orange and pink. It was a beautiful sight, and normally it brought him some comfort. Not today. Dennis sat there, lost in his own thoughts, thinking of the night before. He had spent it deep in his cups again. His life had become a blur; his days and nights spent drinking. Sharing his bed with various women; some he knew, many he didn't.

Dennis was drinking to forget. He had been drinking a great deal for years, but he never really saw it as a problem before. He liked to drink; he liked how it made him feel. It elevated him from the everyday monotony of his life; it was a mood changer, a mood enhancer. He liked the way he felt when he was drinking; until he didn't. Until he drank too much, until he went too far, and he would wake up in the morning full of regret, shame, and, on too often an occasion, despair. Today was one of those occasions. He felt regret for last night's drinking and his behaviour; it came back to him in dark, anxious, embarrassing bursts. He was not proud of last night, not proud of many nights. In his despondent, anxious state, he thought back to one such night three Moons ago.

That night, he had gone too far and said too much. He had let his emotions and the drink get to him; the drink worst of all. Ruperk and Madnan had ridden off early the next morning without a word. He had spent the time since drinking to forget. He had heard no news since then. Dennis knew this meant trouble. Trouble for him and trouble for Midscape. He had contemplated sending a message, or even travelling to Magdil himself. His drinking told him not to, and it gave him the courage to resist. His drinking controlled him completely. He continued to look to the east. His wife had hardly spoken to him since that night, too. Normally, this wouldn't be such a concern, but he felt alone. Not that their relationship had ever brought any real comfort to him, but it gave him some security. He had always felt like some kind of imposter; a pretender to the Lordship here in Stoneguard. At least she provided him with a certain amount of cover; he was always able to hide the lack of confidence he felt. Now he felt exposed. Dennis liked sitting in his gardens. He usually enjoyed the contemplation it allowed him, but not today. Today, he was not enjoying any of the thoughts that rose up from his churning stomach. He tried to keep the anguish and gloom down, but they kept rising to torment his mind.

"Lord Greenaway. Lord Greenaway?" The guard's voice penetrated Lord Dennis's thoughts and shook him from his contemplation. "There's a visitor arrived this afternoon. He says he is a friend. He said to tell you the Fighting Bear is here."

Dennis looked up at the guard. His thoughts were just a little slow, a little behind the movement of his head. He stared at the guard a few moments too long, as the guard broke his gaze and looked down at the ground.

"Shall I allow him entry, my lord?" the guard asked, still looking down.

"What?" Lord Greenaway asked, his thoughts still trying to catch up. "What does this man look like?"

"A tall man, my lord. Thin with black hair, blue eyes."

"The Fighting Bear! Well, bless the Sun thrice. Yes, yes, bring him in, quickly now." Dennis's mind and mood suddenly switched to a more positive one. He stood up in anticipation. He felt the dark clouds circling his mind break up and disperse.

In a few minutes, the guard reappeared with a tall man wearing a dark cloak. Dennis instantly recognised him. "Juk Thri! Where in the fucking Moon have you been? And what have you been doing? Leading Runkarn and his Magdil cronies a merry dance!" He walked towards his old friend, arms outstretched.

"Lord Dennis. I wasn't sure you would be happy to see me."

"Happy? Happy? It is beyond my thoughts that you come here today. It is possible this is the only thing that could shake me from my mood this afternoon," Dennis replied.

Juk and Dennis embraced. It was a happy embrace, and Dennis held on as long as he could. Finally, they broke, and both men smiled at each other. "The Fighting

Bear! How long has it been since I called you that? Three years? Four? Sun and Stars, Juk. The whole of Magdil is out for your blood, it seems. What did you do?"

"I've had some trouble. My family, well they..."

"Of course. I'm sorry. I'm sorry for your loss, old friend. Do you know who did this? Who *could* do this?"

"Know? Not for sure. I suspect it came from Magdil, from Runkarn, that's what I suspect." Dennis saw tears forming in Juk's eyes.

"Runkarn, damn his blood. You really think he would do this?"

"I do," Juk replied, not able to make eye contact.

"Why? For what purpose? Forgive me, Juk. You look tired. You've had a long ride, no doubt. Allow me to take you to the guests' quarters. You can wash up, rest if you need, and I'll have some food sent to you." With that, Dennis took Juk by the arm and led him out of the gardens towards the main building.

"Yes, it's been quite a journey. I think a rest is needed. But I also need to talk to you, talk about something very important. And it must remain a secret I'm here," Juk said as they walked.

"Of course."

"And I fear it may put you in some danger, too," Juk said, and half-smiled at his old friend.

"Ha! Me? In trouble with Magdil? No need to worry about that, Juk. I can make enough trouble myself. A tale for later, I think. Let's get you some rest, and we'll talk later."

Two hours after Sundown, Dennis made his way to the guests' quarters. He tapped on the door three times. The door creaked open.

"Lord Dennis," Juk said, holding the door open as Dennis walked in.

"You can cut out that nonsense. How do you feel? Rested? Do you need any more food? Wine?"

"I am rested. And full. And now we need to speak."

"Let's sit over there, on the table by the wall. Away from prying eyes and ears in here. I think we will not want others to hear of what we speak tonight, old friend." Dennis gestured towards the far side of the room as Juk closed the door behind him.

"So, Juk. Tell me, what has happened in this last year? Why is half of Magdil chasing you from west to east and back again, or so it seems?"

Dennis listened as Juk gave his account; from the Midnight Forest over seven Moons past, until he left Stoneguard less than a week ago. He listened and told of his own dealings with Ruperk and Madnan Veerak.

"Well, Dennis. What do you say?" Juk asked.

"They said you were crazy, Juk, but I didn't know how crazy, until now. Sun and Moon. You really think you can take on Magdil? Five thousand men? You'll need to double that, and I can't believe I'm even thinking of it! Sun and Moon."

Juk's eyes were focused on Dennis's. "I know you did well from the War, but what was it like before? In the Greenscape, before Runkarn usurped the Mastertons here in Midscape. Do you remember any trouble?"

"You seem to have it aright. I saw an opportunity back then. We all did. I never had any love for Runkarn or his Magdil cronies, fat Ruperk least of all. Even less so now, I should say. But look what he has given me; Midscape. There is no greater prize outside of Magdil itself."

"And how long until he takes this from you?" Juk asked.

"I used to think that what I did for him in the War would see me through most troubles. Now, I'm not so sure," Dennis replied.

"Be careful, Dennis. Look what he did to my family when I stepped away. When he hears of your words and actions, he could do the same to you." Dennis could hear the pain in Juk's words.

Dennis looked at Juk carefully. He saw the sincerity in his blue eyes. "Your family? The 2nd Regiment, you say."

"That's what I believe. They were there, in Chinsap before me, I think. And they'd do it, you know they would. It shames me to say, we did as much, worse some would say, before that is, before and under Magdil orders." Juk stood up and walked away from the table they were sitting at, keeping his eyes on the floor.

Dennis remained sitting down, thinking, turning

over the possibilities in his mind. After a while, he spoke. "That snake Ruperk has long-coveted this place. That is true. His cronies, the Veerak brothers, are cut from the same oily skin as that snake. That is also true. But where would these men come from? Ten thousand men? Even five, from where would they come? Bloody hell, I can't believe I'm even thinking of this thing."

"The west has no love for Magdil, the Wetlands and the men down on the coast. Even in the east, Dawngate holds no love for Runkarn either." Juk turned to face his friend as he answered.

"Even so, Juk. Against Magdil? Runkarn? Nowhere near enough. It's suicide. Once word got out, he'd crush any uprising. You've seen it done, Moon and Stars, we bloody did it ourselves!"

"Then we'll find more. What do you say? I think we were on the wrong side, Dennis. I think we can change that. I think I *must* change that. For my family, and for me. We can rid Areekya of Runkarn. We can bring true peace."

"Juk, maybe your reasons are true and noble, but I cannot do this thing. What we are speaking about tonight must not leave this room. It would spell the end for us if it does, even talking about such things, well..." Dennis stopped halfway through his sentence and started another. "Give me some time, some time to think and..." Dennis stopped again.

"Yes?" Juk said, trying to encourage his friend.

Lord Dennis continued. "I will travel to Dawngate. I know Lord Wilton. He is good friends with my wife.

He was a close ally of her father. He has no great love for me, but even less for Magdil and Runkarn. But ten thousand men? I'm not sure this can be done."

"We have another ally, Dennis. One who knows of what we speak."

"One more? Who?"

"His name is Rivan; a mage from the west. He pulled me out of my despair in the Northern Hills. He has power in healing, this I can say, and he is close with the Wetlanders. Rivan accompanied me to Stoneguard."

"A mage? I thought they had long gone. In the Greenscape, we say it is all horse shit and hogwash." Dennis's face creased up. "Sun Magick, Moon Magick, you don't believe in all that, do you? Superstition and ceremony, nothing more."

"Maybe so. He has some power, though from where it comes, I don't know. He can be trusted and he can bring the west, I believe. He counselled me to come to Midscape. You can meet him if you wish."

"No, if you say he can be trusted, then mage or not, that'll do for me. Take him to the west and find who you can, but Juk, for Sun's sake, be careful. Remember, we cannot let any word of this out. And I have not yet agreed to anything."

"Magdil has been chasing me for many Moons. They haven't caught me yet, and nor do I intend to let them."

Dennis Greenaway looked at his old friend, smiled, and looked away. "I'd love to get old Veerak on the end of my sword, and that snake Ruperk, let me tell you." As these words came from his lips he allowed a laugh to escape. He wasn't sure if it was genuine, but it felt good to laugh.

"I'll leave in the morning. Before First Sun, unnoticed. Rivan is waiting in the hills, south from here. We'll head west from there."

"Yes, and I'll get a few men together and head east tomorrow. I'll sound Lord William Wilton out, see which way the wind blows, as it were; pretentious prick that he is. I'll have to tell Livian something, off on tax and administrative business, or some such thing. That should do it. But this is not set until we know we have support and I have given it some more thought. I must ask you to agree to that." Dennis stared at Juk.

"We'll get the support, Dennis. But, you have my word, we'll do nothing until we meet next, in three Moons."

The two men smiled at each other once more. Juk walked over to the window and stared out into the night. Dennis got up from the table and made his way towards the door.

"Good luck, Juk. Send word when you can. And try to return by the full Moon, three Moons from now or at least a message. Then we'll see what we can see and see what we have."

"Good luck, Dennis."

Dennis left the room and made his way back to his chambers. "Sun and Moon, what have we started?" he said to himself. "What have we started?"

MADNAN VEERAK

Madnan Veerak rushed across the courtyard. He had been summoned to an early morning meeting in Lord Runkarn's dining hall. He was not late, but he always liked to get to his appointments early. The guards waved him through, and he entered the dining hall to find Lord Runkarn already seated, talking to Lord Ruperk Stonefish.

The dining room was large and rectangular, decorated in purple with hanging banners from the ceiling to the floor on one side and full-length windows on the other. It was now the tenth Moon, so the windows were closed, and the chill of the air was taken away by a roaring fire burning away in the hearth at one end of the room.

"Good morning, my lords," Madnan greeted the two men as he walked towards the long dining table.

"Ah, Madnan, my good man. Please sit here, next to Lord Ruperk. We have much to discuss this morning."

"My lord." Madnan sat as he was bid.

"And where is your brother? Is he not with you?" Lord Runkarn asked.

"No. Not with me, my lord. Coming soon, I'm sure, my lord."

"He had an interesting visit to Stoneguard to

see Lord Brok, I hear?" Lord Runkarn continued his questions.

"Yes, my lord. Yes, he did," Madnan answered. Just as he did so, the doors opened behind him and in walked his brother, Walnak.

"Well, there he is now. Walnak, please come and join us." Lord Runkarn gestured for Walnak to sit next to him.

"My lords," said Walnak. "Brother." Walnak smiled at Madnan as he walked past him and sat next to Lord Runkarn. Madnan observed his brother as he walked around him to the other side of the long oak table.

"So, here we are," Lord Runkarn said. "I assume you are all well rested after your journeys?"

All three men smiled and nodded.

"It is always invigorating to be back in the capital, my lord," Lord Ruperk replied, as Madnan and Walnak continued to nod.

"Yes, my lord. My brother and I totally concur with the good Lord Ruperk. Even though I have not been back for long, it is indeed as Lord Ruperk says, totally invigorating to be back in your presence," Madnan said, as Walnak continued to nod energetically.

"Good, good." Lord Runkarn smiled as he spoke. "Now, all this business with our good ex-Captain. Lord Ruperk has been enlightening me over the last few days with all the details. It seems we have a problem."

"One we can deal with, my lord." Madnan looked at Lord Ruperk as he spoke. "It seems Lord Greenaway will have to be dealt with. I don't believe he knows more than he said, but the man is a drunken oaf."

"A drunkard he may be, but a tough fighting man. Be careful with Lord Dennis. His bite might be even worse than his bark, so to speak." Lord Runkarn locked eyes with Lord Ruperk as he spoke.

"His wife will be of some use to us," Lord Ruperk said. "She despises him as much as we do, more even."

"Ah, Lady Livian," Lord Runkarn added. "She is a feisty one, as I remember. So, what is to be done, then?"

"Well, Madnan has a good relationship with Lady Livian. I suggest we use this to our advantage," Lord Ruperk answered.

Madnan nodded in agreement. "Her father offered me her hand before the end of the War, you know, desperate man. And I spent some time with her after we left Midscape. She will easily be swayed."

"Indeed," Lord Runkarn said.

"And Juk Thri? I received word from Lord Janson Brok last week," continued Lord Runkarn. "It seems that Lord Brok had him captured, but he escaped,"

"Allowed to escape more like," Lord Ruperk interjected.

"Well, Lord Brok is on his way here, so you can ask him for yourself. He'll be here by the end of the week."

"He was awfully defensive when I spoke to him about Juk Thri," Walnak added. "Wouldn't surprise me if he were aided by Lord Brok."

"It seems my closest advisors are a cynical and suspicious bunch. It appears I chose well," Lord Runkarn said, looking at the three men sitting at his table.

"We'll send the 2nd Regiment to Midscape, with Madnan here. He can bring Lord Greenaway under control," Lord Ruperk announced. "We'll talk to Lord Brok when he arrives and devise a plan to get this Juk Thri captured and back under control. We can't have him wandering the land, causing any trouble now."

"My new Captain of the 1st is still stationed at Stoneguard," Lord Runkarn stated. "We'll send an extra hundred from the 2nd up to him, and this shall be his test. Will he bring in his ex-Captain and friend? Is he trustworthy to Magdil? To me?"

"I have my doubts," Walnak said, looking at his brother.

"He is a good man, a good Captain, I think," Lord Ruperk said. "It will indeed be his test, and we shall send some senior men from the 2nd, just in case," he continued, looking at Lord Runkarn.

"So, there it is. That's done," Lord Runkarn announced. "Lord Ruperk, you and Walnak can deal with Juk Thri. Leave us now. Please, Madnan, remain and eat with me."

Lord Ruperk and Walnak stood up and said their goodbyes, and left the dining hall.

"Guards!" shouted Lord Runkarn. "Get the serving boy to bring in breakfast."

"My dear Madnan, come closer. Please sit here," Lord Runkarn said and gestured to his left.

Madnan moved and sat next to Lord Runkarn. He had no idea why he had been asked to wait behind; he had never dined alone with Lord Runkarn before, and he felt uncomfortable. Madnan could feel the sweat build up on the back of his neck and his palms felt damp to the touch as he rubbed them on his trousers.

The serving boy brought the food out and placed it in front of the two men: dark bread and fried fresh fish, with a jug of water and two silver goblets.

"Please, let's eat," Lord Runkarn said.

"My lord."

As Madnan grabbed a small loaf and one whole fish and placed them onto his plate, Lord Runkarn spoke. "So, you are close with the Lady Livian?"

"Yes, my lord. She seemed very accommodating at Midscape. And after. She holds no great affection for Lord Dennis anymore, if indeed she did at all."

Madnan felt the weight of Lord Runkarn's stare. "She holds great ambition still. You should be wary. The Mastertons have great pride; the family goes back generations. They ruled this land for a very long time. The demise of her family will not easily be emptied from her thoughts."

"What can she do? That was in the past. Her family is dead. My Lord Runkarn rules the land now. She'll be no match for me, my lord. Do not worry about that."

"I do not doubt your guile, charm and cunning,

Madnan. Just make sure she is not underestimated. Her family were tough adversaries, and her father's blood runs in her veins. Lord Sydric Masterton was a tough man once."

"I can handle her, my lord. Her family's time has gone, her father is dead, as is her husband, her brothers, all her family, gone."

"Well, not all gone."

"My lord?" asked Madnan, surprised at the sudden tone in Lord Runkarn's voice.

"Come with me," Lord Runkarn said as he got up and gestured Madnan to follow.

Madnan quickly put down the half-eaten loaf and fish, wiped his hands on the napkin by his side, and followed Lord Runkarn out of the dining hall. Across the courtyard, they walked into the guardhouse across the way. They walked past the heavily guarded entrance and at once, Madnan could feel the floor slope downwards. Down they went, down four flights of stairs. Now they were deep under the city, with cold, bricked passageways leading off in all directions. Finally, they came to a steel gate guarded by four men. The gate was unlocked and opened from inside, and Madnan followed two of the guards and Lord Runkarn to the end of the passageway. As they walked down the hall, the two guards picked up lit torches from the wall. They passed empty jail cells on both sides until they reached the cell at the very end on the right. The smell was horrendous; it was an obnoxious odour of rotting flesh, excrement and something else Madnan couldn't place; something extremely unpleasant. The cell looked dark and empty until one of the guards rattled the bars. Then, in the corner, movement; a bundle of rags, somehow animated by the light shone from the torches the two guards were carrying, moved in the darkness.

"Fine day, sirs," came a gravelly voiced greeting from the corner.

Madnan peered in, his eyes squinting and straining. Slowly, his eyes were able to perceive a shape, a man-sized shape. It was hunched over and appeared to be chained to the wall. Madnan could see that it was indeed a man, an elderly man, with a long, grey beard.

"Is that Lord Runkarn?" came the rasping voice from the darkness. "Indeed, I am honoured this day, the Lord of Areekya himself." The old man moved towards the light of the torches.

"My lord?" said Madnan, as he kept his eyes fixed on the figure hunched over in the corner, who was now smiling widely; a flicker of recognition igniting within Madnan. "Who is this man?"

"Why, do you not recognise him? This, Madnan, is Lord Sydric Masterton. I thought he may now be of some use to us."

JUK THRI

Juk rode out of Midscape before dawn as agreed with Lord Dennis the previous night. He covered his head with the hood of his cloak and passed out of the city, seen only by the gate guards. They had been pre-warned by Lord Dennis, so they posed no obstruction. It was the eleventh Moon of the year and the pre-dawn conditions made Juk glad he had his bearskin overcoat on beneath his cloak; he felt the crisp, cool, early morning breeze on his face as he rode. It had a restorative effect on him today, though. It gave him the extra energy he needed. Juk passed the tall Mountain Tower with no problems, and by the end of the day had met up with Rivan in the foothills of the Mountain of Serenity after Last Sun.

"Well met!" Rivan cried out from atop his large, grey horse. He was wearing a long, thick beige coat.

"Yes, well met, Rivan." Juk smiled at the mage. "It's as you said it would be. Lord Dennis is willing to help. He will ride east, to Dawngate, and speak to Lord Wilton. He is no friend of Runkarn."

"Yes, that is good to hear. And we must head south, Juk, to Deadtown first, and to the Nikrid Desert." Rivan's soft and melodic voice flowed through the air like a sweet song.

"South? I told Dennis we would go west, to the

Wetlands and the towns on the coast of the Endless Ocean."

"There is no need of that. Messages have been sent, men will come. We must head to Deadtown to meet Ashran. He will bring some of the Clan Grash with him."

"Ashran will be in Deadtown?" Juk asked.

"It has been arranged. We must make a start. Deadtown is half a swift Moon's ride from here. The wind will be biting, so you had better brace yourself. It will be better if we ride tonight. We can stop for rest in the morning, after dawn. Ashran will be in Deadtown by the end of the Moon." Rivan smiled as he spoke.

Juk fidgeted in his saddle and looked to the south and then back to Rivan. "Deadtown? Nikrid? This makes no sense, Rivan. There is nothing in the Nikrid Desert but rocks and sand. And our death, more than likely, if we try to pass through it."

"Many paths lead to death and more besides, Juk. No one fully knows the end of a road until the journey is complete. However, you are right and wrong. Our objective is not through the desert. We intend to find what we are looking for *in* the desert. And it's not sand or rocks. Our death neither, not if I have any say on the matter," Rivan replied. His voice had a calming effect on Juk.

"In the desert, through the desert, it will be the same when the Sun beats down and there is no water to be found."

Rivan continued to smile. "Our journey in the desert will take four days, five at most. We can carry water and supplies enough for that. Ashran will have a hundred men with him. That's a hundred horses, and a hundred horses can carry a lot of water."

"And what will we find in the Nikrid Desert?" Juk asked.

Rivan looked intensely at Juk, and he could feel the penetrating stare. "An army, I hope. It will not be easy, but it can be done. Long ago, many Moons, many years before Runkarn, before nearly everything and everyone in Areekya, there was a tribe of people, of men. Well, half-men, half... well, half something else."

"Half-men?" Juk interjected. "Half something else?"

Rivan's smile became wider. "This was a long time ago. Things were true then, that many believe cannot be now."

"Magick? Are you talking about Magick?" Juk asked.

"Magick *is* one of those things," the mage answered. "Magick is as real as the air you breathe, the food you eat, and the water you drink. Sun Magick, which we use for healing, and then Moon Magick, a more aggressive, malignant, war-like Magick. This is still used today by some, to deceive or other nefarious purposes, although it was not always used so. But to have one Magick is to have both. They are counter-balanced, you see."

Juk half-smiled. "Sun Magick, Moon Magick, sounds like a child's tale out of some old book."

"You've witnessed it Juk. You felt my healing power over you in the Northern Hills. This was Sun Magick."

"We'll yes, I felt something that day. But healing a man is one thing. These things you talk about, well... something else."

"You experienced just the tip of the sword with what Magick can do." Juk noticed that Rivan's smile disappeared for a moment.

"And why haven't we heard more or seen more of this Magick? If it has any use for good?"

"Yes, good. And bad. The power of the Magick was mistreated by some. Its power was abused, as in fact Runkarn does so today. In time, there were only a few who knew the secrets. Now, they are mostly gone."

"Well, what has this got to do with this tribe of half-men you speak of? And the Nikrid Desert, more to the point!" Juk could feel himself become frustrated with Rivan's obfuscation and opaque words.

"Well, these people were skilled in Magick, both Sun and Moon. They were blessed with a natural ability for the Magicks. They moved away a long time ago, tired and depressed by the misuse of it. The Magicks became... Well, they became unbalanced. It is to the Nikrid Desert they went. If we could find them and convince them to return, if we could inform them of Runkarn's corruption and abuse, they could be convinced to help, I think."

"Find them?" Juk said, louder than normal, but not quite a shout. "The Nikrid Desert's a big place. Not a place you want to get lost in. Don't you know where they are?"

"Not exactly, but I'm confident we can locate them," the mage replied. His words remained melodic and smooth. This made Juk calmer.

"Can we?" Juk uttered. "Do they have a name?"

"Their tribe was named Deera, a placid people. A peaceful tribe, who lived off the land in central Areekya, growing crops. Very reticent to involve themselves in others' affairs until they were forced, and then their strength could be seen." Rivan's face seemed to change as he spoke of the Deera. His eyes became brighter, and there was a red hue to his cheeks that Juk hadn't noticed before.

"And how can we convince them to fight with us, against Runkarn, if they are as peaceful as you say?"

"You, Juk Thri. You can, I think. You have an honesty to you, an earthiness and a charm. And you have a story to tell, a story that I think will appeal to the Deera. You can convince them, Juk. I feel sure of it."

"Me? Surely you will have more effect. You know their history, it seems."

"Yes, that's true, but it will be you that can make the difference, if I have it right," Rivan replied. "It's time we were on our way. We have two weeks' ride ahead of us. Any questions you have, we can discuss on the way. But now we must ride for Deadtown, Juk. Ashran and his men will be waiting."

"I wonder what the welcome for me will be from

his men." Juk added.

"Ashran is a strong man with a strong character. He will have told them about you, and I'm sure there will be no trouble. Come, let's ride, let's ride until First Sun."

Rivan galloped off atop his proud, grey horse, and Juk dug his heels into his large, grey stallion and followed them. After just two weeks of hard riding, Deadtown came into view. It wasn't a large town; only a few hundred people in total lived there. It was rundown, long past its heyday, when the miners of the Spine moved out from the mountains and harvested the trees of the Dead Forest. That was many years ago, before the forest gained its name, when it was a healthy place with sturdy oaks, beautiful silver birches and large chestnut trees. Now, the town on the border of the moribund area of woodland was mainly out of the mind of most people in Areekya, and home to some of the most destitute.

The town gained its name once the harvesters moved back to the mountains; leaving only the desperate, and those who wished to be forgotten, behind. In the south this late in the year, the weather was warmer than the rest of Areekya. There was no need for Juk's bearskin overcoat. He removed it and neatly laid it securely over his horse's saddle. He was enjoying the late afternoon warmth as they rode to one of the two taverns in the town: the Black Oak, a dark building, with hardly any light emitting from the place even though it was a few hours before Last Sun. There were no windows to be seen, and the paint was peeling away from the tavern's wooden signboard. They tied up their horses outside, walked in, and headed straight to the bar.

"Two jugs of your very finest ale, barman," Rivan said.

"We's only got one ale," came the reply from the tall young man behind the bar.

"And I'm sure it is the finest in town, young man," Rivan responded.

Juk looked around the tavern from the bar. There was one old man slumped over his table in one corner, and a middle-aged woman standing in another. She was wearing too little, even for the late afternoon warmth, and smiling towards the bar. He could see no one else. The place smelled of rotting wood and a sweet, overpowering perfume.

"It be the cheapest," the barman said and poured the beer into two wooden jugs.

Rivan grabbed both jugs, walked over to one of the unoccupied corners, and sat down at a table. Juk followed, looking at the woman as her eyes followed him across the tavern. She smiled, showing a few missing teeth. Juk looked away and, as he sat down to join Rivan, he felt the chair wobble and buckle slightly under his weight.

"So, where's Ashran?" Juk asked, glancing at the woman again before turning to Rivan.

Rivan took a long swallow of ale, wiped his mouth and said, "He will be here by the end of this Moon. That's two days away, yet. We'll stay here until then. I'm sure they have a room or two available."

Juk looked around the tavern again. The man was still slumped over the table, and the woman was still smiling at him.

"Two days here?" Juk said. "What will we do for two days here?"

"We can start by talking." Rivan took another long drink of his ale. "There's something I want to tell you, Juk. Something I need to tell you."

Juk picked up his jug of ale and took a long swallow himself, bracing himself for whatever was about to come from the mage's mouth.

"I have not been altogether truthful with you, Juk Thri." The words felt to Juk like words from a song, melodic and uplifting. He allowed the words to drift over and through him as Rivan continued. "Regarding the motivation for my, and indeed your, involvement in all of this."

Juk took another, smaller drink from his cup and shifted in his chair, keeping silent, but all the time keeping his eyes on Rivan.

"What I mean is, I have reasons as yet unspoken," the mage added.

"And they are?" Juk broke his silence and looked around him to see if anyone could hear their conversation. He saw the drunk still sleeping and the woman now totally ignoring him.

"My relationship with Runkarn goes back many years, many, many years. You see, he was my apprentice.

A long time ago now, when such things were natural, one mage would pass on his secrets and teachings to an apprentice and so on. Over the years, as Magick died out, so did this tradition, and mages such as myself are now rare to find."

"Runkarn was an apprentice mage?" Juk asked.

"An apprentice mage, and then he became a very learned practitioner of the Magick arts, all of them. You see, he always had an inquisitive mind, but this mind became consumed by the dangerous and depraved aspects of the Magick. He started to read in secret, looking for hidden knowledge, hidden powers to be exploited for diabolical means." Rivan's voice remained harmonious to Juk's ears, but it was now tinged with sadness.

"And what happened?" Juk leaned forward; he became oblivious to the tavern and its questionable patrons and smells. He was now totally fixated on Rivan.

"Once the truth became known, I confronted Runkarn with it, and of course he denied it at first," the mage answered. "But in the end he accepted the truth, and I dismissed him at once. He still had so little knowledge, I didn't think he could do any harm with it. I made sure others knew of these dark thoughts and intentions, and I expected never to see him again."

Juk remained transfixed on Rivan, the implications of what he was saying percolating through his mind.

"Alas, he became very prominent. He continued

his studies, where I know not, but many years later he became Lord Masterton's most trusted and listened to advisor. He had worked his way up through Lord Sydric's court, but in secret, he was plotting to bring him down. His Magick was very strong by this time. By the time Lord Masterton realised the truth of it, well, it was too late. And Runkarn had spoken many venomous words into the ears of many powerful lords; pitting one against another, creating chaos, and taking his opportunity when it arose."

"Why didn't you stop all this before it got that far?" Juk sat back carefully in his chair and took another gulp of ale.

"I found out too late. I mainly went about my business in the west. I knew little of the east or the affairs of the land. By this time, mages were looked down upon, mainly seen as old fools, tricksters and charlatans."

"And during the War? Couldn't you stop him then?"

"I tried. I rallied the Wetlanders, and some Hillmen, though the men on the coast wanted no part in a War which didn't involve them. And Runkarn had many lords doing his bidding by then. With his Moon Magick, he was able to win them around and promise them spoils when the War was won."

"And you think I can do something you couldn't do? Why?"

"You are a leader of men, Juk. When I saw you in the Northern Hills, I saw your pain, but I also saw your strength."

"But you are a mage. You say you have this Magick."

"I think it is something we can do together. But it must be done in secret, without Runkarn's knowledge. This will be our biggest weapon, that of surprise and secrecy." Rivan smiled and took a long drink from his cup.

"Two more ales, young man," Rivan ordered from his seat. Juk looked around and saw the barman pouring the drinks. The drunken man had now woken up and was talking to the woman, who was now sitting at his table, smiling. He turned his gaze back to Rivan. "Well, I'm sure no one will think of looking here, anyway."

THE CAPTIVE

The impenetrable darkness had given way to Sunlight, Moonlight and Starlight. He had been moved to a new cell with a window; it had rusty iron bars that separated him from the world outside, but a window that allowed in the glistening rays of the natural universal light bringers. Still, the man inside was in control; ruminating, meditating, building the strength needed to survive. His meals were now two times a day; no more stale bread and water, but fish and fresh loaves. The guards still grunted and spat as they delivered his food. He still returned their actions with a smile, a thank you, knowing that they could do no more harm to him. No more than they had already done, many, many Moons ago. The evil they had afflicted upon him had not penetrated the inner-man; there he understood that evil can only do harm once the man reflects that same evil back. This the inner-man understood and practised, hour by hour, day by day, Moon by Moon.

Knowing that change would come, must come — for what else is there in this world, but enduring change? — pushed the inner-man forward. Waiting for change had been a blessing, a treat, a daily observation and affirmation. The rational mind of the inner-man had control. He had usurped the outer-man long ago, and was witnessing the change that is promised with every Sunrise and setting Moon. The inner-man still had his rational mind. He still worked through the days, minute by minute, hour by hour. The outer man's long grey beard had been trimmed, his rags replaced with a tunic and undergarments. The outer-man was being prepared for change, for some as yet unspoken task, and he complied with the utmost obedience, this outer-man. But he was not in control. This had been given over to the inner-man long ago, many, many Moons ago, and he was ready. He is ready; he is prepared for the change that must come.

His legs and hands no longer chained, he was free to pace his cell or write his meditations with the parchment and ink provided to him by the surly, disdainful, but now obedient guards, and always accepted with a smile.

On each sheet he wrote with fastidious artistry, using the old tongue: Eh sunar te siat gorne. Eh sunar te siat gorne. Eh sunar te siat gorne. Eh sunar te siat gorne. Eh sunar te siat gorne...

Once his parchments had been used up, he turned to the walls. Using the chalk that came with the ink and parchments, he reproduced it with precise elegance onto each wall, in neat lines: Eh sunar te siat gorne. Eh sunar te siat gorne. Eh sunar te siat gorne...

Eh sunar te siat gorne: To live, one first must die.

BOOK 2

THE FOREST

The Full Moon shimmered in the night's sky. It was the eleventh Moon, a special time of the year. The procession of people moving in an eastward direction, wearing full-length, off-white robes, made its way to the tree-lined entrance to the forest. They were wearing masks fashioned from the trees in the surrounding area that covered their eyes and noses. The assembly reached the entrance of the forest and walked past the organic, leaf-covered sentinels; one on each side of the walkway that led to the centre of the dense forest. The vast woodland here in the centre of Areekya was almost an exact replica of the Midnight Forest, far off in the north west of Areekya. Like its older, more sacred progenitor, it took half a day to walk the entire way around it. It had the appearance of a man-made structure; almost exactly circular, with the border trees immaculately trimmed and situated, so that it was extremely difficult to enter the forest at all, apart from the two designated openings. These were created in an exact straight line along the east-west latitude; the western opening used as the ceremonial entrance, and the ornately carved eastern clearance as the exit.

The disciples made their way into the heart of the forest, to the Sacred Place. This Moon day was not only the most important of the year, it was the culmination of the five-year cycle. Tonight, the Sun Star aligned with the Full Moon; they rose and glided across the sky in a silky, harmonious dance precisely as the elongated journey of the Sun Star was complete and the Sacred Shape had been etched out in the night's sky over the previous sixty Moons. The congregation of devotees approached the centre of the forest. They could see the large standing stones, arranged in the Sacred Pentagon, matching the pattern of the Sun Star's five year-long journey in the sky above. One large stone, reaching fifteen feet in height, was placed at the point of each of the five sacred points that made up the five-pointed star. In the centre was an arrangement of three smaller stones; two stones standing upright, about five feet tall, and one stone positioned as a lintel atop the other two. As the disciples reached the Sacred Stones, they fanned out to the left and to the right, standing outside of a circle of smaller, white, natural-looking rocks that surrounded the Sacred Pentagon. These small rocks were evenly distributed, demarcating the Sacred Space; entry to this inner Sacred Space during a ceremony was permitted to only a select, carefully chosen few.

At the rear of the procession, there were two people wearing silver masks and full-length green robes. One walked either side of a naked young man, barely sixteen years of age, wearing only a mask that covered his eyes. His arms were being pulled by the figures to the side of him by a rope tied to each wrist. Behind them was one last silver-masked devotee. He was wearing a full-length purple gown, and he walked five paces behind. When, at last, the rear of the procession reached the Sacred Place, the two figures in green robes tied the ends of the ropes to each standing stone in the centre of the Sacred Pentagon.

The devotees circling the Sacred Space chanted, slowly at first:

"Toooh... Toooh... Toooh..."

While the chanting continued, the two figures in green robes pulled out their knives, with silver blades just shorter than a man's lower forearm and white quartz handles. The light of the Full Moon was now shimmering onto the central Sacred Stones. There was a terrified look on the boy's face. His eyes were wide, although no sound came from his lips. The Cafal, the pre-ceremonial drink, had seen to that. Each knife was raised slowly, as the chanting grew louder and at a quicker rhythm:

"Tooh... Tooh... Tooh..."

The knives were drawn down slowly, repetitively, to the side of the terror-stricken boy tied to the stones, deliberately missing their mark, four, five times the knives were raised and drawn down. The chanting became louder still, quicker than before.

"Toh... Toh... Toh... Toh... Toh... Toh..."

And then each knife found its mark. The boy remained silent, his eyes wide in terror. Each knife slashed at the boy's upper torso, one from the right, the other on the left, five, six, seven times. They slashed quickly until each knife was only a blur to the observer. The blood sprayed out in all directions, the robes of the two attackers quickly becoming covered by the dark red liquid spurting from the severed arteries, turning them a deeper shade of green. The boy's body twitched and convulsed as the blood spurted out. Then the chanting suddenly stopped. The boy's body was lifeless. The two figures lifted their knives up to the Moon. As they did so, the runes engraved on each knife glittered in the moonlight. Now, the silver-masked man in the purple robe came forward and entered the Sacred Space. Slowly, he walked, methodically, towards the limp cadaver. He reached the still, supple body of the young man and stared at the naked, butchered body. Then he reached into the torso, deep into the stomach of the dead boy, and he grabbed at the internal organs and pulled them out. He held the entrails aloft in celebration above his head, blood dripping onto his mask and face as he did so. The congregation cried out in unison:

"From the flesh to the Stars. From the Stars to the Sun. From the Sun to the Moon. From the Moon to the Flesh."

And with that, the purple-robed devotee bit off a chunk from the entrails, and the crowd roared its approval. He then passed the bowels and innards of the young boy to the two figures who had slashed and cut the boy to his death. They too ripped out a chunk of the entrails with their teeth before passing them on to the baying crowd, each devotee, one by one gnawing and biting the remains as they were passed around, as the excitement intensified and the ceremony reached its crescendo.

Finally, one by one, each of the devotees around the circle silently and slowly left in an eastward direction, their blood lust having been satisfied. When all had gone, all that remained were the two figures in the green robes, and the one in purple. The knives were safely sheathed and the lifeless body was still tied to the standing stones; food for crows and other beasts for the next three days, when what remains of the body would be gathered up and burned near the eastern exit of the forest. The last three figures withdrew, their masks and faces still covered in the ceremonial blood of the young victim, following the others slowly, silently, to the eastern exit.

The procession reached the Tower of Nights, situated outside the eastern exit of the forest. All the faithful had surrounded the tower in four concentric circles. The three figures at the back of the procession made their way to the entrance of the tower, opened the door, walked through the hall and ascended the stairs. Up they continued to the Watching Room. There they were joined by a fourth man. A taller man in a full length, dark red robe, wearing a mask of the same colour. There, all four men stood looking out over the balcony. The faithful gathered below held aloft their lit torches and rearranged themselves into the Sacred Spiral. Then the chanting started again:

"Toooh... Toooh... Toooh..."

It continued for a while and gradually, as the rhythm became faster, the sound became louder: "Toh... Toh... Toh... Toh... Toh... Toh..."

On and on it continued before the man in the red mask raised his hands and shouted from the balcony, "All hail the power of the Moon!"

"Hail!" came the reply from below.

"All hail the power of the Lunar Cycle!" he screamed again, this time in a deep, resonating tone.

"Hail!" came the reply from below once more.

A third time he cried, "All hail the power of the Sacred!"

"Hail! Hail! Hail! Toooh! Tooh! Toh!" came the cries from below.

He lowered his arms, slowly, purposefully, until they were by his side and he let out a cry: "Toooh! Tooh! Toh!"

And suddenly, the crowd that had gathered below dispersed. They continued their way eastward, back to the capital city. Back through Magdil's western entrance. The four men came in from the balcony and into the Watching Room. They removed their robes and masks, and one by one drank from a silver goblet covered in Lunar Runes. Then three men left the way they had entered, descended the stairs, and made their way back to the city. The taller man remained alone in the Watching Room, carefully wiping the blood from the Moon Knives left behind. He placed them carefully into a large, ornate, silver and bronze chest , taking care to lay them meticulously at ninety-degree angles to each other, and then he placed his red mask in the chest. He closed it carefully and withdrew to the hall and down the stairs. There, waiting for him, were two guards atop large, black horses. He mounted his own horse, grey and proud, and together they made their way back to the city.

LORD WILLIAM WILTON OF DAWNGATE

William Wilton made his way down from his plush living quarters, with his long retinue trailing as his personal guards led him to the main entrance of Dawngate. A visitor, Lord Dennis Greenaway, had arrived from Midscape late last night, and after a brief supper they had agreed to meet early this morning, just after Sun up. William had decided they would go out hunting. The local game wasn't that numerous at this time of the year, with Midwinter approaching, but it gave them more privacy than Dawngate provided; he had become more suspicious of many occurrences in Moons gone by, and he wanted to be out of earshot of his wife, Ursula.

As he approached the main gates, he saw Dennis Greenaway with six men wearing green and white tunics, and one soldier was holding the banner of Midscape: a white-tipped mountain with a green background. They were waiting for him, as requested the night before, next to the guardhouse. Even at this early hour, the guards announced the departure of the Lord of the City with the clear, bright, powerful blow of the guardhouse trumpets; three clear, tuneful blasts that always accompanied the Lord or the Lady of the City, entering or leaving Dawngate.

Dennis Greenaway nodded and smiled as a

greeting, and slipped in behind the guards, riding at the front to join William. Three of his Midscape soldiers rode either side of the two lords.

"Well met, Lord William. A fine crisp morning." Dennis grinned.

"Well met, Lord Dennis." William gazed directly ahead after briefly returning Dennis's smile. "Good eastern weather this, though maybe colder than you are used to, perhaps, yes?"

"They told me to expect the weather as such, and I've dressed appropriately," Dennis replied, his grin contracting.

William looked at the thick, brown bearskin his riding companion wore, covering his green tunic and portly frame, his flame red hair contrasting with the dark colours of the bearskin, and smiled. "Yes, maybe a touch over the top, but you'll not be too cold with that on."

William was dressed in the standard yellow tunic and overcoat he wore when out hunting. The sigil of his family, a bright Sun rising over three mountains, showed clearly on his breast, as well as on the banners his guards held. His long, brown, curly hair hung down past his shoulders. William was nearly forty years of age, but his privileged lifestyle had been easy on his body and looks. He was still regarded as a handsome man, tall and lordly. He carried the air of a high-born, somewhat aloof and cold, some said. But his outer appearance hid an insecurity he had felt most of his life; a man that never really fitted in or felt accepted. His marriage to Ursula Brackworth had not abated those feelings. She was a woman he had never loved. In fact, the number of intimate nights they had spent together since being married years before were few; William was a man who preferred the company of other men.

His wife's family came from rich mining stock and had provided his father with much needed wealth in the years before and during the War with Runkarn. The joining of their families was one of convenience; in more ways than one. Ursula was not an uncomely woman; she was regarded as the most beautiful lady in the east in her younger days, and the years had been as kind to her as to her husband. The only problem was that she was a woman.

As the party rode through the city gates, the Sun had just climbed above the Mountains of Dawn behind them and was illuminating the early morning sky with a vivid yellow and purple hue. It was a breathtaking sight, one William had witnessed many times, but it still filled him with a sense of wonder and reverence. He loved the early morning Sunrises and late evening Sunsets even more. The vivid colours and mixed feelings of awe and sadness helped him to retain his place within his existence, and a sense of perspective.

"A beautiful morning sky to accompany us as well, Lord William. That's a good omen for the hunting to come, surely." Dennis's smile was back on his face.

"Ah yes, the hunting," William said. "Well, to be frank, that's not the main reason we're heading out today."

"Is it not?" replied Dennis.

"I felt that after last night's supper, some discretion may be called for, and there are not any walls out here for ears to intrude upon, no?" William glanced at his riding partner as he finished his sentence with a question. Dennis nodded silently in agreement.

They continued to ride for about thirty minutes before the guards at the head of the column stopped. They had arrived at the opening of a large woodland area, and after some orders were shouted out, a flurry of activity had the men pitching the tents and getting the hunting gear together. By mid-morning, the two men were riding into the forest with their own guards following behind. They stopped at a small clearance and William gestured to his guards to set up breakfast here.

"So, Lord Dennis. What news is so important you have ridden to the east? A journey you have not made for many Moons, so many in fact that I cannot recall when you were last here?" William was sitting on a wooden bench hastily erected by his guards, who were sitting a good fifty yards away, out of earshot of the two lords' conversation. Dennis Greenaway was sitting on the other bench, separated by a low wooden table with a selection of fruits, cheeses and meats.

"It is true I have not visited for some time. However, my duties keep me busy in Midscape," Dennis replied.

"Ah yes. Midscape, our old, somewhat forgotten capital. Tell me, how is Lady Livian? Do you both ride to Magdil often? And how is Lord Runkarn keeping these days? Well, I hope, yes?"

"My wife is well. I do not travel to Magdil often. In

fact, I have somewhat fallen from favour of Runkarn, I feel. More to the point, fell out with his nest of advisors."

"Ah, I see," replied William. "And I assume this falling out is not insignificant to your visit here, no?"

"There you have it right, Lord William. Let me say that in the past, we have not, well, we haven't been as close as others, let's say."

"Well, as I remember, we were fighting on different sides for some years, for different causes, *let's say*." William picked up some grapes and delicately bit into one.

"There are many who once were enemies become friends, good friends even," Dennis said, smiling.

"Ah! So this is the purpose of your visit: friendship. Seldom is friendship from previous adversaries offered without some price attached. Am I right, Lord Dennis?"

"Well, there maybe you have it right again, but a friendship which could be of benefit to both parties, I feel. Would that you hear me out?" Dennis maintained his smile as he spoke.

"Well then, here we are. Let's hear your proposal then, Lord Dennis." William picked up a small piece of cheese, smiling slightly.

The near-Midwinter Sun glistened overhead. It was a touch warmer now, as the Sun glowed orange in the cloudless sky. After the two men had been talking for a while, William ordered his guards to clear the table and make ready to ride back.

"An interesting proposition, Lord Dennis. A

surprising one, too. And these men you ask of me, how many?" William asked, as the two men rode back to the hunting camp on the outskirts of the forest.

"As many as you could spare, no more than you are willing to offer," Dennis replied, barely above a whisper.

William Wilton stopped his horse as he continued the conversation. "I could spare many thousands if we were certain of victory," he replied. "I am no friend of Runkarn and Magdil. This is no secret. Lord Masterton was a dear friend to my family. His death and that of his family were a painful blow to us in the east."

"Who can be certain of anything in war, Lord William? But the more men we have, the more certain we become. I have friends in the west and I have my own men. With proper planning and patience, we *can be* successful. Will this suffice?" Dennis looked at William as he spoke.

"And this is sensitive information. Magdil will not hear of this, you say. Are you sure?" William held eye contact with his riding companion.

"It is a tightly kept secret between me and one other; Magdil will not hear from us. Can you swear the same, Lord William?"

"We will head back to Dawngate. Have dinner with me and my lady wife tonight. Pray do not mention this until we are alone again. Say you are here on Magdil tax business. I will think it over and give you my answer tomorrow. This is not easy to commit to, however much I might desire it."

Dennis nodded in agreement, and they rode the

rest of the way back to the hunting camp in silence.

ASHRAN

Ashran arrived at Deadtown near the end of the eleventh Moon of the year. He brought with him a hundred men from Lendir. He had left his son, Ashron, back at home together with Bishran to manage things in his absence. Ashran was hoping he would not be gone too long, although he feared he might. Most of his men were camped out in the Dead Forest, as Ashran and half a dozen of the men rode into the town. It was mid-afternoon. As they rode through the deserted main street in the town, Ashran looked around at the impoverished buildings and the handful of people that he saw, and felt a sense of contrition.

He wasn't sure why, but observing the rundown nature of the town and its people made him think back to his shame he had felt at surrendering to Magdil. This feeling of shame and guilt turned to anger. He thought of his own home and family and wondered what lay in store for them. There was a stench in the air, a mixture of burning and something else, thought Ashran, something metallic, something unpleasant. They reached the Black Oak; the tavern, Rivan told him he would be found. The men tied their horses up outside and entered the dark, poorly lit tavern.

As Ashran made his way to the bar, a voice came out from one corner. "Well met!"

Ashran looked over to where the voice came from

and saw, sitting at a small round table, Rivan and Juk Thri.

"Well, here you are," Ashran replied and walked over to the two men, as his men made their way to the bar.

"Sit, sit, dear Ashran," Rivan said, pointing to the chair next to his.

"I came, as you asked, Rivan. It wasn't easy to leave Lendir so close to Midwinter." Ashran sat down and smiled slightly.

"I know, I know. Midwinter is an important time for us all," Rivan replied. "But it is good that you came. Did you bring your men?"

"A hundred, as asked."

"Good, good. Where are they now?"

"They have camped out in the woods near the town. Less than a morning's ride," Ashran replied, looking directly at the mage's dark, almost black eyes. "Rivan, I came here, under some hardship and discomfort, I might add, as you asked. But for what purpose? I told the town and my men it was part of a plan to spurn Magdil's demands, and that brought me some relief. Do I speak it true?"

"There will be time for whys, hows and wherefores, my friend. But you have it true," Rivan replied. Ashran's eyes moved between the mage and Juk sitting opposite him. "We'll be leaving after Last Sun today."

"Leaving? To where? Why so soon? My men are

tired and parched, I dare say. A night's rest would bring benefit," Ashran said.

"Where to? We're heading to the Nikrid Desert. I'll explain the why on the way."

"Nikrid Desert? Sun and Moon!" Ashran exclaimed.

"Ashran, friend," Juk said, "let me get you some ale. It's excellent beer here. Come and join me at the bar. We can talk there." Ashran watched on as Juk stood up and gestured for him to follow as he made his way across the tavern.

"I'll take a drink and then I'll ride to my men. Prepare them for the off after Last Sun." Ashran stood up, looked at Rivan and followed Juk to the bar.

"Good, good," said the mage, as he remained sitting down, smiling.

By late afternoon, Ashran had sent twenty of his men back west, to the towns and villages of the Endless Ocean, at Rivan's behest. Messages had already been sent, and the men were to recruit whoever they could and meet up back in Deadtown after the Winter Solstice.

Just after Last Sun, Ashran and the rest of his men, together with Juk and Rivan, started out on their journey to the Nikrid Desert. It took just over a week to ride through the Dead Forest and reach the edge of the desert. The journey through the forest had been a silent, curious ride. No life at all was to be seen or heard, all the once-proud trees, now withered and lifeless, dead leaves on the ground and broken branches lying scattered throughout. It was aptly named, thought Ashran, and he was glad to reach the end of it.

They camped there for the night, using the dead wood from the outskirts of the forest to make the fire. It was a cold, dark, Moonless night, and the fire needed to be kept burning throughout the night by the men on guard. At first Sun, the fire was still burning brightly, as the men gathered round, warming their tired bodies before the morning's ride.

"Four days, you say?" Ashran asked as he warmed himself by the fire.

"Yes. Five at the most. It has been many a year since anyone has heard of the Deera. However, I have an idea of where they went to and where they are now," Rivan replied. Ashran observed the mage as he spoke. Unlike all the other men around the fire, Rivan wasn't warming himself by the dancing, naked flames of the fire. The mage was a pace or two behind the men and seemed preoccupied with other matters.

"Well, the water bottles have been filled, and we've enough to eat for a week or more, maybe two if we're sensible. We've brought some dry wood for our night time fires, too," Ashran said as he continued to look over at Rivan. He wasn't sure whether or not he'd heard him, when another voice interrupted the silence. It was that of Juk Thri.

"That sounds plenty, if I understand our journey, Ashran. Rivan seems pretty confident he can locate the Deera easily enough. Now, getting them to agree to help us, well, that's another thing entirely." Juk smiled at Ashran and he returned the gesture. They had grown closer during the journey here. Juk was not the closed, aloof figure he appeared to be back when they first met, when he was Captain of the 1st Regiment.

"Yes, yes," answered Rivan after a while. "You and your men have prepared well, Ashran. We'll off soon, when I return. Tell your men to put out the fire and to hide any trace of us as much as they can." With that, Rivan walked off back towards the forest. "I'll be back soon enough."

Within the hour, all was set, and Rivan had returned for the journey into the desert. Ashran's guards rode at the front of the group, followed by Rivan, Juk and Ashran riding side-by-side, with the rest of his men following. As the horses took their first hesitant strides southward into the Nikrid Desert, the tension from the men was palpable. The desert was known as an exotic mystery back in the west. A place to threaten the children with: *if you aren't quiet, the wind will carry you off to the Nikrid Desert,* they were told, and this usually ended any mischievous behaviour in an instant. But it was the parents of those children that were feeling threatened by the desert now. The enigmatic desert was laid out in front of them as far as they could see. The sky above was clear, crystal blue, with not a cloud to be seen. Although the weather was still warm in the south at this time of the year, at night the temperature dropped considerably. The colour of the desert sand was a deep orange and of a very fine consistency. Small plumes of dust exploded into the air as the horses trotted further into the dry expanse of sand. As Ashran looked over his shoulder, he could see a long trail of dust in the air where they had ridden, like a long, winding dark cloud, looming menacingly behind, following the men, acting as a canopy to the clear skies above; It didn't help the mood of the men, as it didn't Ashran's.

At the end of the first day's ride, they had travelled around twenty miles. They had ridden carefully, more to abate the mood of the men than anything else, and by Last Sun, everyone was happy to camp for the night. They made a fire using the wood carried from the Dead Forest, and the men gathered round, using the blankets and sheepskin furs they had brought to keep warm. The fireside mood was bleak that night and the talk was limited.

The next morning they set off early, with the rising of the Sun. They rode their horses harder the second day. The men were getting used to the unchanging, barren landscape, Ashran thought, and the gloomy, menacing image of a mysterious netherworld was moving further and further from Ashran's mind. As the day wore on, the men talked more freely, and by the end of the second day, everyone's mood seemed to be uplifted slightly.

The third day's ride was as uneventful as the first two, if not at a slightly quicker pace. And by the end of the fourth day, as they camped for the night, Ashran saw Rivan walk over towards him, smiling. "Ashran, I feel we are close now. By the end of tomorrow's ride, we shall be at our destination and we shall find what we're looking for." The mage's smile waned.

"The Deera?" replied Ashran.

"Yes, if they still survive. It's been many, many years since anyone has had word from them, and many more since they've been seen."

"If they still survive? Are you saying that all this might be for nothing? This long trek to the ends of the land for naught?" Ashran raised his voice, something he couldn't ever remember doing with Rivan before.

"I am almost certain they remain. They were sturdy people, special in many ways. It would be a great surprise to me if they were no longer where I expect them to be," Rivan replied, his voice sounding smooth and melodic, calming Ashran immediately.

"And where is that, exactly? All we can see is sand. How could anyone exist here, in this?" Ashran's voice returned to its normal pitch and he smiled by way of apology.

"We are almost at the end of the desert. Although that may be somewhat difficult to believe. Soon you shall see, as we all shall see." And with that, the mage turned and sat away from the group huddled around the fire. Ashran walked over to his men and saw Juk Thri there warming himself, standing tall and looking out of place in his long, dark brown, bearskin overcoat, amongst the sheepskin furs of his men.

"Well, Juk. Here we are. In the middle of nowhere, cold, and none the wiser as to what or who we may find tomorrow or the day after that. How are your spirits?"

"My spirits could do with a lift. I was saving this until it was needed, and well, I feel tonight is as good as any other." Juk pulled out a silver flask from his bearskin overcoat, twisted open the top and took a swift drink. "Potato wine. I brought it from the Black Oak." He took another swig and passed it to Ashran. He took a long drink and coughed as he handed it back to Juk.

"Sun be good! I haven't tasted anything like that since only the Moon knows when." Ashran grimaced as he felt the warm sensation plummet down the back of his throat into his stomach.

"It's potent stuff. But I can feel a tough time ahead. It'll be good to get a good night's rest," Juk said as he took another drink from his flask and handed it back to Ashran.

Ashran took a longer drink this time, coughed again, and handed it back. "Aye, I think you may be right there."

CHIK SRIN

Chik Srin was riding back to Stoneguard with fifty men of the 1st Regiment and the same number from the 2nd, who had arrived two weeks ago from Magdil. It was not yet Mid-Sun, but Chik had had enough. They'd been searching the local farmsteads, villages, taverns and hills; they had been searching everywhere for Juk Thri since early morning with no success. Not a trace had been found of him. The villagers had neither seen nor heard anything that could help them in their search. Chik had come to a dead end. In truth, he didn't know what to do next. It had been over a Moon since Juk Thri had ridden out of Stoneguard; to where, he did not know.

"Where to Captain Chik?" asked the Captain from the 2nd Regiment, Hak Krok. Chik detected a certain amount of satisfaction in the question, but ignored it.

"We'll head back to Stoneguard. That's enough for today."

"Enough, is it?" came the reply from the Captain of the 2nd.

"Yes, it is. We've found no sign, and no one's heard anything. There's no use putting any more time into searching round here. We'll head to Stoneguard, and maybe the 1st has returned from Chinsap with news." Chik kept his eyes focused dead ahead, not bothering to look at the man asking the questions riding next to him.

"Okay, lads," Hak said, "let's get back to the comfort of the barracks. It seems these northern lads can't handle a bit of rough riding." Hak started laughing and the 2nd Regiment joined in.

When they reached Stoneguard, they headed to the barracks, stabled the horses and the men of the 1st and the 2nd went to the sleeping quarters. Chik headed to the yard in front of the soldiers' quarters. This dusty, well-worn area was used for training of new recruits and keeping the more experienced men fresh and battle-ready. He sat down on one of the stone benches that had been erected for the man at arms to sit and observe his charges.

As he was sitting there, he received news that the 1st had returned from Chinsap early that morning while they were out riding. His men had found no sign of Juk Thri there. No one had seen him in the town or in the surrounding villages. Chik wasn't really surprised by this, but it disappointed him just the same; it also worried him. The added pressure of the 2nd Regiment sent from Magdil was making him feel worse about his situation. The two Regiments had always had a fierce rivalry, with the mountain men from the north east making up the 1st and the men from the Spine Mountains making up the 2nd. Lord Runkarn had previously favoured the 1st. For good reason: it always delivered. The swift cavalry regiment was sent to the more problematic regions of Areekya. It was the speed of its movement and the effectiveness of the fighting men that made up the 1st which had always given them the edge. The 2nd Regiment was a more cumbersome unit. A combination of heavy-armoured infantry and slower, less careful cavalry. Chik always thought the 2nd's battle tactics were inferior; they got the job done by brute force. The favour the 1st Regiment had from Lord Runkarn seemed to be waning, and with the news of Juk Thri's disloyalty, the 2nd had been pushed to the fore. This was probably helped by the machinations of the Veerak brothers, but with the inability to locate its ex-Captain, the 1st had played its own part in its fall from favour.

"Captain Chik. Shall we ready for the off again this afternoon?" One of Chik's men appeared from the barracks and asked the question.

"No. Not today. Tell the men to stand down. We'll regroup after Last Sun and discuss what's next," Chik said, trying not to give away his somewhat agitated and depressed mood.

"Aye, Captain Chik." And with that, the soldier returned to the barracks.

Chik stood and paced up and down the training yard. They had been searching the local area for a Moon with not even the slightest hint of Juk Thri. He had decided it was useless to continue and had arranged an afternoon meeting with the senior men of the 2nd Regiment to discuss his next move. Chik knew they had been sent by Magdil to be Runkarn's eyes and ears, and he didn't intend to jeopardise his position as Captain of the 1st. He had worked hard for it, and so what if it came to him because of Juk's disloyalty? He still deserved it, and if he were true to himself, he felt it should have happened before it actually did. Chik had hoped to find

Juk and convince him to return, or at least to explain to Runkarn himself. He had failed in that, so now he had to do his soldier's duty, as he had done all of his time spent in the 1st, and would continue to do so.

Chik was sitting at the table in the briefing room at the barracks. Sitting opposite him was the Captain from the 2nd Regiment. Hak Krok was a short, stocky man, with short, dark hair and permanent stubble on his chin. Sitting behind Hak were two of his men. All three were wearing the uniform of the 2nd regiment, with the insignia of two stars against a background of a mountain range, and they had the face tattoo of a mountain tip on their right cheeks men from the Spine had.

"So, Captain Chik, you have failed to find any trace of your absent ex-Captain, eh?" Hak Krok said from across the table.

"We have found no sign here in the north and my men none in Chinsap. It is a waste of time and resource to continue," Chik replied, looking directly into Hak's eyes and maintaining eye contact.

"Well, that will be disappointing for Magdil to hear." Hak looked over his shoulder at his men as he spoke.

"Disappointing or not, that's the truth of it," Chik replied and added, "As I remember, your men found nothing in Chinsap, and you have been out with us here in the north. What were you doing in Chinsap days before we got there?"

"On my Lord Runkarn's business. Perhaps he didn't

trust the 1st, perhaps he wanted the job done by someone else, someone not so close to the deserter," Hak said.

Chik allowed that barb to pass. He looked at Hak and his men standing behind him; they were smiling. Chik didn't like that, and spat back, "Well, it seems you found the same as we did — nothing."

"And what do you intend to do next, Captain Chik?" Chik saw the smile broaden on Hak's face as he spoke, but remained silent. "This deserter, this Juk Thri," Hak continued, "he is not in the north, you say. He is not in Chinsap, you say. *Some* would say, Lord Runkarn perhaps, that maybe you haven't searched enough, or perhaps even wanted to search."

Chik kept his eyes on Hak as the Captain of the 2nd regiment spoke. He observed as he once more looked over his shoulder at his men, and returned his gaze to Chik, with a broad smile all over his face, his tattoo stretching and contorting as he did so.

"Lord Brok will be back soon," Chik replied, keeping his temper under control. "I think it's best to hear what news he brings from Magdil, from Lord Runkarn." Chik saw the smile disappear from Hak's face as ten of the 1st Regiment came in the door from behind Chik and stood behind their Captain, arms crossed.

"Of course, as you say," Hak said. "Well, it seems as if our business is done here, then." With that, he went to get up from his chair.

"If you would, for a moment more." Chik gestured Hak to remain seated. "I want to make this clear, clear to you and clear to your men. I am the Captain of the 1st Regiment. The finest Regiment in the army. As such, I carry out my orders to the best of my ability, the best of anyone's ability, as far as I am concerned. If you feel that I or my Regiment are somewhat lacking in this, then I would have it said true, from your own lips, not tied up in words used to distance yourself from any such slight." Chik's eyes remained fixed on Hak.

"Come, come now, Captain Chik. Just a little jab, and I can see I have offended you. For this, I apologise. You are right. Let's wait for Lord Runkarn's word before committing to our next move." Hak Krok smiled one more time, stood up, and left the room, his men following him.

Chik turned to his men. "Fucking rock smashers. They'll need watching tonight. Make sure they're closely observed and if any of them leave, I want to know about it."

"Aye, Captain," one of his men replied. And with that, Chik left the room. He returned to his bunk in the barracks and laid down, not hoping to sleep — he hadn't had a decent sleep in weeks — but to try to get his mind right. To think things through, to come to terms with what he knew he had to do next.

LORD JANSON BROK

Janson Brok arrived back at Stoneguard just after First Sun, a week before Midwinter. Almost all of Areekya had some kind of celebration for the Winter Solstice. It was a festive time of year; the celebration of the dying world making way for the new, the reborn. The Midwinter Sunrise and Sunset were marked with great reverence in Areekya, and Stoneguard was no different. As Janson rode through the main gates towards the drawbridge and the main tower, he could see the candle-lit lanterns and hollowed-out fruits already being displayed in the streets and houses of the locals. This year, however, the Winter Solstice celebrations would not be filled with the usual merrymaking and joyous celebrations for Janson Brok. This Midwinter brought with it a heavy heart, a sense of duty he knew he had to carry out, for his country, for his family, and for himself.

After lunch, Janson had requested the company of Captain Chik Sri and Captain Hak Krok to his private quarters within the main tower. He had spent the morning with his family, showing none of the burden he carried with him, and allowing his family at least to enjoy his return, even if he did not.

"Enter," Janson said in response to the loud double tap on his door. Lord Brok's personal guard opened the door and the two Captains walked in and sat at the desk on the two chairs prepared for them.

"My Lord Brok," said Chik. "I trust your journey from the capital was uneventful and safe?"

"It was, Chik, thank you."

"My lord," said Hak. "I trust Lord Runkarn is well and business is as it should be in the capital?"

"All is as well as can be expected, given the current situation, and yes, Lord Runkarn is well. Looking forward to the Midwinter festivities, I believe. Celebrations I feel we will have to miss this year."

"What news then, my lord?" Chik asked.

"Ah yes, news. There has been no sighting of Juk. None at all," answered Janson. "There have been some irregular movements in the west of the lands, heading down to the south. Whether this has anything to do with Juk, it is uncertain."

"Wetlanders?" asked Chik.

"Yes, a small band was seen in the villages of the Endless Ocean and heading east."

"Well, that could be anything," added Hak.

"Yes, and it's being investigated by Magdil. Which brings me to our task. There has been no sight of Juk here, in the north or in Chinsap. Is that correct?" Janson asked.

"None," replied Chik. "We stopped looking a couple of days ago. There was no point in continuing. Juk Thri is not in the north, my lord."

"This is a decision Captain Chik came to on his

own, I must add," Hak Krok interjected. "I feel that there is merit still in looking. Who knows what tricks this Juk Thri has played or who he has associated with? Northern Hillmen, brigands, who knows?"

"Yes, who indeed knows?" replied Janson, looking closely at the two Captains sitting in front of him and feeling the tension between them. "Lord Runkarn has dispatched Madnan Veerak with a contingent of the 2nd Regiment to Midscape. He feels that there is merit in bringing Lord Greenaway onside. As you know, Chik, he and Juk are great friends."

"*Are* great friends?" interjected Hak once more. "Surely, *were* my lord? Who could remain friends with a traitor like this?" Janson noticed Hak looked at Chik as he finished his sentence.

"Bonds made in war are difficult to break, Captain Hak. Of this I'm sure you are aware," Janson replied to the jibe aimed at both him and Chik, as well as Lord Greenaway.

"If any of my men were to abandon me, or Lord Runkarn, and murder their family, I'd gladly cut their throats myself. Or more's to the point, I'd treat them to the Spinal Grip. And I'd do it with a smile on my face, too." Hak grinned as he spoke.

"Ah yes, the Spinal Grip," replied Janson, looking at Chik. "A particularly vicious method of death for a stranger, let alone one's friend; tying him up stretched among the rocks covered in honey to allow the creatures and the beasts to eat him alive, slowly, most of the time."

"He'd be no friend if he'd got up to what this Juk Thri had done, I'll tell you that. Let the Moon take him, if it hasn't already." Hak turned and spat on the floor.

"Captain Hak! I'd remind you of where you are and who you are addressing!" Janson stood up and stared at the spittle on his floor.

"Aye, I beg pardon for that, my lord." Hak apologised and wiped the spittle away with his boot. "This talk of traitors and murderers brings it out in me."

"Murderer? Is this the truth of it now? Juk Thri murdered his family." Chik stared at Hak as he asked the question.

"This is what Lord Runkarn believes, Chik," Janson said, trying to get Chik to turn his attention to him. "The gossips of the court and the markets of Magdil are full of the tales of it. As hard as it may be to believe, Chik. This seems to be the truth of it."

"Why? Why would he do such a thing?" Chik asked.

"They say he caught his wife in a tryst with another. The Moon madness took him and in a frenzy, he killed both his wife and her lover, a Chinsap man, as well as his daughters. Terrible." Janson continued looking at Chik as he delivered this horrific news.

"His daughters as well?" Chik exclaimed, almost shouting. "That I find impossible to believe."

"Aye. It's hard to believe, but I've heard and seen worse things when the Moon takes a man, Chik." Janson smiled in sympathy. Chik stared directly back at him for a moment or two and then he looked down and let out a barely audible sigh.

Janson gave the young Captain a few moments to regain his composure before talking again. "Now, we here, the three of us, each of us needs to do a soldier's job. We need to find Juk Thri. This order comes from Lord Runkarn himself. Chik, whatever misgivings you may have had about this, and believe me, it is understandable..."

"Ha!" Hak let out a cackle. Janson looked at the 2nd Regiment Captain, who half-smiled and looked away.

"It is understandable, Chik," Janson repeated. "However, that time has now passed. Now we must carry out our orders. We must find Juk Thri and bring him to Lord Runkarn's justice. Is that understood?" Chik stayed silent, but nodded in agreement.

"What is it that Lord Runkarn bids us to do?" asked Hak.

"We are to ride to Dawngate, to search along the way, and then to speak to Lord William Wilton. If that produces no results, we are to ride on down the Mountains of Dawn to the Mountain of Serenity. There we shall meet up with Lord Ruperk."

"Dawngate?" said Chik, breaking his silence. "Why would Juk go there? He knows no one there. I'm not sure he has even been there in the last five years."

"Well, we've searched everywhere we thought he might be, so maybe we should look in the places he mightn't," Janson replied.

"Well, if he is there or anywhere along the way, we'll find him, and the Spinal Grip will be waiting for him," Hak Krok said with a wide smile all over his face.

"If we find him, he'll face Lord Runkarn's justice," demanded Janson. "They'll be no rough justice for Juk Thri. He may be on the wrong side now, but he was once, maybe still is, the best fighting man I ever saw."

"Well, he's never fought the 2nd regiment now, has he?" Hak said, his smile turning into a laugh.

"You are dismissed, both of you. We'll ride at First Sun tomorrow. Make your men ready to leave, then."

The two Captains left, and Janson remained seated at his desk. He felt a single teardrop fall from his eye. He wiped it away, but it was followed by another and then a few more. Janson Brok cleared the tears from his eyes and sighed to himself.

LORD RUPERK STONEFISH

"Now, tell Lord Runkarn what you told the guards; what you have told me." Ruperk Stonefish was standing behind the man he was talking to, nudging him ever so slightly, barely perceptibly, and pushing him forward towards the desk that Lord Runkarn was sitting behind.

"All of it? Again?" the man uttered.

"Yes. From the start. Tell Lord Runkarn everything." Ruperk gave him another nudge. This one was more obvious.

"Relax, friend," Lord Runkarn said from behind his desk. "Lord Ruperk here tells me your name is Nabak. And you're from Chinsap, is that so?"

"Yes, my lord. Nabak Toll," the man answered. Ruperk walked past him and stood behind Lord Runkarn.

"From Chinsap, yes. Born and bred, my lord," Nabak continued.

"Well, Nabak, you are amongst friends here," Lord Runkarn said. "I need to hear your account of what you saw that night. But, tell me, before you begin, do you know Juk Thri well? Is he, or rather, was he a friend of yours?"

"I know him, my lord. Juk is ten or so years older than me. Chinsap is not such a big place. My brother knew him better back when they were younger. Friends, no. But I know him and knew his family."

Lord Runkarn nodded, before adding, "Please, tell me of that night."

"My lord." Nabak stood up straight in the manner of a soldier giving a report. "It was a normal night, like any other, nothing happening. I was on gate duty, as I say, as normal. Well, there ain't been no trouble for years up there, so it's not really needed, you know. It keeps out the drunks and strangers, mostly."

"I see." Lord Runkarn nodded again.

"Well, as I'm the youngest of my shift, I gets to do the rounders."

"Rounders?" Ruperk said from behind his lord, verbally pushing Nabak now to elicit more information.

"Ah well, you see," Nabak said," every hour or so, one of the gate guards has to do the rounders. Walk round the outside and come back in through the middle. Rounders we call it."

"What time was this?" Lord Runkarn asked, barely above a whisper.

"A few hours before Sun up, my lord. Well, as I was doing the rounders that night, I saw something. Something that, well, didn't look normal. Caught my eye, like. I was at the north end of the city, where the fence is all broken down. Anyone can come in from the north, you know. But as there's mountains and well, not much else really, we don't get no bother from there. Anyway, as I was saying, I saw something. Now, what I saw, I can't be sure, but it caught my eye, if you catch my meaning?"

"I do," Lord Runkarn replied.

"I saw something, someone or maybe more than one, come through into the city. From the north. Well, I thought I did. Bloody big man if he was one, or maybe two or three. So, I walks over there, and has a look. 'Oi!' I shouts, 'Who's there?' Well, no one answers and when I gets there I can't see anyone, anything."

"You saw nobody? Did you see any footprints or marks of any sort?" Lord Runkarn asked.

"No marks, my lord. All rocks and stones there, so no prints or nothing. So I makes my way back. Back to the main gate. On the way, I hears this noise, like a scream only not a scream. Quiet like, but not normal. It could've been a bird or animal, but it didn't sound normal. Well, this scream, this noise came from the lane where Juk Thri lives, over on the left side of the city."

"What kind of noise, Nabak?" Ruperk asked, prompting the young man.

"Well, a scream. Yes, a scream it was, only muffled, it was. Like a man covering a mouth or a rag over a mouth, like. So, as I said, I hears it and goes over to the lane. It's dark, real dark at that time of the night. Tall trees there is all down one side. Very dark, so I gets my sword out and shouts again, 'Who's there?' I shout. Nothing. Well, I walks down the lane, right down the end. Well, that's when I sees it. I sees a man running. Running away, he was. Got scared of my sword, I reckon. He run back towards where I first see him. To the north, where the broken fence is."

"This man you saw, was it Juk?" asked Lord Runkarn, leaning forward.

"Juk Thri? Well, I can't be certain, my lord. But If I had to say, I'd say it was an army man. Tall he was, thin and quick on his feet."

"Was it Juk Thri?" Lord Runkarn repeated his question. This time louder.

Nabak looked at Ruperk, standing behind Lord Runkarn, before answering.

"Yes, my lord. If I had to say, I'd say it was him. I chased him as best I could, but he was too quick for me. He escaped to the north. Well, I walked back down the lane, didn't see anything else out of place. So I goes back to the gate."

"You didn't investigate Juk Thri's house?" Lord Runkarn asked.

"Well, no. Didn't need to. I didn't see nothing wrong there. I just returned to the gate. Didn't think nothing more of it. Well, not till a day or two after. When we heard the news, like. It was well known his wife was very friendly with an outsider. All on her own an' all. A trader who came around once a while. We reckon Juk done her in. He must've found out and done her in. And the kids. Couldn't believe it at first. But when the Moon takes a man, well. Can't really blame him. The kids, well, that's wrong. But his wife with another man? Enough to drive any man to it, I reckon."

"You swear this was Juk Thri. Did you try to arrest

him?" Lord Runkarn asked.

"We looked, my lord. But he had gone. Vanished. Then your men arrived and, well, we let them take over."

"But you can swear to the fact that it was Juk Thri who killed his wife, yes?" Ruperk interjected, extracting as much from Nabak as he could.

"Oh yes, my Lord Ruperk. Swear to it, yes. May the Moon take my eyes, Sir."

"So there we have it, my lord," Ruperk said to Lord Runkarn, as he moved out from behind the desk to stand beside Nabak. "If any proof were needed. Juk Thri committed this awful crime and we have our witness. He must be punished."

"I see," Lord Runkarn said. "Well, Nabak, I thank you for your account. My guards will see you to the barracks. There you may eat and drink before heading back to Chinsap."

"My lord," Nabak said as the two guards entered the room and escorted him out.

Ruperk looked at Lord Runkarn and smiled. "Well, Ruperk, it seems we have work to do," Lord Runkarn said, staring over Ruperk's head to the closed door.

CHIK SRIN

Chik had ridden for half a Moon with his men from the 1st, as well as the men from the 2nd. He rode up front with Lord Janson Brok and Hak Krok, the Captain of the 2nd Regiment. They had searched for Juk from Stoneguard, down past the Green Mountains and through the barren country until the Yellow Mountains came into view in the east. From there, they had explored every small village, town, forest and copse, all the way to Dawngate in the far east of Areekya. They had heard various rumours of unidentified men riding alone or drinking in taverns from strangers, strangers that had mostly told their tales after accepting coin or tankards of ale. Nothing that could be acted upon, and nothing that was likely true.

Towards the end of the day's ride, the large, high-walled city of Dawngate came into view. The glorious sight of the Mountains of Dawn as a backdrop to one of the oldest cities in Areekya at any other time would have been one to behold and relish. Today was not one of those times. The tall mountain peaks breached the snowy white clouds high in the eastern sky. Dawngate had become rich from mining those mountains. Many generations of mining families had made their fortunes mining the iron ore, copper and tin found deep within the Mountains of Dawn. The early blacksmiths of Dawngate were renowned for their mastery of these metals, and the weaponry of Dawngate had been much sought after. Much of this wealth and renown became diminished, even lost in recent years, mostly due to the rich deposits of precious metals in other parts of Areekya; The Spine region in particular. But the city still did a good trade with the Eastern Isles off the coast of Areekya. Eastport had been constructed when the demand for Dawngate metals waned on the mainland. The blacksmiths still maintained their pride in the weaponry they produced; a Dawngate sword was still a thing to be prized.

As the five hundred men of the 1st and two hundred of the 2nd approached the main gates to Dawngate, a delegation of six of Lord William Wilton's personal guards were there to meet them. The men from the regiments were led to the barracks of the city by three of the delegation. Lord Brok was asked to follow the remaining three through the city to the main tower. After feeding his horse, Chik made his way into the barracks, took off his boots and lay down on the bed. It had been a while since he had slept well and he felt the urge to sleep wash over him.

"Captain Chik! Captain Chik!" yelled a soldier from the 1st regiment as he shook Chik awake.

Chik opened his eyes and took a moment to get his bearings and remember where he was. "Yes, what is it?" Chik grunted.

"A message from the tower, Captain. A request from the Lord of the City. You are to follow the guard waiting outside. As quick as you can, he said."

Chik sat up and took a deep breath. He put on his boots, briefly washed his face and neck, and made his way outside.

"Captain Chik Srin?" the guard asked.

Chik nodded, and the guard gestured to follow him on foot. Chik followed him through the main city square where he could see the preparations for the Winter Solstice being made; the candles in the windows, and the fruits in the street. He briefly thought of Chinsap, but this brought only upsetting memories to him, so he quickly blotted these out and continued following the guard with his head down. After a short while, they had reached the inner gates of the city. They were let through and Chik was shown to the personal quarters of the Lord of the City, Lord William Wilton. Chik knew little about Lord Wilton. He had heard rumours and stories during his days with the Regiment. Lord Wilton was said to be a man who wore fancy attire and covered himself in sweet-smelling perfumes. There were more sordid stories of his sexual proclivities that Chik mostly ignored. What a person does in his own bed was not of much interest to Chik.

"Captain Chik Srin. Please sit down here, next to Lord Janson," said a curly, dark-haired man wearing a plush silver tunic from behind a desk as Chik entered the room.

"Allow me to introduce myself," the man continued. "I'm Lord William Wilton, Lord of Dawngate. I've heard a lot about you from the good Lord Brok here."

"Well met, my lord," Chik replied and smiled at Lord Brok as he sat down.

"Now, my good Captain," Lord William said. "Lord Janson here has been telling me of your problems. About your ex-Captain. Terrible business. Terrible indeed."

"It *is* a terrible business, my lord," Chik replied. He studied Lord William closely: hardly any blemishes on his entire face, fair, and wrinkle free. He had a warm smile and dark brown eyes that matched his hair.

"And Lord Brok feels that he may have headed here," Lord William continued. "I have had no reports of such a man in my city, alas. As I've told Lord Janson here."

"I see, my lord," Chik replied. Then, looking at Lord Brok, he said, "Pardon my directness, but why is it I am here, then?"

"Ah, the brashness of the younger man," Lord William said, smiling.

"There's news from Magdil, Juk." Lord Brok answered Chik's question. "A witness has come forward, a reliable witness. A member of the Chinsap Guard reports he saw Juk ride into Chinsap. He looked distressed and didn't answer his greeting, so he followed him."

"Who is this man? This guard?" Chik asked.

Lord Brok looked down at the parchment on his lap and read from it. "Nabak Toll, it says here. Do you know him?"

"Nabak? Yes, he was just a youngling when we left for the War. I saw him on guard duty just a couple of

Moons ago. He said nothing then. Why is he saying this now?"

"He was scared to come forward. He knew how respected Juk is, or was, and he thought, perhaps not unsoundly, that the 1st were there to cover his tracks," replied Lord Brok.

"Then who did he report this to? And when?" Chik asked, this time more firmly, somewhat annoyed by the implication in Lord Brok's words.

"To the 2nd Regiment. They reported this to Lord Ruperk and took the man with them to Magdil. He gave his account to Lord Ruperk himself."

Chik sat quietly for a minute, then two minutes, his head in his hands, his thoughts racing and spinning through his mind. He didn't trust the 2nd regiment, especially its Captain, and he was equally suspicious of Lord Ruperk's motives. But this news hadn't shocked him as much as he'd expected. Deep down, somewhere in his thoughts, there had been a creeping thought. Stalking, crawling its way to the surface of his mind. Juk *was* guilty of these things. He did murder his family. The Moon *had* taken him.

"We wanted to tell you this in private, Chik," Lord William said, breaking the silence. "Without, let's say, other parties present. Although the soldiers will no doubt hear of it soon, and that's the 2nd as well as your own men."

"I thank you, my lords." Chik remained seated, looking down, holding his head in his hands for a moment longer. Then standing up, he said, "Will my lords require anything else?"

"Rest up today and tonight, Chik," Lord Brok answered. "Your presence is requested at breakfast tomorrow, at the pleasure of Lord William and Lady Ursula."

Chik nodded. "With your leave, Lord William, Lord Brok," Chik said as he turned and left. He wandered back to the barracks in a daze. The darkest thoughts he had been denying for so long, were suddenly realised. The anger he felt towards the 2nd Regiment and Lord Ruperk was now focused on his one-time friend and Captain, Juk Thri. Chik's thoughts turned to Juk's slain family, and then his own family came into his mind, his wife and son, back in Chinsap. A solitary tear fell down his cheek. He wiped it away and regained his composure.

Chik made his way back through the main city square, ignoring the people as they prepared for the Midwinter celebrations. He walked back to the barracks, back to his bunk, and lay down once more. He thought of his fighting days, the early days in the War when he fought side by side with Juk. Chik enjoyed those days. He thought Juk did, too. Chik had always embraced the chaos; the darkness. He needed it back then. The enjoyment from the killing would make him a better person; his land free, his family safe. He had always acknowledged this darker-self. This admission had allowed him to reconcile his soldier's life and his family life. He kept them separate. He had to insulate one from the other; not allow the dark to invade the light. Now, consumed by the darkness, he saw the need to search for the light; to do the right thing. He turned his face, so no one could see, and more tears fell. Sad tears for Juk's deceased family and frustrated tears for his own. And then angry tears fell for Juk Thri, his ex-friend. His ex-Captain. It was then that he decided he would find Juk himself. He would find him and he would kill him.

Chik woke early the next morning. He had awoken in a dark mood, the words and actions of the previous night still weighing heavily on his mind. He was escorted to the main dining hall and found Lord William and Lady Ursula already seated at opposite ends of the elongated dining table. Lord Brok and Hak Krok were also seated across from each other in the centre of the table.

"Welcome, Captain," Lord William greeted Chik and gestured for him to sit.

Chik sat down at the place already made for him, with a bowl of hot, steaming soup and a silver spoon placed there. He was sitting next to Hak, and this made his foul mood even darker. Chik spooned the soup into his mouth without saying a word as polite morning small talk was made around the table.

"Captain Chik? What say you? What do you think about Juk Thri's whereabouts?"

The words had come from the end of the table to his right; Lady Ursula. Chik looked over and for a moment observed her without speaking. She had long blonde hair and the bluest eyes he had ever seen. She wore a blue shawl wrapped around her shoulders, and this made her eyes even more striking.

"Ha! Captain Chik's not speaking today. Cat got

your tongue, Captain?" The harsh sound of Hak's words brought Chik out of his observation.

"I think, my lady, that Juk has gone west," Chik said, looking into her blue eyes. "We've searched the east, and my best guess is that he has ridden back to the Wetlands." Chik took another spoonful of soup.

"I see, I see," Lady Ursula replied. "And why is it we don't leave him there? What trouble could he cause? What damage could he do in the Wetlands?"

"Same trouble he's already done," Hak replied before anyone else could answer. "Murderers like him shouldn't and won't be allowed to go here and there as they please. Lord Runkarn's justice will see to that."

"I see," Lady Ursula said in reply, but looking at Chik. He could feel her gaze upon him. "Yes, of course. I'm sure you will see to that, Captain Hak," she continued. "Of course, in Lord Masterton's days, there was no standing army to go raging around the country. We had local answers to our problems. And dare I say, peace. All this long before Lord Runkarn brought it to us."

"Well, alls the better now you have people like me to protect you. And the peace," Hak Krok said, staring at Lady Ursula. "No more need for local answers. Lord Runkarn has real men doing his business now."

"Indeed he does," Lady Ursula replied, smiling, adding, "and anyway, the good Lord Greenaway was here just last week. He didn't seem concerned regarding this trifling matter. Did he, my love?" Lady Ursula looked down at Lord William at the other end of the table.

"Lord Dennis was here?" asked Lord Janson, looking up at Lady Ursula.

"Ah, yes. Indeed he was. He is here on occasion, tax business and trade mainly," replied Lord William, before his wife could answer.

"And what did he say on the matter?" asked Lord Janson. Chik noticed a look of confusion come over Lord Brok's face.

"Only that Juk Thri was missing, and that he thought he would soon be found and brought to justice," Lord William answered. After briefly glancing at his wife, Chik noticed.

"This is of surprise, Lord William. Surprise you did not comment earlier." Chik could see Lord Brok staring at Lord William and felt uncomfortable as moments went by before Lord Wilton finally answered.

"My apologies, Lord Brok. It slipped my mind. And forgive me for saying so, but we have seldom cared too much in the east for affairs of the capital. It has been long since we were in the thoughts of Magdil, and so Magdil is rarely in ours."

Chik saw Hak focus his attention on Lord William during this exchange. His face turned to a scowl, but the Captain of the 2nd Regiment kept his silence.

"I see," said Lord Brok, breaking some of the tension.

Another long silence followed before Lady Ursula finally spoke again. "Soon, Sun be praised, the Winter

Solstice will be upon us."

"Always my favourite time of the year," Lord Janson added. "Just a few days now, and I do wish I was at home with my family."

"And will you share the festivities with us, Lord Brok?" Lady Ursula asked. "With the clear skies we've had recently, I believe it shall be a fine Sunrise. And you and your men are most welcome."

"Alas, my lady. We must leave before Midwinter. Tomorrow morning, we ride west on Lord Runkarn's business."

"Well, that is a shame. You will miss a treat indeed," Lord William said.

Lady Ursula added, "In my late father's day, the streets would be filled with lighted candles, all manner of colours and scents. Fruits and berries hanging from trees. It really was a wonderful sight back then. But then again, most things were better back then. Lord Masterton was still alive, his family were very close to mine, you know," she said directly to Chik, who stayed silent, ignoring the comment as Lady Ursula continued, "Yes, Before Runkarn brought his peace, many things were... how shall I put it? Peaceful."

Chik noticed Hak was staring at Lady Ursula with the scowl still on his face. Lord Brok continued to eat his breakfast in silence, as Lord William spoke up. "And now we have our peace again, thanks to Lord Runkarn." He then clapped his hands, and the serving girls and boys arrived to clear the table. Lady Ursula stood up and bid everyone a good morning, and left the dining room.

"You must please excuse my wife," Lord William said to the room. "She took the loss of the Mastertons very hard. Her family was very close, you know. And she speaks in poor taste this morning. She is not her true self today. Let's say it's a special time of the Moon for her, yes?"

Chik noticed Hak staring at Lord William with the same look he had when looking at Lady Ursula.

"Well, Lord William, we must be off in an hour or so," Lord Brok said. "Thank you for your hospitality."

"Pass on my regards to Lord Runkarn," Lord William replied. "Dawngate is here should he have need of us, should that he remember us, of course."

"That I will do, I definitely will do." With that, Lord Brok stood up and shook Lord William's hand, and made his way to the exit. Hak Krok nodded — with a forced smile, thought Chik — and followed. Chik sat for a moment longer, still lost in his own mind. Then he too stood up and thanked Lord William and left the room.

JUK THRI

Juk, Rivan, and Ashran, together with his men, had been riding through the Nikrid Desert for four days. In the early afternoon, the Sun began to creep down in the western sky, as it did this late in the year. This was a special time, a sacred time for many in Areekya; the twelfth Moon of the year brought with it the Winter Solstice — Midwinter.

The procession of men riding south east, as instructed by Rivan, could feel the weakening of the Sun's rays at this time of the year. Midwinter was drawing near, and Juk had dropped to the back of the group. He was thinking back to his Winter Solstice celebrations back home in the north east, in happier times, with his family. He was lost in this bitter-sweet memory when Rivan rode up beside him.

"Juk, we are close now," the mage said.

"Close? I can see nought but orange. If we're close, then this Deera are well hidden," Juk replied, squinting to see any change in the landscape up ahead. "You said we were to ride through the desert? I can see no end to the sand and dust for miles."

"Tomorrow is Midwinter. With the rising of the Sun, the New Year will be upon us. A special time for many." Rivan smiled as Juk looked across at him. "It will be a very special day for us all here to witness it.

Tomorrow, Juk. Wait till then, you'll see."

"Midwinter? I thought it was close," Juk replied. "A lot of fond memories for me and my family, feasting and dancing at the rise of the New Sun. Long ago they seem now, in time and place."

"The rebirth of the Sun was, and hopefully still is, a special time for the Deera. Us being here now is no accident, Juk. We will see something very special, come the Sunrise tomorrow. The power of the New Sun has properties that a man could scarcely believe: wondrous, mesmerising, unimaginable to most."

"I've seen many a new Sunrise on Midwinter's morning. What will be so special about this one?" Juk asked the mage, noticing the flushing red cheeks of Rivan that he had never seen before.

"This one will be unlike any other you have seen or are likely to see again, Juk." With that, the mage trotted off up ahead. Juk saw him speak to Ashran for a few moments, and Ashran ordered his men to stop riding for the day. Juk gently pulled on the reins of his horse and waited for a while. Ashran's men were busy lighting a fire. Juk also noticed the men arranging perimeter guard duties, and was impressed with the efficiency of their actions as he watched from atop his horse. After a while, he rode over to where Ashran had dismounted and was talking to three of his men. Juk climbed down from his tall, grey horse and attached the nosebag over its head, and gently stroked its neck while it quietly munched away at the grain.

"An early finish to the day, Ashran." Juk walked over to where Ashran was talking to his men.

"Aye. Rivan instructed us to stop here for the night and to prepare for the Midwinter Sunrise. He promised something special," Ashran replied.

Juk noticed a look of concern on the clan leader's face. "Did he say anything else? He wasn't very clear to me."

"Ha! You'll get a straight answer from a mage when you get the Sunrise at midnight," answered Ashran, letting out a laugh as he spoke. "I've learned to stop guessing the answers to his riddles. He has steered us right over the years. Most of the time."

"Well, he assured us we'll see something spectacular," Juk said. "Let's wait and see what the dawn brings."

"Indeed, my friend. In the meantime, let's keep warm by this fire the men are building. And maybe a small drop of that potato wine of yours." Ashran had a considerable smile on his face.

"A drink to bring in the New Sun, eh?" Juk pulled out his silver flask from his long, thick bearskin coat and offered it to Ashran.

"Yes, that warms the throat and more besides," Ashran said and coughed as he handed the flask back to Juk.

Juk took a small sip and replaced the cap and put it back into his coat. "Let's save the rest for the Sunrise, eh?" Juk smiled as he walked over to the fire and held his hands out to warm himself. As he was standing there, allowing himself to think back to Chinsap again and to the Midwinter celebrations, Rivan walked over and stood next to him.

"I've instructed Ashran to have the men ready an hour before First Sun. We'll all sleep early tonight. Tomorrow will be a wonderful day, Juk. A wonderful day." The mage stood for a while staring into the fire before walking off and talking to all the men in turn. Juk observed him as he walked.

Rivan had a languid, graceful gait. Almost floating over the dry, dusty sand, hardly leaving any footprints behind him. Juk caught his thoughts drifting again, back to the first time he met the mage. It was back in the Northern Hills, and he remembered the tranquil, soothing presence he felt then and felt almost every time he was near. He hadn't paid it that much attention until this moment. Maybe it was the hazy setting Sun on the far western horizon, or the potato wine having its effect. But he felt intoxicated and sleepy. Juk found himself a clean patch of sand near the fire and prepared a sleeping area for himself. He laid down and almost immediately he felt as if sleep was upon him. He looked up at the last remnants of the late-afternoon light as the sky prepared itself for the impending re-birth of the Sun.

The twilight of the late-afternoon sky looked beautiful to Juk. He gazed up in awe at the orange and blue tinge, the first of the evening stars glistening and blinking in the western sky. He had seen many Midwinter Eve Sunsets, but none had been as soft and tranquil as this one. He found his waking mind drifting into the advancing calm of sleep, and as it did so, waking dreams filled his mind; colours swirled and danced around in front of him and behind his eyes. He felt himself filled with a restful bliss. It washed over him completely and he felt himself drifting into it, drifting away into ecstasy, into sleep.

Juk was awoken by a soft shaking. He sat up immediately and looked ahead. It was still dark; the first rays of the New Sun were yet to be seen in the eastern sky. The morning stars were still flickering in the pre-dawn sky above. He gathered his things and made his way to his horse. He saw Rivan already atop his horse, waiting with Ashran.

"Juk. Are you rested?" Rivan asked, smiling.

"Yes. Yes, I am. Very much so. I haven't slept like that since I don't know when."

"Good, good. Now, come now. Mount your horse and ride with us, just a short while."

Juk climbed on his tall horse and rode slowly beside Ashran and the mage at the head of the group. All Ashran's men were following closely behind.

"The Midwinter Sun will rise soon, very soon," the mage said. "We need to be in exactly the right place when that occurs."

"And what shall we see?" Juk asked.

"That is something you will have to see for yourselves," the mage replied.

They had been riding for only ten minutes when Rivan signalled to stop. "Now we wait for the Sun," the mage said softly.

Ashran shouted to his men to halt. And everyone

sat atop their horses, not a word spoken, waiting for the Sun to rise in the eastern sky. In a moment or two, there was a flicker of red light in the distance. Then another in the same place on the horizon. These flickers became more numerous and changed colours; orange and then blue, green, pink and back to red again. Then the flickering lights transmogrified into an explosion of colour. Bright, fluorescent, swirling waves of light rising and falling in the sky. Juk looked on in amazement, silent, as the sky continued to transform in front of his eyes. Then the constellation of colours converged and the sight that was created was unlike anything else Juk had ever seen before. Incandescent, the lights radiated and twirled, circling each other and intertwining until they contracted into one small flickering red light that hovered right above Juk and the rest of the men. And then, in one eruption of brilliant colour, the small flickering light exploded, and the sky seemed to tear apart. Juk had to turn his eyes away from the light. The luminosity was so overwhelming. Finally, after shielding his eyes for a few moments, the lights and colours contracted again, allowing Juk to look once more in amazement. There, standing in front of him, where the orange, dusty desert once was, stood a vast horde, thousands strong, an army of people standing in front of a forest so green it shone with magnificence in the early morning twilight.

LADY URSULA WILTON

Lady Ursula, the Lady of Dawngate, stared at the letter that had arrived the night before. She read it twice before delicately placing it back in the envelope it had arrived in. She then concealed it inside of her gown and called for her maid. Almost instantaneously, a short, fair-haired girl of teenage years appeared at the door of Lady Ursula's private chambers.

"M'lady?" the petite maid asked.

"Prepare my riding attire and send word to the stable-master. I shall ride out this morning."

"Yes, M'lady. Will you be riding alone this morning?"

"I will. Tell the Master of the Guards to allow only two to follow me. And I do not want to see them. Make that understood, girl."

"Yes, M'lady. Straight away, M'lady."

Within the hour, Ursula was at the stables. She mounted her elegant black mare and rode towards the main gates of Dawngate. The guards on duty blew on their trumpets as she trotted out, with two guards of the city a safe distance behind her. She pulled on her reins and veered off to the left, then kicked her heels into the horse's side as the mare and its rider set off at a fair pace back towards the Mountains of Dawn. It was a glorious sight; the late-morning Sun glistening off the mountains, a clear blue sky above, and despite the biting wind Ursula felt on her face, she felt exhilarated as she pushed her horse as fast as she could towards the huge mountain range that stretched out before her. She had been riding for almost half an hour when she stopped near a stream next to a large wooded area in the foothills of the mountains. As she dismounted her beautiful riding companion, it let out a loud snort, and Ursula patted her on the nose.

"There's a good girl. You enjoyed that, I think." She reached into a pocket in the saddle and pulled out a small iron box and a large carrot. She fed the carrot to the excited mare and put the small box in her trouser pocket.

Ursula looked back in the direction from which they had ridden but saw no sign of her guards, and smiled. She walked into the small forest for a few hundred yards and pulled out the envelope from her riding trousers and took out the letter once more. After reading the letter in full one final time, she placed it on the floor. She found a few dried twigs and leaves and covered the paper with them. Then she pulled out the small iron box from her pocket and opened it. Inside the box were neatly placed a flint, a small fire striker and some tinder wood. She removed the objects and, after checking over her shoulder for any sign of her guards, she struck the flint against the steel and sparks flew out onto the tinder wood and parchment in front of her. She blew two or three times on the single embryonic glowing orange flame until it spread into a small fire. Within a minute, the flames had caught and she could see the white parchment curl up and begin to char, its colour changing to black and then exploding into a blaze of red flame.

"M'lady?"

Ursula heard a man call out from at least fifty yards away. She knew she had time yet. Patiently, she watched as the letter shrivelled and metamorphosed into grey ashes, the small, black spirals of smoke reaching up to the forest canopy in front of her eyes. Then she stamped out the fire. She made her way back to her waiting, obedient mare and saw the two guards sitting atop their tall horses.

"I thought I said I did not want to see you," Ursula said without looking at either of the guards. "Both of you wait here until you can no longer see me. Then, and only then, may you follow me back to Dawngate. Is that understood?"

"M'lady," the two guards said in unison.

With that, she climbed back onto her horse, patted her on the head as the mare let out an excited sigh, and rode off at pace. Before long the glorious, high-walled sight of her home city appeared on the horizon. As she rode through the gates, the guards once more let their trumpets ring out. Ursula passed through without comment and was met at the stables by her ladies-in-waiting. The stable boy took the horse and Ursula made her way back to her private quarters, pursued by the four young ladies in her service. Once she was out of her riding attire and into a blue silk dress, she made her way to her husband's quarters. Without knocking, she walked in and saw William Wilton sitting at his desk, reading a document.

"Husband," she said and greeted William with a smile on her face.

"My dear. I trust you had a pleasant ride," William replied, smiling, although Ursula thought it looked as fake as her own.

"My ride was fine," she replied. "More importantly, how did you handle Lord Brok this morning after breakfast?"

"Lord Brok was not a problem. It would not have been so uncomfortable for me if you had not have mentioned Lord Dennis's visit, my dear," he replied, holding his smile.

"Ha!" she spat back. "I enjoy watching you flounder, husband. I thought it might warm the conversation up somewhat."

"I'm sure Magdil would have found out anyway, though I would have preferred not to have to explain it. It was an innocent enough visit. I had nothing to hide." William's smile had disappeared.

"If it was such an innocent visit, then why not mention it?"

"An honest slip of the mind. One makes these more and more these days. It must be age, my dear, yes?"

"Well, I hope you made a better job of convincing them of that than you just have with me, my dear." Ursula's smile grew wider as she finished her sentence. "If you think your *hunting trip* was outside my realm of awareness, then you underestimate the reach of my little lovelies."

"My dear?"

"As long as you remember who holds the reins of power in this city. It is my family's money that kept your father in his position, and keeps you in yours, *my dear*."

"I am forever grateful to your family, Ursula. You know that. As I am to you." William's smile returned.

"To me?" she replied. "If you showed me how grateful you are in the bedroom, as a husband should do, then that would be a start. Those days are gone, I know. Long gone. But, I still remember the days before we were married. How I looked upon your fair face from afar. We all did, all the young girls of the city. And when my father told me I was to be wed to William Wilton, to me it seemed like my fairy tale had come true."

Ursula was not smiling anymore. She looked at her husband, as he couldn't look up from his desk. His eyes remained fixed on the document. He remained silent. Not a word came from his mouth for a minute or two. They both maintained the silence until at last he spoke.

"My dear. Is there anything I can do for you?" He continued to look down at his desk as he spoke.

"That time has long past. But I enjoy your embarrassment; I revel in it. As some tiny piece of atonement. For what *you* did to *my* fairy tale. At least you managed to produce a child. The one good thing that has come from our union. That, and the city of Dawngate for my family to take. Our son will be Lord of the City one day. Lord Brackworth, we shall name him. How does that sound, *my dear*?"

"As you wish," replied William, looking up at last. "My name is of little concern to me. My father and mother are long gone. If my name dies with me, then so be it. I shall not mourn its passing, at least."

"It *will* die with you, *my dear.* You just be careful *when* it dies. That should be of some concern to you." Ursula smiled one last time as she turned and left the room.

She walked down the hall into her sleeping son's room, Nathan. He was seven years old and had the blond hair of his mother. Still too young to rule, still too young for the city to accept, even with her ruling in his place until he came of age. She would have to wait; wait, and watch. Plan her movements carefully. With most of the city's guard in her pay, she did not concern herself with her own well-being. She knew she was safe from harm. Too many people depended on her. Betrayal would not be an option. It was her family's money that gave her Dawngate, and together with the news she had burned in the forest, the city would be kept in her control for some time yet.

JUK THRI

Standing in front of Juk, Ashran, and the men was a sight that was difficult to believe. From out of nothing, a vast horde of men, women, horses and an entire community of people and dwellings had appeared out of nowhere. The orange, dusty sand of the Nikrid Desert was gone, and had been replaced by a wide expanse of lush, vivid green fields, myriad vegetation and tall trees. There was an aroma in the air, too. A sweet smell of jasmine mingled with something else, something less fragrant Juk couldn't quite detect. Standing at the front of this changed vista was a wall of people.

Rivan rode from behind Juk to the fore and spoke. "Good blessings on this Midwinter Sunrise, friends."

The vast throng of people standing in front of him parted and a small, elderly man wearing a green tunic which almost matched the colour of the trees, and trimmed with shining silver cuffs, walked forward. He was almost bent over double, less than five feet in height, with whispers of grey hair at the side of his head and a friendly looking, wrinkled face.

"Well met. This morning has long been awaited. Awaited and feared," the old man said, looking at the mage and then past him at Juk, Ashran and the men behind. "Tell me, *friends*, is fear an appropriate emotion for this meeting?"

Juk looked on, still in amazement at what had just happened. Then a familiar, melodic voice replied to the old man's question.

"You have nought to fear from us, my friend," Rivan answered the old man. "We have travelled to meet you and ask for your guidance. Counsel on that which you escaped and which now faces us, the people you see here before you." Rivan gestured to the men behind him.

"I see you are well trained in the art of persuasion, *my friend*," the old man replied. "A voice melodic and pleasurable to the ears. I haven't heard this device used for many, many years. And it is not needed here."

"Forgive me. My meaning is to be friendly, nothing more," the mage replied. "My name is Rivan. I'm from Areekya, as you were before. These are my travelling companions, Juk Thri and Ashran, of the Clan Grash. The men are from Ashran's tribe." Juk noticed the change in Rivan's voice. It wasn't totally discernable, but it didn't sound as musical or as pleasant as before.

"Well, Rivan from Areekya, the fact you are here means you know who we are. Your voice gives away much of your intention, maybe more than you wish to. Let me return the courtesy. My name is Tunrah. This is my tribe, the Deera, as you know." The old man turned his head towards the throng of people behind him, who remained completely silent, with expressionless faces. "Areekya? Is that what it is named now?" Tunrah continued. "We left that land a long time ago. We have never felt any desire to return nor seek out its fate. The counsel you seek falls on ears that do not wish to hear it."

"We come asking for help to save lives. Many lives have been lost and many more will continue to be lost," Juk found himself speaking. He hadn't planned it. He felt surprised to hear these words come out of his mouth.

"And so will it forever be," Tunrah replied, looking at Juk and holding his gaze for a moment too long, which made Juk feel uncomfortable.

To his continued surprise, Juk added, "I see and feel a power here I have never experienced. Is this Magick? If this is it, then the stories and legends from the past have come to life."

"Magick? There is much Magick in this world, young man. There was much more many years ago. To have forgotten this is no bad fate, for you and your people," Tunrah answered. "Magick is dangerous when misused, and it *is always* misused."

"And here we get to it," Rivan interjected. "We are here because it has been and is being misused, as you have it correct. This is why we need your help."

"The land is interdependent," Tunrah replied. "The Sun, the Moon and the Stars are intertwined. This is true for humans and animals, land, trees, soil, mountains. When this is understood, that we are part of the whole cosmos; the Magicks are part of the whole cosmos, that we are all part of this interdependence. Then we shall know peace. This was never understood before, as I'm sure it is not now. Why encourage one course of action, which may aid one chain of events or another when this fundamental truth is not understood?"

Juk kept his eyes on the old man the whole time. He noticed the silver bands he wore on each wrist. They were covered with intricate designs he had never seen before; intertwined lines with no beginning or end. The same elaborate patterns were replicated on the cuffs of the old man's tunic. The old man showed no emotion in his speech, but his eyes contradicted this indifferent exterior. Juk thought he saw some sadness there and spoke up. "There are those who would learn. Or try to learn to understand."

"Who are these you speak of? You, young man?" Tunrah concentrated his gaze on Juk as he spoke.

"For one, yes. There are more I'm sure, given the chance. Given the chance to end the War, misery, to bring about the end of one man ruling over many," Juk replied, holding the older man's gaze.

"And you would have many rulers in place of one?" The old man smiled as he spoke.

"I would have peace. I would have enough food and shelter without the need to fight or steal from one another," Juk replied, mirroring the old man's smile.

"And how about your mage here? Is this what he desires?" Tunrah directed his attention to Rivan.

"Peace, yes," Rivan replied. "We have come here for your help to bring this about."

"And the understanding. Is this your wish also?" Tunrah asked. "You have beguiling speech. No doubt you have Sun Magick and Moon Magick, too. All mages did many years ago. Have you disclosed all to your friends, I wonder?" Tunrah's smile and gaze now switched to one which was not so friendly, thought Juk.

"I have as much as I can without misunderstanding," the mage answered.

"Ah! You are not one to confuse others, then. That is good. And you have told of the third Magick? The Secret Magick, the Magick that controls, beguiles and destroys?"

"This Magick was lost, known only to a few, too dangerous to study," answered Rivan.

Juk observed this interaction between the two: the smaller, older man spoke with an authority that had Rivan sounding more guarded than usual, his voice less harmonious, less definite.

At this moment, a tall, younger woman stepped through the crowd behind Tunrah. She was dressed the same as the old man, and wearing the beautiful wrist bands with the same complicated designs. She also wore a green headband, lifting her long black hair away from her oval-shaped face.

"Come, Father. That's enough for now. Invite the guests to the feast. They have travelled far and not without some knowledge of us. I feel they pose no immediate danger. We can continue to talk while we eat." The younger woman took Tunrah by the hand and squeezed tightly.

"Ah yes, the Midwinter feast. Welcome all. There is enough food and drink for you and your men. You will be shown the way. Come join and refresh your horses and yourselves," Tunrah said and was led away by his daughter.

After the men were shown where to stable their horses, they were led to three large canvas dwellings. These were used for the men to rest awhile, and cool, clean water was supplied to wash. Before long, two men came to the dwellings and requested all to attend the Midwinter feast. Juk felt fresh after washing and resting, and was looking forward to some food, as well as finding out more about their mysterious hosts.

Juk was seated with Ashran on one side of him and Tunrah on the other. Rivan was on the opposite side of the table, sitting next to Tunrah's daughter. Juk observed as she sat down and offered the various dishes to her guest. She had large, dark eyes which matched her hair, and a flawless complexion, which almost glowed in the early Midwinter morning's Sun.

Tunrah instructed Juk and Ashran to help themselves to the many dishes laid out on the table. Juk filled his plate with the various fruits and vegetables.

"I see a glorious array of fresh vegetables and many fine fruits, Tunrah," Ashran commented. "But a man cannot live on grass and berries alone. Is the meat coming soon?"

"We Deera eat no animal flesh, my friend. We can find nourishment enough without enduring any suffering on the other inhabitants of these lands," Tunrah said as he bit into a ripe apple.

Ashran stared at Juk for a moment and smiled.

"Well then, grass and berries it is." Juk smiled at his friend as Ashran filled his plate.

"So, how are the berries? How is the grass?" Tunrah asked after a short while.

"Good enough for this Wetlander. I can't remember when I had a meal so refreshing," Ashran said through a mouthful of vegetables.

"Ah. Then all is well," replied the old man, smiling.

During the meal, Juk frequently looked across the table at Tunrah's daughter sitting across from him. Her green clothing reflected the early morning light. She was deep in conversation with Rivan most of the time he looked over. He felt himself drawn to the woman. He felt attracted to her in a way he had not expected, in a way that wasn't just physical. She seemed to have a presence, a quality that he couldn't quite define. She caught him staring and flashed a smile back at him. Juk looked away and continued eating.

"So, Juk, is it?" Tunrah asked.

"It is. And I wish to thank you for this. This feast, this welcome. We, I, did not know what to expect," Juk replied.

"It is Midwinter, and all are welcome during the Midwinter feast. The return of the Sun is that which should be feasted."

"Yes, of course. We held, hold, celebrations where I come from at Midwinter and Midsummer. Though Midwinter is the one we look forward to more," Juk said, still munching on the delicious food in front of him.

"What is of concern to me, however, is how you found us. We have hidden away for many years, undisturbed, unhindered in our simple lives." Tunrah spoke in a slightly hushed tone. "That itself fills me with unease."

"We mean you no ill will, Tunrah. Rivan said you may be able to help." Juk looked at the old man and could see the concern on his face.

"Ah, the mage. Tell me, what do you know of this mage? Is he well known to you? Is he of honour?"

"Rivan? Well, he has helped me," answered Juk. "He helped me when I needed help. He has done right by me, and Ashran and his clan, it seems. I have no reason to doubt his word."

"And what word is that, I wonder? That he will help you. That he will see your wrongs righted. Does that sound right?" The old man had stopped eating a while ago and was smiling again, softly.

"Well, yes, but is that wrong? To offer a man help when he is down. To help him gain revenge on those who have wronged him. That sounds like honour to me."

"I have known many mages in my life, Juk," Tunrah replied. "None have always been honest, but some have less dishonesty in their words and actions than others. Their true motives are always enigmatic and opaque."

"I know little of this. I didn't even know mages

still lived until I met him," Juk said, draining his cup of the effervescent, fruity liquid it contained. "They had been confined to bedtime stories and fairy tales. No one believed they existed now, or indeed ever.

"They were many, and that there are now fewer, as you say, means there is some right in the world yet," Tunrah replied, taking a sip from his cup.

"He helped me when I was at my lowest. You were talking about Magick this morning." Juk looked at the smaller, older man next to him.

"I was," Tunrah said.

"Well, I know nothing about that either. But if it was Magick he used, then it was well used," Juk added.

"I tell you this, Juk. He is not to be trusted. His voice already has some hold over you, whether you know it or not." Tunrah looked over at Rivan and his daughter engaged in conversation across the table. "When we are finished here, please come to my dwelling. And come alone."

Juk looked at Tunrah for a moment. He then looked over at Rivan and saw the mage was looking directly back at him. "Alone you say?"

"Yes, it is time for answers. And maybe some questions."

SOORAN

The Midwinter Sun was climbing slowly in the eastern sky. The small droplets of dew dripping from the leaves of the forest trees were making the leafy woodland moist underfoot. Sooran was sitting outside her father's house, if it could be called such. The dwellings of the Deera were almost part of the forest itself. They merged in with the trees so much that they appeared to be large, dense branches stretching out into the woodlands, but they looked independent enough to be recognised as a home. A very comfortable-looking home at that. Sooran was waiting for Juk Thri. As she sat waiting on a tree stump, she observed the golden rays of the sun reflecting down on the trees. She smiled as she felt its modest warmth on her face and was pulled out of her mini trance-like state by footsteps coming towards her.

"Good Morning, Juk Thri. We have been expecting you. Are you alone?"

"Good morning. I'm afraid I do not know your name, but, yes, I am alone," Juk Thri replied, smiling.

"My name is Sooran. I am Tunrah's daughter. I was bid to take you inside. My father is waiting."

Sooran pulled back a green veil made of vine and gestured for Juk to follow her inside. The dwelling comprised one large circular living area, a lot bigger than it appeared from the outside.

"Ah, welcome Juk. Welcome," Tunrah greeted Juk, smiling as he sat in a large wooden chair at the back of the room.

"Thank you for your invitation, Tunrah. I am still in awe of this, of all this, the forest, your home, you."

"Ha! Well, awe is not such a terrible reaction. There are a lot worse that could have been expected." Tunrah remained seated and motioned for Juk to sit in the empty chair across from him. "I take it you have met my daughter, Sooran?"

"I have," Juk replied.

"And you are alone?"

"I am."

"He was not accompanied by anyone, nor was he followed, Father," Sooran confirmed. "I would have seen them if that were so." Sooran looked at her father and smiled. She walked towards Juk and Tunrah, and sat next to her father, opposite Juk.

"So, Juk Thri. I think it is time to talk. To talk about many things of which you may not be aware. Things I would rather say with your friend the mage not around to hear," Tunrah said.

"Rivan?" answered Juk. "This is the second time you have spoken of him in such a way. Why is it you do not trust him?"

"I could ask of you," said Sooran, interjecting, "why is it you trust him so?"

"He has done me no harm. In fact, he has helped me. I told your father so this morning, during the feast." Juk turned his attention to Sooran as he spoke. She returned his gaze, and held it until Juk looked away, looking back at Tunrah. "What is it you dislike so much in him?"

"It is not so much him, but his kind," Tunrah replied.

"His kind, mages like him, are the reason we left our home so long ago," Added Sooran. "They are seldom truthful, never to be trusted, and always to be questioned. What has he told you of the Magicks? Very little, I would say."

"Magick is something from a child's storybook. At least it was until I met him. He has some power, he claims," replied Juk.

"He has some power. This is in no doubt," Sooran said, standing up and walking behind Juk as she spoke. "It's what power he has and how he intends to use it that interests us." She walked past Juk and picked up a knife from a table near the wall.

"Have you seen this before?" She held out a silver-bladed knife and handed it to Juk.

"I have not," Juk said as he looked at the knife.

"Can you see the runes on it, the words scratched onto the blade?" Sooran continued.

"I see them, but I do not understand them, or you. What is it you are asking of me, and what is it you're not telling me?" Juk looked at Sooran and then at Tunrah.

"Well, Juk," Tunrah said, "this is Moon Magick. The runes give it power. Terrible power. Power to destruct. To create chaos. This Magick, in the hands of a learned practitioner, can cause terrible damage."

"And what has that to do with me? Or Rivan?" asked Juk.

"There are three Magicks in this world: Sun Magick, the healing Magick, the Magick I believe you said the mage used to help you."

"Well, Rivan helped me. If it was Magick or not, I don't know, but he has some power in healing."

"Yes, Sun Magick," Tunrah said. "It's more benevolent than the other two. It can be used to great effect. Indeed it was, for a time, the only Magick. There were people born who naturally felt this Magick flow through the rays of the Sun; Naturals we called them. It gave them the power to heal. They learned to wield it, to control, and teach this process. It gave benefit to all. This was the Magick that you felt, I believe."

"Then what's the harm?" Juk asked.

"There is also Moon Magick. This is the inevitable counterbalance; the duality. The Light and the Dark. Moon Magick is very ancient Magick, too. Much more aggressive, more violent. You have just seen the Lunar Runes on the silver knife my daughter showed you."

Sooran looked at Juk as her father explained all this, and noticed the lack of any expression on his face. She held up the knife once more. "This," she explained, "is used not for healing, not for peaceful means. This is the device of the mage."

"Rivan?" answered Juk.

"Maybe not your mage," replied Sooran. "But before mages, writing was not allowed by those who practised, it was forbidden. Those that had learned from the Naturals developed this; Mages, they called themselves. They created the Lunar Runes, these!" She held up the knife so Juk could see them on the blade. "This led to the third Magick, the hidden Dark Magick. This Magick was not aligned with the other two. It created chaos. This Dark Magick has no counterbalance. This is why it is so volatile, so dangerous. It is the reason we had to abandon our home. What you call Areekya." Sooran felt her face flush. It was an emotive subject for her, and she always struggled to control herself when speaking of it.

"Come now, Sooran," her father said. "Come and sit down. Let me explain to Juk here. I fear we have him a little confused."

Sooran walked back to her seat and sat down, feeling the eyes of Juk following her.

"You see, Juk, what my daughter is trying to tell you is that the mages have brought nothing but anguish and despair to us. We lived and farmed in our home for many, many years, in peace and tranquillity. We had many Naturals; those who had the gift. We used this Sun Magick to heal and help our land grow and prosper. We used the Moon Magick rarely, only when we had to, to defend ourselves from those outsiders who would wish to do harm. The two Magicks are two heads of the same creature. They balance with each other. It was the natural way of things."

"And what does this have to do with Rivan?" Juk asked.

"Well, maybe it has nothing to do with Rivan, but it has everything to do with mages. There were some of our clan who wrote down the Magicks, put it in books, so it could be studied, enhanced, evolved, they said. They did this in secret, telling no one but the small cabal who had decided this was the way forward."

"And why is the written word so harmful? This sounds like wise counsel to me," Juk replied.

"Ah, well, you see, Juk," Tunrah continued, "we had always agreed that the learning would be passed on orally, in full, from master to apprentice. Until the apprentice was fully learned in it. To ensure that there would always be one with the full knowledge to pass on, to ensure it would not be corrupted, or enhanced and evolved, as they would have it. It was to protect against this corruption that the spoken word was favoured, was insisted upon; to safeguard against the dangers of the Magicks. The written word can be, and is so often, misinterpreted. Like the roots of a tree twisting itself into the ground, reaching out deeper and deeper into the darkness. The written word *was* twisted so, to suit the readers' own desires, thoughts, motives, paths.

"So, the old ways were all but abandoned by most. The cabal grew larger. Mages they named themselves; protectors of the Magicks. They became the guardians of the mysteries, holders of the secrets. They convinced some it was the right path, the way to conserve the sacred, to protect the secrets for future generations. Books and books they wrote, some to be read, but others, many others for the initiated only. These were the books the mages hid the secrets in, keeping them concealed, and they developed a Secret Magick, the third Magick that has the power to corrupt, destroy and bring about total ruination. This they kept for themselves, hidden away, known to very few, which became even fewer; an exclusive group of dark mages."

"What is this Secret Magick? What is it used for?" Juk asked.

Sooran stood up again and replied, "Not for peace. To study it at all risks the learner in ways that are dark. It twists and corrupts the seeker. We saw this Dark Magick used to erect an unseen flaming wall around one of our villages. It destroyed anything or anyone that touched it, and many who dwelt within. They were burned to ashes. This was the Dark Magick wielded by the mages. Used for control and destruction. This was long, long ago." Sooran walked over to her father and continued. "Many years passed. During this time, they used this Hidden Magick, the diabolical amalgamation and corruption of the Sun and Moon Magick, to push us away. We had always seen ourselves as the guardians of Magick. We did not create it, although we had many Naturals in our clan. But the mages used their corruption to deceive them. The power of the Naturals, when turned to this abomination, was even more potent. Before long, we found we had been usurped. We fled. It was that, or be utterly annihilated. This is what mages did to us, what they do. So when one arrives, you can understand our deep concern and mistrust."

"You talk of this," interjected Juk, "of happening many, many years ago, yet you are still young. How can you speak of this with such knowledge?"

"Sun Magick has healing properties. As you know, it can, and does, prolong life, too," replied Sooran. "If used correctly, or I should say, in the correct way. We have our stories, too. Passed down from generation to generation."

"And you think Rivan is of danger to you? How? How could he be dangerous to ones such as you that can do the things I've seen with my own eyes, yet scarcely believe? You appear from nowhere, and I assume you could disappear just as quickly. Does he have this Dark Magick you are talking about?"

Sooran sat down and looked at her father.

"The fact he knew how to find us reveals much, Juk," Tunrah said, turning from his daughter to look at Juk. "It concerns me greatly, and he gives away more than he wishes in his speech. Does he possess this Dark Magick? I don't know, but it is wise for us to distrust him. I wanted to talk to you, his travelling companion, to see what could be learned, if anything."

"And," replied Juk, "what have you learned?"

"This I will discuss with my daughter, I think. But there is in you great trust, I believe," Tunrah answered. "And before you leave us, could you tell us what it is you want? What you travelled all this way for?"

"Men," answered Juk. "Fighting men. The type of mage you talk about, I see none of in Rivan. However, there is another, in Areekya. And the things he has done, and continues to do, seem to align with the dark mages you speak of from the past. And it is men we need to defeat him, to defeat his army, to claim back our land. We do not have the know-how to disappear into an unseen, safe haven such as this. If we are to regain our lands, it's help we will need, Tunrah."

"Well, it is no small favour that you ask," Tunrah said. "And I do not know if it is something I can give. But Juk Thri, give me some time. The Midwinter Sunset is a few hours from now. We can talk again then. But please, keep this meeting between us three here."

"You have my word," Juk said and smiled.

Sooran stood up and looked at Juk. "Please follow me," she said and walked towards the door.

Juk followed and as he did so, Tunrah said, "And remember, not a word to the mage."

LADY LIVIAN

Livian stood by the side of her mother's grave. She laid the flowers she had plucked from her garden in Midscape earlier that morning down delicately; yellow tulips, her mother's favourite. As she did so, she looked around the peaceful place at the base of the Mountain of Serenity. The beauty brought her solace. The burial garden was full of striking, brightly coloured flowers: vivid yellows, reds, blues and purples of the blossoms, although the scent of the flowers also filled her senses with melancholy memories of her youth.

With the foothills of the Mountains of Dawn in the background, there was an aura of wonder and other-worldly beauty that possessed this garden. It had always brought her comfort to have such natural beauty in a place that also held such bitter-sweet memories. Her thoughts turned to the more precious memories she held of her mother. A kind woman, a good mother to her children and, from what she could make out, a good wife to her husband, her father, Lord Sydric Masterton. As much as she loved her mother, Livian was always a daddy's girl. Her father's favourite, something he would admit even in earshot of her two older brothers. She always thought it was because she had appeared last and, of course, because she was a girl. Livian idolised her father, too. Lord of Midscape, ruling with an even hand, fairly and as generous as the Lord of the City could be. Those were her memories of her father. The memories she thought she would have to cherish and no longer add to. That was until Madnan Veerak had astounded her with the news that he was still alive. News that she still could scarcely allow herself to believe. Tentatively, she permitted herself to accept it could be true. She had been overwhelmed with confusion, anger, excitement and fear. Fear that if she allowed herself to believe it were true, she would have to grieve once again.

She remembered the time, years ago, when she was told of her father's and brothers' murder. She remained silent, unable to scream in grief or anger. No tears were shed for days, either. Shock was the state that had hold of her for three days after the terrible news. Then the tears and anger came. Alone in Midscape, surrounded by advisors and handmaids scrambling to adapt to the new power that would now sweep into the capital. But that was nearly four years ago. She had grown strong in those years. She had to live with the loss of her dignity and power, but she grew strong with it. After suffering such a devastating loss, there was not much more that could crack her exterior. She had retreated inward, growing stronger, planning her future, biding her time, and waiting for the opportunity to present itself.

Livian lived estranged from the husband who was forced upon her by Runkarn. She carried out all the expected duties of the Lady of the City, but never consented to any of them inwardly. She presented the face of the Mastertons to the people, to maintain peace, peace that the Mastertons had always ensured before the War with Runkarn, but dutifully she carried out her responsibilities with the grace and refinement expected from her. All this while she was waiting for the opportunity. Livian had been planning for years. Planning for a chance to get back at all those who had wronged her and her family. Everyone who did her harm, intentionally or not, she would have her revenge on them all. But she had not expected the opportunity that arose to be this one that now presented itself. Still, she knew she had to remain cautious. She must not abandon her resolute preparedness. She would hold fast to her plans, and stay resolute and prudent.

She would bide her time, play along with Madnan's plan, one she was sure Runkarn was behind. But she would keep her confidence. Allow none but those she selected in on her secret, a very select few: the innermost circle of circles. First, she required proof. The words of Madnan Veerak would not suffice. No words of any of her enemies would satisfy her. She needed to see her father. To believe it was real, to allow herself to accept the utter impossibility of the situation. Today would bring that proof. She had arranged to meet here. A spot of her choosing. A place of significance to her family. At least this she could control. They had agreed to her demand, and this told her they needed her. Livian knew this would not come for free, but it gave her an edge. She was needed by Magdil, and that was enough to keep her engaged. And this, she knew, she could use to her advantage. Livian had been standing at her mother's grave for some minutes, remembering, ruminating, planning, when a noise from behind her brought her back to the present.

"My Lady Livian. Are you alone, as agreed?" The

voice was that of Madnan Veerak. She turned and smiled at the tattooed-faced man entering through the main gate of the burial garden. Behind him, she could see a group of soldiers walking in formation, eight or ten of them. They were walking on either side of a white horse. She tried to see who was sitting atop the large horse, but her view was blocked by the banners being held aloft by the soldiers; the purple banners of Magdil.

"I am," Livian replied. "As agreed." She tried to remain calm, but she could feel her heartbeat racing and sweat formed on her palms and on the nape of her neck.

"Well, then. Also, as agreed, here is your father, Lord Sydric Masterton." Madnan gestured to the group of soldiers. And with that, the man was helped down from the horse, and took a few steps towards her.

Livian stared, eyes wide, as she tried to comprehend the scene that was playing out in front of her disbelieving eyes. She stood there, unable to move, tears running down her cheeks as time stopped. Her mind was struggling with the sheer absurdity of this reality. She took one step forward before quietly allowing words to form and escape her lips. "Father." This was the only word she could summon before collapsing in a heap on the ground.

JUK THRI

Juk had been resting in the large canvas marquees provided by the Deera and had been thinking over the conversation with Tunrah and Sooran earlier in the day. The expectation of the news Tunrah had agreed to give him at the Midwinter Sunset weighed on his mind, but his mind was preoccupied with other things, too. He had reassessed his relationship with Rivan and their meeting in the Northern Hills four Moons ago. Many questions were seeping into his thoughts, and most of them went unanswered. He also felt a powerful attraction to the Deera, to Tunrah, and to Sooran in particular. Juk was not sure what this attraction was, and it made him feel uncomfortable.

He put all thoughts out of his mind as he rose from the bed he had been lying on and made his way to the exit. As he looked out, he saw Ashran and his men talking happily. This was the most relaxed he had seen them. He smiled and his thoughts drifted to Chinsap, his own people, his lost family, and he felt the weight upon him grow heavier. The pale Midwinter Sun was dropping in the western sky. As it slowly made its journey from the east to its resting place in the west, the sky grew dim, the bright blue making way for the dusky, pre-Sunset orange and red vista now developing overhead.

"Juk, you feel better now you're rested?" It was

Ashran's deep baritone voice. Juk looked towards the men and saw their leader walking over to where he was standing.

"Yes. Better," Juk said, looking to the floor.

"Well. It looks like we're in for another treat this evening," Ashran continued. "They've been preparing another feast all afternoon. And I've been told there's a special honey wine prepared for us."

"Well, let's hope it holds up against that potato brew from Deadtown, eh?" replied Juk, managing a small smile and looking up to the slowly sinking Sun in the west.

"Yes, I'm told it hits the spot," answered Ashran. "Come, friend. Let's walk together. The Sun is nearly down. It's time."

The two men walked in the direction of where the feast was held earlier that morning. The sight that beheld them made both of the men stop and stare at what was in front of them. Juk took in the sight and looked at Ashran, who returned his gaze. In front of the two men, just beyond where they had feasted earlier, a monument had been erected or had appeared from somewhere. It comprised twelve tall, dark grey stones, almost twenty-five feet in height, arranged in what looked to Juk like a perfect circle. At the western and eastern axis of the circle, two of the large stones were joined by a lintel about five feet wide, sitting atop the two stones. How such a structure could have been arranged in the time since the feast hardly registered in Juk's awareness as he stared in astonishment at the stone circle.

"What in Sun and Moon is this?" asked Ashran as he turned to Juk.

Juk remained silent for a long moment before replying, "This feels familiar. I have seen smaller circles on my travels occasionally, ruins mostly. But the size was nothing like this. So different they appear, I'm not sure they're even connected. Yet, it feels like they are, somehow."

They both remained silent for a while before Juk noticed Ashran staring at him.

"It reminds me of the Midnight Forest," Ashran said as his eyes flitted from Juk to the huge structure and back again. "Different, but similar, I think. Different shapes, I mean. But alike."

"It feels familiar, in a way I cannot put words to," Juk replied, meeting his friend's gaze.

"Welcome friends." The voice came from behind them. It was Sooran with four of the Deera with her. "Come, let's take a seat at the tables and watch the ceremony."

"The ceremony?" replied Juk.

"Yes, the Midwinter Sunset ceremony. To us Deera, this is just as important as the Midwinter Sunrise." Sooran and the men walked past Ashran and Juk, signalling them to follow and sit down.

From his seat at the feasting tables, Juk saw that Ashran's men had joined them and were sitting at adjacent tables, looking just as excited and confused as he felt. He looked around and saw Ashran next to him on one side and Sooran on the other. Juk glanced about, but he could not see Rivan anywhere. He was not sitting at any of the tables, nor was he standing anywhere that Juk could see. As his eyes darted around quickly, looking for the mage, a deep booming sound came from the direction of the vast stone circle. There, as Juk turned his attention to it, was a solitary man blowing on a large circular horn. Twice more the sound rang out, powerful and melodious blasts on the horn which stood around four feet in height as the man remained unmoving, waiting, it seemed, for what though Juk didn't know.

From the eastern entrance of the stone circle, where the stones were joined by the lintel, a man appeared. He was small in stature, but behind him, a group of taller men followed. They were dressed in green robes. Each man held out in his hands a round object. To Juk, they looked like globes made from some sort of crystal. He half-remembered seeing something similar at Magdil one time, in his discussions with Runkarn. As the men walked to the centre of the circle in unison, they held up the globes to the dusky, pre-Sunset sky, orange and red light reflecting through them. The light that was reflected shot straight up into the sky, as if being guided by some unseen force. The lights merged into one small ball of light directly above the centre of the circle. At this point, the horn sounded out one more time. One more booming, tuneful blast came from it, and as the sound reverberated throughout the circle, the sphere of light which had been concentrated high above reorientated itself to the west. It now hovered over the western entrance of the circle.

At that very moment, the last, dying rays of the

setting Midwinter Sun were illuminated as they aligned exactly with the gap in the two western stones marking the entrance. For a few moments, which to Juk felt like hours, the two lights combined. The appearance of a luminous, kaleidoscopic shaft of light held Juk in awe. He could not take his eyes from it. As bright as it was, the light infused him with a sense of wonder. He felt he had been taken away to another place in time and space. The light brought with it an energy he felt flow through every sinew of his body and emotion of his mind. He felt elevated and ecstatic. He felt his arms reaching out towards the setting Sun, not by his own will, but pulled towards the dying light source by something outside of him. His senses were overloaded, and he drifted out of his own mind. Then he felt the light drift away from his own conscious awareness. His arms dropped slowly, unwillingly back down by his side, returning to their previous positions. A fleeting sense of loss then engulfed him, lasting only for a moment before the ecstasy returned. He looked around and saw all the men smiling. They were showing the same emotions on their faces that he felt inside. He turned to Sooran, who was looking at him intensely.

"Well," she said, "what do you have to say about that, Juk Thri?"

Juk sat motionless. Words could not form in his mind. He was still lost in the rapture of the experience he had just felt. Juk turned away from Sooran and looked back towards the stone circle. He saw the men walking back out towards the western exit. As they passed through the two large standing stones, he counted them. Twelve men there were in total; eleven taller men and one man shorter than the rest. They walked through the portal in turn and out of view. Juk then turned back to Sooran and smiled.

"I have never seen such a thing as that. What happened? What was it?" Juk asked, his smile widening with each word.

"The power of the Sun," replied Sooran as she reached out and picked up one of the wooden drinking cups that had been placed on the table. She gestured to Juk to do the same and as he did, Sooran drank from her cup. Juk followed, and he felt a sweet, honey-like liquid trickle down the back of his throat. It heightened his already elevated mood, and the sensation was similar to the one he had just experienced, albeit less intense. He quickly took another drink from his cup and turned to Ashran as he did so. He saw Ashran beaming back at him, cup in hand.

"I think we can leave your potato wine in Deadtown, Juk," Ashran said, the smile lighting up his entire face.

Juk Smiled back and took another long drink from his cup.

"Come now, Juk," Sooran said. "My father is waiting for you." She lightly touched Juk on his arm.

Juk looked at her as she did this, and she smiled. She got up from the table and walked off to the west. Juk followed Sooran to her father's dwelling. Standing at the end of the large living area, in front of the chairs that they had all been sitting in earlier that day, was Tunrah. As he stood, looking at Juk and Sooran as they walked towards him, Juk noticed he was no longer hunched over. He was standing up straight with his shoulders back and most of the years he had held in his face previously had fallen away. Juk stared in wonder. At first, he thought it might be a trick of the light. Then Tunrah spoke. "Yes, I am changed. To your eyes I look younger, yes?" Tunrah half-smiled.

Juk stared at the older man in amazement. "I would say the years have been turned back. You look younger, stronger. More vibrant. The lines and cares you carried this morning have disappeared. How is this?"

"This, Juk Thri, is as we have oft said now, the power of the Sun. The Midwinter ceremony is a life-giving, energetic, renewal event. It is how we have kept hidden, strong and secret for all these long years." Tunrah took a sip from a wooden goblet he was holding.

"This day becomes stranger and more astounding with each passing hour," Juk said, still staring at Tunrah.

Sooran appeared from behind Juk with two wooden goblets. They appeared to contain the same drink as the cups at the ceremony. Juk took a sip and found that it was. The same powerful sensations came back to him, and he smiled.

"You like our mead, yes?" Tunrah asked, smiling back at Juk.

"I do not think *like* honours this drink fully," replied Juk. "I have tasted nothing like it. Tell me, what is it?"

"It's a honey mead we brought with us from years

gone by. There was a time when this was brewed throughout the land. But as I said before, the old ways have not been observed for many long years."

"Well, it is a heavy loss." Juk took another sip and felt his smile widen further.

"There are many things which have been lost that we mourn. Which brings us to it." Tunrah took another drink from his cup and sat down on the chair behind him. Sooran sat next to her father and motioned for Juk to sit opposite them.

"I noticed," said Sooran, "your mage, Rivan, was not at the ceremony. I did not see him there, anyway."

"I didn't see him there either," Juk answered, looking at Sooran.

"This fills me with concern," Tunrah said. "Concern for you most of all, Juk."

"For me? Why?"

"Well, it seems to me, to us, that you have been brought here to do a mage's bidding."

"I don't think that's true," Juk said.

"Well, where is he, this mage of yours? I have not seen him all day, yet this morning, he seemed to be most concerned with us," Tunrah asked.

"I do not know where he is, but I still don't see what that has to do with me."

"A question has been weighing heavily on my mind all day, Juk Thri. A question perhaps with no answer. But it is still on my mind."

"Go on," Juk said and nodded.

"This problem you have in Areekya. It sounds very familiar, similar to our own one, many years gone. We did not know how to confront it then. I'm not sure we could now."

"You'll leave us to it, then. To confront it on our own. Without your help." Juk looked from Tunrah to Sooran and back to the older man again.

"I did not say this." Tunrah looked at his daughter as he spoke.

"Then what do you say?" Juk's smile turned into a frown.

"I say this," Tunrah replied. "I do not trust this mage of yours. Nor do I know what we *could* do to aid you. I do not know if we have the strength or power to. But there is something that tells me you need our help, Juk Thri."

"Then you will help. You'll send men with us back to Areekya?" Juk's smile returned as he took another sip of his mead.

"I cannot send the men you request. This would bring too much peril to us. I will send my daughter, Sooran. And with her will go twenty of our best men."

Juk looked at Sooran and half-smiled before speaking. "Tunrah, I thank you for this. I really do, but twenty? What can we do with such a low number?"

"They will report on the plight of your land. On the situation. They will be my eyes and ears, and twenty may become thousands if, and only if, it is right for us

Deera to do so." Tunrah smiled at Juk.

"Then this is glad tidings indeed. It is not as we would have wished, but it seems the next best thing. I thank you on behalf of Areekya, Tunrah. And you, too, Sooran. For agreeing to come back with us. I thank you with all my heart."

Juk looked and smiled at Tunrah and Sooran in turn. He held Sooran's gaze a little longer than he expected to and held his wooden cup aloft. "To peace, then."

Father and daughter both raised their cups and together repeated Juk's words: "To peace."

They all took one last drink from their cups and Juk felt his troubles and cares lifted from his mind.

"We'll leave tomorrow, Juk," Sooran said. "So get a good night's rest tonight. We'll be off before Sun up."

"I have a feeling I shall sleep as well as I have for many a Moon tonight," Juk replied, and he made his way back to his dwellings. As he passed the stone circle, he saw Ashran and his men enjoying the night. He walked past them unnoticed and walked straight into the canvas dwelling and fell onto the bed.

LORD DENNIS GREENAWAY

Dennis Greenaway arrived home from Dawngate early that morning, two days after Midwinter. He had ridden back at a leisurely pace. Together with his men, they took advantage of the taverns along the Great Road that runs all the way from the harbours of the Endless Ocean, to Dawngate. He had enjoyed the ride back to Midscape. It had brought back memories of his life as a soldier years before. Dennis was renowned as a great fighter, one of the best in Areekya, and not without good reason. He was short in stature, but he had an insatiable appetite for blood. Dennis keenly launched himself first in to every battle and always stayed until it had finished.

He remained steadfast to Runkarn until the end of the War. His reward was Midscape: the former capital of Areekya and the seat of the Masterton family before the War. He enjoyed his spoils at first. His body had grown tired of the fighting. He was the Lord of the City, and his fighting days were over. There were times he missed them, but for the first year, he enjoyed his more placid lifestyle. He knew now that his old self was going to be required. The fighting self, the bloodier self, and if he were to be true to himself, his better self.

Dennis had also used the time riding back from Dawngate to plan his upcoming campaign. While eagerly awaiting news of Juk's recruitment in the west, he had already begun to plan his own moves. He knew that secrecy was the key. Runkarn could not get word of any of this or he would send the full weight of his army down on Midscape, he had no doubt about that. Besides having a well-earned reputation for being a great fighter, Dennis was also renowned for his tactical prowess; and he knew how Runkarn thought. That would help him. How much, he wasn't sure. But if he had enough men, he felt confident it would give him the edge.

As he approached his private quarters, he heard voices coming from the main dining hall. One was unmistakably his wife's. He could recognise Livian's cackle anywhere. The other voice wasn't as clear. He entered the dining hall and saw his wife, as expected, sitting at one end of the table, and was shocked to see the tattooed face of Madnan Veerak sitting at the other.

"Good morning, my Lord Greenaway," Madnan said and smiled from his seat.

"Is it?" Dennis looked at Madnan as he spoke, and then looked at Livian. "What is it I see here? Speak, quickly."

"My good Lord Dennis," Madnan replied. "Please allow me to apologise for our last meeting. I feel we were not conscious enough of your long friendship with Juk Thri. I came here to make amends for that."

"I see." Dennis stared at the tattooed man occupying the seat reserved for the Lord of the City.

"And," added Madnan, "I took breakfast with your lovely wife, the Lady Livian. Just as I have for the last three days now." Madnan stood up and walked towards the opposite end of the table where Livian remained seated.

"You've been here three days?" Dennis continued to stare at Madnan as he spoke. He could feel his fighting self stirring within him.

"Yes, I wanted to clear the air. I wanted to wait for your return. From Dawngate, Lady Livian tells me."

"Does she? What else does she tell you, I wonder?" Dennis turned his attention to his wife.

"Ha! You jest, of course," Madnan answered. "We arrived just before Midwinter, so we thought we might stay and enjoy the festivities, too."

"We?" Dennis turned back to Madnan.

"Ah yes, the 2nd Regiment and I. They are stationed in the barracks. On Lord Runkarn's orders, of course," Madnan said with his ever present cursory smile clear on his face. "We thought we might find news of the ex-Captain's whereabouts on our way here."

"And did you? Find anything, I mean," Dennis asked.

"Alas, no. Nothing of note, nothing we could investigate at any rate. However, there has been a witness to the murder in Chinsap," Madnan continued.

"Witness?" Dennis was getting irritated.

"Yes," added Madnan. "A Chinsap man, a guard of the city. He says he saw the whole thing. A crime of passion, it seems. Juk found his wife with another and killed them all. This he recounted to Lord Ruperk."

"Killed them all? His children, for the crimes of the mother?"

"So it seems. It would not be the first time such a thing had occurred, now would it? You, being a soldier, should understand this most of all."

"And who was this man found with his wife? What of him?"

"A merchant, the guard described him as. Also dead. The body was never found."

"Was it not?" Dennis noticed the smile had disappeared from Madnan's face. He also observed his tattooed face had turned towards his wife.

"Well then. It seems it is done. Proof, if proof were needed. He is guilty of the crime. Let that be the end to it, then." Dennis walked towards his seat at the end of the table and sat down as he finished his sentence. A serving boy brought bread and beer.

"No beer, lad. Bring me some water." The boy scurried away with the goblet of beer and brought back one of water.

"How went the celebrations, my dear?" Dennis took a bite of his bread.

"Fabulous, husband," Livian answered, a huge smile on her face.

"I trust our guests were impressed," Dennis said as he continued to eat his breakfast.

"The Winter Solstice was a fabulous affair, my

dear."

Dennis noticed his wife was using one of her fake smiles. The one she always used to mask her contempt for him. "Wonderful!" he replied, smiling in reciprocation.

"The rebirth of the Sun is always a marvel, isn't it?" Madnan added, now standing behind Livian. "And I was certainly impressed. The famous Midscape celebrations are renowned throughout Areekya."

"And not without good reason, either," replied Livian. "My family has always held the Midwinter celebration in the highest regard. Much more so than the Summer Solstice, even."

"It was not a disappointment, Lord Dennis. I can assure you of that." Madnan's smile was as fake as his wife's, Dennis thought. "And now you must excuse me. I have business in the city. I beg your leave and perhaps we can dine together this evening." Madnan walked back towards Dennis and bowed ever so slightly. Dennis smiled and carried on eating his breakfast.

"A lovely idea, Madnan. Let's do that," said Livian, who continued to smile.

After Madnan had left the dining hall, Dennis looked over at his wife. "What in the name of the Sun and Moon has been going on here?"

"I've been trying to keep the peace. Fending off his slippery questions, as obvious and objectionable as his advances."

"Have you indeed. And how's that going?"

"Well, you never know with the Veeraks. But I think he's satisfied you know nothing."

Dennis continued to eat. "Perhaps I should have him beaten. Beat him myself, even. Making advances on the Lord of Midscape's wife. Who does he think he is?"

"Ruperk's closest counsellor is who," Livian answered. "And that would be a terrible idea," she said, in reply to his first comment.

"You told him I was in Dawngate."

"I had to tell him something. I told him you were on a hunting trip. He learned nothing he didn't already know, anyway. My dear husband, my hatred for Magdil and its cronies runs even deeper than my contempt for you. That you can take some solace in."

"Well, I assume you're having him watched."

"Of course, as I do all guests, even those here on your request, my dear."

"I wouldn't expect anything else, Livian," Dennis said. "But there's something going on here. He's not here to apologise. That much I know. What have your little doves reported?"

"Nothing. He moves from the barracks to here and visits the markets. He goes nowhere near the taverns or brothels. Unlike that uncivilised bunch of brutes he has with him. They have kept the City Guard busy."

"The 2nd always were a bunch of cunts. Fucking rock breakers from the arsehole of Areekya. We need to find out what he wants. Sun and Moon!"

"Well, he's being watched. I think it's a good idea for you to keep drinking that water until this evening. We don't want a repeat of last time, dear husband." With that, Livian got up and left.

Dennis sat there, finishing his breakfast, thoughts turning over in his mind. He didn't trust Madnan Veerak, but worse than that was that he didn't trust his wife either. After his breakfast, he went to his private quarters. As much as he had enjoyed the ride back from Dawngate, it had left him exhausted. He needed a good rest, and instructed his personal guards not to disturb him until dinner.

Dennis awoke just before last Sun. He looked out of the western-facing window and saw the low-lying Sun just about to drop behind the mountains in the far distance. He got dressed and headed for the main gardens. Dennis enjoyed them at this time of the day, and they brought him some comfort. He felt apprehensive about this evening's upcoming dinner.

"My lord?" came a voice from behind him.

"Yes, what is it? Can a man not get some peace in this city anymore?"

"My lord. Lady Livian has told me to give you this note." The guard handed the note to Lord Dennis and backed away.

Dennis read the note slowly and carefully.

"Sun and Moon!" He walked back into the main building and headed to his wife's living quarters in the eastern wing of the castle. Without knocking, he burst in and saw Livian sitting by the window looking out towards the mountains.

"What's this?" Dennis shouted. "He's gone? Did he not leave any reason?"

"None. But why would he?" Livian answered without turning away from the window.

"Sun and Moon! What does he think he's playing at?"

"At Runkarn's games, I would imagine," Livian replied, still looking out of her window.

"Well, this is not good for us. I can tell you that," Dennis said, a number of embryonic thoughts rushing through his mind. "Not good at all."

"Not good for you, Dennis," Livian said as she turned and smiled at her husband. "Not good for you at all."

CHIK SRIN

It was four days past Midwinter when Chik and the five hundred riders of the 1st Regiment, together with Lord Brok, Hak Krok and the 2nd, reached the Mountain of Serenity. They had spent the Winter Solstice camped together outside a small village on the route from Dawngate. It had been a tense and downbeat affair. The tensions between the 1st and the 2nd Regiments had not improved, and Lord Brok was showing signs of missing his home and family in the north. In fact, he had confided as much to Chik at sunrise on Midwinter's morning.

As they approached the towering solitary mountain, standing like an iridescent sentinel shining in the mid-morning Sun amongst the foothills surrounding it, a group of riders appeared on the horizon riding towards them. After a few minutes' ride, Lord Ruperk Stonefish, with a hundred or so of his personal guards from his home city of the Gate, together with the two Veerak brothers, halted in front of Chik's group.

"Well met, my lords," Lord Brok cried out from atop his horse.

Chik and Hak did likewise as Lord Ruperk nodded in reply.

"And what did you discover in Dawngate, Lord

Brok?" Lord Ruperk asked, his face showing no emotion.

"Not much, I'm afraid to say, Lord Ruperk," replied Lord Brok. "We found no trace of Juk Thri. No reports of any certainty. Nothing we could act upon."

"We found out that the east can't be trusted," Hak added to Lord Brok's last sentence.

"Go on, Captain," Lord Ruperk urged. Chik noticed the intense look that Lord Brok gave the Captain of the 2nd regiment.

"Well, that Lord William is not a man of his word. As for his cunt of a wife, well, it's obvious who wields the sword in that city."

"Please refine your language, Captain. But continue." Lord Ruperk's face scrunched up in disgust.

"Beg pardon, my lord. Greenaway visited him not long before we got there. He forgot to tell us that, until his whore... sorry, his wife, let slip."

"Is that so?" replied Lord Ruperk.

"And what's more," Hak continued, not letting anyone else speak, "she has no respect for Lord Runkarn or Magdil. She made that clear, wanted us to know it, too, if you ask me."

"I think Captain Hak is getting a little carried away with his report, somewhat," Lord Brok said, finally inserting himself back into the conversation.

"So, this is not true, Lord Brok?" Lord Ruperk asked.

"True, yes, without the colourful language and

biased perspective. It is true that Lord Dennis had visited Dawngate before us. On tax business, Lord William said."

"This is known to us. That Lord Greenaway visited Dawngate. Though it was not on tax business." Lord Ruperk looked directly at Lord Janson Brok. "I have a summons here from Lord Runkarn himself. It is for Lord William to present himself in Magdil. To explain this visit in, let's say, more conducive surroundings."

"Do you expect me to ride back to Dawngate? We're tired and cold. We need refreshment and rest," Lord Brok declared.

His bad mood's getting the better of him, thought Chik.

"You, Lord Brok, no. I do not expect you to travel back to Dawngate. You are to come to Midscape with me and Lords Madnan and Walnak. We have business with Lord Greenaway to contend with." The slightest of smiles showing on Lord Ruperk's face as he spoke. "Captain Hak and the 2nd Regiment will return to Dawngate, together with Captain Chik and his men."

"Aye, Sir. My Lord Ruperk," replied Hak, beaming, "maybes we'll get to show him the Spinal Grip, eh, lads?" Hak turned and laughed along with his men.

"Lord William is to be brought back to Magdil. Mostly unharmed, Captain. If he were to incur some minor riding injuries, well, that cannot always be helped," Lord Ruperk said, his face emotionless once more.

"He is the Lord of Dawngate, Lord Ruperk," Janson

Brok said. "His family has a long and rich history here. Let's not forget that."

"That is why he will be brought to Magdil, my good Lord Brok," Ruperk replied, looking at Captain Hak. Then, turning to Chik, he said, "Captain Chik. You are to support Captain Hak in this. Send two hundred of your men to Magdil. There they will be met by men of the 2nd. There have been rumours of some movement in the west and south. They are to ride out to investigate. You and the remainder of the 1st ride with Captain Hak. Is that understood?"

"It is, my lord," replied Chik, mirroring the lack of emotion in Ruperk's face.

"Then make ready to be off within the hour," Ruperk barked. Then turning his gaze to the Captain of the 2nd Regiment, he said, "Captain Hak, an extra three hundred men from the 2nd will be here shortly. Be ready to leave when they arrive." Ruperk nodded and pulled on the reins of his horse and turned away, adding, "Lord Brok, please follow me. We are heading back to Midscape."

Chik observed as Lord Brok, after saying his farewells, together with his twenty-five Stoneguard men, and two hundred of the 1st, rode away to the west.

"Well then, Chik. Looks like it's just you and me." Hak Krok smiled as he looked directly at Chik. "Make ready. We'll be off when my men get here. And they'll be none of that 1st dilly dallying. We'll ride hard and we'll ride all day."

Chik said nothing in reply. He turned his horse

and, together with his men, trotted away to about a hundred yards from the 2nd Regiment.

"Okay men. We don't have to like it, but we'll do our soldier's duty. Stay close to me, and take no orders from anyone *but* me," Chik addressed his men. "We've an hour. Give your horses some rest and let them graze a while. We face a hard ride back east." With that, Chik climbed down from his horse and allowed it to graze in the grass-rich surroundings.

Within the hour, the call came from a junior man in the 2nd Regiment to make ready to leave. Chik and his men, together with the 2nd Regiment being led by Hak, rode hard all the way back to Dawngate, stopping only at night for a few hours' rest. This made the horses groan and whine in displeasure every morning upon setting out. Chik despised this, but remained silent. He saw Hak took some depraved pleasure in this, but Chik did not want to give him any comfort in his own resentment of this ill-treatment of the horses. By mid-afternoon on the fourth day, they reached Dawngate. Surprisingly, Lord William was at the gates to meet them.

"Well met, Captains. So soon after our last meeting," Lord William greeted them. "I see Lord Runkarn has decided to pay us in the east more attention already, yes?" Lord William smiled as he spoke, almost laughing.

"I have here a summons from Lord Runkarn. It might knock that smile off your face," Hak spat back.

"Yes, yes, we'll have time for all that," replied Lord William, continuing to smile. "I think that first you shall need some rest before our ride back west. Take your men to the barracks. Rest your horses and refresh yourselves. We can ride out tomorrow, yes? "

"Our orders are to ride back immediately," Hak replied, shaking his head.

"Well, our horses could do with the rest, Lord William. We thank you for your kind offer." Chik smiled as he spoke, contradicting Hak.

Chik saw Hak look at his men before speaking once more. "One night, then. My men could do with some refreshment. I take it the brothels and taverns will be at our host's pleasure tonight."

"Indeed, they are," replied Lord William. "Then it is settled. We shall meet here, at the gate at First Sun." With that, Lord William and his guards rode back into the city. Chik noticed Hak did not take his eyes off Lord William until he was out of sight.

"Well, men, enjoy tonight, we have another hard ride in the morning," Hak said, and then rode off with his men to the barracks.

When the 2nd Regiment had ridden away, Chik addressed his own men. "I think it best if we stay fresh for the ride tomorrow, lads. Let's stay within the barracks tonight. Get some rest, give your horses some respite. Stay battle-ready. We need to be very careful over the next twenty-four hours."

LORD DENNIS GREENAWAY

Lord Dennis Greenaway awoke late in the afternoon. As he pulled open the curtains in his bedroom, he could see the pale yellow Sun dropping behind the Mountains in the west. He hadn't been sleeping well since Madnan Veerak abruptly left two days before. His mind had been clouded with competing thoughts. Opposing positions battling with one another inside his mind. He had been waiting for news from Juk before he could take action and act on his plans, to start putting the pieces together, which would allow himself some peace, give his mind some respite from the raging battles taking place within. Then last night, just before midnight, a messenger had arrived with orders to speak only to the Lord of the City, alone. He was taken to the guest's quarters and Lord Greenaway was brought to him. There, the messenger revealed what Dennis had been waiting for: confirmation from Juk. The messenger was from one of the Wetland tribes in the west. He had handed Dennis the news that Juk had secured assistance from the west and south. Not the numbers he had wished for, but it was positive, and that gave Dennis encouragement. It gave him confidence that he could now make his move, make ready his battle plans, and begin his campaign.

Dennis got dressed and went to the dining hall for a late lunch. He hadn't been eating very well either, but last night's news brought his appetite back. As he entered the hall, his mind preoccupied with the plans he must make, he was surprised to see his wife sitting at one end of the table. An empty plate sat in front of her.

"Husband," Livian greeted her husband as he entered, smiling one of her fake smiles.

"Livian. What're you doing here at this hour?" Dennis sat down at the other end of the table.

"Having a late lunch. As are you, it seems."

"Indeed. Why so late?" Dennis asked. He knew his wife did very little without good reason.

"Late night," Livian replied. "And I could ask the same of you, my dear."

"Well, I haven't been eating well lately. I've got my appetite back," Dennis answered as a young, blond serving boy brought him a plate with two large fish and half a loaf of dark bread.

"Ah, I see. And does that have anything to do with your late night visitor?"

He put down the loaf that he was just about to bite into. "Well, yes, actually it does." Dennis knew his wife would have heard about the messenger, but he was surprised she let on about it.

"I see. Good news then, was it?" Livian continued to smile as she spoke.

"Yes, very. It allowed me to clear a few things that had been in my thoughts; money matters, mostly. It allayed my mind somewhat and permitted me to get some sleep. And I woke up with an appetite." Dennis bit into his bread and pulled some flesh from one of the fish.

"Come now, husband. Let's start to be honest with each other, shall we?"

"Well now. Are you sure honesty is the secret to a happy marriage?" Dennis continued to eat as he answered his wife's question.

"Ha!" Livian exclaimed. "Very good. No, maybe not a happy marriage, but we were never going to have one of those now, were we?"

"I was willing." Dennis stopped eating for a moment as he looked up at his wife.

"So, this messenger didn't bring you news about Juk Thri? About his army in the west, and your plans for Magdil? Is that what you're saying to me?"

Dennis pushed his plate to one side, looking closely at his wife at the other end of the table. She had stopped smiling. He had to react quickly. He knew she had all the answers to the questions she had asked. Dennis now had to decide how honest to be. He had to think and act swiftly.

"You know it did. That's why you are asking." Dennis decided to play along with his wife to buy him some time. Time to think. Time to act.

"And your visit to Dawngate before Midwinter. Also, to discuss these same plans. When did you intend to tell me, your wife?"

"I withheld this to keep you from danger, Livian." Dennis felt an unexpected flush of kindness towards his wife, like an echo from some distant, forgotten feeling. He hadn't always been so estranged from her, not at the beginning; he thought he'd even loved her once.

"To protect me?" Livian replied. "To bring down the whole weight of Magdil and Runkarn on *my* city. To destroy what *my* family spent generations building. To be put through this agony once again. All this would have protected *me*? Husband, do not take me for a fool or my indifference for weakness. I would never allow you to destroy this *city*. My *home*. *Me*."

"I do not intend to destroy this city. I plan to protect it. To defend it against Magdil, Runkarn, that pair of cunts, the Veeraks, the whole fucking nest of them. I was waiting for more certainty until I told you, until I moved on my plans."

"It's a shame you had not these intentions five years ago. This city could have been saved from Runkarn then," Livian said, the sadness clear in her eyes.

"Yes, it is a shame," Dennis admitted. "Shame and resentment, that's how I feel. I was wrong back then, though I didn't know that until recently. Until Juk visited. Until it was nearly too late."

"*Nearly* too late?" "For whom? It is too late for my family. *Nearly too late* for you, you mean."

"For us, wife. Your fate, and this city's, is coupled to my own. We must do this to protect us both. To keep this city safe."

A long silence followed. For two or three minutes, neither Dennis nor Livian said anything. Sat at opposite ends of the table, looking in turn at each other and the floor. Dennis was struggling with the thoughts rushing through his mind. *Had he said too much? Not enough? How would Livian react?* Dennis was reflecting furtively when his wife spoke.

"Dennis. It seems to me that you have involved me in something I would rather not have become embroiled in." Livian stood up from the table and made her way towards him. "You have placed me in a rather dangerous position. One which is difficult to see extrication from." She walked closer still, almost within touching distance. "Extrication from alone, that is. It seems we are entangled in this, for good or ill."

"What then do you propose, Livian?"

"That you fully reveal to me your plans. Those I do not already know. And then we move forward, with caution and cunning. In such a way that we can pay back all those who have wronged me, my family, my home."

"That I can do," Dennis replied, smiling.

"Then we shall take a drink together. To seal this pact of honesty and union. Will you join me?" Livian clapped her hands.

"When have you known me to refuse a drink?" Dennis smiled as a young, lithe serving girl appeared with two silver goblets of wine. She handed one to Livian, and one to him.

"Then, here's to the future. To a more honest and fulfilling one." Livian held out her goblet and met Dennis's. Then, in unison, they moved them to their lips, and they both drained their half-filled goblets.

"So, Livian," said Dennis, continuing to smile, "where do you want me to begin? What do you wish to know, my dear?" As Dennis was talking, the blond-haired serving boy reappeared and filled both their goblets with wine. Dennis greedily took another long gulp.

Livian walked back towards her seat and sat down. "From you? Nothing," she spat, and she threw her goblet onto the floor. "What I need from you is the same as it has always been, *my dear.*"

There was a brief moment of confusion for Dennis, in which his face switched from a smile to a grimace before the full weight of understanding fell down on him. He looked over at his wife. He saw the blond-haired boy standing at her side.

"You look confused, husband. Allow me to clarify a few things, shall I?" Livian was now smiling again, although this one looked genuine. "I have known your plans in full for some time. Do you really think you could skulk around my city and play your little games of war without my knowledge?"

Dennis tried to stand, but felt his legs give way and he sank back down onto his chair.

"This is Midscape. A city I have allowed you to be a temporary resident of. It is *my* city. It belongs to *my* family. And it will never be taken from *me.*"

Dennis felt a wave of nausea rise from the pit of his stomach. He felt dizzy and tried to stand once again, this time falling to the floor, coughing. Small droplets of blood exploded from his mouth and nose.

"*My* family," Livian continued as Dennis writhed in agony on the floor," will always be Lords and Ladies of this City."

Dennis was doubled up in pain. He felt intense pressure in his head, like it was in an ironmonger's vice and would be crushed and split in two at any moment. He cried out in anger and helplessness.

"Father!" Livian cried out. And into the room, Dennis saw a tall, grey-haired man walk in.

"Wh... What's this?" Dennis managed to spit out before coughing up a volley of red vomit. The man walked towards him as he felt his body twitching uncontrollably. Dennis saw a glinting steel blade in the man's hand. The man came ever closer and was now standing over Dennis's convulsing body.

"This is from my sons." And then Dennis felt a sharp pain in his stomach and then again, and again, and again. He felt his body punctured many times as he sensed his life ebbing away. Then Dennis Greenaway cried out in excruciating pain one last time.

LORD JANSON BROK

Janson Brok was soaking in the bath inside the guests' quarters at Midscape. He had arrived late last night, with Ruperk and the Veeraks. He was so tired he fell into bed fully clothed. It had been a long ride from Dawngate, and even longer still since he rode out from Stoneguard, before the Winter Solstice.

It was now almost a week past Midwinter, and Janson was weary. Gone now was his previous longing for a return to his soldier's life. He was tired of following orders from men he no longer respected. And he missed his family. Janson wanted to go home. He lay in the bath with all these thoughts going through his mind as the tepid, dirty brown water seeped into his skin, producing wrinkles on his hands and feet. He stood up and grabbed a towel from the hook on the back of the bathroom door. After drying himself, Janson stared at the clothes available to him: his still dirty, weather-worn uniform from Stoneguard, crumpled on the bed, or the purple tunic of Magdil hanging off the hook on the back of the main door to his room. He picked up his uniform, dusted off the dry mud, and tried to stretch out as many of the creases as he could. Then he got dressed. He had been requested to have breakfast with the Lord and Lady of the City, and despite his careworn feelings, he made his way out of the room, forcing himself to conceal any dissenting emotions or behaviour. As he left his room, he was surprised to see two members of the city guard on either side of the door.

"Good morning, my lord," said one of the guards.

"Yes, it is," said Janson as he closed the door behind him. "What are you doing here? Have you been here all night?"

"Yes, Sir. For my Lord Brok's protection. By order of the Lord of the City."

"Protection? From who? Who do I need protection from?" Janson looked at both guards then looked up and down the hall.

"Don't know, my lord. We're to show you to the dining hall, my lord."

"I know where the dining hall is. Many times have I eaten there. I can find it myself, if it please the city guards."

"Lord of the City's orders, my lord. Please follow us," the guard said, ignoring the request.

Janson followed the guards, feeling for his sword by his side.

"My lord," the guard said as they approached the dining hall. The other guard opened the door and gestured for Janson to enter.

As he entered the dining hall, he saw Ruperk Stonefish directly opposite the door, seated at the middle of the dining table. Next to him was the younger Veerak brother, Walnak. They were deep in conversation while eating their breakfast.

"My Lord Janson," came a voice from one end of the long oak dining table. There, smiling as he drained his cup, sat Madnan Veerak.

"Welcome to Midscape. I trust you rested well last night, Lord Brok. I hope you feel better than you look. You chose not to wear the fresh clothes put out for you?"

"Yes, I rested," Janson said, ignoring the last question. As he looked around the hall, he saw Lady Livian Greenaway sitting at the other end of the table, and to his astonishment, he saw an older man with grey hair, who looked a lot like her father, Lord Sydric Masterton, sitting next to her. He stood paralysed as he stared at a sight he had trouble making any sense of.

"My good Lord Janson. You seem confused," Madnan continued from the other end of the table. "Here is Lord Sydric Masterton. Father of my wife, Lady Livian."

Lord Janson stood there, still incapacitated by confusion. He switched his gaze from the Mastertons to Madnan.

"Lord Sydric? How can this be? He fell at the Moon Bridge," Janson articulated, just one of the disconcerting thoughts he was experiencing.

"Ah, no. Not quite," came the reply from Ruperk. "Lord Sydric was wounded at the Battle of the Moon Bridge. Yes, this is true. But he surrendered himself to Lord Runkarn and has been helping him with his efforts to bring peace to Areekya ever since."

"Helping? Why was this not known? Why were we not told?" Janson was still trying to come to terms with what he saw and heard.

"Well, my good Lord Janson. Some were told, those that had to know, knew, as it were. There were reasons that others were not told. This was on the orders of Lord Runkarn. But please sit. Take some wine. Maybe this will help with the shock."

As he sat down opposite Ruperk and Walnak Veerak, he took a sip from the goblet of wine that was already on the table in front of him. He looked back down the table at Lady Livian and her father sitting together, smiling silently. Then he looked back at Madnan. "Your wife?" Janson could not mask the shock in his voice.

"Yes, Lady Livian agreed to become my wife, with her father's blessing, of course. We were married last night in a private ceremony. We thought it best to let you rest."

"Lord Dennis! What has happened to Lord Dennis?" Janson felt as if he were still asleep, his reality changing with every utterance and action.

"Ah," replied Ruperk. "Lord Dennis took the news of Lord Sydric's return rather badly."

"Yes," added Lady Livian. "When Lord Dennis saw my father was still breathing, that he hadn't murdered him at the Moon Bridge as he had my husband and brothers, he fell into madness. The Moon took him and would not believe what his own eyes could see. He was not himself, and he tried to cut out his own eyes with his very own blade. He was restrained, of course, by his guards, but he threw them off, and in his madness killed two of them before moving towards me and my father. There was little choice. The Moon had truly taken him. As he lunged towards my dear father here, the guards ended his madness."

"Ended his madness?" Janson replied.

"Yes, Lord Janson," added Madnan. "They cut him down. Ended his madness, which unfortunately ended his life."

"Lord Dennis, dead? What is this that I wake to this morning? exclaimed Janson. "I have awoken in some nightmare. Where the dead walk and the living are no more."

"It is shocking news, Lord Brok," said Ruperk, staring intently at Janson. "But we hope you are capable of comprehending the need for urgency in such a situation. Order must be preserved at all costs. We have Juk Thri wandering the land, rabble-rousing, creating tension and anxiety."

"You have news of Juk?" Janson switched his attention immediately.

"Well, there are reports of armies he has encouraged, moving in the south and west. Burning towns and villages as they go. We sent out the 1st and 2nd Regiments to deal with these troublemakers."

"And Juk?" asked Janson again.

"Well, my Lord Brok. This is where you come in," Ruperk replied.

"Continue." Janson stared at Ruperk, still trying to grapple with the slew of extraordinary thoughts rampaging through his mind.

"We have it on good authority that Juk Thri is at the head of a small rag-tag army heading this way. Lord Dennis was good enough to disclose this information. It seems he had been in constant communication with our ex-Captain. He is planning on some kind of uprising. We need to know who is involved. We thought you could help with this."

"How so?" Janson looked around the hall. All eyes were fixed on him.

"We could send a small army to crush Juk and his rebel band before they reach us easily enough." Ruperk glanced at Madnan. "But why cut off just one head of the snake when there are many more to be hewn? We need you to bring Juk in. To save his life, so that he can tell us who else is engaged in this madness."

Janson sat at the table, reflecting on what he had seen and all that he had heard. His head was swirling in turmoil. He hardly believed what he saw and did not believe what he was told, but he was caught. He had allowed himself to be situated in a position he should have seen coming. Janson looked up and down the table. Enemies in both directions. He refocused and looked across to Ruperk. "Whatever needs to be done, I will do my soldier's duty."

"Excellent," replied Ruperk, smiling at Madnan Veerak as he spoke. "Then we need you to ride out with your men to meet Juk Thri. Meet him at the Mountain Tower. There will be men there to assist if the need should arise."

"To meet Juk, and then?" Janson replied, choosing to say as little as possible.

"To bring him to us, here. You will have to play the part of Lord Dennis in this. Go along with Juk Thri's madness. With his plan. Tell him Lord Dennis is waiting here for him. And bring Juk and his bedraggled band to us."

"Lie? You want me to lie to him. To trick him into your arms."

"We need you to do your soldier's duty, Lord Brok. This madness cannot go unchecked. You must see this. You must think of your own city, your own people, your own family."

"My family? What have they to do with this?"

"There are brigands roaming the land, Lord Janson. But do not worry. We have sent four hundred men to Stoneguard. To protect your family, should these rabble-rousers head north."

Janson knew now that he was truly caught. He did not allow this to show on his face as he replied. "Thank you, Lord Ruperk. This gives me some comfort, at least. I now know what I must do. When am I to leave?"

"Our scouts say Juk will be at the Mountain Tower at the end of next week. You have some time to rest up," Ruperk answered.

"Finish your breakfast, Lord Brok," Madnan Veerak added. "Speak to your men. Allow them to enjoy a week's rest at the pleasure of the new Lord of the City."

Janson found his appetite had left him. He forced

down a piece of bread and a small fish, and washed it down with two goblets of wine, all the time feeling the eyes of the room upon him. Watching him as he put each small handful of food into his mouth. He sensed their close observation as he brought the goblet up to his mouth and took a sip of the wine. He did all this without giving away any discomfort. Betraying none of what he felt inside: the fear, the anger, the resentment. The fear for his family in the north, the anger he held for the people around the table, and the resentment of allowing himself to be caught in this situation. He finished his meal in silence, smiling and nodding in response to polite questions before finally shaking his head at offers of more wine and food.

When Janson finished, he excused himself and made his way back to his room. He sat at the desk in front of the window facing the mountains. He pulled open a drawer and found a pile of off-white parchments. He took one and wrote on it using the quill that was on the desk. He scratched his words quickly, dipping the quill in the ink repeatedly, and looking towards the door at every noise he heard, or thought he heard. When he had finished, he folded it into the smallest size he could, and placed it under his outer garments, inside his trousers. There it would be safe. Safe from the enemies that he found himself surrounded by.

LORD WILLIAM WILTON

The Moon's glimmering reflection in the pool was a near perfect imitation of the astral original. Paler than the brilliant Full Moon shimmering in the firmament above, but not losing any of its ethereal beauty. Standing in Dawngate's water gardens was Lord William Wilton. He was transfixed by this natural spectacle as it calmly floated on the surface of the water in between the brightly coloured water lotus flowers and the dark green lily pads. As he stood there, deep in contemplation, staring at the transcendent beauty of the Moon's watery representation, he heard footsteps from behind him. This brought William out of his reverie. He waited for the footsteps until they were three or four steps away and without turning around, he said, "Good evening, my dear. Are you here to observe the beauty of the gardens?"

"I'm here to make sure you know what you have to do tonight, *my dear*," said William's wife, Ursula, from behind him, and with a harsh tone in her words.

"Ah. I've been thinking about that," William replied. "We will do well to throw that brutish Captain off of our scent."

"You will do what is necessary," replied Ursula.

"Of course. Let's hope that what is necessary is not too disagreeable, yes?"

"Magdil already knows Lord Dennis was here. They know he wasn't here to talk about tax. You have to save your skin. Our skin, disagreeable or not." Ursula was now so close to William he could feel her breath on his neck.

"And you are certain that Midscape is with us?" William took one step back and turned to look at his wife, taking in her long blonde hair, neatly parted in the centre and running down each side of her flawless, symmetrical face. Her lips were red and generous. And with the Full Moon above reflecting light into the water gardens, her eyes sparkled. She was a beautiful woman, but William found her impenetrable. Despite the physical proximity they shared tonight, emotionally they had been estranged for a long time. She was cold and aloof, and William was unsure if he could trust her.

"My bond with Lady Livian is one that is years old. I know her mind, as she knows mine. Midscape will not fail us. You just make sure that this Captain leaves here with no more knowledge than when he arrived. You should be able to outwit some rock smasher from the Spine who can barely form a coherent sentence. And he is as transparent as the shirts you wear in summer." Ursula stared ahead at the Moon's reflection before continuing. "You can leave the other one to me. This Chik Srin. He has something about him. I saw it in his eyes. I will deal with him, my dear."

"Of course," William replied. "In an hour or so, this Captain Krok will be deep in his cups. I'll pay him a visit then."

"Good. And take the two Jacks with you. Your

words and gold should do the trick, but they will ensure your message gets through. When you have finished with that rock breaker, come to my quarters."

"My dear." And with that, Ursula made her way out of the water gardens.

William stayed a while longer. He looked up at the luminous Full Moon for a moment, and then down at its watery imitation as it crawled into the bunch of brightly coloured lotus flowers. He let out a sigh and then made his own way inside.

William was walking through the city's main thoroughfare. This was not that unusual, as he often walked about the city and, once in a while, he paid a visit to the more squalid parts of Dawngate. On either side of him was an enormous man: the Jacks brothers: Andre and Henrik. They weren't actually brothers, but they were so alike in appearance that they were called so. They were, in fact, cousins who grew up next door to each other in the small village of Huntingcoom, just to the north of Dawngate. Their kin came from across the Endless Ocean two generations ago and settled in the east. Over six feet in height and almost half that in width at the shoulders, both with long, dark-blond hair and piercing blue eyes. Huge individuals that found their way into William's service purely on their size alone. William also had six of his personal guards walking in front, and six behind.

The guards in front entered the tavern first; The Mountain Tip, an establishment William had not frequented before, but its reputation had reached his ears, and the city's guards' attention many times.

William and the Jacks brothers followed and six men remained outside. Instantly William's senses were overrun with a penetrating, sweet aroma of a pungent perfume mixed with the acrid odour of stale beer. William scanned the tavern and at the bar were a handful of Magdil men. Whether they were from the 1st or 2nd regiment, William couldn't tell from this distance. Sitting in one corner, he saw the tattooed face of Hak Krok, surrounded by four of his men, each of them engaged with a woman from the tavern. Three of the guards walked to the bar and ordered drinks for all the patrons. The remaining three stood at the entrance. All the Regiments' drinks were on William tonight anyway, but he wanted to make the gesture. He walked over to the corner of the tavern where Hak was sitting, followed by Andre and Henrik Jacks.

"Well, Captain, I hope you're enjoying yourself. I trust the hospitality of my city is up to scratch for you and your men."

Hak Krok looked up and pushed the girl sitting on his knee to one side. "Well, look who it is, lads. Our good Lord William. Aye, the beer's flowing and you have good women here in the east. Not like those Magdil cunts; all arse, they are. Nice and skinny here. Just how we likes 'em." Hak looked across at his men as he spoke and William saw they were indeed enjoying themselves.

"Well, that is good to hear," replied William. A soldier from the bar brought four cups of beer over, spilling some as he heavy-handedly set them down on the table. William saw the insignia of the 2nd Regiment on his shoulder.

"Drink up, Captain," the man said, smiling widely.

"Ah yes, drink up indeed. Tonight is the time to relax and refresh, yes?" William spoke directly to Hak.

"Yep. Refresh and relax. Early start in the morning," Hak growled back, repositioning the girl on his lap with an ungainly action, all the time continuing to look at his men.

"Well, Captain. I was thinking," added William. "Might it be best to delay tomorrow's ride somewhat?"

"Fuck delay, we ride at Sun up."

William squeezed himself on to the bench where Hak was sitting and placed his arm around the Captain, and barely above a whisper, he said, "Well, it seems to me your lads are somewhat enjoying themselves. It would be a shame to curtail their enjoyment with an early start, no?"

Hak looked at William, then glanced at the two giant men standing next to him. He looked back at William and said, "You wouldn't be trying something now, would you? I've six hundred men with me here, Wilton. And orders from Magdil for you to return. That's what we're gonna do tomorrow."

"Of course, Captain. We shall leave tomorrow, of course we shall. What could I do against this, even if I wanted to, which I don't." William looked at the Jacks brothers and then back at Hak. "All I am proposing is a later start. A civilized breakfast with you and Captain Chik together with my wife and I. I think you will find it to your advantage, Captain."

"You couldn't do nothing, is what you could do. We've run through easterners before easily enough. We'll do it again if needs be. No matter what size of men you put in front of us." Hak looked up at the two men standing just to the left of him. "It seems to me you're trying to say something your mouth can't with those two big bastards standing there. I'll tell you what we'll do. *I'll* give my men a lie in tomorrow. And you'll give me a nice size bag of gold for our delay. How does that sound?"

"That sounds agreeable enough to me, Captain," replied William, smiling. "You'll have your gold at breakfast tomorrow. Let's say a couple of hours after Sun up?"

Hak nodded in agreement. With that, Hak turned and faced his men once more, laughing out loud as he announced his news.

William got up and headed for the exit. He heard the raucous cheers of the 2nd Regiment in reaction to their Captain's news. He was followed by his men, and together they made their way out of the tavern and back through the city streets to the main castle.

The next morning, William was in the dining hall, sitting at the table enjoying his breakfast of eggs, dark bread and chicken. Sitting directly opposite him at the other end was his wife. She was wearing a bright yellow full-length dress, which complimented the colour of her hair and made her eyes shine. She was smiling between each delicate bite of her food at the two guests sitting across from one another in the centre of the table, Captain Chik Srin and Captain Hak Krok.

"Is the breakfast up to the task of restoring your energy after last night's exertions, Captain?" Ursula asked Hak.

"The beer is," Hak replied as he drained his half-full goblet. "Hair of the Dog. Always does the trick."

"And you Captain Chik? How are your eggs? Freshly laid and brought to our table." Ursula turned her attention to the Captain of the 1st Regiment.

"They are fine. Better than fine, my lady. Very nice. Some of the best I've had."

"Good, good. We pride ourselves here in the east with our chicken rearing. Generations of chicken farming here in Dawngate. We're known for our mining and metals, but most of the villagers take great pride in their relationships with the land and its creatures. Chickens in particular."

"You can tell in the taste, my lady." Chik smiled at both of his hosts as he spooned a chunk of egg into his mouth.

"Now," interjected Hak, "what's this breakfast all about, then? And where's my gold?"

"Gold?" asked Chik with a confused look on his face.

"Yes, gold," replied Hak. "Lord William here promised me a bag of gold for our delay today. Don't worry, you'll get yours."

"Ah yes. Your gold," said William. As he finished his sentence, Andre, one of the Jacks brothers, walked in and placed a fair-sized bag on the table in front of Hak.

Hak opened up the bag, glanced inside, and smiled. "That'll do."

William observed closely as Hak continued his breakfast, devouring his eggs, meat and bread with hardly any chewing visible. He only stopped briefly to gulp down his dark beer. Chik had stopped eating.

"So, Captains. Let's get to it, shall we?" William said, looking directly at his wife at the other end of the table.

"To what?" replied Hak. "I've got my gold. As soon as this breakfast is finished, we'll be off. I've told the men to be ready within the hour, sober or not."

"Yes, this is the *it*, Captain. Our leaving," replied William.

"What's this shit? I've six men outside this door. Six hundred more in the barracks. As I said last night, it don't matter how big your gold carriers are. You can't go up against Magdil."

William smiled as Chik spoke directly to Hak. "I had a very informative chat with Lady Ursula last night, Hak."

Hak put down the beer he'd just finished and looked across the table to the Captain of the 1st Regiment. "What? I hope you've not been taken in by these easterners."

"I'd say, been made *aware* of the situation, rather than taken in," Chik replied, as William and his wife watched on closely. "It seems that Magdil had not altogether told us the truth about Juk and what happened in Chinsap. But then, you knew that already."

"What do you you know about what I know? Fuck all. So best keep your mouth shut, northerner. Before someone does it for you. This won't go down well with Runkarn and Ruperk, now will it. Best you quiet yourself. One word from me and six of the 2nd's best will come through this door and shut you up." Hak stared at Chik and then at the door.

"I shouldn't rely on the six men outside the door, Captain," interjected William. With that, Andre and Henrik Jacks walked in, each carrying a sack. In turn, each man emptied the contents on the table: the severed heads of the 2nd Regiment guards, three in each sack.

Hak leapt up from his chair, looking at each huge man before drawing his sword. "You'll not get away with this. My men in the barracks. They'll gut you all like mountain hogs."

"Is that so, Captain? Are you sure of that?" Ursula asked from her seat at the end of the table. "We have Captain Chik here to give our side of the story of what happened here."

"Fucking cunt! You should keep your mouth shut," Hak spat back, his eyes darting from one end of the room to the other.

"Yes, our story," continued Ursula. "The Captain of the 2nd Regiment demanding payment from the Lord of Dawngate, so that he would allow him to remain here. A bribe not to be taken to Magdil. A bag of gold, no less. And using your men to extract said gold. But our good Captain of the 1st Regiment, upon hearing such a demand, interceded on account of upholding Magdil's honour. A scuffle ensued, and unfortunately, our guards were just too strong for your men and overpowered them. Regretfully, they attacked the Lord of the City himself and were dealt with appropriately."

Hak pulled his eyes away from Ursula and stared at Chik. "You go along with this? These were Magdil men. Fighting men."

"These were 2nd Regiment men," replied Chik, standing up from his chair. "Liars, cheats, and a disgrace to the uniform they wear."

William observed as Hak, with his left hand, reached down to his leg and pulled out a dagger. He tried to shout a warning, but Hak was too quick. From an underhand position, he flicked his wrist out towards Chik and the dagger flew out of his hand. In an instant, William saw it hit its mark. Chik fell back with the dagger nestled deep in his right eye, and his chair, unable to absorb the shock, fell backward to the ground. Hak, with his right hand, unsheathed his long sword and slashed wildly at the Jacks brothers to his right, catching Andre with a glancing blow on the shoulder, knocking him to the ground. Hak then jumped up onto the table. He kicked the six severed heads that were lying there in multiple directions, and in the confusion strode down the table towards William. He came within reach after a few long strides as William stood up and moved backwards. Hak made a final leap to reach the end of the table and as his landing foot made contact with the table, he thrust his sword out directly in front of him at William, who dodged to the left, narrowly avoiding the attack.

Hak then immediately followed that by bringing the sword back around his head, positioning it to be swung from his shoulder down towards the head of his target. Just as the sword was about to come down, the table shuddered. Henrik Jacks had lifted the table in the centre, knocking Hak off balance and sending him to the floor. For a moment, Hak remained stationary as William pulled his sword from its scabbard and hacked downwards at the man on the floor. Hak quickly rolled to the left, narrowly avoiding the blow, and reached out for his own sword. He jumped to his feet, sword in hand, eyes darting around the room. As Hak turned his head in the direction of Ursula at the other end of the table, William saw a flash of metal leave his wife's hand. Almost instantaneously, it pierced Hak's left temple. The knife plunged deep into its target, almost to the hilt. Hak stopped completely still for a moment, dropped his sword, and raised his hands to pluck the dagger from his head. He placed his hands on the hilt, and as he did so, fell backwards to the floor. He lay motionless, his hands still on the dagger embedded in his temple, as William lifted up his sword and slashed at Hak's torso, once, twice, three times, and then he plunged his sword into the lifeless body of the Captain of the 2nd Regiment.

William took a step back and steadied himself. It had been a long time since he had swung a sword in anger. His heart was racing, and sweat was dripping from his brow. He saw Ursula walk towards him from the other end of the hall. She stopped halfway down the hall and knelt down to check on Chik. She lifted his head gently from the floor and wiped away the blood that was flowing from his right eye.

"Is he alive?" William asked.

Ursula shook her head. She wiped the crimson blood from her hands onto her bright yellow dress as she delicately laid Chik's head back down. She stood up and walked towards her husband. When she reached him at the end of the hall, he was still standing over the lifeless corpse of Hak Krok. Ursula picked up the long sword from next to his body and plunged it deep into the dead man's heart.

ASHRAN

Ashran woke early. It was the morning after the night before, but to his surprise, given the amount of honey mead he had drunk, he felt fine. In fact, he felt better than fine; Ashran felt utterly invigorated. He hadn't felt as good for a long time, years in fact. He quickly washed and went outside to tend to his horse. There, he was greeted by a hive of activity all around him. The Deera were busily preparing their horses for the journey ahead, carefully loading the animals with just as much as each could manage. He saw his men helping the Deera in this undertaking and were loading their own horses with supplies for the journey. As he walked over to his large grey horse, Grace, he saw Rivan walking towards him.

"Ashran. My, you are looking well this fine morning," the mage said, his face beaming as he spoke.

"Rivan. Where have you been? I expected to see you at the celebrations last night."

"Ah yes. I was disappointed to miss it. I found myself walking among the trees and the journey here tired me, beyond that which I expected. Sleep took me while I was lying under the shade of a great oak. I must admit, I haven't had such a sleep for many a Moon."

"Well, you were missed. And I feel even you would have been filled with wonder at the events."

"Indeed. I heard it was quite a show," Rivan replied, his eyes scanning the area, as if searching for something.

"Well, that would be an understatement. Have you heard the Deera are sending just twenty of their men? Together with Tunrah's daughter, Sooran."

"Yes, a lot fewer than I'd hoped for."

"Well, some is always better than none, as we say in the Wetlands."

"Yes, well, it depends what some is, I suppose." And with that, Rivan's eyes seemed to settle on something over Ashran's shoulder and he set off in that direction.

Ashran reached his horse and fed her a few rosy red apples he had kept from last night's feast. The horse whinnied and neighed in delight as she devoured the fruit.

"Well, old girl. Another long ride awaits us," Ashran said as he placed his hand on his horse's head and gently brought it down to her nose.

"Ashran. How's the head this morning?" came a voice from behind. He looked around and saw Juk smiling at him.

"Ha! A lot better than if I'd been drinking that old potato wine, Juk." Ashran returned the smile. "To tell you the truth, I feel ten years younger this morning."

"I know what you mean. Sun knows how they make that stuff, but I need to find out. I haven't felt so rested in a long time. I feel rejuvenated," Juk said, and walked past Ashran and placed his saddle on Noble.

"So, what do you make of these Deera people?" Ashran asked Juk, still stroking his horse.

"I've never seen their like before, Ashran. The things I have seen these past two days, well if you had told me, I would've said the Moon had taken you."

"I know. It's strange," said Ashran. "But they fill me with the same thoughts and feelings that Rivan does, only more friendly. If you understand me. Not to say, Rivan isn't. But they are more. If you follow me."

"Hmm. Yes, I think I know what you mean. Have you seen Rivan? I didn't see him last night."

"Yes, he was just over there a moment or two ago." Ashran pointed back in the direction Juk had come from. "I'm surprised you didn't see him. He seemed preoccupied with something. He walked over here looking for something. Or someone. He went over there." Ashran pointed with his head over his shoulder.

"How was he? I mean, did he say why he missed last night's feast?"

"He went walking and fell asleep. Tired, he said he was."

"Asleep?" answered Juk, scrunching his face slightly.

"Now, about this journey north. How long do you think it will take?" Ashran asked.

"About two weeks, my friend. If the pace is quick, maybe shorter."

"Well, let's hope they bring that honey mead, eh?"

"No need," replied Juk as he opened his coat to reveal a large bottle of yellow liquid poking out from his inside pocket. "I reckon we'll keep this for special occasions, eh?"

Ashran laughed and nodded his approval.

"Looks like we're off," Juk said and gestured with his head over Ashran's shoulder.

Ashran turned and saw Sooran and the twenty Deera riders riding towards him. Ashran noticed that up close the green clothing they wore looked a different shade from last night; lighter in colour, it seemed more attuned to the light this morning in a natural, yet somehow curious manner. The decorations on the silver cuffs were clearer, too. Ornate, intertwining designs that Ashran found entrancing. He climbed up onto his horse, gave her a pat on the head, and rode slowly over to his men. Sooran and Juk rode up beside him.

"Good morning and well met," Sooran greeted both men atop her tall white horse. She had a long wooden bow protruding out of a pouch over one of her shoulders. As did all the Deera, Ashran noticed. The bows were about four to five feet in length, and the end that was sticking out looked like it had been fashioned to a sharp point. Just below the point were strange markings that had been scratched into the wood.

Ashran nodded, and Juk brought his horse to the front of the group. "Sooran, will you ride with me and Juk up front?" asked Ashran, before adding, "Where's Rivan?" And with that, the mage came trotting up on his horse.

"So, we're ready?" said Rivan. "Let's go. We'll head straight north until we leave the desert. Hopefully, in three days we'll be out and then we'll head north west until we reach the Mountain Tower. Then Juk, it'll be up to you." Rivan turned and half-smiled at Juk as he finished his sentence.

Juk returned the smile. He looked at Sooran and Ashran in turn, and together they headed off northwards.

The first three days and nights were uneventful. They camped by firelight every evening after Sundown and rose early each morning, just before First Sun. Once the desert was behind them, they picked up their pace and near the end of the thirteenth day's ride, the large, looming Mountain of Serenity was close. They would reach the Mountain Tower by the end of the next day's ride. Juk had told Ashran that his friend, Lord Dennis Greenaway, would be waiting there for them.

"Let's camp here for the night," Rivan said, his eyes seemingly searching the local area.

"We've still a couple of hours of daylight left," replied Juk, as he looked up at the late afternoon sky.

Rivan continued to look around. "Yes, but I think we could do with a nice rest. Tomorrow's ride will see us arrive at our destination and we are close enough yet not too close, so we may discuss our plans."

Ashran signalled to his men to make camp for the night. Juk climbed down from his horse and tied its reins to a nearby tree stump. Ashran did the same and smiled at Juk as he did so. He saw Juk wasn't smiling and seemed to be thinking about something other than his horse. Ashran observed the Deera. They were all unloading their horses, as they did at the end of every day's ride, reloading the supplies every morning. Sooran, Ashran noticed, was staring at Rivan as he dismounted his horse and sat on the ground. He too looked distracted, thought Ashran.

He turned to Juk. "So, Juk. How about some of that honey mead? If you've any left."

Juk opened his coat, pulled the bottle out from his pocket and tossed it gently to Ashran. "Help yourself. Share it with your men." With that, Juk walked off towards the Deera. Ashran pulled the cork from the bottle, took a drink and almost instantly felt revived after the long journey. He walked over to his men and passed the bottle around, instructing each man to take only a small swig of the mead. That night, as they all sat around the campfire warming themselves in the chilly night air, Ashran still felt the effects of the mead. His body was free from any aches and pains, and his mind was full of hope and optimism. He looked up into the night sky and saw the Moon beginning its journey from east to west. He thought about his family back home in Lendir. It had been nearly three Moons since he'd seen them. The Midwinter celebrations had come and gone, but he still managed a smile, thinking about Tinkar and Ashron back in the Wetlands. He wasn't sure if it was the mead or his true self, but he held only warm, uplifting thoughts tonight. Across the campfire, he saw Rivan and Juk deep in discussion. Sooran was looking on close by, he noticed. Her green garb reflected the bright flames of the fire and the Moonlight cast a radiance around her that made Ashran's smile wider. After a while, he felt the pull of sleep come over him and laid down where he was. He pulled his thick sheepskin coat over his large frame, and fell asleep.

In the morning, Ashran was woken by a gentle nudge. It was Rivan. "I think it's best if you and your men wait here for a day or so. In fact, ride south west for a few miles, where you will find a small forest. Wait there for us to return."

Ashran shrugged off the last of the sleep. He felt clear-headed, but was confused by Rivan's suggestion. "Wait? Wait for what?" Ashran asked.

"Maybe for nothing. But Juk hasn't seen his friend for over a Moon. It is prudent to take a few precautions."

"They'll only be twenty or so of you. If there's going to be trouble, my men will help."

"If there's going to be trouble, I fear a hundred or even five hundred wouldn't help," replied the mage. "Let's hope my fears are unfounded, and it doesn't come to that. When it's safe, I'll send word. We'll reach the Mountain Tower tomorrow, mid-afternoon. I'll send word by the end of the second day from now. If you do not hear by then, leave for Lendir. Go by way of Deadtown and meet up with the men you sent west there. From there, you'll know what to do."

"It doesn't feel right, coming all this way and leaving you here," Ashran said, looking over at Juk and the Deera.

"Well, it is best if you do. Now we have to be off.

Remember, two days at the most."

Ashran walked over to Juk and the Deera. "Safe travels. I hope this Lord Greenaway of yours can be trusted, Juk."

"He can be trusted, if anyone can. He will not let us down. Not while he has breath in his body." Juk smiled and Ashran returned the gesture. Juk then pulled on the reins of his horse and rode away in a north west direction together with Rivan and the Deera.

Ashran turned to his men. "Okay, let's have a decent breakfast and we'll ride off in within the hour." He heard a rumble of thunder off to the west and saw dark clouds heading his way. "Hurry up, lads, let's get that breakfast done before the weather sets in." Ashran looked to the west and then back north, his smile gone, replaced by a frown. He felt uneasy and anxiety had filled his mind.

LADY LIVIAN VEERAK

Livian held her right ear against the wall, as she had done many times in the past, to hear words that the speakers thought were private. For twenty minutes, she had listened intently. She heard the unmistakable nasal, whiny voice of Ruperk Stonefish together with her recently attained husband, Madnan Veerak, and his younger brother, Walnak. They discussed their plans for Juk Thri and his cohorts. She listened and digested it all, all the time thinking, planning, trying to manoeuvre her own plans to fit with the ones she heard. Quietly, actively, assiduously, she paid attention to every word she could hear, until there were no more. She heard the door open and close, and then silence. This was her cue to return the way she came. The way she always returned, back through the parlour, always careful not to be seen as she made her way back to her bedroom. Even though she was now married again, she had kept her room. She insisted on it. Not for the reasons she had given her newly gained husband, but for her own reasons. Here she could sit. Sit, think and plan. Sitting by her window, looking out to the Mountain of Serenity, was her place. Her special place, and nobody would take this away from her. Just as no one would ever take away her city; Midscape. Her family's city.

Tonight, they would hold celebrations for her wedding. A small number of guests would attend, nothing too lavish, Ruperk had insisted. In a time of turmoil, the people needed to feel safe. They should see the Lord and Lady of the city, embodiments of grace and restraint, not appear too extravagant. Word would have reached the city gossips of the recent happenings, and order needed to be maintained. So it was to be two- or three-dozen guests, no more. Her father, of course, would be there, as would Runkarn. He had made the trip from Magdil. One of his rare ventures out of the capital in recent years. Tomorrow, he and Ruperk would move on to the Mountain Tower, that much she had gleaned from her surreptitious manoeuvres earlier in the day. Her husband would stay in the city with his brother, no doubt to watch over her and her father. *To ensure we keep to our side of the agreement.*

Allowing herself to become another pawn in men's schemes did not feel so bitter this time around. She had her father back. It had moved her one step closer to her purpose. If she had to play the wife of another man she had no love for, what of it? She had done so for years. Carrying out the duties expected of her would not be too much of a burden to bear. She was well rehearsed, a master at deception. She allowed only a select few in on her own intrigues.

Lady Livian had a few hours to rest before she would have to prepare for the evening's festivities. She sat at her window for a few minutes more, allowing herself to think back to happier times, with her mother and brothers. When life was simpler, it was to be enjoyed and a time when no cares or worries were upon her. She allowed herself this time. After a short while, she climbed onto her bed and laid her head down to rest.

She turned her thoughts to the upcoming celebrations, her father, her city, and then finally her new husband. She carried these thoughts for a short time until she drifted off, smiling.

Later that evening, Lady Livian was escorted to the dining hall by her father, Sydric Masterton. She smiled all the way down the stairs as the guests looked on. Her father was wearing his military dress. The same livery he had worn when he rode off to the War that last time with her brothers, many years ago. He, too, was smiling the same smile she had on her face. As they walked down the stairs and through the hallway to the dining hall, the guests clapped and remarked at how beautiful she looked. Normally, these words aimed at a woman on her third husband in her mid-thirties would be mere platitudes, but Lady Livian knew she still maintained her beauty. She felt it had been wasted on her previous marriage, but now, tonight, her elegance, charm and glamour were moving her ever closer to her purpose, and she smiled. She knew that her family, her city, would benefit from tonight. And that was the most important aspect to her.

As the guards, similarly dressed in the military uniform of Midscape, held the dining hall door open for her and her father, she saw her husband, Madnan Veerak, standing at the head of the table. Standing directly behind him was Runkarn. Both men were dressed in the colour of Magdil; purple. To Madnan's right was Ruperk Stonefish and to his left, her husband's younger brother Walnak.

She was escorted over to her husband's side, at which point Runkarn placed a chair next to the one already situated in front of Madnan. Her father officially handed Livian over to her new husband, and both bride and groom sat down at the head of the table. Runkarn walked the length of the long, oak table and sat at the other end. He was joined by Ruperk, who sat to his immediate left. Walnak remained where he was and took his place on the bride and groom's left. Livian's father sat down to the right of his daughter. Once all the main dignitaries were seated, the remaining guests sat down. Most of the other invitees were the nobles from Midscape, with a few exceptions; Lord Brok from Stoneguard was seated at the table, wearing the purple colours of Magdil. Drinks were served and toasts were made. All throughout, Livian's smile remained, and her poise and grace were impeccable. Towards the end of the evening, Runkarn made one final toast to the bride and groom, and Livian and Madnan Veerak were ushered off to their matrimonial bed. As Midscape tradition dictated, the guests stood up and cheered and shouted various suggestions for their night to be a success, but none left the dining hall. All the guests remained standing as the bride and groom walked alone to the bedroom.

Once they reached their bedroom, Livian acquiesced to all her husband's requests. This was no hardship for her. Many times she had given it away, but never for such an important cause as tonight. Madnan Veerak turned out to be an insatiable lover, difficult to fully accommodate, but she persisted and was patient. There were things she had never done before, things she had only heard the whores of the taverns and brothels commit. But she did them just the same, with a smile and a moan of delight and pleasure as required. The smile remained all throughout, not for the acts, not for her husband, but for her family and her city.

Just tonight, she told herself. Just for one night, she allowed herself to be whored again. To be taken advantage of willingly, just tonight. Tonight would be the last time.

JUK THRI

By mid-afternoon, Juk could see the Mountain Tower a few hundred yards in the distance. He pulled his horse to a halt and called Rivan over.

"Well, there it is. This is where I agreed to meet Lord Dennis. I can't see any activity, can you?" Juk asked, cupping both his hands above his eyes, squinting into the distance.

"No. Does that concern you?" replied the mage.

"Dennis will not let us down. Let's ride to the tower and see." Juk kicked his heels and set off again at a gentle pace. Sooran and the Deera were a few yards behind, and he looked over his shoulder and smiled. He noticed that all the Deera had removed their wooden bows from the protective casings. Juk spotted the scratchings on the bows.

"What are those markings on your weapons?" he asked.

"For our protection," Sooran replied.

"They look alike to the Lunar Runes you showed me. Are they?"

"We use the Magick as we have to. Our weapons are old; no match for the metal that you have, that no doubt your enemies carry. These runes give us some protection against such weapons."

"I shan't think you'll be needing those," Juk said, continuing to look at the bows closely.

"They give us some solace, Juk. We are far from home. I shall be happy if we do not have to use them," replied Sooran, adjusting hers so that it hung over her shoulder, about a foot from the floor.

"So be it, Sooran. But Dennis Greenaway has never let me down. I don't expect him to start now." Juk smiled, and Sooran smiled back, but her eyes were looking into the distance, towards the tower.

After a few minutes, they reached the tower. Two guards came walking out of the guardroom. Behind them, Juk saw Janson Brok.

"Janson!" exclaimed Juk, eyes wide and with a big smile on his face. "What are you doing here? Where is Lord Dennis?"

"Well met, Juk. I've been sent in place of the Lord of Midscape. He has urgent business in the city." As Janson delivered this news, Juk heard noises behind him. He turned to see Sooran and the Deera pull their bows from their resting places and grab an arrow each and ready their bows.

"Sooran, that is unnecessary," Juk said, using his hands to gesture for them to relax. "Lord Janson is an old friend." Regardless, the Deera kept their bows trained on the three men. They had positioned their horses in a small, tight circle.

"You have some uneasy riding partners, Juk. It is good to see you have protective friends." Janson looked over his shoulder before continuing. "I'm to escort you to the city, if you'll have me." Janson smiled at Sooran and then turned his attention back to Juk. As he finished, twenty of his men came out from behind the tower on horseback.

"Do you need so many to escort a friend less than a hundred miles?" Rivan interjected from the rear of the group. He rode to the front as he continued to speak. "A journey he has made many times before."

"I do as I'm bid, friend," replied Janson, walking towards Juk, who was still sitting atop his horse.

Sooran pulled back her bowstring, the Deera all following her lead. Each rider drew their bows, strings at full tension, ready to release. "Prudence is valued where we are from, *friend*. Stay where you are," Sooran shouted.

Juk turned to look at Sooran again, smiled, and slowly climbed down from his horse and embraced Janson in greeting. The two firmly patted each other on the back. Juk noticed Janson was not smiling anymore.

"Sooran, Lord Janson is a friend," Juk said. "Has been for many years." Juk looked closely into Janson's eyes. He didn't like what he saw there. He continued, "We'll not need weapons here, will we, Janson?"

Janson Brok remained silent, eyes on Sooran and the Deera. He held out his hand as the two men finished their embrace, and clasped Juk's. Juk felt Janson put something into his hand. He made eye contact with his friend, who winked at Juk. Juk withdrew his hand and placed the contents into his pocket without looking at it.

"So, Janson. This is Rivan, Sooran, and her men. If you'll forgive me one moment, I have to attend to my horse." With that, Juk turned and reached inside his saddle pouch and pulled out an apple. He fed it to his horse and, as he did so, he examined the small parchment in his hand. He quickly unfolded it and read its one-line content, trying not to draw attention to his actions. The note read: "*You were right.*"

At that moment, the noise of arrows whistling in the air came from behind him. He turned and saw Lord Janson writhing on the floor with three arrows embedded in his back. Janson's men had all been knocked from their horses, all with arrows protruding from their heads, necks and other parts of their bodies. Some horses had been struck as well, but most were overcome by panic and ran off in all directions. The two guards had run back into the tower. The Deera aimed their bows in the direction from which the arrows had come. But before any had a chance to loose any arrows themselves, a warning came from the tower:

"It would be wise for you not to draw your weapons," came the deep baritone voice from one of the balistraria, the arrow slits that were cut into the upper half of the tower. "You are all unhurt because we want it that way. And I'm sure we are all keen for that state of affairs to remain."

Juk looked up in the direction of the voice, but could see no one. He looked at his friend twitching in pain on the ground. He turned to Sooran and saw that the Deera had taken up defensive positions, jumping off their horses, squatting in front of them, bows drawn, arrows ready to loose.

"Sooran, can you see anyone?" Juk moved to aid Janson, still writhing in pain on the floor, when three arrows flew out from the arrow-slits, two landing at his feet half an arrow's distance from him. The third one inserted itself into Janson Brok's left eye.

"Put away your bows. This will be your last chance, Juk Thri. If you want any chance of surviving this, do it now," came the shouted warning again.

Sooran nodded to the Deera, and they all relaxed their bow strings. They remained crouched with their bows by their side. Rivan was still atop his horse, furtively looking up and down the tower. Juk raised his hands before yelling, "We have done as you asked. Will you come down and explain yourself?" Juk shifted his eyes to the now lifeless body of Janson just three feet in front of him. His men were mostly all dead, too, but a few were screaming out in pain.

There was no immediate response. After a few moments, the two guards reappeared from the tower. This time they were joined by a dozen more, and in the middle of the guards came Ruperk Stonefish. From behind the tower about a hundred men on horseback came riding to the front of the tower and circled Juk and his group. Juk saw that some men had tattooed faces, and they wore the insignia of the 2nd Regiment.

"Juk Thri," said Ruperk. "You have been a foolish man. To think you could challenge the might of Magdil, of Lord Runkarn, with a rag-tag band of what, twenty riders?" Ruperk looked at the Deera behind Juk. "The eyes of Lord Runkarn see all in this land. His eyes are everywhere."

"Where's Lord Dennis? What do you want with us?" Juk asked, not taking his eyes off Ruperk.

"What I want from you will become clear soon enough." Ruperk signalled to the guards to fan out. "Your friend, Lord Greenaway, is in the city. But he will not help you. None will. You turned from that path many Moons ago when you deserted your men and Magdil, Juk Thri. That treachery has to be paid for."

At that moment, a number of things happened: First, the ground vibrated, which was accompanied by a loud rumble. A noise that sounded like a large throng of horses making their way towards Juk's position from the east. At this, the Deera took up their defensive positions again, drawing their bows, arrows ready. They had re-made a rough circle, crouching in front of their horses, mirroring the outer circle of the guards, who had now each drawn their swords, ready for battle. There was a distant sound of a horn blowing from the direction of the pounding roar, which was now unmistakably a cavalry charge; three times it rang out a clear, bright note. Out of the corner of his eye, Juk also noticed Rivan ride off to a position in the middle of the Deera, protecting himself.

"Well, it seems we have company," Ruperk said. His guards drawing their bows, readying their arrows. "One word from me, Juk, and it does not matter who you have coming from the east, you will all be dead before they arrive."

"It seems to me," replied Juk," we'll all be dead soon, anyway. Better a soldier's death than rot away in a dungeon, or worse. And we'll take a few of you with us,

Stonefish."

Ruperk Smiled. He looked at his guards surrounding him, and then at the men on horseback, swords ready. He then turned to the east.

The sound of the horses became louder. Juk also turned his head to the east and, coming over the horizon, he saw many men on horseback riding towards the tower. Their bright silver armour reflected the bright Sun in the sky. He looked back at Ruperk, who was still smiling, and saw him raise his hand and bring it down in a vertical direction. Before his arm reached halfway, several arrows flew past Juk and landed in the centre of Ruperk's chest. It knocked him down immediately. They were quickly followed by more arrows, all hitting their targets of the guards surrounding the writhing body of Ruperk. Those that weren't hit retreated to the tower, pulling the now limp body of Ruperk with them. Juk jumped on his horse and quickly rode into the centre of the Deera, pulling his sword from its sheath. The riders surrounding the Deera now moved in, their own swords drawn, slicing and hacking away at their foes. The Deera reloaded and loosed their arrows quickly, but as the riders came amongst them, they were too close for their arrows to be effective. Then the Deera brought their bows in front of their bodies and used the sharpened ends like spears, thrusting them out in front and to the sides. Juk dismounted and hacked away at the riders, too, bringing one off his horse and wounding another on the arm. He observed Sooran using her bow, sweeping it under the legs of the riders' horses, then twisting it above her head and slashing the throats of the riders as they fell from their steeds. Juk saw Rivan riding away to the south, dodging the thrusts of the riders and the arrows that were now flying out of the arrow-slits in the tower again.

The charging cavalry from the east got closer. Now the horses were less than a hundred yards away from the tower, and the bright yellow banners of Dawngate being carried by the vanguard were flapping wildly in the wind. Juk scanned the area for his own horse, Noble; he was nowhere to be seen. As the melee continued, a deep, resounding, humming sound reverberated from the tower. The ground shook and knocked the remaining riders to the ground. Juk and the Deera stumbled to their knees. From above the tower came a blue shaft of light. It had the appearance of Moonlight, but much brighter. Juk thought that contained within the shimmering light were smaller flashes of a glowing substance, star-like in appearance, that were pulsating and projecting the light forwards. It penetrated the ground between the charging horses and Juk and the Deera. It moved in a circular motion, boring into the ground as it travelled in a complete circle.

"This is Mage Magick, or I have not seen it," Sooran cried out.

Where the light had travelled, an enormous semitransparent, dome-like structure had been erected. Sooran shot an arrow into it and it fell to the floor and caught fire on contact. One of Ruperk's men had climbed back onto his horse and tried to ride through it. Upon his horse reaching the edge of the huge, bell-shaped configuration, his horse erupted in flames, screaming out in agony and within seconds both horse and rider were lying on the floor scorched, unrecognisable in form.

Looking from within the newly erected structure, Juk could see the cavalry charge halt. The riders' distorted images were just about visible. A few of the charging men on horseback tried to penetrate the dome and were instantly repelled and engulfed in flame. There were still a handful of Ruperk's men remaining. Once Juk realised they were stuck within the spontaneous dome-like confines, he picked up his sword and charged the men he could see. The Deera also picked up their bows and took on the men in hand to hand combat. Juk plunged his sword into the torsos of three men while they struggled to gain their bearings. The Deera were similarly swift and nimble, and either shot or stabbed the remainder of the men, incurring no casualties themselves.

Juk looked at Sooran and her men. Some of them had wounds to their bodies. Juk looked at his own arm and saw a deep gash near his wrist. The area inside the dome was saturated with the dark crimson blood and the foul smell that close combat brought with it. All of Ruperk's men were either dead or on the floor, writhing in pain. Amongst all the commotion, a voice rang out from outside of the newly constructed configuration.

"None can leave and none can enter. Put down you weapons, Juk. And some peace can be made."

Juk looked around the enclosed space. He saw only Sooran and ten Deera on their feet. In one part of the dome nearest the tower, it took on the appearance of a darker shade of blue. It was the direction that the voice came from. Juk looked at Sooran. "What shall we do? I've seen nothing like this."

"This is Dark Magick. This is what we feared. We have no power over this. This area had been prepared days ago. Lunar Runes have been used, together with the Secret Magick. We were led into a trap, Juk. One with no way out. However, it seems *your* mage found his way out of it." Sooran looked around at her men, gesturing to them to put down their bows. She did the same.

An opening appeared near the tower. The voice came again: "Leave through this door. With no weapons and no horses."

Sooran looked at Juk. "These weapons are dear to us. We have forged and crafted them over many years, yet we will leave them if we must. Our horses, the most dear to us. These we will not leave."

"No weapons. No horses," came the voice again. Then several arrows came through the dome, shimmering with the same light that erected the dome, and all arrows hit their marks: the horses' necks. They screamed out in pain as each arrow pierced the flesh of its target. The elegant, proud steeds fell to the floor, still screaming, legs kicking for a minute or two, until each one became silent. Each Deera kneeled and laid their hands on their steeds, comforting them as they passed from the world.

Finally, Sooran stood up with tears in her eyes. "Juk Thri, what have you done?"

"Now leave, in single file. Through the opening you can see," the voice once more boomed out. And Juk led, holding his injured arm as he walked towards the opening in the dome, followed slowly by Sooran and her ten remaining men. Juk looked behind him to see Sooran take one more look at her horse and her fallen companions before following Juk through the door. As the last of the Deera exited the dome, it changed shape. It now acted as a barrier, from the tower to the Mountain of Serenity on one side, and the foothills on the other side in one long, seemingly impenetrable wall. Juk and the Deera were standing on one side, the Midscape side, and Juk could see the vast horde of riders on the other side.

From the north, a host of riders came towards the tower. Juk noticed they too were the 2nd Regiment. At the head of the host, the rider threw a long, thick rope to Juk.

"Tie your hands, and bind yourself together," he shouted from atop his horse. "Then follow us."

"To where?" asked Juk, staring at the rope on the ground.

"We ride to Midscape. You'll follow on foot. And be silent." With that, the rider pointed at the rope. "And be quick about it."

ASHRAN

It had been one day and night since Juk, Rivan and the Deera rode off to the Mountain Tower. Ashran had a dozen men constantly on guard, in shifts, looking towards the north. Looking for a sign. Any sign. Since the time they had left, there had been none. Late in the morning on the second day, Ashran and his men were warming themselves around the campfire when he heard a shout from the north. All the men stood up and prepared themselves, swords at the ready, shields in hand. Two guards came in from the scouting point, and with them rode Rivan.

"Well met indeed, Rivan," said Ashran, smiling.

"Hail, Ashran," came the reply from the mage. "I wish the tidings were less dark."

"Tell me, Rivan. What happened? Where's Juk? The others?" Ashran's smile disappeared from his face.

"It was a trap. I escaped, just. Juk and the Deera, well, they were not so fortunate." Rivan looked to the floor as he spoke.

"That is grave news. Are they still alive, do you think?" Ashran asked.

"I know not," came the reply from the mage. "If I had to guess, I would say not. I do not know for sure."

"All of them? Dead?" Ashran looked at his men and

then back to Rivan. "What can we do?"

"Now, nothing. We must withdraw. Back to Deadtown, collect your men. Then we shall decide our next steps."

"It doesn't feel right leaving Juk. If he is still alive, he will need our help." Ashran felt his resolve grow. He regretted allowing them to leave him behind in the first place. He didn't want it to happen again.

"Eighty men would not be enough to confront what I saw, Ashran. Eight hundred would not suffice."

"What is it you saw, Rivan? Tell me."

"Something I had not seen for many years. Magick from a powerful source. Magick, that had been planned to have a devastating effect."

"Magick? What Magick?" Ashran replied, a look of confusion on his face.

"Dark Magick. Magick, which the might of an army can do little against. We must regroup. Withdraw and rethink." Rivan looked tired. He had dark rings under his eyes and lines on his face that Ashran had not noticed before. "We must ride out at once," continued the mage. "I do not know if I was followed. I was careful riding back, but we cannot take the chance that I was."

Ashran ordered his men to prepare to leave. They had maintained a constant state of readiness, so it took less than fifteen minutes before they were able to ride off. They rode south. Ashran sent ten men in front, with the quickest horses and the lightest loads. They encountered no one that day or night, stopping briefly after First Sun for a small breakfast. And they were soon on the road again, not stopping again until nightfall. They slept for only three hours before they were off again. They followed this pattern all the way to Deadtown, avoiding being seen by almost anyone for the entire journey. At night, they passed a few quiet villages, but their presence did not seem to raise any suspicion.

By the end of the tenth day, they reached their destination. Ashran was tired, cold and hungry. A few hundred yards before Deadtown, a group of riders rode towards them from the direction of the Dead Forest. Ashran recognised them immediately as the riders he had sent to the towns on the coast of the Endless Ocean. The men rode up next to Ashran and greeted the group warmly.

"Well met. We have been camped here for days. Waiting for you to return," one rider said. "How goes it Ashran?"

"We'll have time for tales soon. First, tell me, how many men did you recruit from the coast?" Ashran replied.

"Five hundred. From Jutstown and Rockgarden mostly. They are riding two to a horse. They are camped in the forest over yonder. Hearty men, they are. Men you would want on your side in a fight."

"Five hundred," Ashran echoed his rider. "Have you visited Deadtown?"

"We checked it out a few days ago. It is quiet."

"Good. We will head there for the night. Get some

food, wash ourselves and we need a good night's sleep. Tomorrow we head for Lendir."

"We'll be ready," came the rider's reply. And he rode off back south.

JUK THRI

Juk, Sooran and the ten remaining Deera were walked hard all the way back to Midscape. They had barely stopped during the daily eighteen-hour marches and barely left alone to get any sleep during the six hours of rest at night. They had been dragged along by the riders of the 2nd Regiment. Tormented and ridiculed all the way. They were kicked if they moved too slowly. Punched if they stopped for any reason, and abuse was hurled at them no matter what they did. In the times of rest, Sooran tended the wounded. She received no help from the 2nd Regiment. Juk's pain from the wound on his arm had been relieved by Sooran, but the pain he felt for his dead friend Janson Brok weighed heavily on him. The guilt he carried made him somewhat numb to the torrent of abuse he received from the 2nd.

At the head of the procession back to Midscape rode Runkarn and his private guards. For the first two days, Ruperk had been carried in a palanquin, but on the third day, Juk noticed he had seemingly made a complete recovery and rode the rest of the way at the front of the group, at Runkarn's side. For the entire journey, Juk and the Deera had been completely ignored by Runkarn and Ruperk. They were wholly left to the whims of the 2nd Regiment.

After four days, they reached Midscape. They rode

in through the main gate with a huge crowd awaiting them. The head of the column was cheered as it entered the city. Once Juk and the Deera reached the crowd, the cheers turned to jeers. Rotten fruit, which had been arranged and placed in baskets by the side of the road, was thrown. Most of the fruit was soft and putrid, leaving Juk's dirty clothes damp and foul-smelling. Occasionally, a less rotten piece of fruit which was not so soft, an apple or a pear, would hit Juk and cause to almost flinch; but flinch he wouldn't do.

They were taken to the main market square near the centre of the city. Juk had been here many times in the past, never as a captive, though. He was made to sit on the floor together with Sooran and her ten men. There they were pounded with more rotting fruit and vegetables. They were jeered and cursed at and made to sit there for the rest of the day. A town guard was brought up to read from a list of offences they were supposed to have committed. As each one was bellowed out by the guard, a chorus of hisses and boos was followed by a barrage of fruit and vegetables. An hour or two after Last Sun, they were dragged to their feet and marched off to a courtyard within the main castle. There they stood while four or five men of the 2nd Regiment threw water over them from large buckets that were constantly refilled after being emptied. After a while, when most of the fruit and vegetables mush had been washed away, they were told to sit again, shivering in their wet clothes, watched over by the 2nd Regiment, who continued their taunting and ridicule.

A few hours after Sunset, just as the waxing crescent Moon was rising in the east, Runkarn and

Ruperk came walking into the courtyard surrounded by a dozen soldiers of the 2nd Regiment, plus a detachment of Runkarn's personal guards, dressed in the purple uniforms of the capital.

"So, Juk Thri. How long has it been since you deserted my army?" Runkarn came close to where Juk was sitting, shivering.

Juk remained silent.

"Do not think your associations with mages and these," — Runkarn looked at the ten Deera — "... this reawakening of some long past dream of history will serve you well. It will not."

Juk looked at Sooran. She kept her eyes firmly fixed on Runkarn.

"You always were a deep thinker," continued Runkarn, switching his gaze back to Juk. "Be sure you don't make it unnecessarily difficult on your *friends*, Juk. Even if your fate is already decided." Runkarn finished his sentence and looked again at the Deera sitting on the floor with Juk, then he turned to one soldier of the 2nd and nodded. The soldier walked over to the Deera. He stood next to the last man sitting in the line, pulled out his long sword, swung it over his shoulder and cleaved off his head. Blood exploded from the convulsing, now headless neck of the Deera, as the severed head fell to the floor, rolled, and came to a stop at the feet of the soldier of the 2nd Regiment. There the head lie there, as a pool of dark red blood trickled out and slowly encircled it.

"That's one from the pages of history who died

needlessly," said Runkarn, looking directly at Juk.

Juk looked over at Sooran. Her head hung down, eyes staring at the ground. He turned to meet Runkarn's gaze. "What is it you want?"

A man from the 2nd walked over to Juk and kicked him hard in the back. "What is you want, *Lord Runkarn*," the soldier said.

"I need to know what your plans are, or I should say *were*. Who has helped you? And who else is involved? Give me the answers to these three questions, and no more heads will be cut." Runkarn smiled as he finished his questions.

"If I tell you the answers you need, the people here will go free?" Juk said, his eyes on the Deera.

"I did not say go free. I said their heads will not come off."

"Then take my head now. My life has been finished for some time. It is of no value to me anymore. All I care for is those who sit with me now. Tell me, where is Lord Dennis Greenaway?"

"There was a reason you were made Captain of the 1st Regiment. What a disappointment you are to me now," Runkarn said, keeping his eyes fixed on Juk, ignoring his question. "Showing the true quality of a Magdil soldier to the end."

Juk remained silent. Head down, eyes fixed on the cold, still-damp courtyard floor.

"This is what we will do," continued Runkarn. "You will sit in a cell. You will stay there and think until First Sun. If you are wise, you will then give me my answers. If you are not, two of your friends will lose their heads every hour until you do. We'll start with the woman. At Sunrise."

Runkarn then gestured to the soldiers of the 2nd. They came towards Juk and the Deera, and pulled hard on the rope still binding their hands to bring them to their feet. The dead, headless cadaver was still bound to them at the end of the line, no longer twitching; a lifeless weight added to their burden as they were led away. They were placed in a large dungeon under the main tower of Midscape. Juk had never visited the underground cells, but knew of their existence and knew well the cruelty of the guards. Once the cell door was locked, they were left alone. They were sitting in a dark, dank cell with only the faintest of lights coming from the door with vertical bars, less than a man's hand gap between each strut. The light of the hallway seeped into the cell, giving those inside a dim light to see each other. A jarring stench of excrement and decay filled the cell and overpowered Juk's senses.

"Juk, do not tell this mage what he wants," Sooran said.

Juk looked at Sooran tied next to him and saw a single tear fall from her left eye.

"He is not to be trusted," she continued. "That much is clear in his opaque words. His dark speech might pass for mercy with some, but when you have heard the twisted words of mages before, it is unmistakable. Your own mage did his own disappearing trick at the tower; these people are not honourable. Their words and actions reveal their true meaning. Do not do as he asks."

"Then we all wait here to die. Is that what we do?" Juk replied, turning his eyes towards the other Deera before looking down at the ground. "I have failed utterly. My own life is no value to me. But you. Your men. I cannot carry that burden."

"Listen, Juk. I can assure you that neither I, nor the men you see here, have any fear. We have all lived a long, fruitful life. We have spent many happy days with our friends and families. If our journey ends here, with the new Sun, then we have lived a good life. There is no fear. Maybe anger or resentment, but you will not find fear here. We are prepared, have been prepared for this all of our lives: to live, first one must die."

Juk remained silent. He leaned back against the wall and kept his mouth closed. His head turned upwards, staring at the dark, damp ceiling of the cell. He stayed there, watching the water drip from one corner. His eyes were fixed on the repetitive splash of the water as it hit the floor. Where the water gathered, a small black rat came running from its dark hiding place. It furtively looked around before bowing its head and sipping the water with a tiny squeak and a shaking of its whiskers. Juk sat there, watching and reflecting; the stench of decaying flesh, blood, and despondency no longer penetrating his senses. Juk sat there, thinking. Lost in his own thoughts about what to do next, when he heard the noise of footsteps and talking coming towards the cell.

A number of soldiers from the 2nd Regiment

appeared at the door. A dozen of them come into the room. In groups of three, the soldiers meted out a beating on each of the prisoners. They struck with their fists, feet, and some had wooden clubs in their hands. They attacked their heads, torsos, and legs: no part of the body was left untouched. Each man in turn took his beating. In silence. Not one word of pain, not one utterance of discomfort came from the Deera. After a time, they reached Sooran. She looked at Juk, half-smiled, and looked straight up at the attackers. The first blow reigned down, a punch catching her on the side of her head. She lifted her head again, staring straight at the aggressor. Another blow landed. This time to her throat. One soldier thrust a wooden club into her stomach and the blow knocked her back. Her head dropped and instinctively she tried to pull her hands up to protect herself, pulling Juk's hand up with her own. Still she made no sound. At this point, Juk could hear more footsteps and voices coming towards the cell.

"They're in the cell down the end here," came one voice from the hall.

Juk saw three men approach the cell door. In the light, he could see there were two guards. They were wearing the dark brown uniforms of Midscape that Juk noticed on the way down here. They were standing on either side of an older man. He had short, grey hair, a familiar face to Juk, but one he couldn't place. This man stared at the occupants of the cell. He paid particular attention to Juk, fixing his eyes on him. Juk returned the stare, trying hard to remember the vague, almost recognisable face peering in from the hallway at him. The older man then turned his attention to Sooran.

"That's enough of that," the older man shouted at the soldiers, just as one was about to land a blow with his knee.

"We take our orders from Lord Runkarn," came the reply. Ignoring the older man's words, the soldier made contact with Sooran, his knee catching her under her chin, knocking her head back onto the wall. This jerked Juk back with her.

"Well then. I shall tell Lord Runkarn you have obviously hardened the prisoners' resolve. How do you think he would take that news?" The old man's voice carried a timbre of authority. He sounded like a man who had given orders to men on many other occasions. "Back to your barracks. You can try again in the morning. Before First Sun."

After a moment or two, one of the soldiers held up his hand. "I think they've had enough for now." He looked at Sooran and Juk. "We'll be back. You can count on that." He spat on the floor and led his men out of the cell, all laughing as they left.

"Juk Thri?" said the older man from outside the cell.

"I am," Juk replied, straining his eyes and memory. He saw the older man looking at the Deera all bound together, and he saw him notice the headless corpse at the end.

"Cut him free," came the voice again. "And the body at the end." This he said to the guards. And with that, the two guards entered the cell. One walked over to Juk and cut the rope from his hands. The other cut free the dead man from the end of the line.

"Up," said one guard, and pulled Juk to his feet. Juk stumbled slightly, but stayed upright. "Out," the guard continued and gestured to Juk to leave the cell.

"Where to?" replied Juk, staying where he was. Not moving.

"Out." One guard pushed him from behind.

"They'll be no need for that," the voice from outside the door said. "Bring him over to me."

The guards took one arm each and walked Juk out of the cell. As Juk left, he saw the Deera moving. They surrounded their fallen companion, and all placed their hands on him as they uttered some words in an unknown language.

In the light of the hall, Juk studied the older man's appearance again, looking up and down, and although he looked many years older than he remembered, the resemblance to Lord Sydric Masterton was unmistakable.

"Who are you?" asked Juk, holding his hands up to shield the bright light from his eyes.

"A friend," came the reply. "And you need one of those right now, Juk Thri."

LORD SYDRIC MASTERTON

Sydric Masterton was sitting at the small wooden table in the guardroom. The room itself was only six feet by eight. With the two guards standing by the door and Juk sitting opposite Sydric at the table, it made for a cramped environment.

"Well Juk Thri," Lord Sydric said, "what have you been up to?"

Sydric stared at Juk. His face was dirty, unwashed, and his eyes were narrowed, his brow furrowed.

"How is this possible?" Juk finally asked after a few moments of staring. "How can you be alive? At the Moon Bridge years past. You were killed. Is this more Magick from a children's tale?"

Sydric grinned and stared back at the man sitting opposite him.

"It's no Magick, Juk. But the story could be from a tale, yes. A true one, that is."

"Well, how? Dennis Greenaway said he saw you and your sons fall."

"The battle at the Moon Bridge. The battle that proved to be the downfall of my family was hard. It was where the Mastertons suffered a grave defeat. I lost my sons. They both fell that day. I lost my city. I lost my kingdom. It was a dark day for my family. But I did not fall. I was captured. As you see, breath I still draw, blood still ripples through my body. Just."

"Captured? Why did nobody know of this?" Juk replied, his brow still crumpled with lines.

"I was kept in secret, for what reason, at first I did not know. But I was kept for four years in a dungeon. Not unlike the one you were sent. But smaller. Much smaller and with less light."

"Kept where?"

"I was taken to Magdil. To be broken. To be kept in darkness and secret until my spirit was destroyed. Until I could be of use to him once more. Just as I was of use to him many years before. Albeit, not to my knowledge."

"And when were you released?"

"I should not say released. That implies some freedom for myself. I was brought out of captivity this Moon just past. Before Midwinter."

"Why? For what reason now?"

"It is difficult to be sure. If I were to give my guess, I'd say that Dennis Greenaway had outlived his usefulness. He was not very competent in keeping your secrets. I would say that word had reached Magdil of your plans. That was the trigger for my reappearance. If I had my guess."

Juk looked down at the floor for a moment. Sydric stood up and walked behind Juk, towards the door. "To give you a lesson in history is not my reason for bringing you into this room, Juk. You have probably guessed that."

"What is it you want?"

"My lord," came the voice of one guard at the door. "What is it you want, *my lord*?"

Juk remained silent. He turned his head to look at the guard, and then back at Sydric.

"We are not at different purposes, Juk." Sydric returned to his seat and looked past Juk to the guards, and smiled. "As foolish as your plans have been so far, we share similar ambitions, I think."

"What do you know of my plans? Where is Dennis? Why is he not here with you?"

"Dennis Greenaway is dead." Juk's head dropped when hearing this news, the colour of his face physically changing to grey before Sydric's eyes. "As for your plans, I should say not all, but most. Dennis was not as discreet as he thought. I know of the Wetlanders. I know of Lord William of Dawngate. Although, I admit, I know little of the strange folk in my dungeon. Here *you* have brought a children's tale to life, I think."

"What have I done? First Janson. Now Dennis. Have all my plans brought down all my friends?" Juk took a while, staring at the floor, before continuing. "What are your plans for me?"

Sydric looked once more over Juk's shoulder. He nodded his head, and one guard left the room. The other stood directly in front of the closed door. Sydric pulled out a large square parchment from the inside of his tunic. He unfolded it and laid it out on the table. It was a map of Areekya.

"Here in the centre is where Runkarn holds most of his power; Magdil, the Gate, and the Spine are where he is at his strongest. The north is also his. He has men stationed at Stoneguard and within Chinsap."

Juk studied the map, keeping silent, showing no emotion on his face.

"It's here in the east where we have some advantage." Sydric pointed at Dawngate. "Lord William's family has long been supporters of Midscape. It was his charge which precipitated the spectacular events at the Mountain Tower. He was recruited by Dennis; one of his few right steps."

Juk maintained his silence. His eyes remained fixed on the map.

"The west you can tell me about, I think. And the Endless Ocean. How goes it there?" Sydric smiled at Juk.

"Magdil is not strong in the west. The Wetlanders were with me, are still with me, as far as I know. The Endless Ocean, I could not say for sure. I do not think they are friendly to Magdil, though."

"So we have the east, west and maybe the south west. What of your silent companions in the cell? From where do they come? I heard talk of only twenty taking on the 2nd Regiment and not coming off poorly. That is some outcome if it's true."

"It is no lie. From where they come is not for me to say. After the events at the tower, I do not know if they would still be willing to help."

"There are more of them, then?" Sydric's eyes

widened as he spoke.

"I'll say no more until they are all safe from harm. Away from here. Do you have this within your power? Where is Runkarn? Ruperk? Are they not in Midscape?"

"They are here. And yes, I have that power. This is my family's city. My city. I say who comes and goes in my own dungeons."

"And Runkarn?" replied Juk, lifting his eyes from the map to meet Sydric's.

"He can be dealt with. In the short term, at least. Maybe giving you enough time to flee. You and your mysterious companions."

"How? He has the 2nd Regiment here. I assume more are on the way, after their rout at the Mountain Tower. And what of the 1st? Where are they? Can you tell me of Captain Chik Srin?"

"I have Lord William standing by in the foothills. His army of three thousand will be here before dawn. The Veerak brothers are already dead. Their throats were cut in their sleep this very night. Runkarn sent the 1st and the 2nd Regiments east and west. He has less than a hundred of the 2nd remaining. Maybe a hundred more personal guards. He has no idea of Dawngate's numbers and relies on Midscape for protection. As for the Captains of both the 1st and the 2nd, they are dead."

Juk's eyes opened wide. Sydric could see his pupils dilate. "Chik? Dead?" This news seemed to overwhelm Juk. He remained sitting, holding his head in his hands for a long time. Sydric allowed him to grieve. Many minutes passed before he raised his head once more, tears flowing from his eyes.

"So many friends dead. First my family, now my friends. When will it end? How will it end?" Juk muttered, just loud enough for Sydric to hear.

"Juk, they did not break my fighting spirit in their dungeon as they thought they had. I had to kill the outer-man, Juk. So the inner-man could survive. I do not plan on dying again. Not yet. There will be time for your grief; it cannot be now. Your friends need you. I need you." Sydric stood up. "The Veeraks will be missed at breakfast. Runkarn and Ruperk are too well protected while they sleep. It will be at breakfast when we will have our chance. Sun up is in about three hours. So we need to be quick." Sydric walked behind Juk to the door. The guard opened it and Sydric walked out.

"Juk, come with me. Quickly now. Time is pressing." Juk stood up and followed the older man back down the hall to the cell. The guard unlocked the door and entered.

"Juk, tell your friends here what is happening." Sydric looked at Juk as he spoke.

"I'm not sure I know myself."

"You are being set free. I will show you the way. You will not be seen. This city holds many secrets. Many that only one or two know."

Juk looked at the nine men and one woman on the floor of the cell. "He tells it true." There was no reply. They sat silently as the guards cut their bonds. As one guard cut the rope from the woman's wrist, she reached out her hand and grabbed him round the neck. As she did this, the other guard was immediately set upon by the remaining nine men. Within seconds, both guards were pinned to the floor.

"Impressive," said Lord Sydric. "They'll be no need for that. Not here. Not now."

"Leave them be, Sooran. It was not Sydric's men that attacked us. They're here to help." The woman looked at Sydric and then at Juk. She raised her hand, and the Deera stepped back from the guards.

"Quickly now," Sydric said as he looked at Juk. "Follow me."

Juk nodded at the group and they followed Sydric down the hall. The guards picked themselves up and were at the rear of the group. Sydric led as they went down the hall, first to the right and then to the left, for about a few hundred yards. After that, the ground sloped upwards. They travelled for about another five hundred yards before they reached a dead end. Sydric reached out and pulled out a solitary brick from about half-way up the wall. A part of the wall swivelled, and an entrance appeared. Sydric walked through it, picked up a lit torch from the wall, and stopped. He turned to face Juk and his friends.

"About three hundred yards down this passageway, you will see an exit. There is rubble surrounding it, but it is clear enough. There you will find six of my men. They are holding half a dozen horses for you. Ride to your friends in the west. Wait there for a message. It might take weeks or Moons. But it will come. When it does, make sure you are ready, Juk Thri. And the more of your friends you have, the better."

LORD SYDRIC MASTERTON | 381

"And you? How will you deal with Runkarn and Ruperk?"

"I'm hoping I won't have to." One guard at the back of the group called out a warning to Sydric, who nodded. "Go now Juk Thri. Lord William is nearly here. And I need to be elsewhere."

With that, Sydric held out his arm and grabbed Juk's. They shook in agreement. Sydric looked into Juk's eyes one last time and turned and walked back the way from which they had come, with all the speed his elderly frame could muster.

He looked over his shoulder just before the passage twisted to the right and he saw Juk and his companions running for the exit.

LORD WILLIAM WILTON

William Wilton took off his fur-lined leather gloves and placed them on the table. He took a long drink from the goblet of wine he picked up from the same table and stared out of the window. It faced to the south, and through it he could see the moat. The drawbridge was raised. Beyond that, he could see the narrow streets of the city. It was an hour before First Sun and the pre-dawn gloom that descended on Midscape made his view an unpleasant one.

"So, your men have surrounded the barracks?" William turned his head towards the soft voice of Lady Livian Masterton. They were standing in an ancillary room adjoined to her bedroom. It was accessible through the dressing area and felt very private.

"Yes, I have my men there explaining the situation," replied William. "They'll give us no trouble when they see the number of men we have surrounding them. I have Henrik Jacks there. A bloody enormous giant of a man. His brother was hurt rather badly back in Dawngate, so he is very motivated to bring the situation under control." William smiled warmly.

"And the rest of your men?" Livian's eyes were red, with dark circles under them.

"I have a thousand outside the city gate. The rest are in the castle walls. Combined with your troops, I'd say we have near on five thousand in total. More than a match for Magdil." William turned to look out the window again. He took another drink of his wine. "You know, we should have done this years ago."

"Do not think I hadn't thought of it," said Livian. "Although, I don't think I had the courage until my father was returned to me."

"That was a blessing unlooked for, no? Though we should've never have left him in the first place. How was it that no one knew?" William replied.

"There were not any survivors at the Moon Bridge all those years ago," Livian said. "Well, almost none. I'm sure even that oaf Greenaway didn't even know my father lived still. Runkarn kept this secret very close."

"Well, he's back now. We should be grateful for that. Will he be long? We need to talk before Sun up."

"My father shall be here presently."

At that moment, William heard muffled cries coming from the bedroom. He put down his goblet and drew his sword, then walked to the back of the room.

"Stand back, my lady." He waved his left hand at Lady Livian, gesturing her to move to the window.

"Livian? Livian? Where are you?" the voice from the bedroom called out.

"Father! I'm in here." Livian went to the door, pulled the two bolts from right to left, and opened the door.

"My dear," came the voice, and William saw Lord

Sydric Masterton embrace his daughter. He looked a lot older than he remembered: a shock of white hair, and he looked shorter, too. He had the same regal-looking face, maybe a few more lines than before, but Lord Masterton was unmistakable.

"My Lord Sydric." William walked towards the door and held out his hand.

"Lord William," came Lord Sydric's reply. "Is everything in place?"

"It is." They shook hands and smiled at each other. "Whatever that was at the Mountain Tower disappeared yesterday. We rode as quickly as we could and arrived early this morning."

"You have done well, Lord William. What *that* was, we can discuss later." Lord Sydric turned back to his daughter. "My dear. Tell me about the Veeraks. Is it done? Are they dead?"

"Madnan and Veerak's bodies were taken to the east of the city and burned two hours ago. They suffered before they died. I saw them both scream in pain before the end. It did not satisfy me as I thought it would. Perhaps that is yet to come." Livian's face remained passive as she gave her father the news.

"So, we have Runkarn and Ruperk to deal with," William said. "How many personal guards will they have?"

"They brought only a hundred from Magdil. The 2nd are all in the barracks," Lord Sydric replied.

"Which is surrounded as we speak." William

smiled at both Livian and Sydric.

"Good, good." Sydric looked directly at William. "We plan to have breakfast early, just after dawn. Runkarn and Ruperk plan to bring their dealings with Juk Thri to a swift end."

"Where is he? Where is Juk Thri?" Lord William asked.

"He has gone. Back west with his travelling companions. More of which we must talk later." Sydric raise his eyebrows as he finished his sentence.

"The Sun will be up within the hour. We had best start our plans." William picked up his gloves, nodded to both Sydric and Livian, and left the room. He headed through the bedroom, down the hall and out of the main castle. There, by the main gates, next to the living quarters, were a large number of his men.

"Has Jacks returned yet?" he asked the men.

"No," one answered. "I've heard a few of the 2nd didn't take kindly to seeing their ex-Captain's head on a spike."

"No, I suppose, they wouldn't." William smiled.

"Henrik enjoyed showing it, though." The man laughed as he replied and turned to his comrades, who all joined in.

"Remember what we said." William got his men's attention. "Two hundred in the room next to the dining hall. The rest remain here for Jacks."

"Yes, my lord," they all replied. Two hundred of his

men walked off, back the way from which William had come.

"Now, let's wait for Henrik. And then we'll make our way." William looked to the east and saw the first cerise rays of the Sun shooting up into the sky, ruby red shafts of light climbing over the mountains. By the time the Sun's rays had multiplied and lit up the sky in the east, Henrik Jacks appeared with about fifty men.

"Lord William. The barracks have been subdued. All the 2nd that remain alive are confined there. Outnumbered, five to one at least." Henrik Jacks was smiling and had splatters of blood on his face.

"Good. Let's go. Jacks, bring a hundred," William said. "The rest stay on guard here. No one, and I mean no one, is to enter or leave. Is that understood?"

"My lord," his men replied in unison.

William made his way back into the castle and entered the dining hall. There he saw Livian and Sydric sitting at either ends of the long table. Henrik Jacks took his men through into the kitchen behind where Livian was sitting. William sat down next to Lord Sydric, waiting for their breakfast guests. The room was silent, but William could sense the air of tension mixed with fear. He took a sip of his wine and kept his eyes fixed on the door. All present remained silent. All eyes on the door. Waiting. William saw Livian biting her top lip. His own hands felt clammy.

Finally, Lord Sydric spoke. "It is most unusual for Runkarn to be late." William nodded, wrung his hands together, and half-smiled.

"Guards!" Lord Sydric called out. Six men came through the door.

"Take fifty of the men and visit Lord Runkarn's and Lord Ruperk's rooms. Please tell them the Lord and Lady of the city are waiting for them."

"Sir!" the six men replied.

"This doesn't feel right," Livian said, standing up and walking to the window.

"No. It does not." Sydric remained sitting down, but he was fidgeting in his seat.

"All we can do is wait," said William. "They'll be here soon. Or not."

After a short while, a loud knock rattled the door. Livian sat back down. Sydric's back straightened as he sat up. William's eyes were drawn to the door.

"Enter," said Lord Sydric. In walked the six men from minutes before.

"They have gone, my lord," said one of the guards. "They must have left in the night. There is no sign. None of their possessions remain. It's as if they have vanished."

Sydric smiled. "It seems Runkarn learned more of the city than I imagined he did."

"Lord Sydric?" William said, tilting his head slightly.

"There are many ways out of Midscape. Put there by my ancestors, and a few by me over the years. To aid escape if the need should ever arise," Sydric explained.

"It appears Runkarn has made use of one of these, at least."

"But how did he know?" asked Livian. "To leave, I mean."

"How indeed," replied Sydric. "Lord William, send your men to the main gate. Ask if they have seen anything. Guards, send men to all the exits of the city. Bring word quickly. Off you go." With that, the guards left the room.

William walked into the kitchen and ordered Henrik Jacks to take half the men to the main gate. He then returned to the dining hall and sat down again before speaking, "Well, it seems your murders of the Veeraks were not as discreet as you thought, Lady Livian."

Livian looked at her father, scowled, and then looked at William. "I know not how they could have found out. I would swear not from any of my people."

"It matters not," said Sydric, standing up. "We will wait for reports to come back. We have to decide what we do next."

William smiled and nodded. He took another sip from his goblet, this time a longer swig.

He had finished the contents of his cup by the time the reports came back; nobody had seen or heard anything. Henrik Jacks returned with the same news: nothing.

"They must have left before Lord William entered the city," Sydric said. "Cunning and careful, Runkarn has always been."

"I have three thousand men here in Midscape. The question I need answering is, what do I do with them?" William looked directly at Lord Sydric.

"We shall put the 2nd Regiment into the cells. My men will take care of that," Sydric replied. "Your men can make themselves at home in the barracks for now, Lord William. There should be ample space."

"My lord," replied William. "They will not keep there for long. A rest will be welcome. But more than a few days, they will become restless."

"A few days is more than we need to decide our next step," replied Livian. "I do not think Runkarn will be at ease losing two of his close advisors and having to flee. Maybe he will decide our next move for us. We have ears and eyes in places other than Midscape. We'll obtain news soon, Lord William."

"I shall inform my men." William stood up, and nodded his farewells before continuing. "Then I shall retire and rest a while. Is there a room suitable for this?"

"It shall be prepared," answered Livian.

William left the dining hall with the remainder of his men. They walked to the castle's entrance. There, he informed his men of the plans. He ordered Henrik Jacks to bring twenty of the finest men with him as he turned and walked back into the castle. He was met by three guards of Midscape who escorted him to the guests' quarters and was shown to his room. The Midscape men returned the way they'd come.

Standing outside the room, William looked up and down the hall. "Henrik, inform the men to be very careful what they do while we remain in Midscape. And in particular, nobody is to say anything of importance when they visit me here; nothing they would not want overheard. Is that understood?"

"Yes, Lord William."

"Put the men in shifts and keep five on guard outside this door at all times," William said, issuing his final order of the day. He opened his door, entered the room, and released a heavy sigh. After stripping off his outer garments, and without washing, he lay on the bed. William stared up at the ceiling for a few minutes before falling asleep.

ASHRAN

Ashran and his men spent one night in Deadtown. They got rooms at the Black Oak. They had to sleep five or six to a room, but it made for a more comfortable night's sleep than they'd had for many a week. The next morning, after a quick breakfast, they left. They were joined by the men from the previous night, together with the five hundred from the coast, and made their way north west towards the Spine Mountains. At the end of the day, they camped a few miles north of a small town with the mountains visible in the distance.

"Ashran, we have to take the Bloody Pass." Rivan was standing next to Ashran as the men built a small campfire. "It will take us close to Magdil. I expect it to be manned. With luck, there will not be many there, but prepare your men." Ashran looked at the mage. He looked better than he had. The night at Deadtown had put some life back into his face. His cheeks looked ruddier and his eyes looked brighter than they did.

"Aye. I was thinking the same. The extra men will help." Ashran looked over at the men recruited from the towns and villages on the coast. They were mainly fisher folk by trade. Most of the men had a weather-beaten look about them with tanned skins and dark blond hair. Many of their families had come to Areekya from across the Endless Ocean. They did some trade with Lendir, and Ashran had visited the coast once or twice in the past. He was glad to have them by his side.

As it turned out, they found the Bloody Pass completely empty of Magdil troops. They passed the odd villager with his cart on his way from Magdil, back to Deadtown or one of the other towns in the south, but they saw no soldiers. Ashran had mixed feelings about this. He felt relieved there was no fighting, but he found it difficult to shake the nervous feeling he'd carried for some time. After what Rivan had told him about the Mountain Tower, he had expected Magdil to be vigilant. He had anticipated at least a scouting party at the Bloody Pass. But none were seen or reported. It didn't feel right.

They kept close to the mountains in the south and then headed west to the Endless Ocean, towards Wettown, to stay as far away from Magdil as they could. After two days, they headed north again, keeping close to the coast. After a few miles of travelling in this direction, a scout rider appeared on the horizon, riding back south towards Ashran and his men.

"Ashran," the rider said. He was out of breath and sweat was dripping from his forehead. "We've spotted an army up ahead. Magdil. Looks like the 1st or the 2nd Regiment. Maybe both."

"How many?" Rivan asked from behind Ashran.

"We guess three hundred. All on horseback."

"Have they seen our scouts? Which direction are they headed?"

"No, we don't think they've spotted us. We've hidden out in the hills just to the north. They look like they're coming from Harbour Bay and are about ten miles from here. Heading right towards you."

"Three hundred you say?" Ashran asked.

"Aye."

"We have two choices, then. Fight or run?" Ashran looked at Rivan and then turned to his men. "I'm tired of running. We're double their number. I say we stand here. Prepare ourselves. They are still ten miles away. We have time to get dug in and give them a surprise or two. What do you say, men?"

There was some unintelligible muttering, but after a minute or two the cries were heard: "Aye, let's get ready. Let's bloody our swords and axes."

Ashran jumped from his horse and began ordering his men. He found the extra five hundred men from the coast to be enthusiastic and undaunted. They followed all orders with a fervour he hadn't seen in his own men for a long while.

Within the hour, all plans were set and Ashran stood in front of his men, who were all atop their horses, one hundred of them. Two hundred and fifty of the extra men were protecting the right flank on their steeds. The others were standing behind Ashran. In their hands were a mixture of spears, axes and swords. Not ideal against a charging cavalry, but if they held firm to his plans, they should do the job.

It didn't take long before a handful of enemy scouts were spotted. They quickly did an about-turn and galloped back the way they had come. Not long after this, the army appeared, galloping over the horizon. They stopped about five hundred yards in front of Ashran and his men. The ground between the two armies was solid grassland. If this was going to be the battleground, it would suit the men Ashran had as much as any. The two armies faced off against each other. Ashran waited patiently. Rivan had moved himself to the back of the infantry, waiting. They were all waiting for the cavalry charge that would surely come at any moment. Still they waited. Minutes went by with no movement from the Magdil army just five hundred yards away. Rivan rode from the back to the front and stopped next to Ashran.

"Why don't they charge?" the mage asked.

"I do not know. Is it the numbers? Inferior numbers never stopped them before."

As they were talking, the Magdil army turned and rode back northwards. Ashran turned to look at Rivan, eyes open wide. He then signalled to ten of his men.

"Follow them. From a distance. I want to make sure this is no trap."

Ten of his men rode north, following the Magdil army.

"Stand ready, men," Ashran shouted, not yet believing the battle was over before it began.

After a short while, two of the riders came back.

"They're moving east," one said. "It looks like they're headed for the road back to Magdil."

"Well, I'll be. What can have caused that?" Ashran looked at Rivan with a confused look on his face.

"This is a mystery to me, also. Though it cannot seem anything but good news," came the mage's reply. "I think we should ride north. Back to Lendir. At a good pace, we can be there in a week."

At that point, three of the Jutstown men approached Ashran.

"It's time we left. Seeing Magdil riders here has unnerved some of the men. They wish to return to their homes and families," said a tall blond-haired man holding an axe in his right hand.

"We thank you for your loyalty," came Ashran's reply as he climbed down from his horse and shook each of the men by the hand.

"We will return to our towns and ready ourselves if your call should come again. We are but five hundred. There are many more willing to fight to keep Magdil at bay."

Ashran smiled. "That is good to hear."

"Yes, very good," added Rivan. "We're returning north. Expect us to return within two Moons at the latest."

"We'll be ready," came the reply from the tall axe-wielding man.

Ashran climbed back onto his horse. He signalled for his men to follow him and he galloped off. Riding side by side with Rivan, they set out northwards, for Lendir. They stayed close to the coast until they reached the wetlands and then headed north west to Lendir. It took just over a week's swift ride to reach the borders.

The men were in good spirits. They had no encounter with soldiers from Magdil or had any trouble on the journey home. Ashran's mind was still preoccupied with the fate of Juk Thri, but the closer he got to home, the more his thoughts turned to Tinker, Ashron and his people. They were a mile outside of Lendir when Ashran saw smoke rising from the village.

"What's this?" Ashran cried out, then kicked his horse with his heels and galloped off. He continued to press his horse as fast as he could until he reached the town, and a wave of anguish overcame him. The smell was terrible. The whole town was smouldering. There was a huge pile of waste in the centre of the town that still had flames flickering, but all the houses and buildings were nothing more than smouldering ash. As Ashran galloped closer to the flaming pile in the centre of town, he realised it consisted of burning bodies. He jumped from his horse and erratically tried to stamp out the flames. In his anguish, he was fighting to put out the flames with no success. His men rushed over, and with buckets of water they doused the blaze. After a few minutes, the fire was out and all that remained were lifeless, unrecognisable, charred corpses.

Ashran fell to his knees. He was rooted to the spot, paralysed. Then, he sprung to his feet, and ran as fast as he could to his home. Before he got within fifty yards of his house, he saw there was nothing left of it. It had been razed to the ground. Ashran looked around at the devastation. Ash smouldering where homes once stood. His family, friends, gone, a charred pile of indistinguishable bodies. He fell to his knees.

And on his knees, he sobbed.

RUNKARN THE LORD OF AREEKYA

Runkarn disembarked the ship and stormed past the waiting soldiers from the Gate, assembled there on either side of the ship's ramp to welcome him. He strode directly to the waiting horses that had been prepared. Ruperk Stonefish hurriedly followed, struggling to keep up. There, sitting atop their horses, were men of the Gate's City Guard, wearing the dark blue livery of The Gate.

"Is everything prepared? As requested?" Ruperk barked at one man holding two horses, wearing a long blue cloak hanging down from his shoulders, almost reaching the floor.

"It is, my lords. The way is clear. And safe."

Runkarn climbed onto one horse and, kicking his heels into its side, rode off towards the city. He could hear Ruperk being helped onto his waiting horse, and heard the group of riders follow him. Runkarn had brought the ship ashore at Eastmount, the port used for trade between The Gate and Midscape, rather than Magdil, as a precaution. It was closer. And safer. After the events at Midscape yesterday morning, he wanted to take no chances. He needed to regroup and rethink. The battle at the Mountain Tower had surprised him. They had captured Juk Thri, and Janson Brok was dead;

this went to plan. He knew Juk Thri to be tough. He had expected and prepared for a difficult confrontation. The charge of Dawngate was not unforeseen, either. It was those who had accompanied Juk which held surprise for Runkarn. This he ruminated on as he rode. He also thought deeply about what had transpired at Stoneguard. How had he underestimated Sydric? He had kept the man in his dungeon for years, breaking him further with each Moon. Controlling him with the Magicks; even speaking the words into his daily bread to bend him to his will. He had even used the Dark Magick to manipulate his dreams. He *was* broken. Runkarn saw it. How had he been deceived?

Runkarn continued riding west. He had now been joined by the group of the riders from the Gate; three flanking him on both sides, and six behind, with Ruperk. After a morning and afternoon's swift ride, they reached The Gate. Magdil's second city since the War, and home to Ruperk Stonefish. The group was ushered in through the city's ancillary gates. They were rarely used, intended as support when the grain shipments were too much for the main gates to handle. However, Ruperk had them reinforced and refitted to be used solely as a secret entrance on occasions such as this. They led directly and safely into the heart of the inner city. Runkarn dismounted and marched into the main counsel room, outpacing his retinue. He sat behind the desk in the corner and threw his gloves onto it. After a few moments, Ruperk came blustering in, ordering his guards to bring food and drink.

"Leave. All of you," Runkarn said, barely above a whisper. "Ruperk, you stay."

"My lord."

"There is much that troubles me, Ruperk."

"My lord. If I can explain —"

"Silence." Runkarn held up his hand, palm open, his back to Ruperk, staring out of the window. "There is much that troubles me," he repeated. "Your incompetence, luckily for you, is not uppermost in my thoughts. We will get to that later." Runkarn turned to look at Ruperk. "What troubles me most is who we saw at the Mountain Tower."

Ruperk stood still, not moving at all, eyes down, his body stooping.

"I paid it little attention at the time. But given what transpired at Midscape, of which I hold you accountable, it has grown in my mind. It may be the answer to the questions that have had me puzzled." Runkarn was now staring through Ruperk, focusing on nothing in particular, contemplating, examining his own thoughts and trying to make sense of them. "Did you see the rider on the tall grey horse? He rode away, as the battle at the tower commenced."

Ruperk stayed silent. His body remained hunched over.

"Ruperk! Did you see him?"

"My lord?"

"The rider. Did you see him?"

"I did not." Ruperk was still staring at the floor.

"It was one I assumed dead. His reappearance is

like that from a dream; a nightmare. That he brought the Deera with him also fills me with great concern."

"My lord? The Deera?"

"They are no concern now. He is."

"He, my lord?" Ruperk was now engaged in the conversation. He looked, his head at an angle, gazing at Runkarn from the corner of his eye.

"He! He that should not have been. Could not be. He that died many years ago. From my own hand. My old apprentice. I plunged the knife into him myself. I left him there on my steps, dying. Dead, I thought. When I returned from the ceremony the next day, I saw the trail of blood lead into the forest and end at the river. I assumed he had drowned or some other fate had taken him to his end. This was my error. And this we must remedy."

APPENDIX A: MAIN CHARACTERS

Ashran of the Clan Grash - Leader of the Clan Grash in Lendir, the West of Areekya.

Chik Srin - Lieutenant to Captain Juk Thri of the 1st Regiment.

Dennis Greenaway - Lord of Midscape, wife of Lady Livian Masterton-Greenaway.

Hak Krok - Captain of the 2nd Regiment.

Janson Brok - Lord of Stoneguard in the North of Areekya.

Juk Thri - Captain of the 1st Regiment.

Livian Masterton-Greenaway - the last living member of the Masterton family. Wife of Dennis Greenaway.

Madnan Veerak - Son of Berak Veerak from the Spine region of Areekya.

Rivan - Mage

Runkarn - The Lord of Areekya

Ruperk Stonefish - Lord of the Gate, Areekya's second city.

Ursula Wilton - Lady of Dawngate, Wife of Lord William Wilton.

Walnak Veerak - Brother of Walnak.

William Wilton - Lord of Dawngate in the East of Areekya.

APPENDIX B: LOCATIONS IN AREEKYA

Chinsap – In the NE of Areekya. Home to Juk Thri, Chik Srin and the 1st Regiment.

Dawngate – In the East. Home of Lord William and Ursula Wilton.

Dead Forest In the SW of Areekya.

East Sea – East of the Mountains of Dawn..

Greenscape – In the N of Areekya.

Lendir – In the Wetlands. Home to Ashran of the Clan Grash.

Magdil – The centre of power in Areekya. Home to Lord Runkarn.

Midnight Forest – Ancient, mystical forest.

Midscape – Home of Lord Dennis Greenaway and the former home of the Mastertons former rulers of Areekya.

Nikrid Desert – In the SW of Areekya.

Northern Hills – Home of the Hillmen.

Spine Mountains – The range of mountains in the S of Areekya. Home of the Veeraks.

Stoneguard – Home of Lord Janson Brok.

The Gate – Home of Lord Ruperk Stonefish, principle advisor to Lord Runkarn.

Valley of Widows – At the entrance of Chinsap.

Wetlands – In the far W of Areekya.

Windwatch – In the N of Areekya. A tower used to protect against the Hillmen.

———

ACKNOWLEDGEMENT

A special thanks to Yosbe Design for the wonderful cover and to Steven who helped with the edit. You both made the book better.

ABOUT THE AUTHOR

Barry S Markwick

An English Language Teacher by profession who graduated from The Open University in the UK with a BA (English) and MEd (Applied Linguistics).

I've taught in various countries around the world, and I've now found time to embark on my second passion - writing. My first novel, The Waxing Moon: The Areekyan Chronicles Volume 1.

Creating the Land of Areekya with its many compelling characters has been an enjoyable and rewarding labour of love. I hope you enjoy reading about them as much as I did telling their stories.

https://www.theareekyanchronicles.com

Printed in Great Britain
by Amazon

21113612R00243